THE CRIMES OF HECTOR TOMÁS

THE
CRIMES
OF
HECTOR
TOMÁS

Ian Colford

Canada Council **Conseil des Arts**
for the Arts **du Canada**

Freehand Books gratefully acknowledges the support of the Canada Council for the Arts for its publishing program. ⁋ Freehand Books, an imprint of Broadview Press Inc., acknowledges the financial support for its publishing program provided by the Government of Canada through the Canada Book Fund.

Freehand Books
515 – 815 1st Street SW   Calgary, Alberta   T2P 1N3
www.freehand-books.com

Book orders: LitDistCo
100 Armstrong Avenue   Georgetown, Ontario   L7G 5S4
Telephone: 1-800-591-6250   Fax: 1-800-591-6251
orders@litdistco.ca
www.litdistco.ca

Library and Archives Canada Cataloguing In Publication

Colford, Ian
The crimes of Hector Tomás / Ian Colford.

ISBN 978-1-55481-109-0

I. Title.

PS8555.O44C75 2012   C813'.54   C2012-904884-4

Edited by Robyn Read
Book design by Natalie Olsen, kisscutdesign.com
Cover photography copyright of but beautiful°, time.,*princessa*, jonibe.de, halb-blind, inkje, ringo / photocase.com
Author photo by Tina Usmiani

Printed on FSC recycled paper and bound in Canada

To Collette

Now I understand why the movies, literature, and historical accounts, even the word-of-mouth tales that are passed down to their grandchildren by eyewitnesses to events like these, always leave a false impression of spinning, dizzy motion, although curiously enough, the horror of such periods actually lies in the slow motion, the snail's pace of events. An insatiable, tense expectancy controls the situation, stretching the minutes, the hours, the days, the weeks, and the months to intolerable length. Yet the man who is telling the story piles murder on arson, arson on rape, rape on robbery, without meaning to, and so everything agglomerates, whirls, and is pressed together in very concentrated form, whereas he would be more accurate if he said that as matters actually developed, in reality, there were no such mobs or mob scenes, no such violent commotions, whirling action, or marching or trampling feet.

FRANCISCO AYALA
Muertes de Perro

Sometimes good things
fall apart. So better
things can fall together.

—Marilyn Monroe

ONE

The Tomás family occupied a roomy flat on the fifth floor of the apartment building at 53 Rua Santa Maria in the provincial capital of B——. The flat belonged to Enrique Tomás, whose family had moved there when he was a young man.

Enrique Tomás had been a solitary child, a precocious scholar who, as he grew into adulthood, developed an abiding interest in philosophical conundrums that had puzzled the ancients, questions such as, *Where do our words go after we have spoken them?* and *How do we decide to make a decision?* He read thick tomes devoted to these questions and wrote papers, which nobody would publish. In his late teens his everyday attire consisted of a heavy black flannel suit with a vest and dark jacket and a black hat. He grew a beard and carried a watch on a chain and wore glasses even though his eyesight was perfect, and he looked so much like the Hasidim who inhabited the Jewish quarter that he was often mistaken for one.

There was no question he was eccentric, but he was their only child and his liberal-minded parents indulged him, much to the detriment of his character. They allowed him to remain at home throughout his twenties and into his thirties, where he secluded himself in a spare bedroom he had converted into an office and scribbled his unfathomable dissections of the reality that the rest of us take for granted.

When his parents died, his mother quite suddenly, his father after a lengthy stay in an expensive nursing facility, he was shocked to learn that the income from the estate was hardly adequate to support the style of life to which he had grown accustomed, and that if he continued as he was, he would run out of money in no more than two or three years.

In order to avoid selling the flat he had to take a job, and he was very fortunate that the archivist at the university was about to retire, because when the time came he was able to convince the Dean of Arts and Sciences, a family acquaintance, that his research into spiritual regeneration and Gnostic rituals was perfect training for this sort of position. He was given the job of archivist and held it until shortly before his death nearly forty years later.

For his entire life his mother had retained the services of a housekeeper and a cook, but it was not long after his parents were laid to rest that the cook, who was very old, suffered a stroke. Enrique had already decided he could no longer afford the housekeeper, so he let her go, and for those long and painful months that he spent searching for a means to support himself, he lived completely alone, cooking his own meals, doing his own laundry, cleaning the flat when the need grew so urgent that he could no longer reasonably avoid it.

After being employed by the university he decided that the income gave him the flexibility to once again hire a housekeeper. He composed an anonymous but detailed advertisement and posted copies of it around the campus. The wage he was offering seemed fair to him, but he had no way of knowing that it was almost five times the customary wage offered to the girls and young women who normally took on this kind of work. As a result, his mailbox was bursting with letters of application when he returned home from the library on the second day after the advertisement had been posted. He spent an entire evening going through them. He did not know about the agencies one consults when one desires the services of a housekeeper; he did not know that these agencies bring girls into the city from the provinces, illiterate and ignorant country girls who are only too happy to give their sweat for a wage that is barely enough to keep them alive. The applications that Enrique Tomás sorted through on that fateful evening had been, without exception, prepared by articulate and intelligent people, not all of them young, not all of them female. There were students on the verge of graduation, several grade school teachers, sales clerks, an actor, an unemployed lawyer, even a librarian. He shook his head as he set aside these applications, which he regarded as misguided and inappropriate, unaware that the fault was his, not theirs.

He settled on two applicants and notified the young women, by letter post, of his decision to grant each of them an interview at the flat at an appointed day and time. On the day in question, he put on his best suit and waited. He resisted the impulse to tidy the place, to dust his mother's collection of miniature Chinese warriors and Portuguese dancing figures, to take out soap and water and have another go at the wine stain under the coffee table, to finally discard the newspapers that had accumulated on his father's desk in the months he had spent waiting for the old man to regain his health and return home. These were tasks, after all, that the girl would be expected to perform.

But as he waited for the first stranger to arrive, the flat seemed to expand before his eyes and grow huge and cluttered. It occurred to him —not for the first time—that the wage he'd offered was insufficient to make the job attractive, and he worried that neither of the applicants would accept the position after being in the apartment and seeing what she would be up against. His office would pose a particular challenge, because his papers now filled ten shelves and had overflowed into piles on the floor. He had books that he hadn't touched for twenty years. He sometimes ate while he worked, and he was often coming across bits of petrified food that he didn't recognize and couldn't recall ever having cooked. In fact, the whole notion of allowing another person into the flat after all this time left him feeling vaguely imperilled—as if he were plotting his own demise—and he was suddenly conscious of a sweetly cloying taste rolling off the edges of his tongue. By the time the buzzer rang, promptly at the appointed hour, he had convinced himself that he didn't need a housekeeper after all but decided that he had to go through with the interviews, if only to be polite. Once they were concluded he would inform both applicants that, regretfully, he had hired someone else.

He opened the door and let the first girl into the flat.

She was taller than he expected, almost as tall as he was. And pretty, rather than beautiful, in the winsome, pasty complexioned manner of some aristocrats. Her dark hair fell in soft curls and rested on her shoulders. For the interview she had chosen practicality over sparkle and was dressed in a white blouse and grey skirt cinched at her tiny waistline. But her smile was dazzling. She met his eyes and smiled broadly as she held out her hand for him to shake and introduced herself as Lucinda Machado.

"I've come about the position of housekeeper?" The question in her voice, which was mirrored in her eyes, brought him back to himself.

"Please," he said, falsely calm, indicating the parlour where he had been waiting. The roaring in his chest resounded so clearly in his ears that he thought he would not be able to make himself heard above the ruckus.

When they were seated, he on the antique divan, she in the slender wingback chair preferred by his mother in her later years, it occurred to him that he had given no thought to the questions he would ask. He had never really had any exposure to young women, having spent most of his youth in his room with his books. At the archives, his two assistants were men, one of them grey-haired and older than himself. He glanced at the smooth skin of her neck, which still bore traces of the glow it had acquired with the exertion of quickly mounting five flights of stairs, and then at her eyes, which gazed at him with the naive eagerness of youth.

He could think of nothing to say.

When he was growing up all his friends had been boys, some his own age, some older, some younger. They ventured to the outskirts of the city where they played in the remains of buildings damaged by earthquakes or destroyed in the uprisings and conflicts of the previous decades, enjoyed alliances that crumbled as quickly as they were formed, used sticks to torment the dogs that ran wild in the streets. With the onset of puberty he joined a closely knit group of boys who, though it was unstated, preferred each other's companionship over anyone else's. Together they shoplifted and raided the clotheslines in the back yards of houses in the exclusive river district. Later on, avoiding the girls in the neighbourhood, he and his friends went swimming in a secret water hole in the hills outside the city, and here they explored each other's bodies and learned to sodomize and masturbate each other. For a while he thought this was love and that it was all he would ever need. But the group dispersed as they grew older; he retreated into his books, where he had remained ever since. These had been his first, and only, sexual encounters, and looking at Lucinda perched like a child-queen on his mother's chair, he blushed ferociously.

"Would you like a cup of tea?" he asked, making a sweeping yet strangely indecisive motion with one arm.

"Would you like me to get it for you?" She stood quickly and bustled away, instinctively it seemed, in the direction of the kitchen. He realized she'd taken his query as the beginning of the interview, as a test of sorts.

Unable to relax in her presence, he now felt the tension lift from his shoulders as he listened to the clatter she made opening cupboards and searching for the tea tin and the cups and saucers. And surprisingly he found himself growing comfortable with the idea that someone else was in the flat doing something that needed to be done. The novelty of interacting on a meaningful level with another human being struck him with its freshness, and for the first time in his life he suffered the vaguest twinge of regret over all the weeks and months and years he'd spent alone with his books.

When she returned with the tray he noticed that she'd brought tea for him—as well as milk, sugar, biscuits—but none for herself.

"You're not having any?" he asked.

She set the tray on the table and stood before him, still wearing her coat. A small imitation-leather purse, grey to match her skirt, hung by its strap from her shoulder.

"I didn't want to presume," she said, and she opened her hands in a gesture of helplessness.

Aware, finally, of his obligations as host, he removed her coat from her shoulders and hung it in the closet and asked her to bring another cup and saucer from the cabinet in the kitchen. He served her tea and they talked. He asked how old she was.

"Seventeen," she said.

"How did you find out about the job? It was only advertised at the university."

"My brother brought home a copy of the advertisement." This seemed to cause her some embarrassment and she lowered her eyes. "I hope you don't mind."

"Not at all," he said.

Her brother was taking biology classes in preparation for medical school. Her father was a dentist. Enrique told her a few things about himself, about the various projects he was working on. She sighed and gazed wistfully around the room.

"It's so cozy here," she said, her eyes darting from side to side, and he found himself trying to catch a glimpse of her small tongue as it moved about in her small mouth.

When the apartment buzzer sounded again he leapt to his feet and almost cried out in alarm. Never before had he suffered such a lapse of memory or intellect. He had allowed this Lucinda, with her flawless skin and her haughty allure, to distract him from the scheduled second interview.

"Is that another applicant?" Lucinda asked calmly.

"Yes, yes," he muttered, looking this way and that. It was plain to them both that he didn't know what to do.

He steadied himself, one hand gripping the divan, while Lucinda went to the door and found the button on the panel that activated the front door release. Soon he heard a series of timid knocks, and Lucinda opened the door and admitted the girl into the flat. When Lucinda introduced herself as his niece and explained that she was helping with the interviews, he seated himself and wiped the sweat from his brow with a handkerchief. His breathing slowed to its normal pace as she showed the girl around the flat, which he had neglected to do with her. Finally they came into the parlour.

"Uncle, this is Dominique Rodriguez."

He smiled and inclined his head though he disliked this girl instantly because she was short and fat and had a snub nose.

Enrique said nothing while Lucinda conducted the interview herself, making notes on a scrap of paper with a pen that she had found in another room. As he watched her flex her slender wrist and listened to the soft music of her voice, his heart turned over, not once, not twice, but three times.

TWO

Enrique and Lucinda married less than a year after her interview. It was 1947. He was exactly twice her age, thirty-six to her eighteen. Her parents had explained about children and the rigors of raising a family. But Lucinda was a dreamer who had allowed romance novels to fill her head with radiant, fantastical notions of married life, which, on the morning of her wedding day, appeared before her as a series of empty months and years waiting to be filled, a mysterious and wonderful adventure that left her breathless at her own daring and feeling as if she were boarding a train with no ticket. However, Enrique appeared to believe not only that marriage would allow him to continue with his research, but that having a wife would present no obstacle to him shutting the door to his office for six, seven, eight hours at a stretch. That upon his reappearance the house would be clean and tidy, the laundry done and stowed, the silver polished, and his evening meal well along on its journey to the table did not seem to him unreasonable expectations. In short, he appeared to believe he would resume his old life, and not simply as a bachelor, but one who had hired a maid and a cook.

Despite her aristocratic bearing, Lucinda was a girl who demanded neither trinkets nor attention. Her family was of modest means for though her father was a dentist, he was not a very good one. But she had been raised in an enlightened household, in a home filled with poetry and music, where generosity was expected and encouraged. Her parents often gave food and clothing to their poorer neighbours, and her father was known for travelling to poverty-stricken corners of the province and donating his services. The Machados taught their children to enjoy the simple gifts of the beautiful world in which they were

15

privileged to live: a warm summer night, the song of the nightingale, the scent of wild roses.

But simple gifts are one thing and being ignored and neglected by your husband is something else. For the first months after the wedding, Enrique took pleasure in undressing her every night and paying homage to her body with his lips and tongue. But once the demands of domestic living supplanted the connubial rigors of the marriage bed, Lucinda realized that she had tethered herself to a supremely selfish man, one who ate whenever and whatever he wanted and who made no inquiries into how she was feeling or spending her time from one day to the next.

The first child came; then the second. Enrique spent more and more hours secluded in his office, the door shut and bolted, but still the children arrived—as if heavenly floodgates had been opened—a total of seven when the final count was tallied. The flat in the building at the end of Rua Santa Maria was now swarming with bodies, seething with the squall of babies, and foul with the stench of childrearing.

The boys, Carlos, Hector, and Julio, slept in one room, the girls, Dulciana, Cesara, Rosaria, and Helena, in another. There was one bathroom for the nine members of the Tomás family. Enrique and Lucinda continued to share a bedchamber, but it was a matter of convenience and nothing else. After only fifteen years their marriage bed had ceased to be a sensual retreat or a font of conjugal bliss. Only in her early thirties, Lucinda was still a very attractive woman, but her husband had reverted to the lusts of his youth and after his fiftieth birthday took a series of lovers, boys not much older than his own sons. Without the least warning he sometimes brought his companions to the flat for dinner, and Lucinda was compelled to prepare meals for a succession of slender, effeminate youths who drew curious stares from her own children and whose presence in her home made her supremely uncomfortable.

In addition, the neighbourhood around Rua Santa Maria was no longer as desirable as it had once been. When Enrique's parents had moved into the flat some forty years earlier, the rot was confined to the city's outer margins where earthquakes had rendered many buildings uninhabitable; the Tomás family lived in a community strictly of the elite, filled with doctors and lawyers and politicians, as well as oil industry executives and musicians from the state opera company. There was a public garden with a bandstand and a duck pond, and a number of monstrous estates owned by some of the city's wealthiest residents. The trees along all the streets were tended regularly, there was no loose litter blowing around, and animals were kept on leashes. Over many years, however, the decay made furtive inroads into the very heart of the city. Patriarchs and matriarchs died off. Families that had lived in one house for generations splintered and dispersed and developers bought the huge old dwellings, demolished them, divided the properties, then divided them again. Flimsy apartment complexes shot up offering affordable rents. A rezoning project allowed the streets near Rua Santa Maria to become cluttered with businesses, most of which failed, leaving behind vacant storefronts and smashed windows covered with sheets of plywood that were soon spray-painted with revolutionary slogans. Older structures that had not been maintained were condemned and abandoned. It was at about this time that a burgeoning awareness gripped people of all classes and income levels that the country was seething with unrest, that rebel factions were organizing and arming themselves, though nobody dared to voice their fears. Certainly not Enrique, engrossed as he was in his liaisons. And not Lucinda, engaged in a daily struggle to raise seven children on a budget that never varied, even after the currency was devalued by a quarter, and then again by a third.

basement of the Lutheran church and deeply influenced by their passions, which struck him as profound and meaningful. He spoke to his friend Nikos about his plan to build a bomb and use it to destroy some government target that would get a lot of attention, and Nikos passed this news along to his friends at school. Carlos told his little brothers, Hector and Julio, that he was soon going to go away and join the rebels, who were setting up camps in the hills. But Carlos did not know that all over the country the situation was rapidly deteriorating and that the government, desperate to maintain order along with its international credibility, had spies everywhere. All he really wanted to do was impress Isabel. But he was profligate and boastful, and soon word had spread from one end of Rua Santa Maria to the other that he was constructing a bomb and, depending upon who was telling the story, was going to use it to blow up a school or a bus filled with American tourists or a government office building. The truth was that he had done nothing but talk.

One night when he went to the church basement, they were all waiting for him and eyed him coldly as he entered. He began setting out the cups and the urn for brewing coffee, but nobody said a word and as the silence stretched he grew nervous because of the tension in the room. Eventually he turned and confronted them.

"Is something the matter?" he asked.

Isabel would not meet his eyes. For the first time that he could remember the radio had not been switched on.

His legs began to quiver and he fought to control his bladder.

Luis, the man who had been their chief organizer from the beginning, spoke first.

"Carlos, we have heard some disturbing things. There is word going about that you are preparing to engage in some terrorist activity. Is this true?"

He glanced from one face to the next and then shook his head.

Luis continued. "I'm glad to know that, Carlos. I hope you understand that we conduct our activities in secrecy because technically we are enemies of the state. You've noticed the soldiers on every street corner. If they knew we were here right now, they would break down the door and kill us all. You would not be spared just because you are the youngest. By association, you are one of us. And because you are one of us, when you say you are building bombs and planning to blow things up, people believe you. Do you understand?"

Carlos nodded. His throat had swelled and he was unable to speak.

Luis leaned forward and linked his hands together in the manner of a priest. "We're living in a very dangerous world, Carlos, and I will explain this to you even though I thought I had already made it clear. We do not speak of our work here. Each one of us conducts another life apart from this group, and it is important that we do not allow our roles to become mixed up with one another. I live with my mother and my idiot brother, and if anyone were to ask them where I spend my nights they would tell them that I am at the university, in the laboratory conducting experiments and monitoring the animals. They would say that because that is what I told them and they believe it to be true. Not because I have asked them to lie. When the time comes for the state to arrest me, my family will know nothing of my activities here. I have arranged it that way to ensure their safety and to leave the possibility open for them to escape. Now, I don't know what you have been saying to people—" He held up his hand when Carlos attempted to speak. "I don't know if you have divulged any facts that constitute a risk to our operation. But, Carlos, I cannot take that chance. I know you will understand. You are an intelligent boy. You will see that lives are at stake and that the movement we have gone to great trouble to build has been compromised by your actions. We have no choice but to move our operation elsewhere and you will no longer have the privilege of making coffee and fetching newspapers for us. After tonight, there is no place for you in our organization. Your only duty now, Carlos, is to return to your life of playing stickball and going to school and doing what your parents tell you to. I want you to be innocent and to make it plain to anyone who asks that you made a great mistake when you tried to gain the attention of the adults who have been ignoring you by telling stories about bombs and guns. Do you understand me?"

Carlos nodded. He wanted to catch Isabel's eye, but she was watching Luis.

"Now, Carlos," Luis continued in an unhurried manner. "Do you have anything to say in your own defence?"

He looked around the room. The plaster was cracked and there were spider webs hanging from every corner of the ceiling and the tables were coated with dust, but he had found happiness here along with a sense that the duties he performed, though menial, carried with them a ponderous burden of history. He didn't want to give up any of this.

"I won't do it again," he said, his voice distorted by the dryness of his throat. "I'll be quiet. I promise." But he knew his cause was a lost one when Isabel finally looked at him with eyes that were as hard and blank as slate.

Luis stood. His khakis were wrinkled and his gun was evident in the belt resting at his hip.

"You will come here, Carlos," he said, extending his arm and motioning with one hand. "Come to me." The others remained seated.

Carlos stepped carefully around the tables and broken chairs and debris and stood in front of Luis, who drew a black cloth from his back pocket. This he held lengthwise before Carlos and then placed it over the boy's eyes. He tied the ends together behind Carlos' head. Carlos did not resist. No light penetrated the cloth. He was blinded.

"Because you are no longer a member of this group, we must conceal our activities from you, as we would from any outsider. I trust I do not have to ask you to remain quiet."

Carlos was crying now and soon the cloth was wet with his tears.

He felt hands on his shoulders and was forced to march forward. He stumbled. Nobody said anything. After walking briefly he heard a door creak open on rusty hinges. They had left the main room and had entered a space that was damp and smelled of spoilage. He sensed walls close by on either side. Someone held his arms behind his back while his wrists were bound tightly together with twine. Then he was thrust forward and collided heavily with a wall and fell to his knees. He whimpered but did not cry out. The door was shut behind him and he heard it being locked from the outside. Steps receded into the distance, but he was not convinced that he was alone, and after a minute during which he remained absolutely still despite his discomfort he heard Luis say through the door, "Carlos, I am no longer responsible for your safety. I am sorry for this. I wish you the best of luck."

After a moment he shifted his body and sat on the floor. He had urinated in his pants and his shame was such that he dared not make a sound in case they came back and Isabel saw what he had done. The brackish foulness of his urine flooded his nostrils. He listened for sounds of movement but heard nothing. He wondered why they had not killed him and could think only that they pitied him and this made him angry and even more ashamed of himself. Why had he told stories about building bombs and blowing things up when he'd no intention of doing anything? Of course, he knew why. By speaking this way he made the other boys fear and respect him, and when he saw the fear in their eyes he said other things that also were not true. He had made sure they all knew that he was a trusted and valued member of a faction that hoped one day to topple the government, for this made him brave and important in their eyes. Even now he could not imagine his life without the other boys gazing at him with awe and admiration and he decided, as he struggled with his bindings, that he would not stop telling stories. When he left here tonight he would behave as if nothing had happened.

It was some minutes after Luis had spoken to him through the door that he was at last able to twist his hands free of the string that bound his wrists. He pulled off the blindfold and stood. He put his hands out and felt the walls of a closet. There was no light. Above him was the wooden rod used for suspending garments on hangers. He lifted this out of the slots where it rested at either end and held it like a baseball bat. It occurred to him that he had been put through a trial or test. They were probably waiting for him. Even now Luis was looking at his watch, counting how many minutes it was taking him to free himself. He reached for the doorknob and gave it a twist, but it held fast. With his shoulder he applied pressure against the door, measuring the resistance it offered. Finally he slid the rod back into place and, grasping it with both hands, lifted himself and pressed his feet flat against the door. He battered the door with both feet again and again until the wood cracked and then the lock gave. He had made a lot of noise and he hoped this would not be counted against him. But when he burst into the room where their meetings had been held there was nobody in sight. It was dark. The communications equipment was gone, as were the coffee urn and the electric generator. He was alone.

They had left the room as they'd found it, in a state of dilapidation, so that if government troops were ever to conduct a search it would look as if it had been abandoned a long time ago, and this was how it appeared to him now, like nobody had been there for many years. All the tables were either broken or upended. Chunks of plaster and concrete littered the floor. Carlos scuffed through the vacated space, unbelieving at first, but in the end persuaded that his friends had forsaken him. A few more tears dropped from his cheeks and mingled with the dust that coated the floor. His sopping underwear chafed against his skin. He became angry again and uttered a curse, but his anger changed nothing. When he lifted his eyes the room was still dark and empty, and in the midst of the stony and indifferent silence of the four walls surrounding him his anger soon died away and was replaced by twinges of helplessness and spasms of remorse. He bowed his head and admitted finally that he had behaved with the kind of reckless stupidity that gets people killed and that it was unlikely he would ever see Isabel again.

He walked home hoping that his pants would dry before he got there. The day had been warm and the air still held its warmth against his skin. The rains of October and November had come and gone and people would soon be enjoying the hot dry days of early summer, and like every-one else he was looking forward to this. Normally he moved quickly and silently, counting his steps as he passed through side streets and narrow alleyways, but tonight he defied the curfew and walked straight up the broad Avenida Independencia towards Plaza des Patriotas, where the monument to dead soldiers stood in front of the austere stone build-ing that housed the military academy. Though empty, the *avenida* was brightly lit by lamps mounted on steel poles and he felt no danger being alone. As he approached Rua Santa Maria, he heard laughter and passed a cluster of young soldiers smoking in a recessed doorway beneath a tattered awning. Their guns glinted in the light as, unconcerned, they watched him pass by, and he realized that he could easily become one of them, that his passions and loyalties, as pliable as chewing gum, could be turned in an instant to the service of those who, only moments before, he had been plotting to destroy. He understood as well that politics were of no interest to him, that he didn't care about his country or its people, and it came to him as he rounded the last corner and observed the building where he had lived his entire life that what he desired above even love or money was to carry a gun and have others look at him and be afraid. These thoughts gave him hope, and as he crept up the stairs to his family's flat and let himself in, he envisioned the kneeling figure of Luis and saw himself pressing the muzzle of a gun against the terrified man's head.

Hector awoke when his brother entered the bedroom. He always woke up when Carlos returned from his nocturnal rambles, and as always his feelings were a mixture of relief, curiosity, and envy. Remaining still, he watched as his brother undressed in the shower of silver moonlight that flooded the small room. Carlos removed his clothes quickly and let them drop to the floor. His movements were jerky and his lips trembled as if he were speaking with someone. He made no sounds. His naked body was sinewy, no longer that of a boy. Hector saw a smile flicker across his brother's face, but it was a smile without mirth and when he saw this, the muscles of his belly clenched and he was afraid. But his fear was gone a moment later when Carlos drew back the blanket and crawled into the bed beside their youngest brother, Julio, who slept in between them.

Hector wanted to tell his brother where he had been that day and what he had seen. After spending a tedious morning in school, during which he dreamed and thought of anything except the work that was put in front of him, he did not go back in the afternoon. Instead he joined some of his friends in a vacant lot in the old factory district where they played a game of stickball. Afterward they explored an abandoned apartment building where one of the children claimed vagrants were living and where someone else had told them there was a dead body in the basement. He arrived home late in the afternoon, tired but enthralled by what he had seen, sticky with the sweat of his childish pursuits. The dead body stood comparison to his brother's tales of guns and radios and throwing rocks at soldiers. He had seen it with his own eyes. But because he'd been out exploring all afternoon he had arrived home later than usual, just in time to sit down for dinner. He found it impossible to talk when the rest of the family was there, especially his mother and father. They never listened to what he said. The girls chattered all through the meal, and afterward Carlos vanished without saying goodbye or even excuse me. For some reason Carlos was allowed to do whatever he wanted. Nobody asked him where he was going or when he was coming home. His parents were always distracted by something, his father with his studies and his young companions, his mother with cooking and cleaning and trying to keep the house in order. They rarely spoke to one another and hardly seemed aware of the fact that their oldest son was almost never at home. Hector's sisters played together and sometimes let him and Julio join them, though Hector was older now and disdained their dolls and plush toys and girls' adventure books, cherishing instead the plastic revolver and cowboy hat that his father had given him. Carlos roamed the margin of the family unit like an unwelcome guest. When Carlos began leaving the flat most evenings and not returning until dawn, Hector looked at his parents and remaining siblings and guessed he was the only one to whom it made any difference. In the last few months his brother had grown elusive and mysterious. Hector valued his presence all the more because of its rarity.

He whispered, "Carlos!" then drew in his breath and waited for a reply. Between them Julio's rhythmic exhalations continued. Hector raised himself up and rested his weight on one elbow.

"Carlos!"

"What? Go to sleep."

"I saw a body today. In the old apartment building on Avenida Castelia, out past the fish market. You know the one?"

"I've seen lots of bodies. Go to sleep."

"It was in the basement. The rats had got it. Joaquin threw up, but it didn't bother me."

"You shouldn't go into those places!"

"You go into those places."

"I'm older. Go to sleep."

Julio sighed and rearranged himself beneath the bedclothes. Hector waited.

"Carlos!"

"What?"

"I want to be with you, when you go out at night."

"Don't be crazy. You're too young."

"I'm not. I'm ten."

There was silence. Hector watched the back of his brother's head, which rested on the pillow and was quite still. The moon's silver light mingled with and gave depth to the tangle of black hair. Hector wondered what his brother was thinking. This was more important to him than anything else.

"Carlos—"

"In the morning," Carlos said wearily.

"Yes?"

"In the morning we will go and see your body. Now go to sleep."

Hector lay back and closed his eyes. He smiled, even though it was

26

dark and nobody would see him. Warmth spread outward from his heart and into his limbs and made his feet tingle. He glowed with the triumph of having made himself heard. He'd detected interest in Carlos' voice, seriousness in his tone. After tomorrow he would join his brother at night and together they would roam the city. What they would do, where they would go—he gave no thought to this. But he knew they would have to be careful. The soldiers patrolling the streets and enforcing the curfew would not hesitate to shoot if provoked.

Hector did not understand the unrest gripping his country, but he knew that his mother was often angry at having to stand in line for food that had once been plentiful. The whole family was subjected to her complaints, which were endless and repetitive. How many times had he listened to her complain about empty shelves in the supermarket and about having to pay 150 pesetas for a loaf of stale bread? How many times had he heard her say the fishmonger was a liar and a fool? This year he was fortunate: he had new shoes. But some of his friends had no shoes, and in his mind this was linked to the sporadic gunfire that punctuated the night and the radio and television blackouts that were becoming more frequent and that seemed to declare that life was changing in ways that no one could foresee. He overheard conversations among his teachers and among adults in his apartment building; he heard people everywhere talking of other places, other countries, especially America. He didn't really understand where or what America was, but like many of his friends, he listened to these words and had come to regard America as a bastion of freedom and opportunity where he might someday live and make money and buy a big house. This is what people were saying you could do there. The government would give you a place to live and find a job for you, and you would have more money in your pocket in a month than you could make at home in a year.

The hope of going to live in America seemed to be a hope shared by everyone, and Hector wondered what would happen to his own country if everyone left. It seemed a terrible thing, to wish so badly to leave your home, even for such a paradise as America. But when he looked around he could see why people would want to go somewhere else. The only city he had ever lived in was falling to pieces, and though he had never ventured beyond its precincts, he had no reason to believe the rest of the country was not similarly afflicted. When his teachers and his parents spoke of a time not long ago when the streets were safe and clean, and goods of every imaginable sort were available at reasonable prices, and there was no need for curfews or soldiers, he could scarcely believe they weren't making it up. For Hector Tomás, the military was a daily presence and even food that was stale or beginning to spoil was consumed zealously because it was better than nothing.

He had fallen back to sleep, but was awakened by a sound. It was the hour when the first pink flush of daylight could be detected above the eastern horizon, along that distant rim where the hills rolled down to meet the city. He adjusted his pillow and listened. The street below the bedroom window seemed quiet, but he was aware of a deliberate hush, as if voices somewhere had been silenced. He knew that in the flat next door old Señor Volos would soon be rousing himself to go up to the roof and feed his pigeons, and he thought maybe he would follow and, as he had in the past, help the old man scrape the droppings from the floor of the pen and spread out the new seed. The hollow sonorities of his brothers' breathing filled the room. He dozed.

It happened with the swiftness of a bird taking flight and he was still barely awake when it was over. There was a crash that somehow seemed a part of his dream, though it did not belong. In the dream he was walking beside his classmate Nadia, who was from Warsaw, across a field fragrant with wild thyme, gathering pink daisies for her into a bouquet. When the crash sounded they looked to each other and then upward, as if the answer to the mystery resided in the clouds gliding across the blue sky. He heard voices. The vision of himself with Nadia dissolved as he was thrust towards consciousness. His fist was still clenched around the stems of the dream flowers, but the bed was being jostled and he knew that someone had been in the room. He sat up. Carlos was no longer there. Julio was standing in the doorway.

"Carlos," Julio cried. "No! Carlos!"

Hector jumped from the bed and pushed past Julio. A dark huddle of figures stood in the hallway. Carlos was struggling to cover his nakedness with a pair of trousers. Two men were with him. One gripped him by the arm.

Hector heard a brutish voice command: "Hurry!"

The glint of metal caught his eye just as the door of his parents' bedroom swung open. The unshaven face of the man who held the gun was suddenly visible. Hector saw his black beard and eyebrows, the crooked scar below his eye. The man looked straight at him and at that moment Hector lost his voice. With a sweeping motion the man raised the gun and, pointing past Enrique, who stood in the open doorway trying to speak, fired. The blast knocked Hector to the floor and in the same instant the light went out. Voices raging and crying filled his ears—he heard Carlos, his father, and his mother—and then the grunt of someone receiving a blow, and the terrifying thud of a body hitting the floor. A second later it was over. The two men were gone and had taken Carlos with them. For just a moment a brittle silence prevailed. Hector went to his father, who with Lucinda's help had raised himself to his knees. There was blood on his face and his eyes were wet and wild. The door of the girls' bedroom opened slowly, and then they poured out, sounding a general lamentation. Julio resumed wailing and refused to be comforted until finally Dulciana had to go to him. The morning was growing brighter and soon neighbours arrived from throughout the building, all of them asking what had happened. Hector heard his mother: "They've taken him. They've taken my Carlos!"

"But Lucinda, who? Who has taken him?"

"I don't know. They looked like criminals."

Later in the morning Hector observed his father in the front room, sitting perfectly still in his chair. He held a pad of gauze to the yellow bruise that encircled his eye. He seemed dazed. He looked at Hector but said nothing.

Nobody went to school that day. The girls stayed in their room. Hector loitered outside their door, but all was silent within.

His mother sat in the kitchen with the other women.

"You must go to the police and report this! Tell them! Demand an explanation!"

"Why would they take him? He's just a boy."

"Do you think it was the police?"

"None of us are safe. The other day? My Ricardo was coming home from school and saw a man being pushed into the back of a truck. It wasn't the police, he said, but they had guns."

Hector went into his parents' bedroom and looked at the ceiling light, which had been shattered by the bullet. Nobody had done the cleaning up. The bullet had taken a chunk out of the ceiling and glass and flakes of plaster littered the unmade sheets and the floor. He went into his own room. Julio lay on the bed covered by a thick blanket. His mother had given him a pill and Julio whimpered lightly and twitched in his sleep. The shirt and underwear that Carlos had discarded the night before lay where he'd dropped them. Outside, the day was bright and when Hector looked down to the street he could see people walking with a light step, riding in buses, stopping to talk, laughing as if all were normal. But it was not a normal day, and he wondered why they pretended it was.

FOUR

Many months passed before the Tomás family returned to something resembling their normal state of affairs, though, of course, they would never be the same. Carlos did not return and nothing was heard of him. Enrique claimed to have made inquiries into the abduction of his son. He reported to his wife that the police were not interested in the disappearance of a teenager and threatened to arrest him if he didn't let the matter drop. Lucinda suspected that he had done nothing. He went about his life as always, back and forth to work, shutting himself in his office when he returned home. His manner did not change; he remained by turns inward and reserved, or childishly petulant and demanding. The only difference she noticed was the circle of rouge that appeared on his cheek whenever he was expecting company—one of his depraved young companions— or was planning to go out for the evening, where she did not ask.

By now it was clear that civil unrest would not be avoided. The number of soldiers deployed in the streets continued to grow. People were being detained or arrested simply because they aroused suspicion, and because those with a cleft lip or a club foot or one eye turned inward had never been trusted to begin with, the prisons were soon filled with these unfortunates. Hector's geography teacher, a gaunt young man with a beard who had spoken with enthusiasm of other countries and cultures, and who often brought photographs and slides from his travels to share with the class, vanished without a word of warning.

Hector's mother reminded him again and again, until he was sick of hearing it, that he must not dawdle on his way to and from school. "It's dangerous," was all she would say when he asked what she was afraid of. Then one of his classmates—a gentle boy with no enemies—failed to report to school for an entire week. Hector and some friends followed some of the older boys to his house on Avenida de Suarez, and they found it open and abandoned, with slogans and insignia in black and red paint sprayed on the walls, all the furniture smashed and overturned, and what looked like smears of blood. Later, Hector learned the boy's father wrote for the newspaper. After this he respected the pleas of his mother and ceased his wandering and his search for dead bodies and did not stay out any longer than necessary. He did what he was told and escorted his sisters and his little brother whenever they had to go out. Lucinda had a new look in her eyes, a haunted look that made him think of a wild animal that was always on the alert. It made him long for life as it had been before Carlos had disappeared.

But the worst thing was that after the initial shock and outrage had died away, and his absence had become to their everyday lives what darkness is to the night, nobody spoke of Carlos. Nobody said his name out loud. To Hector, it seemed the entire family was pretending his brother had never existed. They hung their heads, pursed their lips, and avoided eye contact as if the events of that night had cast a pall of shame over the Tomás home. His parents offered no explanation and responded to his questions with silence. Because she was the oldest, one quiet evening Hector approached Dulciana and asked if she had been told what happened to Carlos. All at once she was unable to look him in the eye. With her head tilted downward and her face concealed behind an impenetrable veil of thick dark hair, she choked back a sob and concentrated even harder on her sewing.

Hector now shared a bed only with little Julio, and as he lay there each night he wondered where Carlos had gone and what he was doing. It did not occur to him that Carlos might be dead. In his mind he conjured an image of the hero rebel that Carlos had become. When Julio asked where Carlos was, he told the boy all about the raids and dangerous incursions that Carlos and his friends were carrying out from their headquarters, which was concealed in the hills, miles from the city, deep in the countryside. Who were they fighting against? Julio wanted to know, and Hector discovered he had no answer to this question. All he knew was that there used to be food and now there was none; that they used to be well off and now they were poor; that his mother made herself sick with worry and that on the way home from school his sisters were often afraid when they found themselves being followed by groups of insolent young soldiers, all of them with the same hungry, jealous look in their eyes. It was this, he told his brother, that Carlos and his friends were fighting against. Have you been to see him? Julio asked. Yes, Hector said. Carlos had come one night and taken him to the headquarters. Carlos had been driving a Jeep and it took hours to get there because it was dark and because they had to follow the back roads in order to avoid the military checkpoints, and these roads were narrow and winding and in bad repair. They had guns, he went on, and they all lived, men and women together, in a cabin with many rooms, and women from nearby villages brought them food and water because they were so brave. They spent their time planning raids and talking about the people they would kill and what they would do with their prisoners. They smoked cigarettes and laughed out loud because they weren't afraid of anything. Julio asked when he and Hector would go to visit, and Hector told him soon. He mustn't tell anyone, but they would go very soon. And after Julio was asleep Hector rested his head on the pillow and was ashamed because now that Carlos was gone the bed was spacious and cool, and he was glad because of this.

FIVE

Señor Volos leaned against the wall and extended his finger towards the cloudy horizon, which blushed with early morning light, pointing at something Hector couldn't see. As if continuing a conversation that had only been interrupted a short time ago, he said, "When I was a boy, there were no tall buildings and no factories. It was all pine trees, tall monkey-puzzle trees, right down to the ocean. But you're much too young to know about this, it was all so long ago. The water was clean too. We had a beautiful country once." He shook his head and made a clicking sound with his tongue. "Now they've made it ugly."

Hector had come up to the roof early to tend the pigeons. He found their cooing cheered him. It was as if the birds, like old men, were grateful for the opportunity to gather together and converse, and he felt lucky to be in the midst of their chatter. They didn't seem troubled by his invasion of their space. As he scraped the floor of the pens and filled the metal bowls with seed, they observed him with beady eyes.

It was early July and growing colder by the day. The rains had begun and Hector knew they would not let up for many weeks. Often he felt the damp and the chill penetrate through to his bones and it sometimes seemed as if this were a condition of being alive, of being human. Señor Volos seemed not to notice the cold. His tweed hat with the black band was perched on top of his sparse white hair, but it never blew off, not even in strong winds. He wore an old brown suit jacket that had been patched and patched again at the elbows, the collar of his pink shirt was frayed, and he smoked cigarettes, one after another until he started coughing with an explosive urgency that began deep in his throat and seized his entire body with spasms. Once the outburst had passed, he would resume smoking, struggling to light the match with trembling hands.

"Do you think there will be a war?" Hector asked. He frowned and held his voice steady in an effort to not sound too hopeful.

Señor Volos rested his elbows on the wall and glanced at his young companion, whose eyes and hair were as black as the coal he used to shovel into the stove when he was Hector's age. The boy puzzled him, and not only because he posed disturbing questions, but also because he was willing to perform menial chores without being asked—chores that were unpleasant and required a strong stomach, like removing pigeon dung from the bottom of the coop and filling plastic bags with it and leaving those bags by the curb to be taken away. Why a boy of twelve would want to dirty his hands in such a way made Señor Volos think there must be something wrong with him. Hector was small for his age as well and had to work very hard to pry the cement-like droppings away from the wooden base of the pen. His scrawny arms protruded from the short sleeves of a shirt that, at least two sizes too big for him, enfolded his torso loosely, like a tent. The shirt was a garish blue with crooked yellow-green stripes, something no sane person would buy at full price. It was probably left behind in a hotel room by an American tourist and made its way to the flea market, where Hector's mother would have bought it for ten pesetas and thought herself ill-used. But Señor Volos did not like to speculate about the fortunes of the Tomás family, who had fallen several notches in rank since he had known them. And though the boy could be a nuisance with his questions, he would not trade Hector's companionship for solitude, with which he was only too familiar. Señor Volos knew that, though only in his sixties, his life was approaching its end. He had lost interest in his pigeons long ago and would have dismantled the pens, burned the wood in his stove, and allowed the birds to take their chances with nature, if not for young Hector Tomás, whose father everyone called *esta inútil,* "the useless one." For many months now Hector had been doing almost all the work. Occasionally Señor Volos would take a handful of seed and scatter it over the rooftop just for the pleasure of watching the birds demonstrate their affection for him by clustering at his feet, but his back was stiff and sore all the time now and would not tolerate the stooping and bending these activities demanded. Most of the time he simply watched Hector work. He knew that Hector would not be with him for much longer, that if fighting broke out his parents would send their children away to live with relatives, or maybe to stay in a Christian shelter. He had made up his mind: the pigeons would go when Hector did, but not before.

"You should be asking your father these questions."

Hector lowered his gaze. "My father never talks about things like war. I can't ask him anything. He won't talk to me. All he ever does is give me books and tell me to go away and read them."

"Books are good, Hector. Don't you like to read?"

"No." Hector pursed his lips and spat in imitation of the older boys at school. He thought of his sister Cesara with her thick glasses, always going to the library. "I hate reading. Books are for girls."

They had been through this sort of thing before, and so Señor Volos simply nodded. He had no patience to argue a point like this. It was up to the boy's parents to explain to him that if he neglected his intellect he'd grow up to be a dumb animal. Still, he felt more than fondness for Hector Tomás, and sometimes had to fight back an impulse to ruffle the boy's hair or pinch his cheek as an uncle or grandfather might. He understood that these feelings placed him in an awkward position and that they had sprung from the bottomless well of loneliness in which he had been immersed since his wife died seven years ago. But he was unable to quell them, and now, after all this time, was unsure that he wanted to. His own children were scattered across the globe; he never saw them and hardly ever heard from them, and there were times when their names, to his shame, escaped him altogether.

Above the sounds of the morning traffic, Hector asked, "If there is a war, what will you do?"

"There's nowhere for me to go. I suppose I'll stay right here."

"Will it be safe here?"

Señor Volos regarded Hector with a stern eye. "Who can say? Every war is different."

Hector nodded. He knew his questions sometimes annoyed the old man, like a mosquito on its insatiable quest for blood, but he could not help himself. Other than Señor Volos his life was empty of adults to whom he could direct his inquiries.

"What was the last war like?"

Señor Volos drew thoughtfully on his cigarette and exhaled the smoke through his nose. "You do not want to know the answer to that question," he said.

Hector nodded. "Were there bodies everywhere?"

The old man tipped his head downward in order to observe something on the street. Hector waited for his hat to fall off, but once again it defied gravity. Behind them the pigeons pecked at the fresh seed Hector had put out and, settling on their perches, made sounds of contentment.

"It wasn't like that," Señor Volos muttered. "It wasn't that kind of war."

"What kind of war was it?"

Hector watched his friend, eagerly awaiting a response. He knew that if he persisted he would eventually break down the old man's reserve and get an answer. It often happened this way and their conversations were typically filled with lengthy pauses during which it seemed that Señor Volos had successfully evaded the thrust of Hector's curiosity, only to give way to it in the end. Just one time Señor Volos had held his silence—and indeed had demonstrated his displeasure by tossing his cigarette over the side of the building and going indoors. This was when Hector had asked question after question about his family. Hector had never again allowed his inquisitiveness to stray in that direction.

"For most of us it was a war we didn't know we were fighting." Señor Volos lit another cigarette and drew the smoke deep into his lungs. "There were no gun battles on the street. There was nothing to shoot at. They told us there was an enemy, but it wasn't the kind of enemy you could see."

Hector didn't understand, but he said nothing.

"I was very young, a little bit older than you are now. I was engaged to be married to a beautiful girl. I loved her very much. I was only seventeen. She was fifteen. That's the way it was done in those days. You married when you were very young and started a family, and if the grace of God was with you, then you would live to see your grandchildren. I was living with my mother and father in their little house and I had seven brothers and sisters. The only way I was going to get out was to join the army. So I joined the army and they gave me a gun and showed me how to use it. But I used it only in practice. Never once did I fire bullets at a living thing. One day I said goodbye to my Louisa and they put me in a barracks with a hundred other boys and they made us all work so hard some got sick and were sent home. A few died, but they were weaklings and we all knew they didn't belong. You can't imagine it now, but I was a fine specimen in those days. I had long legs and a straight back and I could walk for many miles without getting tired. I didn't smoke then."

Hector had never heard Señor Volos say so many words at one time, especially in a voice that trembled. He watched as the old man drew a new cigarette from the package in his shirt pocket. But there was one already in his mouth and Señor Volos seemed confused to discover this. After a moment he used the glowing end of the old one to light the new one, then threw the old butt away.

Hector looked towards the coast and saw that the sky had brightened. A wind had risen out of the west and carried with it a briny fragrance of decay. Señor Volos had once explained to him that this meant the seas were very rough.

"If you read the history books you will learn about General Aguaria. He was a little man, *enano,* a shrimp. But he always looked taller in his big boots, and he liked to ride on horseback to inspect his troops so they wouldn't see how *pequeño* he was. But everybody knew. Still, all the people were afraid of Aguaria because he had gathered many men around him, the kind of men who will do anything.

"Then the government decided to introduce reforms. They wanted to limit the power of the military because everybody was so scared. But before the lawmakers could pass these reforms and make them into law, Aguaria had the president arrested and charged with treason. This is where the system failed us because nobody knew what to do. You see, we had never seen any president of ours brought before us in shackles and with a hood over his head. Aguaria had a fine speaking voice and he went before the Assembly and said that the president and his friends had been stealing the country's money and that's why everyone was so poor. There was a tribunal and the president was found guilty. Of course, it was rigged. Everybody knew. But it didn't matter because the whole country wanted to believe what Aguaria was saying. He was smart. He had discovered what the people wanted to hear and he said it again and again, each time more loudly than the time before. And the more he said it the more it seemed like the truth. Because it was true that we were poor. And it was much more agreeable to believe that the government was corrupt than to have to accept that people weren't working hard enough.

"After the tribunal delivered its verdict it wasn't over because there were members of the old government who wanted the president freed.

These men went into hiding and organized an opposition. And then the president's wife, who had been an actress once and who was so beautiful you would weep to see her, she spoke about what was happening. After her husband was found guilty of treason, she went on the radio and told everyone that it was all lies, that her husband was innocent. She called Aguaria a troll, a contemptible little man.

"That was when the trouble started. Aguaria installed himself as president and dissolved the Assembly. He gave a speech from the balcony of the state house and said he was going to clean up our country and get rid of the fascists and the anarchists and the communists and anyone else who threatened what he called the "civil law." Soldiers were sent out to keep order, and my unit was put on a train and we ended up in a village a thousand miles away, beyond the mountains. The people who lived there were ignorant peasants. They didn't know anything about what was going on in the capital, but we were instructed to round them up. Most of them ran away when they saw us coming with our rifles, but we captured about thirty of them and locked them in a cattle shed with the animals. None of us knew why we had been sent there, but the rumour was that because Aguaria had unseated a legitimate government that had allies in other countries, he feared an invasion, and we were supposed to keep a lookout for foreign troops. Of course nothing happened."

Señor Volos drew on his cigarette and gazed into the distance. He was silent for a long time before he picked up the thread of his story.

"When winter came it grew very cold, and because we'd kept the peasants from harvesting their crops and catching fish and tending their animals, there was no food. At the beginning the train came once a week with provisions, but then it was once every two weeks, then once a month. People started getting sick. It was the worst feeling because we were far away from home and most of us were just boys. We lived in stone cottages and made our own meals out of whatever we could find. We were supposed to feed the prisoners as well, but, truthfully, this didn't happen very often. One day we discovered the cattle shed was empty. All the peasants had escaped, disappeared into the hills, and taken their animals with them. Our commander was furious, but what could he do? He said someone had let them out. But how could he know this for sure? Anyway it didn't matter because we were having enough trouble keeping ourselves alive, and most of us were glad the peasants had gone and we wished them well. But for our commander it was as if he had suffered a great personal humiliation. He was tall and thin with sunken eyes, and his hair was black and greasy, but he wasn't much older than the rest of us and he didn't know how to be a leader or how to inspire the correct mixture of fear and respect. He took the two boys who had been on duty when the peasants escaped and used his gun to force some of the other boys to torture them. Finally after days of being tortured they both began telling the same story, saying how the other one had fallen in love with a peasant girl and had let all the peasants escape because of fears she would be hurt. It was terrible to hear this because it could so easily be true.

"By this time the train had stopped coming altogether. We had no way to communicate with the rest of the country. It was as if nobody knew or cared where we were. The commander decided to have both soldiers executed as an example to the rest of us. He said we would soon learn to obey orders. On the day this was to happen he came to the cottage where I was and said I would be part of the firing squad. I followed him into the snow. It was very cold that day. I remember the sky was dark and there were black birds that looked like ravens circling around. None of us had seen these birds before. The two boys who were to be executed were standing with their backs against a stone wall at the edge of a field. They had been stripped down to their shirts because, we were told, their overcoats could be used for something else once they were dead. The snow was two feet deep. I went to join the six others in the firing squad. The commander marched around and around talking to himself. We were all looking at each other and none of us could hide the fear in our eyes. Maybe something had happened in the capital. Maybe he'd heard news of some sort, but I didn't know how this could be. I was getting my rifle ready, but it was such a long time since I'd used it even in target practice that I didn't know if it would fire, and I wondered if this too would anger our commander. I was scared and my hands were shaking. It felt to me like the world was coming to an end. I was just as scared as those two boys at the other end of the field.

"Then there was a shot. It came from somewhere close by, but I didn't see. I looked up and the commander was lying in the snow. There was a gurgling sound coming from his throat and his body was pitching back and forth. He had been hit in the neck and his blood stained the snow a colour that I will never forget. He struggled for a bit then stopped moving. None of us went to him. Instead we helped the two condemned boys back to the cottages and dressed them in warm clothes. When we went to drag the commander's body into the forest we had to chase away the birds that had come to peck out his eyes. To this day I don't know who fired that shot."

Señor Volos stopped speaking and in the abrupt silence Hector flinched, as if he'd been awakened from a dream. He looked at his friend, who leaned forward with his elbows resting against the wall, his gaze falling over the city, his hat perched high on his head. The old man's face had relaxed and his eyes seemed clear and untroubled. There was almost nothing left of the cigarette in his hand.

"Someone was guilty of murder, but with our silence we promised we would never talk about it. So then we had to decide what to do next. Since the commander had never trusted anyone to be his lieutenant, there was nobody to take his place. We took an inventory of the supplies we had, and in the commander's cottage we found enough food to last ten men for a week. We also found a radio, but it was broken. Some wanted to stay where we were. Others felt it would be better to leave. The map told us that we were miles from the nearest village and surrounded by mountainous terrain. Some men were sick and would surely perish if they were forced to walk for days through the snow. But we had to come to a decision, and in the end three of us agreed to make the trek. We promised to send help for the others who remained behind. We gathered food and water to last us and then set out.

"The first thing that happened was that a storm descended upon us, with wind so strong it uprooted the trees and threw them around like matchsticks. We found shelter in the caves at the foot of the mountains. By the time we could leave we were many days behind schedule and running out of food. What could we do? We had to go on. We were sure now that we would die, but at least we would die trying to save the others. So on half rations, and then quarter rations, we walked each day and then tried to find shelter at night. When we shared our last food a week later, we watched each other eat with great jealousy, with tears in our eyes. Two days later one man fell and died of exhaustion. By this time we hardly knew where we were. Our map said we should have reached the village, but in the unfamiliar terrain all we could find was snow. I knew then that we were lost and that our mission had failed. We decided to split up, thinking that our chances of finding help were better that way. I took a route to the north, my friend went east. I never saw him again."

Hector turned his face to the wind. The dampness in the air told him that soon there would be rain. He had noticed that Señor Volos had allowed his cigarette to go out and that he had not lit a new one. This struck him as very odd and he was about to make a comment but decided to keep his silence. Señor Volos gazed out over the city, his rough hands clasped together. Hector waited for him to go on.

"My physical strength allowed me to survive. After wandering for a day or two, some peasants found me. They took me in and gave me food and nursed me back to health. I was still miles from any town and they had no means of communicating with the outside world. Weeks went by before I was well enough to travel. By this time the weather was not so cold. A farmer gave me a ride in his cart and from the village I took the train north. People everywhere were talking about Aguaria, about how his own troops had risen up against him. It was not enough that he had declared himself president, he wanted to be prime minister as well. People were saying he would have made himself pope if there had been a way to do it. He was in custody in the capital and our old president had been returned to office and called together the Assembly. The rightful order had been restored, but the country was still in a state of high alert. Laws were passed, limiting the power of the military, and these laws were much harsher and more restrictive than the original ones that had been proposed. The president was now the head of the military and he made all the decisions. But the military was divided. Some still supported Aguaria. There was a great deal of confusion."

For a moment Señor Volos seemed distracted by something in the street. He steadied his hat with one hand and gazed straight down. Hector looked down too but didn't see anything of interest—a few cars, some people walking. Soldiers watching. Señor Volos rubbed his nose and went on.

"I reported to my base as soon as I got back, to tell them about our camp in the south and what had happened. I said to the corporal in charge that our commander had been killed in an accident and that for many months no supplies were delivered. Some men were still there trying to carry out their duties. But time was running out. Something had to be done. I was then shown into a room and told to wait. The room had a desk and some chairs but no windows. I could hear people talking on the other side of the door. Telephones were ringing and I heard many feet stepping rapidly along the passageway. They made me wait for a very long time. I got the feeling that I had stirred something up, that they hadn't expected me to appear, like a visitor from the spirit world, and that for some reason it was very serious. At last the corporal returned with two other men. They were not wearing uniforms, but he introduced them as police and told me to say again what had happened in the southern camp. I did this, and when I was finished they all looked at each other and appeared very satisfied, like the cat after he has eaten the canary, you know? They left me alone again and soon my old barracks commander came and told me to go home and relax and forget about it. He said I could report for duty when I had my strength back. It wasn't until later, when I met some off-duty soldiers in a café, that I learned that my commander in the southern camp was Aguaria's nephew. It seems he was sent there to get him out of the way; because of his hot temper he had made many enemies, even among those who supported his uncle. They wanted to get rid of him before he made trouble, and so with this posting it was intended that he would die, if not of starvation then in a mutiny, because he was known to be the sort of commander who drove his men to rebel. But in order for it to look like a real mission they had sent a whole unit of men to die with him. We were all supposed to die. All of us. Once I knew this, then of course it made sense. The train that stopped coming, the poor provisions, the radio that wouldn't work."

Señor Volos fell silent, and after a moment, when it seemed that the story was over, Hector asked, "What happened to General Aguaria?"

"Ah, yes. The General. He was forced to issue an apology to the nation. This was intended to restore stability, but the war continued, mostly in the hills. The conflict had fired up the communists, and there were other groups as well who saw it as a chance to make a grab for power. But they were disorganized and nobody seemed to know what causes they were fighting for. The soldiers were kept busy for many years, rooting out the rebel factions like rotten teeth, one by one. I had no stomach for military service after my adventures. I was promoted, but after a month I resigned my commission. Louisa and I were married and I went to work with her father in his newspaper kiosk. Aguaria was kept in prison until he died.

He died a very old man. For all the misery he caused, he died warm in his bed with a full belly."

Señor Volos looked towards Hector and smiled. "So, you see, this is what the last war was like. Many innocent people died, but nothing was accomplished. Nothing was gained. One man's lust for power caused misery and suffering all across the country. You should not be so eager for war, Hector." He glanced at his silver Timex watch and clapped his hands. "And now I must go or I will lose my place. The others will not wait. They will start without me. Old men, Hector, we are creatures of habit. I will see you tomorrow."

Hector nodded as Señor Volos laid one hand briefly on his shoulder before leaving him alone. At this time each morning Señor Volos joined his friends in Señor Claudio's *restaurante* where they would while away the morning hours smoking, drinking thick coffee laced with hot milk, playing backgammon, and talking about politics and sports. Before making his move, Hector waited until the clatter of the screen door slamming shut told him the old man had entered the stairwell.

He gathered the cigarette butts that Señor Volos had discarded. This morning the take was good: six uncrushed butts with an inch or so of pure Cuban tobacco left in each one. Cuban was the only kind that Señor Volos smoked and Hector found it less harsh and more aromatic than the local brands his mother and father preferred. Working quickly because of the approaching storm, Hector pulled from his pocket a small length of paper cut from the pages of one of his father's books. The paper was yellow, lightly ribbed, and brittle with age. He turned away from the wind and crouched down, hunching his body to shield his activities from the weather. Using the dusty concrete roof as a work surface, he laid out the piece of paper and broke a cigarette butt open so that the shreds of tobacco spilled onto it. Carefully, he spread the tobacco into a line that fell lengthwise down the middle of the paper. He did the same with a second and then a third butt. Then he rolled the paper, encasing the tobacco in a cylinder. Since there was no adhesive with which to bind the edge of the paper to the roll, he held it in place with his thumb and forefinger as he lifted it and placed it between his lips. The paper was stiff and held its shape as he retrieved from his pocket the package of matches he had taken from his father's bedside table. He lit a match and held it to the end of his homemade cigarette, inhaling deeply. The smoke entered his mouth in a torrent and with conscious effort he swallowed it and coaxed it into his lungs. Because the paper was dry, it burned faster than the tobacco. He sucked on the cigarette until he felt the familiar lightness in his head. The smoke tasted of burning pampas grass, summer, and the skewers of spiced grilled meat sold by street vendors in the market square. It brought tears into his eyes as the heat attacked the tender lining of his throat. The impulse to cough, to vomit the smoke up and out of his mouth, to fill his struggling lungs with the clear morning air, was powerful, but he tensed his body and fought against it as he gripped the wire cage of the pigeon coop to keep from falling. His head felt emptied of all thought, as if his skull had been opened and his brain taken out whole. When he lifted his head and exhaled, watching the stream of smoke rise and vanish, borne off by the wind, he then gulped the air, just as a man who has been thrown overboard will when he breaks the water's surface and is no longer in fear of drowning. But the violence of the moment remained and seemed to echo all around him. There was a rushing sound in his ears and he felt the tingling in his fingers as blood chased the numbness from his extremities, a sensation he found intensely pleasurable. The lightness in his head remained as well, along with a feeling of serene confidence, as if he had glimpsed the devil in his lair or touched some deeper part of himself and come away convinced of his own immortality.

For one moment he was shaken by panic, but the cooing of the pigeons and the rain that began falling at that moment brought him back to the rooftop, and he told himself that he had not done anything this morning that he had not already done many times before.

The other three butts containing the remains of Señor Volos' Cuban tobacco had fallen to the roof, and he gathered these quickly before the rain made them unusable. He thrust them into his pocket and went through the screen door, letting it clatter shut behind him. For a moment he stood in the narrow stairwell. He drew his hand over his face as he tried to calm his heart, which still thumped and kicked as if it would force its way up his throat. Then he continued down the stairs.

SIX

Hector walked so quickly that Nadia had trouble keeping up. He had grown since his fifteenth birthday. A year ago if they had stood facing each other she would be looking straight into the depthless slate grey of his eyes, without straining her neck or standing on tip toe. But since that time Hector had gained inch upon inch while she seemed not to have grown at all. It didn't bother her because boys were naturally taller than girls, but most of his height had gone to his legs. She had recently noticed that whenever they went walking together he often forgot to make allowance for the six inches in height that now separated them.

They had left school at noon to eat their lunch, slipping away to the grassy slope at the rear of the schoolyard where they could hold hands without anyone seeing. But instead of returning for their afternoon session she allowed him to lead her away, across the hilly expanse of Areos Park.

As he pulled her up from the grass and helped her brush the dust and pine needles from her dress, there was in his manner the uneasiness of someone facing a difficult decision. The tension rested on his face, in the ridge between his clenched eyebrows. It was clear that something preyed on his mind. "I want to show you something," were his only words, spoken after a brief hesitation during which his eyes shifted from side to side, never settling on hers. She had nodded, though the time to return to Señora Palermo's classroom was fast approaching and she had never before missed a moment of school for reasons other than illness or mourning. She had given fleeting thought to the notion that he might try to kiss her, but he had only smiled. They gathered their things and he took her hand. Together they passed through the iron gates of the park.

She followed him willingly along the winding paths, wondering where he was taking her but not daring to ask, for that would break the spell and dampen the thrill of expectation that made her heart gallop. They had been friends since they were small and had spent many hours together playing and reading or just idly watching people pass by on the street. She had visited the Tomás apartment and met Hector's mother and his sisters and brothers. She had eaten meals there and been welcomed as if she were a member of the family and with a degree of warmth that left her groping for words adequate to express her gratitude. When Carlos had disappeared, she had mourned the loss as if he had been her own brother. And in the same way, Hector had been made welcome at the little house where she lived with her parents, her younger sister Magda, and older sister Carmel, even though her parents did not speak Spanish very well and conversation was a strain. Her father worked on the trams as a conductor and though she did not understand why a man of simple needs would leave his home in Poland to work on the trams in another country, she did not ask any questions. She could remember very little of Warsaw. Mostly she remembered the stone buildings and the snow and a grey sky hanging over a damp city, and long lineups for food and tall gaunt men with haggard faces and hunger in their eyes. Sometimes her father spoke to his daughters about the war and how the people had suffered, but if her mother was in the house she quickly put an end to such talk and they would argue, exchanging shrill comments in their Warsaw Polish, which Nadia had learned in the first years of her life but which now, having lost contact with its angular intonations, made her feel as if she were standing on the platform of a train station in a foreign country.

For a long time after coming here she was not sure of herself with the other children because her skin was so pale and looked strange against hair that was so black, and when she spoke, they all laughed. She noticed Hector right away. His eyes seemed always turned in her direction, but whether this was because he thought she was pretty or because he thought she was funny looking, she could not tell. He was the first child who tried to talk to her, and soon they began walking home from school together. He taught her some Spanish words, the first that she spoke with confidence, and helped her with her schoolwork because her parents were unable to and her sisters were engaged in similar struggles of their own. He became her friend and she accepted this, but still she could not understand his impulse to be kind because she was an oddity, a foreigner in a place where being foreign was a sin and a curse. More than once she lowered her face in shame and fought back the tears when she saw how the old women, with their wrinkled skin and dressed all in black, crossed themselves and lifted their eyes to the sky if she happened to cross their path. Hector had taken her side against children who wanted to torment her, raising his fists in her defence. After a while they left her alone, but she would always remain grateful to Hector for placing himself in harm's way and once even taking the beating that rightfully should have been hers.

He seemed to know where he was going as they crossed Avenida Independencia and turned down a side street barely wide enough for a single car or two donkeys, where they passed a bright shop selling linens. The day was warm and the *músicos* who played on the street for money strummed their *charangos* and sang in high clear voices. It was almost the end of spring and there would be many holidays and festivals in the coming weeks and months. The Feast of the Virgin. The Feast of All Saints. The Day of the Dead. Even after all these years she could hardly comprehend these celebrations, especially the Day of the Dead, when people went to the cemetery with lit candles and spent all night beside the graves of their relatives. She could not understand the custom of wanting to converse with the dead, and each year as the day approached she would become more and more apprehensive, crying suddenly for no reason and flinching at sudden or strange noises, as if she expected to see rotted corpses rise up out of the earth and walk in the streets. It was silly of her to think such things could happen, but even so she could not shake off the fear, and as the day approached and everyone put on their masks and displayed painted carved death's heads on top of poles and candles in the shape of skulls in the windows of their houses, she refused to look people in the eye in case they really were dead and watching for a chance to steal her soul for their own use. On the day itself she went to bed early and buried her face in the pillow and stayed that way all night long. At these times when her fears were at their worst, she thought longingly of life in Poland, where the dead were consigned to their tombs and quickly forgotten and there were no customs that encouraged them to rejoin the land of the living, not even for one night.

As they proceeded along a network of alleyways, Nadia gripped Hector's hand tighter and felt a surge of warmth flood into her when he returned the pressure. He had taken her into a part of the city that she had never seen before, or, if she had, she did not remember it. They were skirting the very edge of the hill town, a place where she had never ventured and where her mother had warned her never to go. Gone were the clean little shops selling pastries and discounted clothes and handcrafted souvenirs for tourists. Instead, she saw a motorcycle repair shop where a man in grease-stained overalls leered at her as they went by. Next to this was a little gas station with a single pump. The air was filled with shouts and rough laughter and the revving of engines. Diesel fumes invaded her nostrils and made her light-headed. A few doors down from the gas station, two dark-skinned men argued loudly on the steps of a fishmonger. As Hector led her past the open door, the stench of raw fish warming in the sun snagged in her throat. She saw a pawnshop, a shrunken old man with no teeth standing in an open doorway, a dark storefront with some broken wooden boxes, picture frames and old paint cans piled high behind filthy windows. The lane had narrowed, and she felt confined by the tall ramshackle buildings hemming her in on either side. Huge flies hung languidly in the warm air and stray dogs roamed about, urinating against lampposts and sniffing each other. Hector seemed unconcerned by any of this. Coughing, she stumbled along beside him, grateful that he still held her hand and that he seemed content to move at a pace that was dictated by her smaller stature and shortness of breath.

Finally she could take no more.

"Hector, please," she said.

"We're almost there."

"Where?" she asked, looking at him. "Where are we going?"

He didn't answer but did slow down so that she could more easily walk at his side. They stepped around a man lying on the sidewalk and she wondered if he was dead or merely sleeping. When they turned another corner, she saw what looked like a small park ahead of them. There were pine trees and grass and some benches. Nadia thought maybe he had brought her here for privacy, so they would be away from the inquisitive glances of friends and neighbours. She inched closer to Hector so that their shoulders touched with every step. She willed him to put his arm around her, but he did not seem inclined to do this without prompting, so she let his hand go and lifted his arm, and when he stopped and looked inquiringly at her she said, "Hold me, Hector."

His gaze was troubled, but she did not allow herself to imagine that she may have acted rashly or asked too much of him. He put his arm around her, but there was something in his manner, a sullen resistance or lack of enthusiasm, as if he were doing this out of charity, as a reluctant favour. To put him at ease she embraced him with her left arm and slid one finger through a belt loop on his jeans. She gave him a generous smile, and he smiled in return. They walked towards the park, but instead of sitting on a bench he led her up the cobbled walkway past the open area, and soon they were within sight of a small café with outdoor tables. It was not a grand place, and so she thought that maybe they would have a cup of coffee and while away the afternoon gazing into each other's eyes, but again he confounded her expectations by leading her past the café towards a church, near where a stone wall encircled a playground. When they sat on the wall, the café's cluster of outdoor tables was still in view.

Now she thought that maybe he had come here to meet someone, that this was a rendezvous point, and that for some reason he was going to include her in the meeting. She glanced at him and saw that his gaze was set on the open door of the café. There was nobody seated at any of the tables. A moment later a woman in a white cotton dress and floppy sandals walked past them leading a little girl by the hand. Nadia studied the woman and decided she was the girl's mother, but she was very young, not much older than Nadia herself. Then a burst of squawking made her look over her shoulder. A swarm of black birds circled the bell tower of the church, their swooping shapes prominent against the stark blue of the sky. When they were gone her gaze drifted. A few shanty houses huddled close upon one another further up the street. Some people hung about on the front stoop of one of them, but they were too far away for her to see them clearly. Beyond the houses, the street meandered into the hills.

"We're early," Hector said, looking across the road towards the café.

He seemed calm now, strangely at peace, and she hoped that his serenity was due in part to having her at his side. She took his hand, interlacing her fingers with his. She shifted so that her leg rested against his. This time he did not look at her, but he seemed to accept without question or resistance that she should approach him in a manner that implied an intimacy beyond friendship. She could not say why she felt this degree of comfort in his presence because he was a brooder who at all times, even in moments such as this one, remained separate from her, private and watchful. It made her sad because she so loved the physicality of him and thought he was the most beautiful of the boys in the school. His hair was the same liquid black as the pupils of his eyes and at this time of year his skin, which she longed to stroke, shone with a swarthy sun-warmed lustre. Two small moles on the left side of his face seemed to beckon her to touch them. She sometimes stayed behind after school to watch the football team on the practice field because Hector played forward, and when he put himself to the test he could outrun them all. On a hot day she would wait for him to remove his shirt after practice, anticipating the moment when he revealed the lithe tautness of the muscles of his chest and arms. She didn't know if he'd ever noticed her sitting with the other spectators, mostly parents and older siblings of the players. He had never approached her while she sat there and neither of them had spoken of the plays he had made. So in her mind it remained her secret.

"Nadia, you've never met my father, have you?"

He was looking at her now, studying her.

"No," she said.

"You will meet him today."

She took her eyes away from his and settled her gaze on the arrangement of tables and chairs at the café. She noticed that a boy wearing a yellow shirt had taken a seat and she wondered, startled, how he could have appeared without her seeing him.

"Is there something you're not telling me Hector?"

"There's a reason why my father is never around when you come to have dinner with my family. He lives with us but doesn't like to eat with us. He is part of us, but he lives his own life. I can't explain it."

She shook her head. "You don't have to explain, Hector. You don't have to do this."

"But I want you to see." Hector spoke slowly. "I want you to know where I come from."

For a moment his eyes hardened towards her and Nadia realized she could not stop this from happening.

"I don't know what my father does all day. It's something to do with books and papers. He never says anything about it and I've never asked. I know that people talk about him. I know they laugh behind his back. I try to ignore the gossip, but you know how it is. Even though you try, you can never really ignore it."

She wanted to touch his face, to quiet him, but could not make herself do so. She looked down, vaguely ashamed.

"He works at the university and a little while ago I went down there. I'm not sure what was in my head. Maybe I would ask him if he would buy me something to eat. I'd never been to the university before so I had to ask where he was. People showed me the way, but they looked at me strangely, and it made me feel like I shouldn't be there. Then it came to me that they were annoyed since it was the afternoon and I was supposed to be in school. I didn't want to get into trouble, but it was too late to worry about that. I found the building where his office was but I couldn't go up in the elevator because only students and the people who work there have passes. I had to wait. There was a notice board, and I went over to read the notices. After a little while I saw another boy come in. I didn't pay much attention to him, but I thought it was strange because he was younger than me. I knew I didn't belong there, so that meant he didn't belong there either. I don't think he saw me. It was busy and there were a lot of people around. It was like our school, only bigger. The other boy sat on a bench. He had on a white shirt and black pants and a black tie, like he was on his way to church. He was thin. And then I remembered that I had seen other boys who looked like this in our apartment. My father seemed to know lots of boys who were thin and who walked like their shoes pinched their feet. I didn't know where they came from. I remembered one was named Raoul and another one was Domingo. They were always polite, but they seemed to make my mother unhappy when they visited and had dinner with us. She would sit at the table but she wouldn't speak. Then they stopped coming to the apartment and my father stopped eating his meals with us at the same time. It seems so long ago. I waited. I wanted to see what this boy would do. When my father came down in the elevator, he looked around like he was expecting someone to be there. I knew it wasn't me. The boy stood up and went to him and they went out together. I decided to follow. I wanted to see if my father was going to take this boy to a restaurant for a meal even though he'd never done that for me. But they walked past all the restaurants downtown. They weren't in a hurry. My father put his hand on the boy's back. Sometimes they stopped in front of a shop and the boy pointed at the window, but my father would shake his head. Then, at last, they stopped in front of a shop and the boy said something and they went inside. I crossed the street and watched the front of the shop from a doorway. When they came out a little while later, the boy was wearing a new jacket. It was one of those American jackets with the design on the arms. You don't see anyone in our school wearing a jacket like that, but sometimes the teenagers in their big cars have them on. I followed them again and they walked and walked. They came up this street, to this café. They sat outside in the sun and my father bought tea and some cakes. Then they went inside and later, when my father came out, he was alone."

Nadia understood now that they were spying. Spying on Hector's father.

"We don't have to do this, Hector," she said. She was afraid, just a little bit. But she was also excited at the prospect of what was to come. Looking around, she saw that Hector had selected a position that made it possible for them to observe everything that transpired at the café without anyone taking notice of them. The boy in the yellow shirt was still sitting at a table shaded by an umbrella and he was sipping a drink from a tall glass through a straw. She could see him better now because he was interesting to her. His hair was short and she saw that beneath the table his legs and feet were bare. His shirt was so long on him it was almost like a dress.

"Since that first time I've come here over and over again, to watch my father having tea with this boy. I think it's the same boy, but it might not be. I've never gone up to them or said anything. I'm not sure what I should do. I'm not sure I should do anything."

Nadia felt her body stiffen when Hector squeezed her hand and looked into her eyes. Somehow their friendship had attained the intensity and passion that had existed only in her mind before today. She saw this on his face and it heightened both her fear and her excitement. Her heart trembled as she struggled to control an impulse to throw herself against him. Instead, she raised one hand to his face and gently guided his mouth towards hers. When their lips touched it was like hot liquid pouring through her, from her neck down to that mysterious cleft between her legs, which had become for her a source of both pleasure and unspeakable torment. She grew ashamed when the hungers of that part of her body overcame her dread of being discovered, and she let her fingers explore this cavity that performed the most basic of functions, but which, as she had been told in school by an old nun who gave special lessons just for girls, was also the cradle of God's gift of life and as precious as gold. The violation of that gift was a sin, but sometimes, when she lay bathed in sweat in the heat of the night, she was unable to control herself.

But her pleasure ended abruptly when Hector pulled away from her. "What—?"

He was looking towards the café. When she followed his gaze she saw that a man had joined the boy at the table. The man sat with his back to them. He was wearing a dark suit, and even from this distance Nadia could see that the suit was made of some heavy coarse material. Just contemplating that material against her skin in this heat made her squirm. But the man seemed comfortable enough. He inclined his head slightly when, from time to time, he directed a comment towards the boy, but otherwise he seemed content to sit in the shade of the umbrella. She could tell without looking that Hector had focused all his attention on the pair, that for the moment he had forgotten her. She wanted to draw him to her again, but did not dare.

"Is that your father?"

Hector nodded. He jumped down from the wall and surprised her by turning and taking her under the arms and lifting her down.

"We'll do this now," he said.

They joined hands and approached the café as if they were two young lovers enjoying a stroll. It was the hottest part of the day and Nadia felt that if they were going to the café she wouldn't mind taking a seat beneath one of the umbrellas and having a glass of water with ice and lemon. But she refrained from making this suggestion for two reasons. First, she was beginning to sense that Hector's actions were motivated by something more deeply complex than simply wanting to introduce her to his father. And second, as they drew near the café and her view was no longer obstructed by distance and by the spindly trees that lined the street, she saw that the boy wore a bracelet on his ankle and that under the table the man's hand was stroking the boy's bare thigh.

There would be no opportunity for her to back gracefully away from the confrontation she could see was coming. She felt now as if her will had dissolved and she was being carried along by a force that, struggle as she might, would pay her no heed.

They were close enough now that she could hear a soft murmur when Señor Tomás spoke to the boy. Hector was holding her hand so tightly that she felt a twinge of pain, but she said nothing. Then they were standing in front of the table where Enrique Tomás sat with his young companion.

"Hector," Enrique said, glancing up at them. The dry evenness of his voice conveyed the fact that he was both startled and annoyed. Nadia felt a little gasp escape her throat at the sight of his face, which was painted in the manner of a woman who has no shame. His lips were a deep crimson and circles of rouge adorned his clean-shaven cheeks. His eyes were outlined in black, giving them a sinister look, and, as if it had been oiled, his greying hair closely followed the contours of his head. She noticed that the boy in the yellow shirt didn't pay them even the slightest heed. For a moment she felt weak, as if she might collapse, but managed to remain standing as the spell of faintness passed and the strength returned to her legs.

Hector said, "Father, I want you to meet Nadia Wladanski. She's a friend of mine from school. Nadia, this is my father."

She forced her lips into the shape of a smile and was vaguely horrified when Enrique acknowledged her presence, meeting her stricken gaze and stiffly inclining his head. She felt now as if she had awoken, not out of a dream, but into one, and her faintness returned as she wondered what sort of place this was—a café with no waiter or waitress where it seemed acceptable for an old man wearing makeup to fondle the naked leg of a boy younger than his own son.

"What are you doing here?" Enrique asked. "You should be in school."

"It's a holiday," Hector said, and Nadia suffered new horror at the ease with which this lie issued from his lips.

"Hector, it's too hot," she said. "I have to sit down."

She felt herself being guided into a chair, and though she may have lost consciousness for a few seconds, she distinctly heard Hector's father say, "Jorgé, some water for the young lady." She closed her eyes and in the shade of the umbrella allowed herself the luxury of a few moments of repose. The boy's feet on the paving stones made a series of muted slapping sounds that were only faintly audible, but she followed them without difficulty as far as the door of the café since they were the only sounds to be heard as neither Hector nor his father spoke. Hector's fingers stroked the back of her neck and she was thankful for this small gesture of concern. In a moment, as Jorgé emerged from the café, the silence was broken by the soft tinkle of ice in water and then a clunk as the glass was placed before her on the table. She opened her eyes and reached for the glass and sipped the cool water through the plastic straw. Stronger now, she looked about her and saw that Jorgé was watching her, it seemed, with intense interest.

"You have recovered, my dear?" Hector's father was also regarding her closely.

She nodded and tried once again to smile. "Yes, thank you."

"You have been overcome by the heat, no doubt. You would do well to drink your water and then go home and lie down."

Nadia forced herself to meet those eyes circled in black, eyes that seemed to smile upon her benignly from beneath their elaborate ornamentation. He was a thin man, with a thin neck that sagged where the skin was loose, and whose face had the unwholesome pallor of one who rarely sees the light of day. He seemed small within the suit he wore, and when, with a fastidious gesture, he took a package of Derby king-size cigarettes from his breast pocket and lit one with a match, she noticed that the nails of his fingers had been carefully shaped and polished in a manner she had only ever seen in the pages of magazines.

"Hector, I think we should go." She placed her hand on Hector's arm.

"Father, you have not introduced your friend."

Nadia looked from son to father and instantly recognized that the contest being waged was going to be a lengthy one. She could see no common ground, nothing that could serve as a pretext for reconciliation. Their loathing for one another sat plainly on their faces, like a family trait from which there is no escape. A constriction rose up in her throat and she struggled to suppress a cough. She felt the utter helplessness of all those who unwittingly find themselves the only obstacle to an unseemly display of family discord.

"You've met Jorgé—"

"You haven't introduced me. Tell him who I am."

Nadia watched with relief as Jorgé withdrew his unnerving gaze from her face and looked towards Hector's father. Jorgé continued, in his childish manner, to suck noisily on the straw even though his glass was empty.

"Jorgé, my son Hector wishes to make your acquaintance. Say hello to him."

The boy now turned to Hector. His gaze was completely open and without guile, though Nadia could also see that he was basking in the knowledge that, of the two young men seated at the table, he was the favoured and therefore privileged one. "Hello, Hector," he said.

There followed a moment during which Nadia felt the heat of Hector's rising anger almost as if it were her own. She watched as the vein most prominent on the side of his neck pulsed once, twice. How well did she really know him? But even as this question formed in her mind she felt the blush of shame on her cheek because of course she knew him very well. She loved him and would continue to love him. It was his father who puzzled and saddened her.

Hector stood.

"We'll be leaving now, Father," he said in a strained voice. "Nadia has to get home to help her mother and I have things I have to do."

He held the chair for her as she quickly got to her feet. She straightened her skirt.

"Are you quite all right now, my dear?"

Hector's father was standing as well. His smile was gracious and his question sincere, but she would surely swoon again if she were forced to endure his attentions for much longer.

"I'm fine now. Thank you for the water."

"We will meet again, I'm sure." He inclined his head.

She managed a smile as Hector took her hand and led her out to the street. In his anger he walked with rapid steps, and she hurried to keep pace. When she stole a glance over her shoulder, Jorgé, still seated at the table, was apparently listening as Enrique spoke, but observing the two of them out of the corner of his eye. He might have been smiling, but she couldn't tell for sure.

SEVEN

Enrique was unwilling to regard his son as an adversary, but without a doubt this seemed to be how matters stood. He had not missed the sneering disapproval with which Hector had regarded him, and had imagined the seeds of a plan stirring in the boy's brain as he'd sat there with his attractive young friend across the table from himself and Jorgé, a plan to bring shame and ruination down upon his own father's head.

Hector's unexpected intrusion into his other life left Enrique shaken and irritable and his quietly blissful afternoon with Jorgé in tatters. For almost an hour after Hector left them, Enrique said nothing, though he was of course aware of Jorgé sitting at his side waiting for him to utter some endearment or other. Later, when he escorted Jorgé back inside and upstairs to the room with the blue and gold wallpaper, where heavy damask draperies blocked out the light and bowls of gently warmed rose-water perfumed the air, he found he had no patience for the boy's evasive squirming and frolicsome squeals. He was rough with him, pushing him down on the bed and ripping the shirt from his back.

Under normal conditions he would take his time and savour each curve of Jorgé's perfect young body, which he had purchased for his own use from the boy's parents. Sometimes, as he gazed down at a naked youth whose flesh he had rented for an afternoon, it occurred to him to wonder how many boys there had been, and in his mind he would search obscure crevices of memory for faces and names of boys who had enabled him to realize the erotic potential of his own body. How, he would ask, did this one compare to that one? He looked at Jorgé, who was splendid in his own way but who could also drive him to heights of exasperation with his demands for new clothes, his sullen protestations and maddening episodes of petulance. Playing the submissive, Jorgé covered his eyes with his hands and let out a moan. Enrique had never been rough with him before, but the encounter with Hector and his friend had left him fearful and suspicious. Had it really been coincidental, or had Hector known where to find him? Who had told him where to look?

Ever since Lucinda had banished his companions from the flat, Enrique had been conducting his affairs in the furtive manner of all those who in their hearts harbour an unforgivable, ungovernable secret. He was fully aware that the scandalous nature of his appetites could land him in serious trouble, that even though it was not officially a criminal act, it also was not something with which most people could be expected to sympathize. It had been foolish of him to bring his friends home—to expect his wife to cook for them and his own children to accept them, as if into the family. He had not done this often, but at that early point of his career the expense of renting a space for the sole purpose of carrying on such liaisons was still far beyond his means. More than once he'd been compelled to satisfy his lusts in a grimy room in a downtown boarding house, which he could take by the hour, and which offered nothing by way of material comfort or atmosphere. Ever on the hunt for surroundings conducive to seduction and erotic horseplay, he roamed from neighbourhood to neighbourhood, moving his activities from one building to another, and yet often found himself seducing a new boy on soiled sheets amidst a stench of urine and the squall of stalled traffic. His search was a difficult one because it was not something that you could bring up in conversation with a colleague or a casual acquaintance. Knowing full well that exposure could cost him his job, he took pains to conceal his sexual tendencies from the officials to whom he reported at the university. This was simply a precaution, for he no longer felt any particular shame, only the awkwardness of concealment.

So now the word was going to get out. He did not trust Hector to keep his secret, and he was not about to bribe his own son to keep his mouth shut, at least not as a primary course of action. He could try intimidation, but Hector had inherited his mother's unruly streak of independence and, like Carlos, could be counted on to defy authority whenever an opportunity arose. Without a doubt he would get himself into trouble one of these days, but by then the damage would be done. And what of Hector's friend? Had Hector brought her along to bear witness to the depths to which his father had sunk? How would he deal with her if she chose to divulge what she had seen, for instance, to her own parents?

Jorgé raised himself to a sitting position and Enrique pushed him back down on the bed. He began to remove his clothes.

"Is something wrong?" Jorgé spoke in a high-pitched voice that betrayed some anxiety.

"Nothing's wrong."

"I thought the girl was very pretty."

Enrique said nothing. He painstakingly draped his jacket over a wooden hanger and hung it on the rod in the closet. He began loosening his tie.

"I thought she was one of the prettiest girls I've ever seen."

"You are too young to be making judgments like that," Enrique commented. The boy was transparently baiting him. He felt his excitement climb.

"Someday I'll have a girlfriend," Jorgé said. He had turned his attention to the lacy fringe of the pillowcase, stretching and prodding it with his fingers. "My girlfriend will be the most beautiful girl in the whole world. I'll give her everything she wants."

Enrique caught himself before a derisive snicker could escape from his lips. He almost told Jorgé he was a fool, that he would never be able to give any girl everything she wanted, that there wasn't enough money in the world for that. Instead he concentrated on lining up the creases of his trousers as he suspended them over the rod of a wooden hanger.

"I'll get to see her without her clothes on, too. She'll want me to see her without any clothes on before we make babies, won't she?"

"Girls are a different breed, my dear," Enrique said as he removed his socks and his underclothes. "Before you make any babies you will have to make many promises. You will find yourself making so many promises you won't be able to keep them all straight in your head. She will get angry with you because you will break some of your promises and you will forget others. But she will remember every promise you ever made, and she will remind you of these from time to time, especially during those intimate moments when you want to make a baby and she doesn't want to."

He stood naked and aroused before the boy, who stared at him from the bed. Enrique realized that the statement he had just made—perfectly sensible from the perspective of an adult—would be hopelessly confusing for a boy of Jorgé's age.

"My dear friend, you know very little of the ways of the world. Today, you are perfectly innocent. Tomorrow, well, who knows what tomorrow will bring. You should enjoy your childhood while you are still young because someday you will wake up an old man like me wondering where the years have gone."

This was not what he'd intended to say, and in his confusion he felt his engorgement slacken. Puzzled, Jorgé gazed at him and then, in the belief that the game had begun, folded his arms behind his head and smiled.

"I like Hector," he said. "If I'm a good boy, will Hector come back and play with me?"

Enrique started, shocked to be reminded of the connection that only today had been forged between his real life and his false life. His mind raced. Where was Hector now? To whom was he divulging his secrets? To hear Jorgé utter the name of his son in this manner reminded him that he had not been as circumspect as he might have been, that exposure was only a whisper away. He had felt safe for so long that he had allowed himself to be seduced into complacency. It was foolish of him to meet Jorgé at the university. He had been lazy, unwilling to put himself to the trouble of arranging a rendezvous point. But the dangers were real, and they were everywhere. Anger gripped him by the throat and all at once his erection rebounded to its former state of rigidity. He descended upon the bed and took Jorgé in his arms. The boy made no response, even when Enrique pressed his tongue between his thighs. This was part of the game: Jorgé remained limp, a mere plaything. He was not to say anything or to use his hands in any way. Enrique disliked being touched or stroked by someone else and would, if encouragement were needed, do it himself. He flipped Jorgé over so the boy was lying on his stomach. Jorgé's skin was perfect. Not a single blemish. Enrique ran his fingers down the length of Jorgé's spine, over his buttocks, his legs, his feet. He fingered the silver bracelet encircling Jorgé's ankle. He knew that it was too late. He was too old to reform himself. Even if discovery and public castigation were imminent he would likely carry on as if all were well. In another few months Jorgé would be showing the first signs of puberty and Enrique would have to begin searching for a new boy. He had promised himself that Jorgé would be the last, that once Jorgé's skin turned oily and pimply and his body began sprouting those disgusting black hairs he would immerse himself in his work and not surface until the book was finished. But he knew himself well enough by now to realize that any promises he made, especially to himself, were idle and pointless, and that the book would probably never be written.

He straddled the boy and, roughly prying Jorgé's buttocks apart, thrust himself inside. The boy stiffened and uttered a groan but otherwise remained silent. He pressed both palms flat on Jorgé's back to remind him not to squirm. They both knew that these encounters brought with them a degree of pain, but Enrique was familiar with thresholds and limits and could restrain himself if need be. The main thing was to stop well short of any crying or wailing, for that would attract the attention of Jorgé's parents, as ignorant and contemptible a pair as he could ever hope to encounter, who had bartered their only daughter into a similar kind of servitude and who imagined themselves his moral superiors because they only facilitated these assignations and did not actually take part. With their beady eyes and evasive glances he did not trust them. He paid them in cash and had given them a false name. Someday he would see them brought to justice. He would see them both hanging by their necks from a tree for what they had done to their children. But that day was a long way off, and for the moment—as he sought to quiet Jorgé's whimpers by murmuring, "Shhh, my love, shhh," softly in his ear—for the moment he would take his pleasure any way he could get it.

EIGHT

Claudia Acuña Cordoba
Estafeta Postal N° 9
San Gregório
Envigado P.

Dear Aunt Claudia,

Please forgive me for not writing. You know I always mean to, but time will not obey my commands to stand still. How are you? How is Francisco? Is he still dancing the tarantella with Gabriella as we used to say? I hope the recent drought did not affect you and that you are both healthy and that your table is full. I meant to send a greeting on your eightieth birthday and now I have missed five more. I am not a good nephew, I know.

I am writing on a matter of some urgency. It has been many years since your last visit and my children have now reached an age when they are in need of guidance and a kind of rough-hewn discipline. The city is a treacherous place to raise children, especially in these times of unrest in which we find ourselves. I envy you your placid country setting and recall with fondness our visits to your house when I was younger. In my memory the countryside is always green, the sky always blue, and I can remember swimming in the river with Diego Rodriguez and his friends, who always made me feel welcome, even though I was a pale city boy. I was sorry when I heard that Diego had died in the cholera outbreak. He was such a beautiful person. Life is unfair sometimes.

My son Hector has committed an indiscretion and I feel certain that the authorities will soon appear on our doorstep. It is not a serious matter, nothing criminal. He injured another boy in a dispute, an event that would normally be of little importance. However, the incident has been brought to the attention of the police, and having already lost Carlos in such a frightening manner Lucinda and I feel it is incumbent upon us to place Hector out of harm's way as quickly as possible.

I know that at your age having a fifteen-year-old boy in the house will be a strain. I am therefore willing to compensate you for any inconvenience this may cause above and beyond Hector's room and board. God knows that Lucinda and I are hopeful this matter will pass and that Hector will be able to return to us in a month or two. The police, as I'm sure you must know, have many other pressing issues with which to occupy themselves. With the latest devaluation there have been riots. You have no doubt read the accounts and seen the pictures. We are thinking of leaving the city, but at the moment I don't see how this is possible.

Please let me know if this proposal is to your liking. I offer the enclosed as a gift. Use it as you see fit. Be assured there will be more if you agree to have Hector in your house.

I know that one letter cannot make up for a half a decade of silence, but I promise to be a better correspondent and to bring you up to date with the changes that have been taking place in all our lives. In the meantime I remain

Your loving nephew,
Enrique Tomás

NINE

They lumbered into motion and the city quickly fell away as if crumbling before his eyes. Hector had never seen so much nothing. The rickety train skirted the mountains, passing villages that were no more than clusters of huts and shanties, occasionally winding its way up into the hills and chugging laboriously across a high plain. There were frequent stops. Hector could hear and see, in the warmth of greetings and in the eyes of children trying to sell plastic Virgin Mary statues, molasses drops, and dried figs to the passengers, that the train's arrival was a momentous event for the people who inhabited these parts.

Progress was slow. He had plenty of time to drift from one sweltering compartment to another, to watch the ocean pass by on his right and the mountains on his left.

His belongings filled a single small valise: clothes, toiletries, a deck of cards, a few prized superhero comic books: *The Flash, Spiderman*. He wore his only pair of shoes, which still bore traces of Jorgé's blood. The lazy swaying of the train made him restless and he did not like the way his travelling companions looked at him—sullenly, as if he represented all that was troublesome in their lives. The soldiers in particular, of which there were many, seemed annoyed by his presence. He did not trust any of these people and when he roamed from one compartment to another he carried the valise with him. He took it with him to the toilet. He saw how the other passengers watched him and knew they did not trust him either, and for the first time in his life he began to suspect that the black hair and swarthy complexion he had inherited from his mother's family marked him in some way. The man who examined his ticket did so with a wary frown, as if he could hardly believe there wasn't some trick being played on him. Sitting by the window, Hector inadvertently met the glance of a young mother, and at the moment of contact she gathered her baby close to her breast as if to protect her from the evil eye. What did they think? That he was dangerous? Many people had black hair and skin darkened by the sun. It did not mean they were murderers. He smiled at the woman with the baby, but she lifted her chin and did not smile back. A few moments later she stood, collected her things, and left the compartment.

The landscape was parched. The sun beat down without mercy and Hector recalled the geography lesson in which his teacher had told the class that certain regions of the country had not seen a drop of rain for a hundred years. In some areas people working the fields paused and stared as if mystified, watching the train pass them by. Hunched and motionless, they seemed like stumps from huge felled trees. Oxen and goats huddled behind sun-flayed wooden fences had a look of doomed resignation about them.

He had been told the journey would take three days, but among the delays they encountered was an unscheduled twelve-hour stopover in a town he had never heard of where they waited for the delivery of an engine part, and then waited further as the part was installed and tested. To amuse himself he left the train and wandered through the town, where there were almost no people and where each and every one of the cinderblock buildings had suffered some sort of earthquake damage and none was more than a single story in height. He had some money that his father had given him for everyday use, and a further stash of bills that his weeping mother had pressed into his hand at the last moment as he was leaving the apartment, his father having been distracted on some pretext by one of his sisters. But instead of using his limited supply of funds, he targeted a shop away from the main street and helped himself to what he wanted while the ancient shopkeeper snored behind the counter. He didn't take very much. The ease with which he was able to steal a bottle of orange Fanta, some peppermints, and a string of jerky left him maddeningly alert to his own guilt, and he was not able to enjoy his booty while he consumed it. Later in the day, when he returned to the shop, he made sure to waken the shopkeeper by scuffing his feet noisily across the wooden floor. This time he purchased a bottle of spring water and a tin of lima beans in tomato sauce, which he asked the man to open and warm for him on the hotplate he had seen in the back room on his first visit. While the man was doing this, Hector browsed the store shelves, contemplating further thievery, but was almost grateful when a woman entered, thus saving him from having to decide among the meagre produce on display.

He was drowsy when the train resumed its journey and dozed intermittently while the car rattled and shuddered along the tracks. The events of the last few days had left him shaken. Though he had clenched his teeth and given the impression of blasé acceptance of his fate, he still felt an occasional tremor in his gut when he thought of where he was going. Having forbidden the rest of the family the privilege of a formal farewell, his father had seen him off at the station, his face paler than usual in the evening light. There were no embraces.

"You have disgraced each and every one of us," Enrique told his son. "I wouldn't be doing this but for your mother, who is quite out of her mind with the trouble you have caused."

Hector gazed without feeling into his father's eyes, which were level with his own. He had heard of the word hypocrisy, and though he was not sure of its precise meaning, he suspected he was being shown an example of it at this moment.

"Your Aunt Claudia and Uncle Francisco are old and frail and they have seen every one of their ten children into their graves. I hope that you will not be the cause of further heartache for them."

Hector said nothing. He had not apologized and was not inclined to do so. In his mind he had done nothing but defend the honour and good name of the Tomás family. Indeed, he believed he deserved thanks and congratulations for what he had done and that it was his father who had earned a punishment far more severe than the exile that he was being forced to undergo.

"I can see you have nothing to say for yourself," Enrique observed dispassionately. "You are fortunate the boy did not die. If that had happened I would be in no position to help you."

Hector continued to meet his father's eyes.

"You are the type of person who does not learn from your mistakes. You have a temper and you lack self-control. I suspected the same of Carlos, but I failed to act and we continue to mourn that loss. Well, my boy, you are being given the second chance your brother never had, though I dare say you do not deserve it. If you attract the attention of the local authorities in Envigado, then God be with you because I will not."

With that, his father turned on his heel and walked quickly away, leaving Hector to await the arrival of the train on his own. Hector rubbed the tears from his face with clenched fists. The feeling with which he struggled was grief mixed with the shock of betrayal, for while he suffered keenly a child's loss of home, he also sensed that his offence was a minor one and that more could have been done to place it quietly to one side until everyone forgot it had happened.

As he drowsed in an overheated train compartment many miles and many days from home, Hector steeped himself in bitterness, fixing his thoughts on the injustice of his situation. After the encounter with his father and Jorgé at the café, he had returned to the city with Nadia at his side, their hands linked in a desperate grip. In the shelter from the sun provided by a storefront awning, they embraced and pressed their lips together and explored each other's mouths with their tongues. Nadia pushed herself against him, every inch of her body in warm contact with his, her small breasts flattened to his chest. Afterward, he escorted her to her front door with a promise that very soon they would seek out some private space where they could shed their clothes and partake of a ritual that they both saw as inevitable and necessary.

But Hector could not shake the image of Jorgé regarding him serenely across the café table. Thoughts of the boy's indolent gaze stoked the fires of his anger, and against his will he retraced his steps until the café was once again within sight. He concealed himself behind the stone wall where he and Nadia had exchanged their first kiss only an hour earlier and kept vigil over the café entrance. Eventually the light of late afternoon began to dim into evening. The air grew chill. In a short while his father emerged from the doorway and, with glances up and down the street, walked towards the city. A few pedestrians strolled back and forth, but for a long time there were no other signs of habitation. Then it was dark. Hector was missing his supper and his stomach groaned in protest. Still, he kept watch and was soon rewarded by the sight of Jorgé leaving the café in the company of another man. They exchanged a few words and the man laughed, but all he did was touch the back of the boy's head and ruffle his hair. Jorgé was fully dressed now, wearing sandals, jeans, and a white shirt. He took the man's hand and together they walked up the street. Hector allowed them to gain some distance before abandoning his hiding place to follow. He kept to the edge of the road and walked carefully, as the only illumination to guide his way came from the houses lining the street. He stopped when he saw the two turn and follow the walkway to the front door of a small house. They entered. Hector's anger had dissipated as his hunger grew, but he forced himself to continue his watch, and after a time his stomach, convinced there would be no supper, ceased its protests. He took up a position behind a tree across from Jorgé's house and stayed for a period of time that he afterward guessed was several hours.

Stray dogs approached and sniffed his legs, but he remained still and they lost interest. A group of young men went by. They passed a bottle back and forth and spoke and swore in loud voices. Hector was not afraid. The moon came up and in the pale silver light he crept across the street and around to the rear of Jorgé's house. He wasn't certain what his next move would be, but when he saw two open windows he knew at once that he was going to steal into the house. He approached with barely a sound, stepping carefully around the debris littering the property. Through the first window he saw two adults sleeping in one bed. Through the other he saw two smaller beds, a child in each one. Hector searched the ground at his feet for a weapon and found a small piece of wood with the tip of a nail protruding from one end. He inserted this into his pocket and hoisted himself up on the window ledge and pulled himself inside. When his feet touched the floor he remained in a crouched position for a moment, utterly still, watching. The two children slept on as he rose to his full height and circled the beds. He pushed the door to the bedroom into its jamb, shutting out the rest of the house. He could see them clearly now in the moonlight, a boy and a girl, and his breath caught at the sight of Jorgé asleep, his body curled as if for protection, his thumb in his mouth.

He tried to focus his thoughts. Should he take the boy outside and beat him senseless under cover of night, or assault him where he lay? Which of these actions would cause his father the most grief? He stood looking down at Jorgé and tried to make up his mind, but in the end, since it seemed either approach suited his purpose, he decided to let the episode play itself out as it would.

With his finger he prodded Jorgé in the region of his abdomen through the thin blanket. There was no response. He leaned in closely and with his hand shook the boy's shoulder. The eyes fluttered open, but there was no immediate sign of recognition. He put his finger to his lips. Jorgé did not seem to understand. As if he meant to speak, Jorgé's lips parted, and to silence him Hector placed his hand over the boy's mouth. Still, Jorgé showed no signs of knowing who he was.

"Come with me," Hector whispered. "We're going for a walk."

Beneath his hand Hector felt the boy's lips moving. He took his hand away and leaned over.

"I'm afraid," the boy said, speaking into Hector's ear. He closed his eyes.

Hector shook him slightly to get his attention, but, as if he were suffering from a fever that had numbed his brain, Jorgé seemed to fall back into a deep sleep. Hector shook him again, this time more roughly, shook him until his eyes snapped open. A whine issued from between Jorgé's lips, and this time Hector clamped his hand over the boy's mouth. Jorgé seemed to struggle, but his movements were sluggishly inept and not those of someone who has been rudely awakened and in fear for his life.

Confused now, Hector tried to pull Jorgé from the bed, but the boy's foot was caught, and when Hector drew back the blanket, revealing Jorgé's thin body clad only in underwear, he saw that the ankle bracelet, which he had assumed was a decorative accessory meant to heighten his appeal, was attached to a small chain and that the chain was fastened to the metal bed frame.

The worst that could happen, Hector had thought, was that he would lose his resolve—that, faced with the tears and entreaties of a small boy whose only crime was a desire to profit from a physical allure that men like Enrique Tomás could not resist, he would relent and allow Jorgé to escape the beating he so richly deserved. What he had not anticipated was that his sympathies would betray him utterly, that he would find himself stricken by conscience and tempted by the idea of placing himself at risk in order to help the boy. He saw now that Jorgé was watching him, his eyes wide open and tearful with understanding. He began to struggle, pushing at Hector and biting his hand. Hector lost his balance and felt Jorgé slip from his grasp. The boy's yelps and shrieks filled the room, and as he tried to flee towards the door he pulled the entire bed behind him. The legs scraped noisily along the rough wooden floor. The girl in the other bed was screaming. Hector leapt on Jorgé and, trying to silence him, wrapped his arm around his neck. They both slipped and fell. The metal frame of the bed banged into the wall and reverberated, making a sound like heavy chimes being struck by a mallet. Recalled to his original purpose by the struggle, Hector pulled Jorgé to his feet and punched him with his fist, first in the stomach and then in the face. Jorgé's nose erupted in a copious flow of blood. He fell silent and crumpled to the floor. Hector pulled the stick from his pocket and landed a blow across Jorgé's back. In the moonlight he saw blood gush from the wound. The girl shrieked and struggled with the chain holding her leg. Hector was aware of voices and of someone pressing against the door, trying to enter the room, but Jorgé's bed blocked the way. He hit the boy again, on the head this time. He kicked him in the face and the chest and delivered more blows with the stick. The danger of his situation made no impression upon him as he continued to kick wildly at the boy, who was now lying unconscious on the blood-smeared floor. All he knew was the heat of his own blood pulsing behind his eyes. He could not stop. It seemed his anger would never be quenched. And when at last the door burst open and a man entered and struck him across the head, Hector made no attempt to fight back. He could not remember leaving the house and had no idea how he made his way home.

The train had stopped again. Hector gazed through the window at the dusty landscape and the mountains hovering in the distance. His father's anger had followed swiftly upon the event, along with shrill recriminations and a sense of anguish and desperation that pervaded the apartment while preparations were made for his departure. He remembered his mother's tears and the flash of hatred in her eyes as she regarded his father, and him turning away, either in shame or disgust. He remembered his sisters tiptoeing around, afraid to acknowledge his presence, and Julio, silent and troubled as only a ten-year-old boy can be. Hector had been lying on his bed. His mother had given him ice cubes wrapped in a towel, and he held this to the welt that had risen on the side of his face. His father had entered the room and stood looking down at him as he removed his belt. Without a word he struck him, flogging him across his legs and chest. There were tears in his father's eyes. As the flogging continued the tears welled up and overflowed so that Enrique's face dripped tears by the time he retreated from the bed and, with laboured breathing, looped the belt around his waist and left the room. Hector had not cried out and had lain very still during the beating. But once his father was gone he curled into a ball and closed his teeth on a corner of the towel and bit down hard to prevent himself from weeping aloud.

In the end the journey took five days. At each stop Hector had listened as the man who had examined his ticket at the beginning importantly strode the length of the train announcing the name of the station, and when he heard the word Envigado being bellowed in the familiar tuneless baritone, he grabbed his valise and prepared to disembark.

Hector could not recall ever hearing of Envigado prior to his father's declaration that he would be leaving home. But as the train meandered southward through the barren, sun-bleached landscapes, he had slowly built an image in his mind of the town where he would be staying. This imagined Envigado was very much like the city where he had spent his first fifteen years, filled with voices and music and the grinding of engines and the smell of grilled meat mingling with diesel fumes, intricate with streets, crowded with tall buildings and many people, wealthy and impoverished, going about the complex business of day-to-day survival. Likewise, he had formed an impression of his great-aunt and great-uncle, neither of whom he could remember having met. His father had said they were old. But so too was his father. Even his mother, not yet forty, seemed old to him. And since Hector could not conceive of anyone being older than this, the picture of his aunt and uncle that formed in his mind looked very much like his parents. He even imagined they lived in a flat over-looking a city square, close to shops and schools and well-tended parks. He imagined he would make many friends and that life in Envigado would not represent any significant breach with the past.

The Envigado he encountered was the plateau town with which we are all familiar, considerably smaller than B——— and capital of the prov-ince from which it took its name. Hector elbowed his way through the throng of passengers leaving the train, mostly soldiers carrying army issue duffel bags and backpacks, and with the moving crowd filed into the station from the platform. He immediately found himself beneath a high-domed ceiling in a cavernous space that was raucous with the voices of people arriving and people departing, of people selling and buying tickets. He gripped the valise tightly and stretched his neck, hoping to catch a glimpse of someone who might be his uncle or his aunt. He knew that he was two days late, but he also trusted that his relatives would be watching for him, that despite the fact that he was being punished he would not be abandoned.

Hector pushed forward. He had dozed on the train, but in the fitful manner of someone who doesn't trust his travelling companions, and as he threaded his way through the crowd towards the exit he experienced his fatigue as a light-headed sensation and a lack of balance. He was also conscious of not having washed or changed his clothes for a very long time. At this moment he wanted nothing more than a hot meal and a pillow on which to lay his head.

Outside the station he sat on a bench and clutched the valise to his chest. Above him the sky was blue and dotted with only a few clouds, but cool breezes reminded him that he had travelled many miles, to a southern province where the weather was going to be very different from what he was accustomed to. The air held the memory of moisture, as if rain had fallen recently, though every surface around him was dry. He opened the valise and pulled out his jacket, and while he was putting it on, wave upon wave of soldiers left the station and passed him by. They all wore the familiar green uniforms with matching berets, and black lace-up boots. They talked among themselves. Some were light-skinned, others were darker. A few smiled, but most seemed weary or sad, and Hector wondered how many of them were as far from home as he was. He watched them enter the waiting buses. When one bus pulled away, another rolled forward to take its place and was quickly filled as well. He imagined this going on forever, but then, sooner than he would have thought possible, the soldiers were gone and the lane in front of the station was empty except for a taxi whose silver-haired driver stood leaning against the ancient vehicle smoking a cigarette.

The town of Envigado was a disappointment. From his position in front of the train station Hector could see no office complexes or modern apartment houses. The streets—cobbled, not paved—were lined with narrow buildings four or five stories in height, all huddled against one another as if for support. For a few moments the guttural whine of a single motor scooter was the only sound to be heard, and when it rumbled around a corner into view, he was surprised to see that its driver was a young girl with bare legs wearing a denim jacket over a white dress. A cathedral loomed above the broad plaza, where some children were skipping rope and a few old men in rumpled suit jackets and leaning on canes had gathered to converse. The stone cathedral was streaked and weathered with age and it seemed to press its bulk to the earth like some enormous beast squatting silently in wait. Swarms of slate-coloured pigeons circled the bell tower or strutted about pecking at the ground. For a moment Hector's attention was drawn to a boy on a bicycle riding back and forth and back and forth, apparently without aim. Then, as if he'd made a decision or heard someone calling his name, he whirled about and disappeared up a side street. In the distance, to the east, three snow-capped peaks jutted high above the rooftops of Envigado.

Hector did not feel welcome. There was nothing here for him. He was the alien, the one who does not belong, and he cast Envigado a dark glance, as if it had caused him an injury. He thought of his home, many miles to the north, and of the room he shared with Julio, where his brother would now be sleeping alone. Caught up in his own fate and the panic gripping the Tomás household in the days following the assault, he had thought only fleetingly of Nadia and put off contacting her until it was too late to do so. He shuddered to think of the distance that now separated them and of the notions to which she would be falling prey. He realized suddenly that he had taken her for granted, that there was about her something graceful and pure, a quality of modest beauty of which he had hardly been aware until this moment but that he knew he would miss more than anything else in his life. He was ashamed of his neglect and resolved to contact her somehow, by any means that presented itself. And what would happen to his sisters, wise and patient Dulciana—a second mother to him—studious Cesara always with a book in her hand, dark-eyed Rosaria who at fourteen had already begun attracting the attention of boys, and poor Helena, so pale and sickly? He had been watching over them for so long he could not imagine they would continue to exist without his protection. Señor Volos and his pigeons caused him concern as well, because the old man so clearly welcomed Hector's inquiries into his affairs, and the pigeons depended upon him for their care and feeding. And he worried about his mother, who sometimes seemed to lose her way in the middle of a sentence and who was trapped in the apartment on Rua Santa Maria with a husband whose passions and diversions, Hector now understood, were odious to her.

The thought of his father left a bitter residue in his mouth and his muscles hardened as anger took him in its grip. Someday revenge would be his. And this thought gave him strength as he continued to sit on the bench in front of the Envigado train station.

It was on this same bench that his Uncle Francisco, a man many years older than the oldest man Hector had ever seen in his life, found him asleep as afternoon bled its colours into evening.

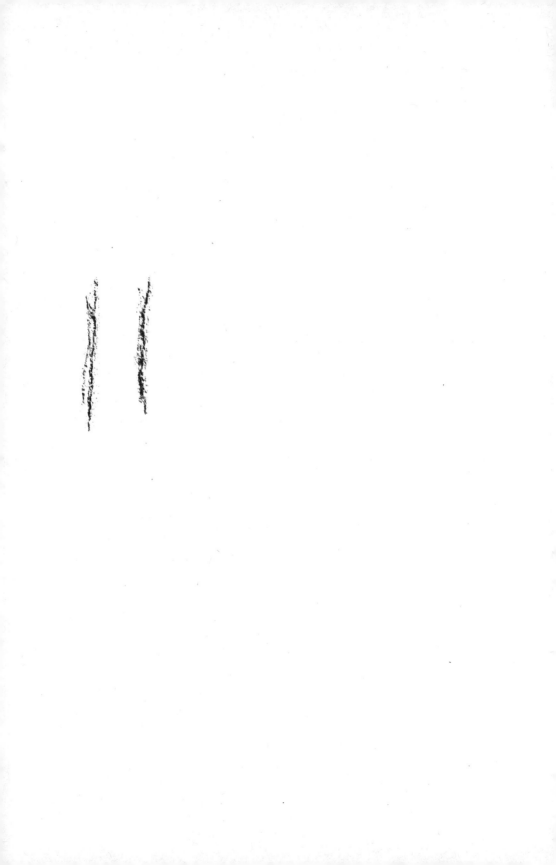

TEN

My Dear Son:

By now you will have settled into your new home. I did not write sooner because I was so distressed over the circumstances of your departure I was unable to express my feelings in words. Now that two weeks have passed I can put this selfishness behind me. I miss you more than I can say, but I am comforted by the knowledge that Claudia and Francisco are good, gentle people who will treat you well.

I hope your journey was not too arduous. I love the idea of travel but the reality frightens me, so I have spent most of my life here, with no ambition to go anywhere else. In a sense you are lucky to have the chance to visit another part of the country. I have heard that Envigado is a beautiful province. I hope you will explore the region and make new friends. I am sad that you are so far away, but I anticipate seeing you again very soon. A mother should not be separated from her children.

Now I must tell you the truth. When I heard from your father what had happened, and that the boy's parents were going to the police, I insisted you be sent away. The arrangements were made in haste and harsh words were said. You should forget all of that because in extreme situations people say things they do not mean. I know we have acted for the best. Rosalinda Cordero, from the third floor (you remember her?), told me her cousin was arrested for stealing an apple and came home blind in one eye and with *cigarette burns all over his back. I was very afraid of what might happen should you be arrested because what you did was much worse than stealing an apple.*

You will be glad to hear that the boy you hurt will make a full recovery, with only minor scarring. Your father is in contact with the parents. I will pass along more news when I hear something.

Only you can tell why you did this thing. Please, Hector, take your mother's advice. I want you to look into yourself, find the source of your anger, and erase it from your heart. Such anger is not healthy. It will get you into trouble and give only grief to the ones you love and who love you. Forgiveness is yours if you ask for it. Please do not be too proud to ask, but remember also that you must be contrite and you must be ready to pay the price for your sins.

My love for you remains as strong as ever. It is a mother's love, given unconditionally. I ask for nothing but your safe return into my arms.

Dulciana, Cesara, Rosaria, and Helena are managing, but they miss you greatly. Julio thinks you have gone to be with Carlos. I cannot make him believe you will be home soon. What kind of stories have you been telling him?

Your friend Nadia has been asking about you. I have offered to pass her letters along to you.

Your father is very worried about you.

As I write this it is raining and my cares weigh heavily upon my heart. But I have good news. Yesterday, as we crossed the plaza next to the Church of Our Saviour, we saw the pious bird of good omen. It was windy and he was hovering high above us, almost touching the clouds. He was crying out, making a sound that was like laughter. Cesara saw him first, so most of the good luck will be hers. But we will all benefit from his protection and the bounty he will bring. I could almost see him casting his eye towards where we stood on the ground. He floated above us for several minutes, and then the breeze quickened and he was carried out over the sea. It was a magnificent sight that has given me strength at a time when I was so weak I felt that I would die. I now know that before long you will be home and that very soon our lives will return to normal.

The stains my tears leave on this paper attest to the sorrow that will not let me be. I deserve this for sending you away, but I could not lose you too. Please write and tell me you do not hate me and that you are safe.

Your mother who loves you more than she can say . . .

ELEVEN

Francisco entered the sleeping boy's room and announced, "Wake up. It is time." When Hector failed to respond, Francisco bent down and jabbed his craggy knuckles into Hector's shoulder.

Hector flinched and rolled over. The narrow wooden bed creaked as his body came to rest.

"It is five o'clock. There is work to be done."

Hector moaned, but after a few seconds tossed the sheets away and pulled himself to a sitting position.

Francisco was already shuffling through the doorway and so was spared the sleepy look of distaste that Hector cast in his direction.

"Two minutes," he warned as he stepped with confidence along the dark passageway towards the kitchen. Francisco had no sympathy for the indolence of youth. He would teach the boy the value of hard work or one of them would die in the effort. Francisco's children had been either impetuous or unlucky or both. They had accomplished nothing. Now they were all dead. He had been unable to save them because youth does not see beyond itself. This boy was no different. After all these months he was every bit as useless as the day Francisco had found him toppled over asleep on a bench in front of the train station. He should have known Hector Tomás would be no good, like that soft-skinned father of his, Enrique Tomás, with his books and papers and eyes like a reptile.

They came from weak stock, this Tomás branch of the family, city people who had never known the virtue of building a stone wall with bare hands under a scorching sun. They were Claudia's relatives, her responsibility, her shame. Thankfully, she rarely mentioned them, and whenever a letter arrived she would put it away and conceal its contents from her husband, who was not interested in what those people had to say. But when almost two years ago, after years of silence, he noticed a city postmark on a letter and read the concern on Claudia's brow, he knew they were once again being asked to do something.

The previous time had been when Claudia's brother José Antonio had brought his wife Maria Christina and son Enrique to visit. They wanted to entice the young Enrique away from his books and introduce him to a healthy world of outdoor activity, and so came to sample the sweet mountain air of Envigado in the hope that the boy would so enjoy himself that he would want to come back again and again. It had worked while they were here. Enrique spent all his time at the river swimming with the Rodriguez boy and his friends. But once they returned to the city it was like nothing had happened. José Antonio wrote to say that the exercise they had thought successful had failed after all. Enrique took up with his books exactly where he had left off before the trip, and that was the last Claudia heard from her northern relatives for a great many years.

The kitchen was dark but it didn't matter because Francisco knew every inch of the room and could navigate his way from one end to the other without the benefit of light. Daylight, he had come to realize in his old age, was an overrated luxury and many people took the lack of day-light as an excuse to be lazy. He was ashamed to think of the days and months and years he had squandered in the pursuit of sleep, because as he grew older and broke free of its tyranny, he imagined he could have done so earlier had he only tried. Years ago, before the time of the terrible earthquake, when he had already gathered many more years than his father had, and after his life in the mines had come to an end and he had retired to the farm, Francisco noticed that working past sunset presented no problem to him. He began doing this frequently, and soon it became habit, and as the years went by his regular working day extended well into the night. This was good, he thought, because he would accomplish more of the things that needed to be done. But he also found that when he finally lay down and closed his eyes, sleep refused to come. Sometimes it was early morning when he returned from tending the crops or repairing a fence, and he would find Claudia fast asleep in their bed. As her husband, it was his duty to join her. But the moment he stretched out beneath the blanket, keeping as still as a corpse, his mind would begin teeming with ideas and visions, his limbs twitching with unspent energy. After twelve months of forcing his body to abide by patterns of light and dark that seemed more alien with each passing day, he finally conceded the futility of the effort and relinquished his spot in the marriage bed. Now, after the passage of more time than it takes for a boy to grow into a man, when he had reached an age so advanced that the years had accumulated beyond his ability to count them, he found that he could function without sleep altogether.

He struck a match, lit a candle, and took the tin of coffee beans down from the shelf. Overnight, the fire had reduced itself to embers while he had been carving the posts for the new fence, but the stove was still warm. When he heard Hector's slow tread approaching from behind he uttered a single word: "Wood."

There was only a brief pause before the treads reversed themselves and traced a path to the door. Francisco did not turn. The door opened and with a clatter of loose hinges slammed shut. Francisco shook his head while he pried the cover from the tin. Seven times already he had told the boy to fetch more wood and place it in the box in the room behind the kitchen. Seven times he had suggested it would be better to gather the wood during daylight hours when it was dry, rather than in the dark of early morning when the wood would be damp. But youth never listens. He poured the roasted beans into the hopper and began cranking the wheel of the old iron coffee mill. He would have gathered the wood himself but for a stubborn streak that prevented him from giving in to the laziness of others. He would rather suffer discomfort than perform a task he had assigned to someone else. Hector was an odd boy who never smiled and rarely spoke, and whose idea of work involved an improbable element of choice. He would do some things without being asked, but he was also capable of ignoring repeated requests to perform a chore that could be completed in a few minutes. Claudia got along with him better than her husband, but Francisco put that down to their common blood. That the boy was no good and would prove himself so in the long run, Francisco was certain. But after eighteen months of living under the same roof he had also begun to wonder if the boy was really impervious to learning or if he, Francisco, had been unwittingly drawn into a battle of wills that would end only when one of them was in his grave.

In his letter, Enrique explained that his son had done something to attract the attention of the authorities. Along with the letter, the envelope contained 10,000 pesetas and a promise of more should they agree to allow him into their home. The decision was not a difficult one. Being well acquainted with the annoyances and frustrations of old age, Francisco and Claudia welcomed the offer of an able-bodied young man who would be placed into their charge—in a position of subservience moreover—and whose gratitude would be expressed in his every word and gesture. Immediately Francisco began planning improvements to the property that the boy could undertake. There were the dying *mañío, tepa,* and *canelo* trees at the edge of the river to cut down and chop up for firewood, a creek to divert, a deep trench created over time by the restlessly shifting earth that needed to be filled so the animals were not in danger of falling in. Claudia imagined him helping around the house, cleaning and washing, thus freeing her to bake more of her fabulous honey almond bread so prized at the Envigado market. But more than simply performing menial chores like a hired labourer, Claudia and Francisco expected that Hector would become a son to them, seeking their advice and absorbing their wisdom, so that when he returned home at the end of a month or two he would be prepared for the challenges all young people face in these uncertain times.

However, despite their eagerness to immediately take Enrique up on his offer, they would not be treated like country fools. Negotiations were in order. Francisco scoffed at the 10,000 peseta note where it lay on the kitchen table while Claudia composed a reply. More than once he called Enrique a "miser" and went outside to spit. It was not a simple thing, to take another person into your house as a boarder, even if he was family. And, as Francisco pointed out, Enrique had been sparing in his description of Hector's offence. They could be allowing a murderer or a rapist into their house for all they knew. With each minute that passed, Francisco found another reason to raise the sum higher, and then higher still. Claudia wrote as quickly as her arthritic fingers would allow and was folding the letter into the envelope just as Francisco opened his mouth to speak yet again.

"No!" she said, and scowled at her husband in exasperation. "If we ask for more he will think we are mad." She licked the envelope and sealed it. "It is done. I understand what you are saying, but if we scare him off and stay poor, we will have no one to blame but ourselves." With a triumphant gleam in her eye she handed the envelope to Francisco to deliver to the post office. "You just wait and see what he says."

Once the deal was struck, and Enrique had agreed to pay a further 100,000 pesetas in addition to 20,000 for every month Hector lived in their care, Francisco went to town and returned in a new cart, with fresh bedding, two dozen tins of Spanish beans in *salsa picante*, enough honey, almonds, and flour to last six months, a box of Cuban cigars and fifteen cartons of cigarillos for himself, and a bottle of rum for his wife.

But far from being a grateful and compliant addition to the household, the boy whom Francisco brought home on that cool, cloudy evening in October had in the subsequent year and a half proven himself a morose, silent, skulking creature, someone Francisco found neither reliable nor trustworthy. Not that he had discovered Hector stealing or plotting against them. And it was not as if Hector were disrespectful or hostile, or even, for that matter, overtly unpleasant. Often Hector did exactly what he was told. It was nothing that Francisco could easily put his finger on. But when he saw the boy at rest, leaning on his shovel, gazing across the open field and into the distance, he couldn't help thinking there was purpose in that gaze, that beneath all the silence there lurked a dark heart and a deceitful mind. He was up to something, this boy, with his false innocence and mulish disposition, that much was certain. Francisco repeated his warnings. But Claudia, blinded by Hector's youthful charms, refused to listen. She was pinning her hopes on a boy who could not be trusted, and he wanted to protect her from disappointment. But he had done everything he could. Where Hector Tomás was concerned, it was clear they had no common ground.

TWELVE

Claudia awoke to a clatter of pots and pans coming from the kitchen. Oh Francisco, she thought, and rolled over.

Then she remembered. Market day. By now Hector will have finished loading the cart with baked goods and the plums, pears, and apples that he had picked during the week.

By the light that had just begun trickling through the window, she judged it was five-thirty. The bedsprings squealed as she heaved herself up. Each morning, when her eyes landed on the wooden crucifix that hung on the wall beside the bed, with its bloody figure of Christ in His death agony, she lamented that she was not strong enough to pitch the thing out the window. Gazing at it now, she muttered a prayer and quickly crossed herself. Her feet had swollen during the night and felt round and heavy on the wooden planks of the floor, like melons. The lavender water had not helped; neither had the corn mash she'd cooked for supper, which seemed even as she ate it to slide down the inside of her legs and puddle into the soles of her feet. As always, Francisco had demanded more salt. So she retrieved the salt shaker from the cupboard and watched with fear and longing as he sprinkled a liberal portion over everything on his plate: the mash, the fried eggplant, and the beans. He did not watch his diet, her Francisco. He did not listen when she told him salt was no good for the blood. When he gave the shaker back to her she could not resist a sprinkle or two over her own food. Then she offered it to Hector, who shook his head in refusal. Of course, she had intended the corn mash to be corn cakes, but they had not held together, so as she spooned it on their plates she pretended it was supposed to be mash. Too much water. Too much oil. Francisco had frowned at her, a silent reprimand. She avoided his gaze and acted as if all were normal. She was suffering such lapses more often lately, her rock-hard memory of the recipes she had been making for seventy years going blurry, like the writing on paper that has gotten wet. She worried that her honey almond bread would also turn out badly, become hard like bricks or crumbly like dried horse dung. But she was safe as long as Hector was there to watch over the ingredients as she mixed them.

She pulled her robe on over her nightgown and stuffed her feet into a pair of tattered slippers. Her knees and ankles ached with the effort of supporting her weight.

Francisco had built the fire in the stove and when she entered the kitchen it was warm. Hector and Francisco sat at the table, not looking at each other, silently sipping black coffee by candlelight. They had fried some beans and eaten this, together with the last fragments of corn bread. There were two empty plates on the table, a pan on the stove, crumbs everywhere.

"I will not be going with you today," Claudia announced as she sank with relief into a chair. Hector rose to pour a cup of coffee for her.

"You are not well, my violet?" Francisco's voice betrayed no surprise.

"It's my legs. My feet. Oh, Hector, we are doing you no favour by showing you what it is like to be old before you should have to know these things."

Without a word Hector placed the cup in front of her. Since the money from Enrique had begun arriving they had sampled coffees from mountainside regions of the north, coffee that nuzzled the tongue with such flavour it had to be sinful. She would never go back to the beverage made from fast dissolving powder that they had endured for all those years and which by comparison tasted like muddy water.

With the first sip Claudia shivered with pleasure and pulled the collar of her robe close into her neck.

"Hector and I baked fifty good loaves this week. Not a broken one in the lot. If you are careful they will bring 50 pesetas each."

Francisco grunted.

"There are eggs too. And the pears and apples are good quality. Hector showed me the baskets. Not so the plums, but if you leave the spotty ones at the bottom people will buy them anyway."

Francisco pushed his cup across the table towards Hector, who wordlessly stood to refill it.

Claudia observed Hector's strong back as he stood at the stove. He wore a clean white T-shirt that she had selected with her own hand from a stall of American imports at the bazaar. The people at the stall had told her they received their goods from a supplier in Panama City who got them from Miami, previously worn but fine quality and hardly any damage that you would notice. In the last year and a half Hector had grown a head taller and the flesh of his arms and chest had thickened with the work he'd been doing. His hair was straight and sleek and black. It was so beautiful she resisted cutting it, even when he asked her to because it was in his eyes. They'd had trouble finding clothes for him, now that he had outgrown everything he had brought. She had written to Enrique, asking for more money to buy the boy clothes that would fit. That was a month or two ago and she was still waiting for a response. In the meantime, she had been able to barter bread and fruit for shirts, pants, underwear, and sandals at the bazaar. The boy had an appetite. Oh, he could eat. But he stayed slim; the muscles of his stomach and buttocks were firm. Often she passed by the stall when he was washing himself and stole a peek between the loose boards. Not for many years had she seen a young man's naked body and she was thankful for the electric thrill that pulsed down her spine. It meant she was still alive. She was thankful as well that he was healthy and that the mountain air agreed with him. He would stay for a long time. Already he had stayed longer than they had anticipated. Too bad Francisco was not capable of being civil. It would make their life as a family so much easier. But no man was perfect.

Suddenly she was overcome by sentiment.

"What is wrong, my pet?" Francisco asked as she wiped tears from her cheek.

She shook her head. "I'm old and foolish. That's what's wrong."

Nobody responded. As dawn advanced Claudia was able to see the distracted expression that Francisco wore on his face, an expression that Hector shared as they both gazed at the scarred kitchen tabletop. Her husband was a handsome man who in old age had grown wiry. He still had every tooth in his mouth and every hair on his head. Perhaps once a year she searched his face and body in vain for signs that he was getting older, but his only concession to the years were the heavy flannel shirts he wore all the time, even during the worst of the hot weather, because he felt cold. The one he wore today was red with black checks. When he walked he carried himself nearly upright, with only a slight stoop. Because of all the time he had spent outdoors since retiring from the mines his skin was leathery and his neck and face deeply scored with wrinkles, but this had not changed for decades. For as long as she could remember he had looked the same, while she had grown stout and lame, the flesh at her neck slack and juddering, her legs like stovepipes. As a girl she could remember calculating how old he would be when she had reached a certain age, because she was conscious all the time of the years that separated them. She had married him at sixteen; Francisco was twenty-three years older. Now, at seventy-seven, she looked at him and wondered if he had been lying, if he had been merely a boy who had dressed like a grown-up to fool her parents into thinking he could support a wife. Because she could not believe the man she had married would be a hundred years old on his next birthday.

Finally the rooster crowed. Scuffling noises came from the barn, where Francisco kept a few pigs and some hens. The goats they used for milk stayed out in the field.

Claudia reached up behind her head and tightened the kerchief that held her hair in place.

"Ow," she said.

Hector looked at her.

She smiled apologetically. "My arms are so stiff, Hector. Pray you do not end up full of arthritis."

Francisco stood. The crowing of the rooster was the signal that there was enough light for the journey into town. This was a concession that Claudia had forced upon him with tears and wailing. Reports had been circulating that bands of outlaws roamed the hills at night, committing acts of plunder and carnage. The army had been called in, but she still did not want her two men travelling when it was dark.

Claudia followed her husband out the door to the patio while Hector cleared the table. She noticed again—it seemed like the hundredth time —that Francisco's denim trousers were too long and that he had to wear them with the cuffs rolled up. She would fix them tonight, for sure.

Hector had already been at work this morning. The earthen floor had been swept and cleared of the debris that the wind deposited every night. Even if Francisco didn't, Claudia recognized Hector's efforts to improve that part of the house. He had built a roof out of discarded planks and thatched it with dried grass from the edge of the field. When the heat of the day was at its worst, they could find relief out here, shaded from the sun in a space that captured the breezes flowing down from the hills.

The cart stood ready, filled with goods to sell at market. Hector had covered the baskets containing fruit and eggs and the bags of bread with oilcloth to protect them from the dust and the sun and tied the cloth down with rope. The mare, Consuelo, eyed her master expectantly.

Claudia touched her husband's shoulder.

"Hector is a good boy, Francisco," she whispered as Francisco ran his hand over Consuelo's shank. The mare had only recently recovered from a limp.

"If he is so good then why was his family so eager to see the last of him?"

"We don't know if that is the truth. Any day now Enrique could ask us to put him on the next train home."

Francisco checked the harness and the reins. "We haven't heard anything for months. They might all be dead."

"You know as well as I they are not dead. The money still comes, as regular as the day. But something is going on. Maybe if you would buy a newspaper we would find out what is happening."

Francisco was silent.

"Who are you going to leave the farm to if not Hector? We have no one else."

"Victor's boys will have it."

"You haven't seen your cousin in fifty years. I wager he is dead and his boys are no longer boys. You forget how old you are. You forget that we are the last."

The kitchen door slammed. Hector approached, crossing the patio.

"We are the last, Francisco," she hissed. "Everything will change once we are gone."

"Again you're talking foolishness—"

"It's true." Though there were tears in her eyes, Claudia smiled. "Please excuse me, Hector. I make myself ridiculous, crying for no reason. Please excuse the stupidity of an old woman."

A canvas bag—one that she had fashioned herself from a potato sack—was slung over Hector's shoulder. It was packed full, its sides stretched and rounded.

"What do you have there?"

"The last of my old clothes. I'll see if I can trade them."

Claudia nodded and glanced towards her husband. But Francisco, occupied with the bit in Consuelo's mouth and the tightness of the harness, was not listening.

"You have my list?"

Hector nodded as he climbed into the cart. He carefully stowed the canvas bag beneath the seat and then took the leather reins into his hands.

"You won't forget anything?"

Hector smiled, and her heart leapt to see this because it happened so seldom. He closed his eyes and began to speak as if reciting a poem.

"Twenty pounds of flour, twenty pounds of sugar, ten pounds of almonds, half a gallon of honey, a bag of dried beans, a dozen sticks of soap, two pounds of cornmeal, and five pounds of coffee from the mountains."

Claudia patted his knee. "It is good that one of us can remember these things."

Francisco climbed nimbly into the cart beside Hector. Consuelo stamped her foot and emitted a snort.

Francisco said, "If we don't leave soon there will be no reason to go."

Hector jiggled the reins and in an instant Consuelo was in motion. The heavy cart jerked forward, the wheels bumping over the uneven terrain.

"Don't forget to feed the pigs," Francisco said without turning, only raising his voice so she would hear him over the clatter.

Claudia watched them go. The morning sun was setting the hills ablaze. Birds circled overhead. She crossed herself again when she saw their shiny feathers were black. The cart's wheels raised thick clouds of dust. Though she stood in the shade, she could already feel the sun's heat. The cart reached the end of their lane and turned onto the main road. In the old days, if she were staying at home and the weather was fair, she walked beside the cart for the first hundred yards or so, talking with Francisco of the day she had planned. But she couldn't do that now, with such an ache in her legs, a constant reminder of age, a portent of death.

She returned to the house. Enough beans remained in the pan on the stove for her breakfast. As she spooned them onto the plate Francisco had used and took a seat at the table, she thought with gratitude of Hector, who acted with generosity and possessed the foresight to cook beans for her too, even though there was no guarantee that she would be out of bed in time to see them off. She did not consider the possibility that he had simply cooked too much for himself and Francisco.

She ate slowly. The beans were bland, and she stood to get the salt shaker, but then returned to the table without it. As the sun rose higher, the noises in the barnyard grew clamorous. She would feed the chickens and the pigs. The goats could fend for themselves.

THIRTEEN

Dearest Hector:

I despair now that I will never hear from you. I want to hear your voice but I will settle for a letter. It has been so long since I last saw you that despite my efforts to cling to your image it is no longer so clear in my mind. This is shameful, I know, and shows how undeserving I am. I hope you will forgive me.

In the months since my previous letter there have been many changes in our lives. Carmel is at last married to her sailor and is living on the naval base in San Sebastián. Magda is still at the Academy but will graduate soon. She has applied to universities in America and is confident that her academic standing will enable her to go. All her friends are trying to leave as well. She tells me there is no future here.

This new government looks with suspicion on young people. They think we are troublemakers, but all we want is justice. It is dangerous to think about justice in times like these and it is reckless of me to write it down, but this is how I feel and if you were here I would tell you to your face. I am not afraid. They can shut down the radio stations and impose all the curfews they want, it will not change the way people feel. My parents are so worried that I worry about them. They have done nothing wrong but even so it is not safe to be foreign. Their crime is their fair European skin and Polish accent. My father continues to work, but his job on the tram was given to someone else, and he can only work as a labourer, mending fences and moving stones. The money he makes is hardly enough to buy food. I know that he is trying hard not to give up.

It is kind of your mother to pass my letters along to you. I wish I knew where you were but she tells me you are safe, and I suppose I must be content with that. I have not seen your father since that day, the day we kissed. He is never at home when I visit. Dulciana's wedding day is fast approaching and I have promised to be a bridesmaid. It's strange how life continues, even when the world is falling apart around us.

There is so much more I want to tell you, but I will leave it for another time and hopefully I will be able to tell you without having to write it down. I want you beside me. I want to be able to touch you. This does not seem like a lot to ask.

Please remember me. I could not bear to be forgotten.

With much love,
Nadia

FOURTEEN

They were heading west, away from the sun. The dirt road followed the snaking contours of the land, descending gently into river valleys, jackknifing steeply down craggy hillsides. The town of Envigado was located in the very centre of the province of Envigado, on a plateau nearer to the coast but still about five hundred feet above sea level. The drop in elevation from the farm was two thousand feet, and Hector always felt light in the head while making the descent. The first time he had travelled into town with Francisco and Claudia, he had passed out and almost toppled from the back of the cart. It must have been this incident that turned the old man against him. From that moment, Francisco had made it a habit to either ignore him or shake his head despairingly at the sight of him. It was as if he believed Hector would go to almost any lengths—even to the point of feigning illness—to avoid work.

Hector was determined not to be regarded in this way, but nothing he did satisfied Francisco Cordoba, who had to be listed among the most ancient citizens in the country, if not the world. Hector had never seen a face like his, with lines incised so deeply into the skin it was impossible for there to be no bleeding. The bags under Francisco's eyes looked like they would burst if squeezed, and when he leaned over the bags leaned with him, drawn downward by gravity. His body appeared to have no fat on it, but the few times Hector had happened upon Francisco stripped to his underwear he had glimpsed prominent ribs above a sagging belly; his knees and elbows protruded from his stick-thin limbs. He tried to convince himself that none of this was unusual. Someday, when he was very old, he would find that his own body was wrinkled and drooping all over. But Hector still avoided looking at his great-uncle because the sight was vaguely horrifying, as if he were gazing upon one of the walking dead.

There had been clouds earlier, but the sky was clear as they left the hills behind and entered the final long stretch of flat road before entering town. As usual, they had not exchanged a single word during the ride. Hector did not know what to make of Francisco's lengthy silences except to think that he had lived for so long that his conception of time had been distorted to accommodate his years, and that a spell that seemed interminable for others was but a minute for him. Francisco would sometimes go an entire day without speaking, and even Claudia would begin to think that something was amiss. But then over supper or breakfast, as if continuing a conversation that had been interrupted only seconds earlier, Francisco would make a comment that harkened back to something one of them had said days ago. He was even capable of referring to an event so distant in time as to be lost to memory as if it were last week, and Claudia would curtly inform him that all the people who would know what he was talking about had been dead for twenty years.

But this was only one aspect of Hector's new world that was puzzling. He had tried to adapt amiably to his new living arrangements because he understood it was temporary and that he would be home in a matter of days, a few weeks at the most. In this spirit, he left his resentments behind and portrayed himself to his hosts as not just willing to cooperate, but willing to complete tasks unbidden and in the process test the limits of his endurance. He swept out the pig sty, built a thatched lean-to over the patio, dug holes for fence posts, harvested the fruit trees, and every week loaded the cart with goods for market, performing these and other tasks happily because soon he would be returning to the city, where Nadia was waiting for him and he could go back to school and not be expected to do work of this sort. At night, while fighting off sleep, he scribbled feverishly, letters full of heartsick longing, mostly to his mother and to Nadia, which his aunt posted once a week. In this way he passed the time while awaiting word that it was safe for him to board a train for home.

But as the weeks slipped by and his letters went unanswered, and as the weeks stretched into months, and the months into a whole year, he began to suspect that his family had given up on him, happy to leave him mouldering in this rural backwater, where every day he strained his bones with unpaid labour and suffered the glowering disapproval of his ancient uncle. He believed now that his present situation was his own fault, and this was a source of pain and, oddly, of comfort as well. It had taken him eighteen months to reach this point, and having reached it he felt a strange and welcome calm descend upon him. Each morning he awoke resigned to the day that lay ahead, to the work that must be done, to the hours he would spend stooped over and exhausted. Thankfully, as the sun rose higher in the sky, his mind was numbed by his labours, and he did not think so much of Nadia's smile, and of his friends and his family and the life he was missing. Day after day he passed in this manner. He blessed his new serenity because it spared him the sting of grief, and like animals that lie down quietly in the night to breathe their last, he gave himself up to his fate. Without warning he might emerge from his cocoon and, with a flash of recognition, see where he was and what he'd become. His mind would spin and tumble as the reminders of his previous life rushed into view and tempted him to longing and to anger. But over time he had learned to master these moments and his emotions, and he was able to nurture the calm that was allowing him to survive. It was the calm of someone who holds his fate in his own hands, and as he glanced at Francisco beside him on the cart he felt a pang of regret for not having bullied his way past the old man's inhospitable exterior and tried to know him as a friend.

He guided the cart down a gradual incline. The sun had risen above the hills and lit their way. To his right, the view was of pine trees, grass, rolling hillocks all the way to the horizon; to his left was a lake that stretched for a mile or more. One afternoon, at the height of summer, on another day when Claudia had not accompanied them, Francisco had bidden Hector to stop the cart as they were passing this way during the journey home. He had then said that it was hot and he would wait if Hector wanted to go for a swim. Hector had looked at the old man, who so rarely acknowledged his existence that he had begun to doubt it himself, and wondered why on this occasion his comfort was something that would cause Francisco concern. Please, Francisco had said, gesturing towards the water, something like a smile passing across his face. Suspicious of a trick, but also grubby and tired after a full day of peddling produce under a scorching sun, Hector had stripped to his skin and enjoyed a brief respite in the chill water of the lake, but not before checking for ghosts, for he had heard that when people drowned it was because their frolicking caused such envy in the spirits inhabiting the water that they pulled them under to their deaths. He had also kept his eye on the road, for a part of him expected Francisco to drive off and leave him there. But nothing had happened. Refreshed, he dressed quickly and returned to the cart, where Francisco was smoking a cigarillo, and they drove off.

As they passed the lake, the sun crept upward. The morning grew warmer. Pretending to scratch his ankle, Hector reached down and felt beneath his seat, checking for the canvas sack that held his belongings. It was there, as he knew it would be, but still a wave of relief swept over him.

Except for their cart the road was deserted, for it was a poor dirt road that passed only the poorest of settlements, the ones that had lost their water because rivers from the mountains had been diverted for the hydroelectric project, and where damage from the last earthquake seven years ago was still evident. The dwellings close to the road were mostly empty shells. Constructed of mud, stone, and grass, they had crumbled to dust as the ground shook beneath them. Rather than rebuild on arid soil that was lifted and carried off by the slightest breeze, many owners had abandoned their ruined homes and moved to the city, where they now lived in crowded tenements or shared quarters with other family members. Those who remained had already patched and repaired their dwellings more times than they could count. But Hector did not know the history, so all he saw were broken-down homes with no roofs and holes for windows, and children crawling in the dirt. The sight of such misery pained him, and he kept his eyes on the road.

The youthful arrogance he had brought with him to Envigado—feelings of uniqueness and privilege, the conviction that he was indispensable—had long since faded and been replaced by desolation and emptiness and a growing suspicion that his future was one of slender prospects. Often his thoughts turned to what he might have done to prevent his capture on the night of the assault. He could have so easily wrapped his fingers around Jorgé's throat and cut off his screams, and then silenced the girl in the same way. But being caught had been crucial to the statement he'd wished to make. Hurting Jorgé and slipping away unseen would have been a betrayal of his true goal, which was to show Enrique Tomás that he had fathered a son who was not afraid of dispensing justice, even at the cost of personal suffering. Many months later, exiled and lonely, he held fast to the conviction that he had acted for the good of his family and in the only responsible manner available to him. His sole regret was that he had not acted sooner.

Still, he longed for word from his family and Nadia, and grew more troubled each day none came; as the months drifted by, taking the seasons with them, he understood, as if someone had informed him of the fact, that the silence he endured could not simply be his father. The explanation was deeper, subtler, fuelled by illness or catastrophe, a breakdown in communications affecting the entire country. While Claudia and Francisco had no telephone, on a number of occasions Hector had brought money with him to use the pay telephone at the Envigado *Telefonica*. However, his time was limited and the lines were always too long, or the phones were broken, or the office had closed unexpectedly. And as time passed and his anxieties mingled with bitterness and finally gave way to the numbness of acquiescence, he came to fear breaking the silence in this fashion. What terrible thing would he learn that he was better off not knowing? What if something had happened to Nadia? What if she didn't love him after all? And then the day arrived when at the *Telefonica* he reached the front of the line. The phone was in his hand, his finger poised to dial the number. With a sinking heart and a constriction in his throat, he laid the phone back in its cradle and turned away, resigning himself to the crushing burden and yet relative safety of ignorance. Early in his exile he had inquired of Claudia every week if a letter arrived and she, in her vague fashion, told him again and again that he would know when a letter came because the envelope would be on the kitchen table waiting for him to open it. Finally, he stopped asking. But he still checked the table in the evening whenever he knew she had visited the post office that day, remaining faithful in his vigil long after he understood that the time for waiting had ended.

The final stretch of road to Envigado was lined with shanties occupied by people of a sort Hector had never beheld in such profusion. The dwellings of the Mapuche were constructed haphazardly, of odd pieces of lumber, tarpaper, corrugated tin, and other materials that Hector guessed had been either discarded or stolen. Trees, bushes, and overgrown grass encroached on many of them. He tried not to stare, but could not resist the impulse. In front of one house a small round woman with dark skin and wearing a multi-coloured headdress was washing a baby in a basin of water. In front of another a man with a dark crumpled face sat chewing an unlit cigar and staring impassively as the cart rolled by. From a few of the houses a spiral of smoke issued lazily through a stovepipe chimney. Here and there a donkey or a goat was tethered to a post. Two children, their clothes torn and filthy, faces smeared with dirt, sat laughing on the front step of one house. As always, Hector took in these sights uneasily, sensitive to the hollow pit opening at the base of his stomach. The reek of poverty was unmistakable and even though his ignorance was profound and his understanding superficial, he felt overcome by despair and, inexplicably, shame. Surely no one would choose to live under such circumstances. It had come to him, after many passes along this road, that the houses shared a tumbledown, provisional quality, as if the people had been hastily moved to this uncongenial setting from somewhere else, prodded along by promises that remained unfulfilled. He had no way of knowing that the country's leaders had never made peace with the native population, that the ritual slaughter of past centuries had never been officially acknowledged, and that the recent flooding of Mapuche homelands, which had taken place to accommodate a hydroelectric project, was widely regarded as an atrocity. He didn't know that years of oppression had given rise to a sentiment among the Mapuche that they had nothing left to lose.

All he knew was that he would never have to pass this way again. And for this he was thankful.

By the time they crossed the town limits, they had been joined by many carts with drivers bringing goods to market, and the road was congested and noisy with voices and the braying of donkeys. Motor vehicles did not often venture along the dirt road they had followed for most of their journey, but once within the precincts of Envigado, all traffic mingled on the cobbled streets, horse-drawn carts and bicycles competing with scooters, buses, pickup trucks, and Jeeps. Hector had learned there was no point trying to hurry. There were no shortcuts to the central plaza where, along with hundreds of others, they would set up shop beneath the imposing stone spires of the Iglesia Corazón de María. Hector followed the stream as it wound slowly along and watched the residents of the town go about their business. Francisco sat quietly as if in a trance.

Having recovered from his initial disappointment, he could now admit that Envigado possessed an allure of its own. B____, though modern and filled with distractions, had lost touch with its past when the colonial buildings were demolished to make room for office towers and the centuries-old cobblestones were paved over with blacktop. But Envigado had eluded the clutches of progress and remained a town where people were not dwarfed by their own creations. The sky seemed nearer to the earth, not pushed out of reach by massive structures. In the shops there were fewer choices—they sold necessities rather than luxuries— but Hector hardly noticed because he had little time and less money. In Envigado he saw no girls strutting along in high-heeled boots, short skirts, and sunglasses; no young men wearing black T-shirts stretched over muscular torsos. In B____ people were always aware of how they looked. Here nobody cared. They dressed simply, the men in everyday shirts and pants, the girls modestly in knee-length skirts. At some point he had noticed the absence of billboard advertisements blotting out the landscape, but welcomed this as an improvement over what he was familiar with. He had at first missed the American fast-food restaurants selling hamburgers in plastic cartons, and for many weeks had craved the taste of processed meat on a dry bun. But this craving faded as he grew to appreciate his Aunt Claudia's home cooking. He had left the train station full of bitterness, thinking he had been sent to the last stop at the far end of the earth. And maybe that was so, but he was going to leave this town with mixed feelings.

As he had for almost a half century, Francisco set up shop near the northwest corner of the plaza, where the shade cast by the church spires would last for an hour or two. The cart itself, one side of which folded down, served as a display space. Months of repeating a mechanical process enabled Hector to complete the transformation from cart to stall in minutes. Francisco had always left everything in baskets in the back of the cart. But using as a model other stalls he had seen at the market, Hector had built a tiered platform that rested on the ground on which to arrange the goods that were for sale, placing all within easy reach. An oilcloth cover, supported by two stakes angled out from the cart, served as an awning to shield their wares from the late morning sun. While Hector was doing this, Francisco led Consuelo to a nearby stable where for a small fee she was fed and watered and sheltered from the sun for the day.

Hector understood how valuable his contribution to the Cordoba household was. Without him Claudia would be forced to make the journey every market day, because the task was more than Francisco could cope with on his own. He was ashamed therefore about his plans to abandon them without a word of warning, but he could no longer support the idea of remaining in Envigado while his family was falling prey to whatever prevented them from communicating with him. Day after day Claudia insisted that no word had come, but Hector was not so innocent that he imagined Claudia and Francisco had agreed to house, feed, and clothe him for nothing. He knew money had changed hands and that it continued to do so. In a few days he would arrive home and discover the truth for himself.

Hector was quick to fill the bags of regular customers and make change for them, performing these acts nimbly and with precision. There were many who expected and cherished Claudia's honey almond bread, and in less than an hour all the loaves—even the damaged ones—had been sold. During brief intervals between tending customers he checked to make sure that the canvas bag was still in its hiding place beneath the seat. Over the months Hector had noticed more soldiers patrolling the market—unsmiling young men in green uniforms wielding semi-automatic weapons—but on market day petty thievery was rampant and nobody expected a few soldiers to change that. Only by making mistakes had Hector learned the importance of vigilance, of being suspicious of everything and alert to commonplace tricks. One of the first times he'd been left alone, he had been fooled by a boy who fell off his bicycle while passing the stall. The boy wailed as the scrape on his knee grew crimson and seeped blood, and Hector, amazed and indignant that no one else had done so, rushed to the boy's aid. He helped the whimpering boy up and back on the bicycle and when he returned to the stall discovered that a good portion of the fruit and vegetables he had been trying to sell had been stolen. It was only when he saw the woman at the next stall laughing toothlessly at him that he realized what had happened, and the blood of humiliation rushed to his face. After that incident he kept his eyes open at all times and never strayed more than a few feet from the stall.

A pair of soldiers—one tall, the other shorter with a thick moustache —entered his vision from the right as he helped an old Mapuche woman place a bag of apples and pears into her two-wheeled metal basket. As she did every week, with a coy smile she asked him to help her home with her purchases so she could introduce him to her daughter. And, as he did every week, Hector gently refused. When she was gone he stepped out from the stall and glanced in both directions. Francisco was nowhere to be seen. He would return eventually, but Hector was not expecting the old man to hurry. Market day was his opportunity to drink fiery home-made *aguardiente* and cheap *grapa* in the company of friends, tell stories that were not true, and smoke cigars out of Claudia's sight.

The church bells tolled the hour. It was now ten a.m. and the arid warmth of another day without rain flowed with the breeze and moved across his skin. The morning rush was over. Across from him the Mapuche man selling wooden carvings of his own design lowered himself onto a stool and, lighting a cigarette, glanced from side to side along the passageway separating the rows of stalls. His long hair fell in a rat's tail braid down the length of his back. A group of tourists, two middle-aged couples, laden with bags and parcels, strolled by discussing something in a language Hector could not understand. He wondered if it was English. They looked like Americans, all four wearing wide-brimmed straw hats, short pants and sandals, their ample bodies straining against their clothes, their heavy legs pale white, like something that has been underground for too long.

A festival air prevailed. From a distant corner, amid echoes of laughter and childish screams, came the strains of a mountain melody being played with robust enthusiasm on traditional instruments. Nearby, someone was blowing a slow tune on pan pipes. Occasionally, a ripple of applause reached him as one event ended or another began. In the past, Hector had seen street performers who could swallow swords and breathe fire and make small animals disappear, and others who could twist their bodies into impossible shapes as onlookers gasped. Men came dressed as women and danced for money. All through the market a hundred kinds of food were being prepared. On other market days he had filled himself with spiced meat and fish on skewers grilled over an open flame, aromatic herbed vegetables folded within rounds of flat bread and lightly toasted, Chinese noodles with vegetables in a warm spicy sauce, Spanish chorizo sausage, cream-filled cakes, deep-fried rings of sweet batter, all kinds of candy that stuck to his teeth. Even now, the peppery smell of grilling meat floated in the air, accompanied by the pungent sweetness of rotting fruit. From beyond the edge of the market, the drone of a motor scooter rose above the other traffic noises and echoed sputtering into the distance. Someone shouted hello to a friend.

At the sight of an old woman who resembled his Aunt Claudia, Hector's stomach lurched, causing him a brief wrenching spasm. He was not naturally deceitful, and whenever he contemplated doing something that he knew was going to displease his elders his guts would grumble and gurgle until he had either changed his mind or completed the deed. He breathed deeply and struggled to subdue his seizing innards. In his imagination, everyone whose eyes he met instantly understood what was on his mind and judged him harshly. He felt like the child in the story, the one who had concealed a stolen coin in his pocket that glowed so brightly everyone could see it. Over the previous weeks he had spent his free time on market days at the bus station, making inquiries and committing the schedule to memory. He knew that if he hoped to reserve a seat on the bus to Villa Real, which left at one p.m., it would be best to purchase his ticket no later than noon. At Villa Real he would board another bus that would take him the rest of the way to B____. A question remained of how he was going to pay for this, but he would face that problem when the time came. Perhaps he could sell something. Or maybe phone his mother, and she would meet him at the station in B____ and pay for the ticket after he had arrived. He had repeated to himself that he was doing nothing wrong. His life was his own and he would do with it as he saw fit. But he had still not committed himself to anything. He could return to the farm with Francisco if, in the end, he chose to do so.

Once more he quickly checked the canvas bag. As he was returning to the front of the stall, the same pair of soldiers strode by again, this time from the left, their expressions earnest and watchful. Without meaning to he met the eye of one, the taller of the two, a young man with thick black brows and features that looked as if chiselled from stone. The soldier gave him a cursory up and down glance before shifting his gaze straight ahead. He seemed with this quick assessment and dismissal to scorn Hector's position as a humble vendor of fruit and vegetables. Hector, conscious of his tattered green apron, of the fact that the apron and his hands were stained with fruit juice, of the flies that continuously swarmed about his face, looked away and felt his blood rise. He was thankful when a small thin woman pushed forward through the meandering crowd, stepped into the shade beneath the awning, and began fingering the pears and apples.

"How much are these?" she demanded, though a card propped in the bin displayed the price prominently.

He pointed at the sign. "A dozen for five pesetas."

She lifted a plum, held it to her nose, and put it back.

"These are not ripe," she declared, scanning the selection. "No good for eating."

"Good for preserves," Hector countered. "The best." Over her head he noticed the soldiers again. They had approached the Mapuche man and were speaking to him. The Mapuche glanced upward but did not stand.

The woman was saying something, but he wasn't listening. He knew her. She was always pushy and bad-tempered, but today seemed more so than usual. He could tell this by the unpleasant set of her thin lips and the jerky way she brushed the mane of unkempt grey hair back from her face.

"I'm sorry?"

"Three pesetas. For these you'll get no more from me."

Hector shrugged. "As you wish," he said, growing weary at the thought of haggling with such a person over two pesetas.

She thrust a plastic bag at him, which he held open. With a series of fussy gestures and the occasional grimace, she made her choices, pushing the rejected fruit to one side and placing the acceptable ones in the bag. She seemed disappointed that he had given in so hastily and maybe thought less of him because of this. Hector did not care.

He continued to watch the two soldiers question the Mapuche man. Standing perfectly straight in their clean uniforms, their hands ready on their weapons, they commanded the respect of all who passed by. A twinge of envy chafed his heart and, as he continued to observe them, spread through his chest to become longing. The soldier with the chiselled features barked questions at the Mapuche while the one with the moustache kept close watch on the activities of market goers passing by. The way they looked about them—they didn't trust anyone. Eager to avoid trouble, people gingerly stepped around the Mapuche and the soldiers, as if the spot were tainted. Nobody approached the Mapuche's wooden carvings.

The presence of soldiers was not something Hector had ever questioned. Armed soldiers patrolled the streets of his earliest memories.
But the idea came to him now that if there was a need for soldiers to
defend the country, there had to be an enemy. In the war movies he had
watched on Saturday afternoons at the B——— cinema with his friends,
the enemies of the hero Americans wore strange helmets. They had guns
but died by the thousands. The cowboy movies were the same, with
the good guys shooting at the bad guys from behind craggy rocks or
out of windows and doorways, defending the ranch or the honour of
their women; they fought a real enemy, one that made itself seen and
felt. It was absurd to even imagine that he stood in the presence of an
enemy, here at the market. It made no sense, until he recalled that in
the middle of the night someone had entered his home and taken his
brother away.

The two soldiers and the Mapuche were arguing now. He could not
escape their angry voices. He wondered what the man had done, because
he must have done something. It was not possible that people who were
guilty of no crime had reason to be afraid.

Confused and growing anxious, he continued to hold the plastic bag
while the thin woman searched her purse for money.

The soldier with the chiselled features had pulled the Mapuche to his
feet and was shouting at him, repeating a question: "Where are they?"
Hector looked towards the ground. He shuffled his feet and, thinking
about the task he had set himself today, felt a raw tingling in his scalp.
The soldiers had no reason to take notice of him. But why were they so
angry? Why were they questioning the Mapuche? The gurgling in his
stomach intensified.

And then he heard it, a loud crack as the soldier with the moustache
struck the Mapuche across the face with the butt of his pistol. Hector
looked up and at the same moment the thin woman turned. The coins
she had retrieved slipped through her fingers and fell to the ground. The
Mapuche lay amidst his wooden carvings supporting himself with one
arm, groping with his other hand for the gash that had opened above
his eye. The soldiers stood above him, their weapons aimed towards the
prone man as if he posed an imminent threat.

Leaving the coins where she'd dropped them, the thin woman crossed
herself, grabbed the bag of fruit from Hector's hand, and vanished into

a cluster of onlookers. But Hector hardly noticed. He could not tear his eyes away as the soldiers pulled the Mapuche to his feet and dragged him off at gunpoint. The man appeared dazed. His mouth hung open and blood from the gash streamed down his face. It was only when they were gone that time, which during the arrest had seemed to pass haltingly, galloped forward. Suddenly there were people everywhere. Those who had witnessed the violence gathered around the Mapuche's vacated stall, pointing at the bloodstains and in loud voices describing what they had seen. Their chatter gradually subsided as they dispersed, carrying the story with them, and seconds later traffic sounds from the street and the general clamour of the market drowned out everything else. Shoppers who had been in another section of the market during the arrest strolled by with their bags and parcels, glancing curiously at the wooden carvings that lay scattered on the ground next to the overturned stool. Into Hector's mind came an image of a pool of water, its surface momentarily disturbed by a dropped stone, quickly returning to a state of mirror-like tranquility.

After a short time the tolling of church bells once again marked the hour. Hector wished that Francisco would return because he knew that if he did not soon act upon his plans he would lose the opportunity together with the nerve to do so. Absently, to distract himself and calm his churning stomach, he selected a plum from the display, a yellow one with no imperfections that was streaked with red like a sunset and that had some softness beneath the skin. But the thin woman was right. It was not ripe and it resisted his teeth unpleasantly when he bit into it. He had picked them at Claudia's insistence, but it was too soon, and now that they were off the tree they would not ripen properly; one day as hard as stones, the next day rotting from the inside out. The best thing to do would be to dump the lot on the way back to the farm. Give the birds a feast.

He dropped the uneaten plum and kicked it towards the back of the stall where it rolled under the cart.

He still had to buy the items that Claudia had asked him to get, and soon people would be packing up their unsold wares. Again, he searched up and down the long aisle for Francisco. The crowds had thinned. Music echoed in the distance, but an eerie quiet had descended over their corner of the market. Across the way, a man in shirt sleeves squatted to get a closer look at the Mapuche's carvings. He picked one up and turned it over in his hands.

Abruptly, the music stopped. As if this were a sort of signal, the vendors around him began immediately to pack up their things. Hector went to the rear of the stall, grabbed the canvas bag from its hiding place, and set out.

FIFTEEN

The clock on the wall told Francisco he had lingered too long. He rose to make his farewells. It was a wonderful thing, to have a seventeenth grandchild. He wrapped Egberto in a close embrace and said, "We will meet again soon, my friend, eh? This celebration will not be our last."

The two ancient men drew apart and looked briefly into each other's eyes. Egberto's face, lined and leathery, was spotted with freckles. His bones were frail. They were so old now that every time they said good-bye they knew the chance was good that they would never see each other again. Ever the sensitive one, Egberto was weeping. Maybe he knew something Francisco did not. Maybe he was drunk.

There had been plenty of whisky and *grapa*. Around and around the bottles went. When they emptied one bottle another appeared, as if by magic, to take its place. Francisco had consumed his share and more. He had smoked an entire cigar. The noise of conversation and laughter all around him was the sound of life being lived. He didn't want to leave, but the time had come.

He stopped at the door. The young man strumming the sad mountain tune "Señora de mi Corazón" on his *guitarrón* looked up and smiled. The women swayed their hips to the rhythm. Francisco lifted his hand in farewell, but Egberto, distracted by one of his young grandchildren, was not looking his way.

On the sidewalk the sun's heat attacked him. The sky was clear. After only half a dozen steps he stumbled on the edge of the curb and nearly fell. As he found his balance and set out towards the spire of the cathedral, Claudia's words returned. They were both very old. Soon they would be dead. Who would fill their place? Who would take over the farm? Their children were gone; weakened by disease or wounded by misfortune, they had withered and turned to dust before the unbelieving eyes of their parents. It had been a remarkable thing to witness. Such bad luck. Everyone said so. Claudia and Francisco had shared a life of virtue and hard work. How could God, claiming to be merciful, point the bony finger of death at them so many times? It was not fair. But who were they, simple peasants, to question the will of God?

Ah, he was tired. He had walked and walked but the market seemed no closer. He sat on a bench and retrieved a cigarillo from the package in his pocket. Traffic noises and the howls of frightened animals filled his ears. A Jeep packed with soldiers sped past. Although Envigado was a raucous place, he sensed something more than the usual hubbub. But he was too tired to think. He closed his eyes and drew the smoke into his lungs.

Francisco was not devout. He could not put his faith in an unjust God. His countless years had seen earthquakes, revolutions, epidemics, floods, and drought. In the mines he had escaped but not eluded death. Friends had been crushed by falling stone, suffocated by gas leaks, impaled on rocks as sharp as spears. He had seen too many men die who deserved to live. And while he laboured at the rock face, Claudia had managed the farm on her own. Then he retired and was free to help. Early in their marriage they had expected that their children, and perhaps grandchildren, would share the work, but instead, he and Claudia had done all the work themselves.

Aguaria's rise to power brought with it a period of turmoil and terror. Suspicion had been the rule. Neighbour could not trust neighbour. Nothing made any sense. He had seen a young girl shot because a raven cried out at the same moment that she denied sympathizing with the rebels, a man because one of his arms was two inches longer than the other. Those were days when an unexpected knock on the door could only mean death.

Luck was with them again. Their farm was difficult to get to and well out of the way of armed conflict. But there had been incidents. One morning he found the body of a soldier beneath an apple tree, arms and legs bound, almost no skin left, the face torn to pieces. He knew at once that the man had been dragged to his death, probably tethered to a horse and hauled for miles across stony terrain. Francisco immediately buried the man beneath that same tree, and by keeping silent about it he hoped to forget. But a few days later, three soldiers came looking for their companion. Other farmers living on the high plains outside Envigado had been caught harbouring and feeding rebels, and in retaliation had been forced to watch their daughters raped and their animals shot. Because she knew nothing of the dead soldier and therefore could not lie, Francisco let Claudia accompany them on their search while he feigned illness. But it had been a cold day, and, finding nothing, they quickly retreated inside. He had not at first noticed their gauntness, the hunger that bleached their skin of colour, and the terror of an enemy that was everywhere and nowhere that never left their eyes. They stayed for a week, drinking gallons of coffee and feasting on pie made from apples taken from the tree beneath which the dead man lay quietly in his grave. They left strengthened and grateful.

Aguaria's downfall had freed people from the shackles of suspicion, and this freedom had lasted for many years. But the country's fortunes had been long in decline and the last government had failed to revitalize the economy as they had promised and were now sharing power with the military. They needed someone to blame, and all the while they searched for an enemy, suspicion was on the rise. This was the reason why he did not discuss the news of the day with his wife and would never bring a newspaper into the house. He could see, in the eyes of mothers searching for food for their children—in the eyes of the children themselves, in the eyes of frightened boy-soldiers that detected an enemy in every unfamiliar face, in the eyes of the son of Enrique Tomás, who was the restless victim of a strange discontent—he could see that more dark times were ahead.

He rose and continued walking in the direction of the cathedral's spire, doggedly placing one foot in front of the other. When he reached the edge of the market he saw that some stalls were already vacant. The sidewalk was strewn with overturned baskets, smashed fruit boxes.

"What's going on?" he asked a woman seller of herbal remedies and spirit cures.

"The soldiers," she said curtly as she placed vials and small paper packages wrapped with twine into plastic bags. She had long straight hair which she swept back from her face to reveal a prominent nose. She did not look at him but her eyes were wide and her hands were trembling.

"They took some people away and searched through their things. I don't know what they are looking for."

She fell silent and continued packing. Francisco pushed forward through a noisy, agitated crowd that seemed to flow in all directions at once. He heard angry voices. Shouts and cries. Soldiers yelling. He was forced backward and jostled without mercy, without deference to his age. Nobody cared. Somewhere, a child howled. Beside a stall where leather boots were sold, two men—one old, one young—raised their fists and struck one another, drawing blood.

Hector was not at the stall where he belonged. The fury that took hold of Francisco sharpened his wits and renewed his energy. He looked around, but there was no one to ask where the boy had gone. People were busy packing up and many of the nearby stalls were abandoned or empty. Meanwhile, the fruit that he and Claudia had laboured to grow sat in the display, free to anyone who cared to take it. He cursed, but at the same moment sensed movement. Hector stood beside him.

"These are for Aunt Claudia," Hector said as he lowered to the ground several bags he'd been carrying.

"You left the stall. Everything could have been stolen."

Hector slowly raised his eyes. Francisco did not like the boy's expression.

"You have to leave now," Hector said. "I will help load the cart but I won't be going with you."

Francisco stared, not believing he had heard correctly. "What do you mean?"

Hector faced him squarely. "I'm not going back to the farm."

As the significance of Hector's declaration dawned on him, Francisco felt a surge of anger rise up within. Though why should he be angry? Wasn't this what he wanted?

"This is not right," he said. "This is not the way to do things."

But Hector had turned his attention to the task of dismantling the stall, folding up the fruit stand and lowering the oilcloth canopy. Francisco grabbed his shoulder.

"Look at me boy! Look at me when I talk to you!"

Hector shook him off.

"There is no time. The soldiers are everywhere. They are closing the market and hurting people who don't move fast enough. We have to hurry."

But Francisco could see only insolence and defiance. It was too much. He grabbed Hector's shoulder again but the boy slapped his hand away.

"Uncle, listen! You hear that, don't you? Use your eyes! Look at what they are doing!"

"You will not speak to me this way!"

Francisco's fist caught Hector on the jaw. Hector's head snapped back and he emitted a grunt. But Francisco swung too slowly the second time. Hector ducked beneath the blow and grasped Francisco's wrist. Hector's grip was strong. Francisco could not break free.

"Boy, you will treat me with respect!" Francisco was mortified when he realized tears were staining his face. He struggled briefly but, exhausted, soon gave up.

"I'm sorry," Hector said. Leaning forward, he spoke into Francisco's ear. "We must put everything back into the cart. I will help you and then I will fetch Consuelo."

Francisco let his arm drop to his side when Hector released it. He nodded. Hector turned away, the altercation apparently forgotten. Looking around for something to do, Francisco spotted the basket of eggs, which was still half full. With more effort than it should have required he lifted it and placed it carefully in the rear of the cart. The force of his rage had set off a ringing in his ears, and as this diminished he grew conscious of an infernal din, as if the world and everyone in it had descended into madness. There was commotion on all sides, of vendors being ejected from the market, of soldiers bellowing orders, of hastening footsteps and revving engines. From nearby came the sound of someone weeping, but Francisco paid no heed and mechanically straightened the boxes in the rear of the cart. Hector worked swiftly and silently. In a few minutes everything was put away. Francisco watched as Hector took the bags he had said were for Claudia and stowed some beneath the seat of the cart and piled others on the seat itself. When he was done it was obvious there was room for only one person. The last thing left on the ground was the canvas sack that the boy had brought with him that morning.

Hector quickly untied the apron from around his waist and lifted it over his head. The pockets of the apron bulged with coins. He handed it to Francisco who, without comment, put it on as he did every week when he relieved Hector at the stall.

Hector drew a roll of bills from his pocket.

"I will go to the stable and pay the money." He selected two 100 peseta notes and pushed what was left into Francisco's hand. He took the canvas sack and thrust it up on the cart in the place where Francisco would be sitting. "Please watch this," he said.

Francisco, still suffering the effects of the alcohol, fought off a spell of dizziness. He blinked and rubbed his eyes.

Hector laid his hand on the bag and said slowly, "This contains my clothes and my money. I will need them."

Francisco nodded. "Why are they closing the market?"

"I don't know."

Francisco tried to hold Hector's gaze so he could see the truth of the matter, but Hector paused too briefly before running off, weaving a path through an unbroken flow of people and vehicles. He watched until Hector was out of sight.

He knows, he thought. But the idea did not hold. He could not convince himself that Hector knew what was going on and chose not to tell. Why would the boy lie? Something was taking place, maybe a government or military crackdown. Who could say for sure? The soldiers with their clubs were probably as ignorant as everyone else. One thing was certain: there would be no market next week, or the week after that. Francisco had seen it all before and often mourned for his country, which could not control its passions, which had not learned from its turbulent and inglorious past, and which time and time again allowed the most vulgar and malignant of its citizens to seize the reigns of power.

So now, as in the past, the market would fall victim to a distrustful government's fears. In Aguaria's day there was a law. The little man and his cronies were so paranoid they thought a dozen old women rinsing clothes in a stream would organize a counter-revolution. This regime would be the same. Events that drew people together would be banned. There would be a curfew. Francisco sighed. The beginning of such a period was always the worst. Because the young soldiers were naive and eager to show their superiors what they were made of, they would take every opportunity to impose discipline. No infraction would be too small and they would enjoy enforcing the new laws. Beating an old woman senseless with metal pipes because they imagined she had cast a spell, or kicking a child's dog until it was dead because it would not stop barking, these were acts they would be proud of, and they would stand tall with their chests thrust out during morning inspection. But these same youths would soon weary of tormenting peasants, especially after finding the rewards to be meagre. The worst of them would seek out more lucrative amusements: raiding farms and shops, drinking stolen liquor until they fell down drunk, and filling their pockets with booty.

Hearing cries and angry shouts close by and sensing the approach of soldiers, Francisco stuffed the roll of bills into the pocket of his pants. He was not afraid, but he wanted Hector to bring Consuelo back so he could be on his way. Shouting echoed throughout the plaza, drowned out only by the sound of heavy objects being dragged. The street was empty of vehicles but littered with the debris of sudden flight: pop cans, plastic bags, scraps of paper, dropped clothing, discarded fruit and vegetables. People did not walk but scurried like mice, shoulders hunched as if under pursuit. Thinking to conceal himself he stepped to the front of the cart and sat down on the cobblestones. He peeked around the wheel of the cart and saw a few soldiers on foot, still a fair distance off, sifting through the remnants of the market, pulling apart the few empty stalls still standing.

He rubbed his hand. It was sore, but in an odd way the pain was reassuring, as if it had resulted from useful labour. He was not sorry. The boy had to be taught discipline and respect. That was why his parents had sent him here. Being lazy and ineffectual, they could not control his outbursts. A youth with strength in his arms and a temper in his brain is a danger to everyone.

Perhaps the boy was right. It was time for him to leave. He and Claudia had done as much as they could for him, but now they would be better off on their own. Claudia was too trusting. She had grown soft on the boy and was losing her courage. Deliberately or not, Hector played on her weakness. Francisco had noticed how she gazed at him, with a dreamy vacant stare, as if imagining she was looking at one of her own children returned from the dead. And it was true there was a resemblance. Hector shared Antonio José's heavy-lidded, dark brooding eyes. But Antonio José was gone and the past was in the past. It had taken all his strength to bury ten children and he was not going to conjure those ghosts for anyone. But he could understand how so much grief could addle anyone's brain. Where else could this notion have come from, that Hector would stay on after they were no more? Had the boy made a promise he had no intention of keeping? Or had she dreamed it up? The things that came out of her mouth! Sometimes he feared for her mind. There was a history in her family—an aunt had spent her declining years talking to a potted plant. How could she even suggest leaving the farm to Hector? Victor's boys would have it. They were prepared to step in. It was better this way. A clean break. The winter was going to be hard. There would be no market. They would have to barter their produce with other families in the mountains. But they would survive. They always did. Hector's parents had never meant for him stay in Envigado forever.

It would break Claudia's heart when she discovered he had run off without so much as a thank you, but she would get over it.

SIXTEEN

The blow had not hurt at the time, but as he led Consuelo along the narrow lane that joined Rua Independência to the plaza in front of the Iglesia Corazón de María, Hector could not ignore the growing tenderness and swelling in his jaw. He had seen Francisco angry and had sometimes taken perverse pleasure in provoking him, but never had this anger risen to the point of using his fists. Sometimes when Hector and Claudia talked as if Francisco weren't present he would rise from the table without a word and leave the room. But it was all in jest. Later, after the sun had gone down, Claudia would say goodnight and go to him in the other room and apologize, and Hector would hear their talk and laughter drift through the open window while he lay in bed waiting for sleep. Their relationship did not seem vulnerable to bouts of temper. They did not raise their voices for any purpose other than to make themselves heard. If Claudia spoke sharply, it was to remind Francisco to scrub the dirt from his hands before sitting down to eat. If Francisco uttered a harsh word, it was only to curse the bad luck that had blighted the potato crop.

He whispered to Consuelo and stroked her nose as they reached the end of the lane. In order to shield her from the sounds of flight and confusion coming from the street he had followed a series of back alleys. As they emerged into the plaza she jerked her head from side to side, resisting his lead.

It was approaching noon and the sun beat down from a position almost directly overhead. Soldiers were still searching the ruins of the market, but had not yet reached their section. Hector's stomach lurched when Francisco was not immediately visible, but then he saw him rise to his feet from where he'd been sitting beside the cart. He was smoking a cigarillo. When Consuelo saw him she fell into a trot.

Francisco said nothing to Hector, but greeted the horse affectionately with a tap on the nose as he took hold of the bridle.

"How's my girl, eh?"

"We must move quickly," Hector said.

As if in defiance of Hector's urging, Francisco continued to stroke Consuelo's nose. Finally, just as Hector was about to speak again, Francisco said, "Yes, yes. I know."

As they were hitching the horse to the cart Francisco asked, "Where will you go?"

"Home," Hector said. "To be with my family."

"We are your family."

Hector looked up. Francisco's expression was grim.

"You know what I mean."

Francisco nodded.

"Thank you for all you have done for me."

His hands busy with the harness, Francisco did not respond.

"Please apologize to Aunt Claudia for me. I'm sorry, but I have to do this."

"Claudia will be disappointed," Francisco commented. "But this decision you have made comes from your heart. She will understand."

"I will write to you when I get home."

Again, Francisco's response was a nearly imperceptible nod.

With Consuelo in position and the harness secure, Francisco and Hector stepped back. Francisco drew deeply on his cigarillo and discarded the butt. The horse snorted and stamped her foot, impatient to be off.

"I must go," Hector said. He took the canvas sack down from the cart.

Francisco retrieved the roll of bills from his pocket and held it out.

"You will be able to use this."

Hector glanced at the money and up at Francisco.

"Take it," Francisco urged, extending his arm towards him. Hector took the bills and pushed them into the pocket of his jeans.

"Thank you."

"Our country has changed since you came here," Francisco said. "Be careful. When soldiers stop you to ask questions, answer them politely. People will always be suspicious of a young man travelling alone. It's the nature of things. Let them be suspicious. They will not be able to dispute the honesty in your eyes."

Hector nodded.

Francisco climbed into the cart and took up the reins.

Looking straight before him he said, "May God grant you a long life."

"Goodbye," Hector said.

The cart trundled forward. With the canvas sack slung over his shoulder, Hector watched briefly before growing aware of a couple of soldiers approaching him. When he turned, they motioned with their guns for him to leave. He backed away and set off at a brisk walk in the direction of the bus station.

SEVENTEEN

My Dear Son,

There is much I wish to say to you. Our parting took place under the worst of circumstances. I should not have allowed that to happen, and yet it did and I cannot alter the past. All I can say is that I am sorry.

You have not written, but Claudia tells me you are working hard and contributing to the household, and that you do not complain. I could not have asked for more. But I wish that we could hear from you in your own words. I must accept your silence as a judgment upon myself, and, to a lesser extent, upon your mother. We understand that you are angry. The time must seem long to someone as young as you. I can remember my own youth, when it seemed an eternity to wait for five schooldays to pass before attaining the coveted weekend. There is nothing I can do to push the clock forward, but I want you to know that if we had any choice in the matter you would be home with us this very moment.

As far as my own behaviour is concerned, I had no intention of seeing you become involved in my personal affairs. There is, however, a lesson to be taken from these unfortunate events. In order to get along with our fellow human beings we must make allowances. We will not always be cheered by the behaviour of our friends and family, and yet we love them. You will see this more clearly as you grow older and learn the ways of the world, and perhaps have children of your own. If we embark on life expecting perfection we set *ourselves up for disappointment. All people are weak, but if we judge them solely on the basis of their weakness we will condemn each and every one. I dare say the worst criminals have their good points. You would do well to remember that your own weakness will enable you to tolerate the weakness of others.*

The reason I am writing is to tell you that with the political and economic situation growing worse from day to day, it is no longer safe for women and children to live here. The rebels have established a foothold in the surrounding hills and make incursions into the city on a regular basis. Francisco must surely have bought a radio by now, so you may have heard reports of bombings and kidnappings. But if not, I will tell you that the power-sharing arrangement that the government negotiated with the military is essentially a coup d'etat. The military is in control. You see the evidence everywhere you look. For now, the university is functioning normally, though I await the day when I arrive at work to find the doors locked tight. I am sending your mother and your brother and sisters away. Your Uncle Javier and Aunt Josefina in Puerto Varas have offered to provide refuge for an indefinite period. Dulciana's husband Roberto, whom you have not met, works with a shipping concern and will stay behind as well. If the worst comes to pass and I am unable to stay here, I will join them and bring Roberto with me. It was not easy to reach this decision because travel has become hazardous. For this reason it is necessary that for the present you remain with Francisco and Claudia. Your position on a farm in the mountains is one of great safety. I hope you can appreciate this.

Please do not imagine that we have forgotten you. None of us anticipated you would be staying in Envigado for longer than a month or two. But over the past year circumstances have changed and to bring you home now would be foolish, considering the dangers.

It may interest you to know that Jorgé has recovered from the beating you gave him. He and his sister are no longer with their parents. At my request the authorities intervened. The parents were arrested and the children were declared wards of the state and placed in a home. It is not an ideal arrangement, but I believe they are better off.

121

Let us pray that the present difficulties pass quickly and that we are together again very soon. Though our circumstances may be reduced, we will thrive once we are living under one roof, as all families must.

This is all I have to say for the moment. Your mother misses you. You would be doing a kindness if you wrote her even the briefest of notes.

I acknowledge our differences. But I remain,
Your loving father . . .

EIGHTEEN

Today, **while Hector and Francisco were at the market,** she would make her weekly visit to the post office in San Gregorio. It was the one task she could not entrust to Hector, and in truth it was the reason she often begged off going to the market. Hector would have gladly performed this chore had she asked him. He would take the cart or even walk the fifteen miles into the village. All she had to do was ask. But this was not possible.

Carissa would be along shortly. Carissa Villégas and her husband Dominic owned a nearby tourist resort, and until recently Claudia had supplied their restaurant with baked goods. Carissa was her lifeline, a young woman of sixty who could drive a car. Francisco, as old as he was and after all he had seen, had only grudgingly accepted the existence of the automobile. The presence of motorized vehicles in town was as unavoidable as it was undeniable. But here on the plains you could sometimes think time stood still. Technology was slow to make the ascent to the lofty heights where their farm sat between the mountains and the sea, and evidence of automobiles was so rare it was possible to regard them as nothing more than a nasty rumour. They had never owned one and Claudia did not know where or how one would go about making such an extravagant purchase.

But she could remember her brother Pablo, who was ten years older than her, the family's high-flying playboy, driving the little black Roadster during his visits back home, giving all the local girls rides, frightening the animals in the streets of Huelva, the village on the coast where she grew up. He was boastful and conceited, but oh so clean and handsome in his white suits, his shirt and tie, all neatly pressed by hand. One morning he put her in the car and they drove out to the hills, just the two of them. She didn't know what he had up his sleeve. And why take her? She was just a skinny teenager with big feet who never said anything and who giggled whenever any boy smiled at her. Not beautiful. She would never be beautiful. Her parents had four children, two girls, Viola and Claudia, and two boys, Pablo and Diego. She was the youngest of the family by three years, so young she could not even remember a time when Pablo had lived with them. He had left home at an early age to make his fortune, and had done well by the look of him, or so her mother said. Claudia only knew him from his infrequent visits and his even less frequent letters. They had nothing in common but their last name, but she admired him from afar, wondering about the life he was leading in the city, wishing she was bold enough to ask him what it was like. He laughed a lot and drank whiskey with Papa. But this one morning he had arrived in the sitting room so early, even before breakfast, and said, Claudia, come with me. We'll go for a drive. Where? she asked. But he didn't answer. Just smiled.

So she dropped her needlework and off they went. Along the narrow winding roads that skirted the coastline, and then inland, up and up, towards the snow-peaked mountains. He'd removed the top from the car and she held her hair in place with a kerchief. He drove with a young man's recklessness, as if nothing bad could ever happen, as if the world would never change, as if they were going to live forever. She could not resist him or his confidence. She was intoxicated by the danger of her situation, because people drove like fools and car wrecks happened all the time. He stopped in a little mountain village where rich people went to buy the hand-crafted carpets and carvings that adorned their huge houses. He spoke to some locals he knew and then took her to an outdoor coffee bar, where he bought two *café con leche*. It was her first time drinking coffee, and she was so in love with her own brother that she could still taste it to this day, still feel the thick foamy heat as it slid down her throat. He gave her a cigarette, wouldn't listen to her protests. He lit it for her and when the tears flooded her eyes and she doubled over coughing, his laughter rang out so that everyone turned to look. You'll learn, he said. You'll learn. Then he grew solemn and told her he'd met a woman. Everyone else in the family is so strict, Claudia, he said. They won't understand. But you will. I'm in love with her. She's an American, a widow. She has two children. He paused. She's not Catholic. It will break

Mama's heart, she said, and then looked down, ashamed to say such a thing on such a beautiful day. But I want you to know, he said. I want you to understand. I'm not doing this to hurt anyone. I tried to tell Papa last night, but I couldn't. I couldn't make myself say the words.

They were silent for a moment. She observed him while he wasn't looking at her. He looked like a dandy, with his neatly trimmed moustache and the cap that he'd said was Irish tweed, which he had not taken off. Maybe he looked like someone you wouldn't trust, but he was finely turned out, like a man of action. He seemed to have everything: money and freedom, and now a woman he could love. But in truth he was a humble bank clerk who lived alone in a small furnished flat with no curtains and a troublesome heating system and whose landlady was forever chasing him for overdue rent. The car he drove was borrowed from a friend. Despite appearances, he lived frugally. He was worried, but not, as Claudia believed, about his family's reaction to his betrothal, but about how he was going to convince his beloved to marry him when he had no money. There were many ways in which his scheme could go wrong, but he remained confident he could bring it off because his greatest asset was an ability to talk his way into people's hearts. Claudia, who knew nothing of his day-to-day existence, looked at him and wondered how her own brother, a boy from Huelva who had left school barely able to read, could have become a successful man of business, as he had claimed. Import, export. Are you going to bring her home for us to meet? she asked. You know I can't do that, Claudia. He thought for a moment. Maybe, he said. After the wedding. And then it occurred to her to ask, Are you going to live with her in America? He smiled. Once I'm there, he said, I will send for you. You'll come, won't you? She nodded. And for now you'll keep my secret? She nodded again. Because, you know, everything is still up in the air. I shouldn't be telling you this, but the next time I see you I'll be married and I don't want it to come as a shock. They fell silent again. Her mind swirled with images of America, or what she thought America might be, because to her it was a word with many wonderful meanings.

Soon they got back into the car and began the descent to the coast, back to Huelva, Claudia praying the secret her brother had shared with her would stay silent in her heart and not creep up her throat while she wasn't looking and jump into the ears of her sisters and friends. Pablo left the following morning for the city. He winked at her from behind the windscreen before setting off, and that was the last any of the family saw of him and his fine car. Did he marry his American widow? Claudia didn't know. Perhaps her parents had somehow learned of his intentions and prevented the marriage, and out of anger he had estranged himself, but if this was the case they never let on to their remaining children. Within a year she had left home and was married to Francisco, and the years since she had spent in houses and apartments and one farm or another, because they had sold up and moved half a dozen times that she could recall.

Now she was crying again. Mourning a brother she had not seen for sixty years. Such a fool, she thought as she dabbed at her eyes. Such a ridiculous old fool.

There was a sound from outside. She took her canvas bag from its hook on the wall and lumbered towards the door.

"Claudia, you're looking peaked," Carissa greeted her. A lit cigarette dangled from her lips. "*Achacoso*. Not your best. Are you feeling quite all right?"

"When you are my age you will understand that it is good to be feeling anything at all."

"But not pain," Carissa said, taking Claudia's arm to steady her as they went slowly down the dusty path from the house. Claudia groaned as she heaved her backside into the seat of the vehicle, an old army Jeep, one without doors, regulation green, pockmarked. Years ago someone had scraped the army insignia off the hood with a pocket knife and the scar had browned deeply with age. The Jeep rocked as Claudia settled into place. "How can pain be a good thing?"

"I feel. It means I am alive."

"You are an optimist. That's all there is to it."

"Ah, me," Claudia sighed. "This heat. Do I imagine things? Is it getting worse?"

Without looking, Carissa backed the Jeep into the main road, stopped, and shifted gears. The Jeep shuddered as if it might stall, then leapt forward like a whipped pony.

"It's still early," Carissa said, shifting gears again. "It's going to get much worse than this. The forecast said without a doubt, the hottest day of the year."

"How can they say these things?" Claudia complained. "How can they know what's going to happen before it happens? What sort of witchcraft is that?"

"The magic of science," Carissa said. "The men on the radio say what the weather will be and they're always right. Who can explain it? I can't." She tossed her cigarette butt out the open side of the Jeep.

Claudia braced herself with one hand against the dashboard. The dirt road was bumpy and uneven and the Jeep bounced from one rut to the next. "Even the fortune teller does not claim to know everything."

"And what did Francisco say when you asked him about the telephone?"

Claudia shifted in the seat, which dug into her back. "You drive very fast," she said.

Carissa applied her sandaled foot to the brake. "I'll slow down then. If that's what you want."

"Thank you."

"So what did he say?" Claudia felt the other woman looking at her. "You didn't ask him, did you?"

Claudia used her hand to wipe sweat from her face. She kept her eyes on the road.

"Why didn't you say anything?"

"If I had known you were going to pester me with questions I would not have asked you to take me."

Carissa released a sigh.

"I'm sorry. But I worry about the two of you on that farm with no way to communicate with the outside world. In this day and age it's a crazy way to live. What will happen when one of you gets sick or has an accident? A telephone is only common sense."

"You forget Hector."

Carissa nodded. "Yes, Hector. He will save the day. What do you expect of a boy barely seventeen? I'm sure he can tie his own shoelaces but do you think he's going to mend a broken leg or carry Francisco on his back if he has a heart attack in the field?"

"You talk like nothing good ever happens."

"Good things happen. I'm not saying they don't. But bad things happen too and it makes sense to be prepared."

Claudia clasped her hands together in her lap.

"What good will a telephone do? Will a telephone mend a broken leg or carry Francisco on its back?"

Carissa glanced at her.

"Is this you talking or is it Francisco?"

"Francisco does not care for such things. I know this. So, you are right. I have not spoken to him. I can hear what he will say. 'Telephone?' he will say. 'You want a telephone? Next you will want to fly to the moon.' That's what he will say."

"You exasperate me, Claudia."

"Or he will say nothing and just stand up and leave the room. That will be my answer."

They were silent. Carissa's hair, which still held traces of brown amidst the grey, blew freely in the breeze of the open Jeep. With one hand she lifted some strands that had fallen into her eyes and persuaded them into place behind her ear.

"Ten minutes," Carissa said. "In ten minutes I would be at your farm, *if* you could call me and ask me to come."

"Hector will take care of us. We have nothing to worry about."

Carissa clucked her tongue and shook her head. "If that's what you say."

"I will ask Francisco. But after living with a man for sixty years I have heard all his answers. What is the point of asking questions when you know what the answer will be? And who will pay for it? We have no money for such things."

"They are not expensive. Even Francisco knows that." Carissa paused. "Why don't you ask Hector what he thinks, you believe he's so wise and useful. I'm sure they have telephones where he comes from."

Claudia made no response. One of the first things Hector had done after arriving at the farm was ask where the telephone was. She was still trying to make up for disappointing him on that occasion.

"You really should have a telephone," Carissa said. "It's only common sense."

Claudia held up her hand. "Please," she said. "No more!"

Carissa shrugged. "What else will we talk about?"

Claudia turned from her friend and watched the grizzled landscape slip by. A telephone would cause problems, just as the post office caused problems and enticed her further within the web of deceit she had constructed. Hector had not stopped asking about letters from his family, but the questions came much less frequently than before. Perhaps this meant he was forgetting them—discarding them as they had discarded him? She knew she was acting for the best but felt no easing of her shame, which followed her throughout her waking hours. Enrique and Lucinda had shamelessly forsaken the boy. They did not deserve to get him back. She had thought it through a hundred times and saw no reason why Hector should not stay with them on the farm. It was only right and proper.

She was dazed by the heat and uncomfortable in the shuddering vehicle. The Jeep had not been designed for people her size. But she had no choice. And now Carissa had found a new topic of conversation. She was complaining about her husband. Claudia wasn't listening. Absently, she nodded in agreement. But her mind was drifting and she did not feel inclined to rein it in.

The morning passed pleasantly enough. Many old friends lived in San Gregório and Carissa did not mind stopping here and there to visit. They went to a shop that sold baked goods and Claudia had the satisfaction of seeing that the pies and loaves on display were inferior to her own. Finally, they went to the post office and Claudia picked up the mail from old Támar Rodriguez. There were some letters. She quickly looked them over and concealed them in the canvas bag.

When they were back at the farm, Claudia let herself down from the vehicle, grunting with the effort of shifting her weight from foot to foot.

"I should come in and help you lie down," Carissa said.

"I am fine," Claudia snapped, and immediately regretted it. But she was impatient to be alone. Placing her hand dramatically on her forehead, she struck a pose and inhaled deeply. For just a moment she closed her eyes. Carissa had recently grown overly solicitous, and Claudia had to be careful when rejecting offers of help that she did so in a way that did not offend. She was grateful for the friendship, which could have ended when Carissa started buying her breads and desserts from a commercial bakery. "There," she said and smiled. "I feel better now. Hector and Francisco will be back soon. I will have something to eat and then a little sleep. You should go home and be with your husband."

Carissa manoeuvred the gearshift into place. "I have enough to keep me busy without worrying about him."

"You worry too much about me and not enough about your Dominic.

I have heard—mind you, these are only stories—that husbands who are neglected by their wives are sometimes snatched away by the spirits of women who were spurned by their lovers. I will sleep better knowing that he is always first in your thoughts."

Carissa was smiling as she backed the Jeep down the long drive. It swung onto the main road. She waved before driving off, and Claudia lifted her arm stiffly in reply. The Jeep left behind a dusty cloud that hung in the air. Claudia watched it settle.

Even though the heat outside had been killing her, the interior of the house had remained so cool that the chill seeped into her bones. She went to the stove, removed the lid, and stoked the embers. She tossed in a couple of the logs that Hector had chopped and soon the fire was crackling nicely. With a sigh she lowered her tired body into a chair at the kitchen table and settled back to read the mail.

Claudia Acuña Cordoba

Estafeta Postal Nº 9

San Gregório

Envigado P.

Dear Aunt Claudia,

I hope this note finds you and Francisco well and quite shielded from the calamities that are taking place in other parts of the country. As per our contract, I enclose the monthly payment. I will keep these up as long as I am able, though we have been warned that our situation at the university is no longer as secure as it once was. I have some money put by, but if everything shuts down, as I fear it might, I will have no choice but to forgo payments for a time, until I can relocate.

In your last letter you said that Hector was, and I quote, "a pleasure and a comfort" to both you and Francisco. I dare say that the boy has undergone a transformation under your tutelage, for he was always somewhat morose and unmanageable, particularly after Carlos disappeared. Perhaps life on a farm in the mountains agrees with him.

Lucinda sends her love. I do not hear from her and the children as often as I would like, but I gather that Puerto Varas, being small and remote, not unlike San Gregório, has been spared the full brunt of the new junta's emergency legislation.

I will avoid making reference to the political crisis again because I hear that correspondence may be monitored. Just let me say that in B____ tensions are at a breaking point. When the junta took power they neglected to crush the opposition, and now find themselves obliged to look behind every door and beneath every rug for those who might be against them. We are living under a dusk-to-dawn curfew and the streets are crowded with soldiers and police at all hours. I also hear rumours of a special unit that operates at night. People are very frightened. Nobody has any idea what might happen next.

I cannot thank you enough for keeping Hector safe. With luck the crisis will soon pass and life will return to normal. I regret that Hector has not seen fit to respond to the letters we have been sending. Perhaps, since you have struck up a rapport, you could impress upon him the importance of maintaining contact with his family.

Lucinda will be sending something your way soon. Hector's silence has affected her deeply.

If I am forced to leave the city I will relay my whereabouts to you and continue the payments by some means. I pray this will not be necessary.

Your loving nephew,
Enrique Tomás

Claudia made a clucking sound and shook her head as she placed the little stack of peseta notes on the table. She folded Enrique's letter and pushed it aside. There were two other letters in separate sealed envelopes, both with Hector's name written on the outside. She would read those and then burn the lot.

In a year and a half Claudia had done her best to obliterate the bad influence of Hector's parents, but it had not been easy. She had tightened the reins on the boy and he now seemed willing to do anything she told him, though Francisco still had trouble getting him to complete chores, no doubt due to his gruff way of giving direction and his stinginess with praise. But Hector was learning and would be ready to take over the farm after they were gone. A few more months of sensitive guidance and Hector would convince even Francisco that he was the one.

She had expected that at some point she would show Hector the letters that his family had written, but it came to her one night in a dream that this would be doing more harm than good. The boy was volatile. She could see that his passions were intensely held, and if he reacted badly to her concealment then all her work would have been for nothing. Of course, she trusted him to understand that it was for his own good that she had kept the letters from him, because it would only make him sad to learn that others were sad on his account. If he was the boy she thought he was, he would not want to know that because of his actions the people closest to him had suffered. Why impose on him an experience that was bound to be hurtful, especially if no good could come of it? No, it was all for the best that she had taken the vision as a literal rendering of God's will and destroyed the letters she had received, along with those he had written to his family and this girl.

In her dream there had been fire burning in a huge furnace, and she was the one who had to keep it going. Everyone depended on her. So she shovelled on all the fuel, and when it was gone she demolished the house and furniture and burned that. And when everything else was ash and the only thing left was her little treasure chest, she knew she had to burn that too or all would be lost.

The morning after the dream, while Hector and Francisco were working in the field, she took the letters out of the dresser in her bedroom, where over the months they had accumulated into a fat bundle, which she kept in the drawer with her underwear, and put them all on the fire. She suffered no regrets as she watched them burn. Hector knew he was loved. She did not want him thinking his home was elsewhere.

"Ah, me," she sighed. She pulled herself to her feet and gathered the letters together.

She went to the window and looked outside. Maybe she would have a little sleep, just as she had told Carissa.

The clouds she had noticed earlier on the horizon now stretched across the sky, their bellies low to the ground, touching the mountains. She could feel the scraping, the searing pain. The land was in shadow and the wind that had risen agitated the spindly branches of the cassava tree in front of the house. The clouds churned threateningly. Soon they would burst and spill their rain over the parched earth. Hector and Francisco would get wet. And Consuelo too, she would need her blanket, and hay and alfalfa.

She would prepare for their return once she had had a little rest.

She hobbled down the hall on her aching legs, but on the way to her room paused briefly in Hector's bedroom doorway. Everything was tidy. The bed was made. To know that the line would continue, that someday these rooms would echo with the laughter of Hector's children, that there was indeed a future, allowed her to breathe with ease.

She went into her room and closed the door behind her.

NINETEEN

My Dear Boy,

Your Aunt Claudia reports that you are well and as happy as can be expected under the circumstances. I trust you have been receiving your mother's letters· from Puerto Varas, and maybe you have found it in your heart to respond to her. If you have not I urge you once again to do so. She has done nothing to deserve this kind of treatment and it is unfair of you to use your anger with me to hurt her.

Your friend Nadia is concerned for you. I am surprised that you have failed to respond to her letters as well. Nevertheless, she is not discouraged and lives in hope that you will soon be home. I know this because I have seen her. She was so distraught that I made her come and sit with me at the little café in the Arroyo Salas Theatre, near the campus. Hector, she is a smart girl but I swear she has no sense, or has been provoked beyond reason by her grief. Once I had assured her that you were safe and healthy and would write to her at the first opportunity, she started talking about the army and the situation here. There were soldiers close by, within earshot, but that didn't stop her. Apparently her father has suffered some sort of persecution. But I would have jumped across the table to stop her mouth if she hadn't finally relented. She insists these things must be said, but my God there's a time and a place. I don't know what will become of her. I'm afraid she will involve herself with a group of hotheads and attract the wrong sort of attention, which can only lead to trouble. The best thing for her would be to remain in the background and stay invisible. That way she will still be alive when the crisis has passed, and then she can carry placards and make all the noise she wants. I said this to her, but the way she looked at me I know she was not convinced.

If you would write to her and urge her not to do anything foolish, I am sure she would listen.

Since your mother, Dulciana, Cesara, Rosaria, Helena, and Julio left, I keep to myself, but it is difficult being alone. There is a chance that I will soon have to shut up the flat and leave the city. The situation grows worse by the day. There are checkpoints at almost every corner, and everyone is required to carry identification. It is not uncommon to hear gunfire after dark, and sometimes you see smoke rising from the hills. Old Juan Carlos, who is still with me at the archives, told me about someone who was leaving for work one morning and found the street outside her building stained with blood. So, you see, you are better off where you are.

I am proud of how you have been conducting yourself. For someone your age, life on a farm located along that lonely stretch of road must seem very tedious. I am glad that you have been contributing and helping out. It is a desolate place, but I am afraid you will have to remain with Claudia and Francisco a while longer, at least until the political situation stabilizes and I can determine what our next step will be. I have considered emigrating, but that hardly seems practical. Most countries will not let you in unless you can demonstrate you possess a skill that they need. Alas, this does not apply in my case.

Take care, my boy. I pray that we will see each other before long.

Your loving father

TWENTY

Dearest Hector,

We are settled now in Puerto Varas and feel lucky to be away from the city. I don't know why we did not come here sooner. It is a lakeside resort town and so peaceful, full of tourists, though many of them are hurriedly packing their bags and leaving. I feel sorry for the hotel and restaurant owners, because when there is nobody left but the people who live here they will have lost their livelihood.

We miss you very much. Julio talks about you all the time and asks when you are coming home. I have to tell him that none of us are home at the moment, but he hardly seems to notice. He has adapted well to life in Puerto Varas. Already he has made many friends and enjoys going to school more than he did in B____. Maybe this is because the school is so much smaller that his teacher can spend time with him. He is making great progress with his mathematics, and I think he will grow up to be a scientist, because he takes jars out to the fields and returns with grasshoppers and ants and other insects that he watches for hours. You would hardly recognize him, he has grown so much. I am sure he would hardly recognize you.

There is exciting news. Dulciana is going to have a baby. You are going to be an uncle. Being only seventeen this is hard for you to grasp, but just think, Julio is twelve and he's going to be an uncle too! We are taking good care of her. She wants you here for the birth, which is still many months away.

But I hope by then things will have settled down so that you can join us. It will be wonderful for our family to all be together again. Your father is still in B_____ , but in his last letter he said he was not certain how much longer he could stay there. His reports are distressing. I know our country has suffered through times like this in the past and survived to become stronger, but it is still sad to be forced out of your home. It is hardest on the children because they do not understand what is happening. But it is not easy for any of us.

I try not to let my mind linger over why you have not written, but it is something that comes into my head when I least expect it, and like the rain that sometimes falls when the sun is shining it catches me unprepared. I hope you are just being lazy and are not still angry. Believe me, Hector, the time for anger is past. What you did to that boy turned out to be the best thing that could have happened for he is no longer with his parents who were abusing him. It is strange how events turn in ways we could never have predicted. A year ago I could not have seen myself living with Javier and Josefina in Puerto Varas, taking walks by the lake and wasting time gazing at the stars. I have plenty to worry about, but this place is so far removed from the things that are going on elsewhere that it seems like another country, and it is greatly against my will that I am reminded of the horrid facts. I try not to dwell on these, for nothing good can come of brooding and I don't want the girls to see me sad. I can say this to you because you know what I mean.

Claudia reports that you are content and working very hard. This makes me happy despite all that has happened. There is nothing better in life than to be useful, and if you have learned nothing else in the last year and a half I hope you have learned this. You are a good, kind-hearted person and I regret more than ever that it was necessary to send you away. But knowing that you are safe, I cannot let myself be upset. It is only a matter of time before we are together.

The girls send their love. They will all write to you again in their own time. But Hector, please write to them and to me. I cannot live without knowing what you are doing and thinking, because you are more dear to me than *life itself. This will sound strange to you, but until you have children of your own you cannot know the pain a mother feels being separated from her child. This is a long and cruel separation, but it does not have to leave lasting scars. We will see each other very soon.*

Take care of yourself and do everything that Claudia and Francisco tell you to. They are wise and can teach you a great deal.

I love you more than words can say.

Your mother

TWENTY-ONE

Dearest Hector,

How do I begin? I miss you and think of you all the time. Is this what I should be saying? Does it make you feel bad to know that thoughts of you are always with me and that I sometimes cry when I realize you are so far away? When your father told me you were in Envigado I didn't know what to say because I didn't know where that was. I had to wait until I was in school to look at the map, and even then it took me a long time to find it. It is hundreds and hundreds of miles away, up in the mountains. He said you were living on a farm with some people who are very old. He said you were ploughing the field and picking fruit off trees and helping the old woman bake her bread. It sounded so funny, the way he said it, I didn't know whether to laugh or cry.

I am glad to know where you are, and also to know that the danger has passed. Your father said that there was a chance you could have been arrested for something you had done, and that's why they sent you away. He did not tell me any more than that, and so I am left wondering, did you steal something? Were you caught somewhere you should not have been? It is terrible for me, not knowing what you have been facing, not knowing if you have suffered pain or loneliness. Not knowing if you ever think of me. Your father said you are doing very well and working hard, and I sometimes imagine that you are in a camp like they have in Russia, and are forced to do many hours of hard labour every day. And I think, foolish romantic that

*I am, that you work yourself so hard because you cannot bear to be apart
from me, just as I cannot bear to be apart from you.*

*I don't know how I have survived this year and a half without you because
just before you left I was sure that we had seen into each other's hearts the
way that lovers do. I know you felt the same because I saw it in your eyes.
If you had not gone away we would have lain down together and become as
man and wife. But you did go away, and I am left with nothing but my dreams.
Is it wrong of me to indulge in fantasies about us being together? Are they only
fantasies, or do they fit somehow with the way things really are? Hector, you
have made me half mad with not knowing and I am getting very bold with my
questions. Why haven't you written to me or to your family? I dread to think
that you want nothing to do with me, that you feel nothing and wish I would
go away and keep all this to myself. It is unbearable to think like that for even
a second, I am surprised to see I wrote it down.*

*I could have torn this letter up and started again, but I want you to know
how I feel. If I am causing you only embarrassment, please forgive me. I say
these things because I love you so much.*

*Each day brings more difficulties but my parents are not giving up hope.
My father is now working regularly at the naval base where Carmel and
Raoul are living. I don't ask him what he does and he does not talk about it,
but it pays money. It takes him two hours to get there in the morning and
two hours to get home at night. He is exhausted all the time. On Sundays
he sleeps until the bells toll at noon and then goes out to do more chores for
people because he thinks we need the money. He is too old to be living such
a life. The year after next year Magda will be going to a university in California.
Already she has applied for a student visa because these things take so long
to be approved. We will miss her but it is for the best. She will study to be
a doctor and get married and live like an American. She wants me to go
with her, but I cannot leave yet. If I can improve my science grades next year
I will apply for a scholarship to la Universidad de Antofagasta. But nothing
is for certain.*

People pray that life will continue in a normal fashion through all the troubles, but I don't see how this can be. Your father said I shouldn't talk this way, but I don't trust the government because they don't trust us. Soldiers and police are everywhere. All you have to do is walk down the street and you see them watching, like we are all criminals trying to get away with something. I have met people who say they will fight the military rule, and because I share their ideas of justice I am tempted to defy the curfew and go out with them at night. But I know my mother would worry and I promised your father that I wouldn't do such a thing. But there have been protests and people have been hurt. I feel I should be doing something, but what can one person do? So much has changed since you went away, I'm not sure I know what normal is anymore. We have lost so many of our rights, you would hope they would let us think our own thoughts. But even this is not allowed.

Oh, Hector, I miss you so much! Please write and tell me if my feelings are worthless to you. I would die if you said you didn't care for me but even knowing the worst would be better than knowing nothing. I don't want to sound like I am complaining, but after all we have shared it's not fair of you to keep your feelings from me.

I know we will see each other again.

With all my heart,
Nadia

TWENTY-TWO

There were soldiers everywhere. Hector felt their eyes on him and left the main street for the back alleys, but they were patrolling here as well. They watched him closely, their eyes narrow slits. Some, at his approach, gripped their snub-nose machine guns as if preparing to fire. He kept walking. He could not imagine what they thought he was up to. They made him feel such shame he could not even look them in the face. At the decisive moment, when he was close enough to read their expressions, he lowered his gaze to the cobbled lane until he was safely past. He understood that looking away made him appear guilty. Probably even the fact that he was alone announced to those inclined to think in such terms that he was up to no good. He was used to this by now—to the child recoiling and lurching into her mother's arms, to the shopkeeper yelling at him to get off the premises, to the old woman averting her eyes and crossing herself. It did not reflect on him but on the people who reacted this way.

The bus station—a grimy cinderblock structure, windows cloudy with soot—occupied three sides of a litter-strewn courtyard accessible from the street through a stone archway. The buses passed into the courtyard and parked at one of more than twenty spots, depending on where they had come from or where they were going. A raised walkway surrounded the parking area, and scattered along the perimeter were a dozen benches where waiting travellers could sit and pass the time. On his previous visits, Hector had strolled beneath the arch and into the courtyard with feigned confidence, hopeful that a smile and a friendly glance are all it takes to open doors that might otherwise remain closed.

He did the same today. There were only five buses parked, but the station was as crowded as he had ever seen it. People stood about in groups or

142

pairs, mostly men but some women too, the day's purchases in bags on the ground at their feet, deep in conversation, arms in constant motion, voices amplified as they argued some point. Almost everyone was smoking and the air was cloudy and pungent with mingling varieties of cigarette and cigar smoke. There were soldiers as well, loitering at the margins and keeping watch, and almost immediately one turned his head and caught Hector's eye. Hector looked away but his step remained steady as he proceeded across the courtyard towards the glass door of the large waiting area where the ticket office was located.

He went inside. The clock said ten minutes past twelve, but he was still able to purchase a ticket for Villa Real from the silent, scowling woman in the booth, who took his request through a round hole cut in a glass window that was reinforced with wire mesh. He took the money out of the canvas bag, 1250 pesetas in paper notes that before leaving the farm he had clipped together with a wooden clothes peg, and pushed it through the slot in the bottom of the window. She paused during the transaction to light a cigarette, but she did not seem suspicious and gave him his ticket as soon as she finished counting the money.

As he left the ticket booth, he saw that the room was crowded with people of all ages, some sitting on the rows of benches, others standing in small groups. Their chatter was loud. Many were smoking, and the smoke spiralled lazily upward, hardly disturbed by the listless movement of four fans suspended from the high ceiling. The warm air shimmered with the sour reek of many bodies. Towards the rear, close to a side exit, three soldiers stood casually observing the room and talking among themselves. They seemed relaxed. One of them cradled a machine gun.

He shoved the ticket into his pocket with the money that Francisco had given him and moved deliberately towards the back. He held the canvas bag slung over his shoulder and aimed his glance downward. He did not look at anyone. This was a precaution—perhaps unnecessary —but he did not want to be distracted or drawn into conversation, and inadvertent eye contact could sometimes lead to this. Yet he also did not want to raise suspicions by behaving as if he were trying to hide something. As a compromise, it made sense to behave naturally, as if nothing mattered.

He pushed open the washroom door and met the stony glare of a young soldier wearing the familiar green uniform. The man was stationed with his back to the wall beside the row of sinks. The soldier's presence stopped Hector in his tracks and for a moment he could not think what to do. Behind his ribs his heart bucked crazily. Should he leave? But why was he afraid? He'd done nothing wrong. He drew in a breath, but it snagged halfway down his throat, stifled by the swampy rot of shit and piss. His gaze fell to the smeared floor but he made himself look up. The stench engulfed him, moist and fetid, a tangible but unseen density thickening the air. Light-headed, he wobbled past the soldier on legs turned to rubber. There were six urinals. He had intended to use one of these but instead hurried into an unoccupied stall. Gasping for breath, he pushed the door closed, but the bolt was broken and the door would not stay shut. He pressed himself against it, a dull roar filling his ears. He had almost forgotten the soreness in his jaw where Francisco's knobby knuckles had made contact with his flesh, but as he struggled for calm the pain returned, swelling and receding in time to the panicked rhythm of his heart. From the next compartment came the grunts of a man completing a satisfactory bowel movement, followed by the hiss of urine streaming copiously into the bowl. Then he heard steps and the gush of water and the groan of pipes as someone vigorously washed his hands. As people entered and left, during the brief intervals when the door stood open the washroom was flooded with the echo of voices from the outer room.

The toilet was a bowl with no seat, caked and smeared with past deposits. Hector held the neck of the canvas bag in his teeth, its bulk slung over his shoulder and pressed lightly against the door of the cubical to keep it from swinging open. Breathing though his mouth, he opened his fly and pulled out his penis and took aim. But it was hopeless. He could not loosen his muscles. His bladder, painfully full, refused to yield a single drop. The man on the other side of the divider flushed and left. The room fell quiet, and when the door closed Hector was absurdly aware that he was the only person in the washroom other than the soldier. He shut his eyes and strained until pinprick lights danced at the edge of his vision and the throbbing in his jaw sharpened to a stabbing pain, but it was another minute before a reluctant trickle issued from his penis. When the washroom door opened again an announcement of an imminent departure was being delivered over the loudspeaker. A group of men entered. They had been talking and laughing, but all at once fell quiet. At long last his bladder was empty and he could breathe. He flushed the toilet, left the cubicle, and went to the sink in the middle of the row. He avoided looking at the soldier and kept his eyes straight before him as he placed the canvas bag on the floor by his feet. He washed his hands and checked his face in the mirror. The spot where Francisco had struck him was puffy and tender. He rubbed it, but this did not soothe the pain, which came and went with a dull rhythmic throb.

It was twenty-five minutes past twelve when he emerged from the washroom. He approached the window and looked into the courtyard. There were now seven buses parked. The bus to Villa Real was supposed to leave from the spot numbered fourteen, but no bus was there yet and he preferred not to think about the possibility of a delay. The weather had been clear all day, but now clouds streamed across the sky above the courtyard. Grim-faced soldiers with guns maintained their watch, but people milled about, apparently unconcerned by their presence. After the frightening and chaotic exodus of vendors from the market, Hector was surprised by the prevailing calm. The day was like any other, and he wondered if his imagination was making the incident at the market worse than it had been. He thought back, to the assault and arrest of the Mapuche man, to the fear that had lit the eyes of the woman who had been buying plums when it happened, to his own sensations of apprehension and disquiet.

Distracted by his recollections, he did not immediately notice that a tall man wearing a dark jacket and smoking a cigarette had approached and was standing close beside him. When the man spoke, Hector's body tensed, but he remained where he was and did not allow his eyes to stray from the buses in the courtyard. "If your bus is late, don't blame me." Unsure if the remark was addressed to him, Hector did not respond. In order not to appear rude he stood his ground for a few seconds before sidling away and leaving the man to himself.

Restless, he debated going outside. But first he wanted to get something to eat. His plan had included buying something from the vending machines to take with him on the bus, and he was also suddenly aware of a rasping thirst. He went over and stood before the three machines and counted his change. He would have a little left over if he bought a bottle of water, a cream-filled cake, and a bag of potato chips. After making his purchases he dropped the food into the canvas bag and opened the plastic bottle, but because he did not want to use the bathroom again, he sipped only enough to relieve the dryness of his throat.

As he turned to go back to the window, a boy carrying a cardboard box the size of a soccer ball entered the ticket area through the door from the courtyard. The boy held the box with both arms and studied the schedule, which was posted on the wall above the ticket booth. Hector judged the boy to be about ten. He wore a red and white striped shirt over a stocky body, and his short pants revealed a pair of chubby tanned legs. With an impatient gesture, he kept sweeping his dark hair away from his eyes.

Hector took a seat on one of the benches near the vending machines. The pain in his jaw had not diminished and was making him dizzy. Every few minutes he rubbed the sore spot, but the relief was fleeting. He tried to sit absolutely still, but his body refused to relax and would not let him be comfortable. He twitched and jumped as if electricity were pulsing through his veins instead of blood. Like poor Consuelo, he hated wait-ing. Too many things could happen. As long as he was not on his bus, the chance of something going wrong cast a grim shadow over his journey. With a jerky movement, he got to his feet and drifted back across the room to the window, where he could observe the movements of people and buses in the courtyard. Finally, there was a bus parked at the num-ber fourteen spot. Relief swept over him like a cool breeze. It was now twenty-five minutes to one. He wondered if it was too early to get on and decided it probably was. He would wait another ten minutes. He had his ticket. They could not refuse him a seat fifteen minutes before the sched-uled departure time.

Smiling, he turned and found himself face to face with two of the soldiers he had seen positioned at the back of the room behind the fern. With them was the man in the dark jacket. The man extended his finger towards him.

"He's the one," the man said, his tone bland, matter-of-fact. He drew on his cigarette and remarked indifferently, as if bored, "He's been here before. Not causing trouble. Just hanging around."

Without taking his eyes from Hector, the lighter skinned of the sol-diers said, "Thank you. You can go."

With a shrug, the man walked away.

The soldier jutted his chin towards Hector. "Boy, are you going some-where?"

146

Hector stared at the soldier who had spoken. He was not thin but not fat either. His hair, cut very short, closely followed the contours of his skull. The other soldier had heavy dark features and a fierce aspect. Neither carried a gun in his hand, but both wore waist holsters.

"I asked you if you are going somewhere."

Hector searched his brain for the answer, but his mind seemed to have been wiped clean. He could neither speak nor move, and yet he felt strangely calm, almost numb. Inexplicably, his eye was drawn to the progress of a fly crawling across the lapel of the soldier's uniform. Then he looked past the soldier to his right. Everyone was watching. The room, which moments before had buzzed with conversation, was almost silent.

"What's in the bag, then? Since the cat seems to have got your tongue."

He held the canvas bag towards them.

"On the floor," the soldier ordered. Abruptly, frighteningly, his expression had become severe. "Empty it on the floor."

Hector set the bottle of water down and did as he was told. That morning he had packed his things hastily, and the clothes tumbled out in a heap, along with his potato chips and the plastic-wrapped cake he had just bought. His comic books fluttered out last and slid off the pile to the floor.

"I have a ticket," he said finally. His voice cracked and in the hushed room seemed very loud. Pain shot from his jaw up the side of his head and made him wince.

The soldier frowned. "Back away," and when Hector did this the fierce soldier stepped forward and prodded the pile with his foot, spreading his pitiable garments around so that each shirt, each piece of underclothing, was clearly visible. As this was going on, a movement caught Hector's eye. He glanced across the room in time to see the boy, still holding the cardboard box, exit through the door leading into the courtyard.

"Let's see your ticket."

Hector reached into his pocket and placed the ticket into the brawny hand extended towards him. He performed these actions mechanically, cushioned from the full meaning of what was happening by the numbness in his brain. As the scene advanced with the inexorable forward motion of a film, he felt his disconnection from it increase until it seemed possible he was not even present. His eyes smarted as if from an intense glare, but his head felt completely empty, his body weightless.

Having found nothing of interest among his belongings, the fierce soldier retreated a few steps and eyed him with what seemed to be genuine dislike.

"You are going to Villa Real." The soldier spoke as if this presented a difficulty.

Hector nodded.

"This ticket cost 1250 pesetas. Where did you get 1250 pesetas?"

"I . . . I saved it up."

"Doing what? How does the likes of you save 1250 pesetas?"

Hector was about to answer when the third soldier, the one with the machine gun, appeared and interrupted the interrogation. The three consulted in whispers, and then, still talking, walked off. Hector observed this dumbly, unsure what had happened. Relief that they had been called away swept over him with such intensity that his body began to tremble. He wanted to know if he was safe. But he was unwilling to establish himself again as the focus of their attention and remained silent and stationary next to the pile of clothes. The empty canvas bag dangled ridiculously from his hand. He waited, and as he did so the room emerged out of the haze of his clouded vision and he saw the people staring at him, their features animated by amusement and contempt.

Moist prickly heat surged from his torso upward into his neck, setting off a fiery itch in his underarms. Furious, fighting back tears, his jaw throbbing, he knelt and began pushing his things into the bag. As he tried to reassemble his thoughts, a blazing realization swept over him that by visiting the bus station every week for the last two months, he had raised suspicions among those who worked here and drawn attention to himself in precisely the way he had hoped to avoid. He muttered a curse and almost struck the floor with his fist. Then, worried he might have spoken too loudly, he cautiously raised his head. The soldiers had retreated to the far end of the waiting area and were conferring among themselves. One gestured in his direction and Hector instantly lowered his eyes and resumed the task of repacking his things.

Without looking back he slung the bag over his shoulder and headed for the door, with each step expecting an outraged voice to bellow an order to halt. But nothing happened. As the door swung shut and he left the waiting area behind, a delightful awareness of the freedom he still enjoyed swept him along like a tide. With a buoyant step he crossed the courtyard towards his bus. Even the pain in his jaw had receded to a dull ache.

As he passed a parked bus with *San Sebastián* printed on a sign in the window, the boy he had noticed earlier jumped carelessly down from the exit and, unable to avoid him, bumped Hector off stride, knocking the bag from his shoulder.

"Hey! Watch it."

"Sorry," the boy said. He swiped his floppy hair away from his eyes and watched as Hector slung the bag across his shoulder again. When Hector resumed walking the boy fell into step beside him.

"What did the soldiers want?"

Hector glanced at the boy. After a disdainful silence he decided to speak. "Nothing," he said.

"It didn't look like nothing."

"Nothing I want to talk about."

"What's your name?"

Hector did not answer. He quickened his step as he neared his bus and without another word joined the line of people waiting to board. He reached into his pocket for the ticket. His fingers grasped the roll of bills that Francisco had given him. He dropped the bag to the ground and reached into the other pocket. It was empty.

"My name's Rico. It's really Federico but everyone calls me Rico. Are you going to Villa Real?"

Hector checked both pockets again. "Yes," he muttered, but his voice betrayed doubt. He pulled the bag open and rummaged through his clothes, turning them over roughly with both hands.

"What's the matter?" Federico asked.

Hector glanced at him and would have told him to get lost, except for a hollow sensation that seemed to emanate from the base of his stomach, which told him that he might find comfort in the fact that someone seemed interested in his plight.

"My ticket's gone. I can't find it."

"What happened to it?"

Hector dragged his bag of belongings out of the way of the other passengers and searched through it again. The line moved quickly as people climbed the steps and took their seats. With a swift upward glance he glimpsed the waiting driver. At that moment the bus shuddered and its engine rumbled into life. All at once the degree of noise and activity around him seemed to swell and multiply. He was besieged by anxious bawling voices, thunderous machinery, and a crush of people pushing by him. The roar of engines scattered his thoughts. Piecing together the scene with the soldiers in his mind, he watched himself—once, twice, three times—place the ticket trustingly into the soldier's hand, and with each repetition his sense of misgiving deepened; because once, twice, three times, he could not find the part where the ticket was returned. Tears welled up in his eyes.

"You must have dropped it somewhere. We can go back and look for it. But if we don't find it, I will buy you another one." Federico skipped eagerly in the direction of the ticket office.

"I didn't drop it," Hector commented sourly, slinging the bag across his shoulder. "The soldier took it. And, anyway, there's no time."

"There's lots of time." Federico came back and, pushing past a woman who was just about to enter the bus, hopped up the steps. "Will you wait while we go and get a ticket?"

Hector stepped forward. The driver nodded towards the office. "One minute." Federico turned to Hector. "You see?" He came down the steps and pushed past the woman again. She muttered crossly and glared at him. "Sorry." He lowered his eyes as if ashamed. "Come on!" he said to Hector and dashed off.

Hector followed. He took the money that Francisco had given him from his pocket. 950 pesetas. Not enough for a ticket. He swore.

"You won't have to spend your own money. I will buy the ticket."

"Why would you do that?"

"You're my friend." The intimacy of Federico's tone and his unguarded openness told Hector that in the boy's mind there was no question that this was true. "And besides, I have the money."

He reached into his pocket and extracted a wad of cash so fat that Hector could not suppress a gasp. Instinctively he extended his hand, as if to touch it.

"Where did you get that?"

"That's not all of it. There's a man waiting and when I go back he's going to give me the rest. It was so easy. He gave me a box and promised me 20,000 pesetas if I brought it here and put it on the bus that's going to San Sebastián. He said it was a present for his brother."

Hector smiled, imagining that his innocence had made the boy an easy mark for a swindler. But his smile faded in an instant because there was no denying that in his hand Federico held a very large sum of money.

"He must be crazy," Hector commented. "Why didn't he do it himself?"

"He said that he used to take the buses all the time without paying and he was caught. He got away, but the police and all the people who work here know who he is, so he can't come down to the bus station anymore."

"Who is he?"

Federico shrugged. "I don't know who he is," he said, speaking as if nothing could be of less interest. "I never saw him before. He was standing outside the store where I go to buy candy and he said I could make some money. I asked him how." Federico grinned. "I didn't think making money was so easy."

Hector opened the door and they went inside. Some dark, spiteful impulse goaded him into envy of Federico's good fortune, but he tried to push this from his thoughts. The soldier with the machine gun stood alone at the back. He surveyed the room, searching for the soldier who had questioned him. But there was no sign of that soldier or the fierce one.

"Do you want me to get a ticket for you?"

Hector nodded. "You still want to?"

Federico looked up at him. Hector imagined for a moment that he must bear a resemblance to Federico's brother or cousin, or someone else to whom the boy was very close. Why else would he go to such trouble?

"Why wouldn't I want to? I said I would. I don't go back on my promises."

Federico ran to the ticket booth and joined a short queue. Hector watched for a moment and tried to think how he had so quickly gained the trust of someone he had just met. It did not happen often and it was a shame that he would not have an opportunity to exploit that trust. Because he had no alternative, he would accept the boy's charity. But he was leaving, and that would be the end of it.

He went over to the window to make sure the bus was still there. It was, and he gave himself over to the belief that the driver would wait until he had returned with his ticket. Federico was next in line. Hector looked down and saw a bottle of water tipped on its side. It was the bottle he had bought and forgotten after the soldiers had finished with him. He picked it up and unscrewed the cap to take a sip when his eyes were drawn to a small rectangle of paper in the middle of the aisle. A woman walking by stepped on it, and once she had passed Hector retrieved it. It was his ticket for the bus to Villa Real. He was going to signal Federico that he could keep his money, but it was too late. The boy was pushing some bills through the slot in the bottom of the window. Hector shoved the ticket into his pocket and returned to the view of the courtyard, where the bus to San Sebastián was backing out of its parking space. It occurred to him that he was free to leave.

But something was wrong with the bus. It halted suddenly in the middle of the courtyard. As he watched, the world seemed to slow on its axis. The bus reared up like a stallion bucking against the bridle. The side of the bus bulged like a balloon filling with air, and then split open, releasing a cloud of black smoke. The bus windows blew into a million pieces and sprayed across the courtyard like water gushing from a hose. As if they had never existed, the people who a second ago had been standing close to the bus waiting for it to pass had vanished. At his back, Hector heard wailing voices, screams, and cries. Outside, people were running from the explosion, but all he could see was a solid wall of smoke and flame hurtling towards him with the velocity of a speeding train.

He dropped to the floor, his back against the wall, his body stiff with an instinctual, animal terror. Without thinking, he covered his head with the canvas bag. Above him, the window burst inward, followed by a torrent of smoke and ash and burning debris. This was accompanied by a sound—the detonation of a hundred thunderclaps—that pierced the thin shell of his skull and emptied the space inside of everything but itself. The building trembled as if knocked loose from its foundation. Flaming wreckage rained down all around him and his nose was filled with a choking, bitter stench. It seemed as if the whole world had caught on fire.

Seconds passed. He became aware of a muffled silence that seemed to reach him not from outside but from somewhere within his head. It told him that his opportunity to run was now, and he saw himself getting to his feet and calmly leaving the station, which was intact, and slowly—so not to attract attention—gathering speed until he was running along the streets of Envigado. But when he came to himself, he remained huddled on the floor, his back to the wall, his arms wrapped around the canvas bag. He could not open his eyes. He could not move his limbs. A sharp pain stabbed his thigh. Another pierced his arm, and then it was like bees had stung him all over his body. He sobbed and fought for breath.

Later—a few minutes or a few hours, he could not tell—a young soldier pulled him to his feet and peered with concern into his eyes. The man spoke but there was no sound, and Hector was passed from one hand to another, and finally put into the back of a truck. He thought vaguely that he should care about what was happening, but he did not care, and as the truck jerked soundlessly into motion, he rested his head against the shoulder of the old man next to him whose forehead was wrapped in gauze and fell into a profound sleep that was as close to oblivion, to death itself, as he would ever come in this life.

TWENTY-THREE

Hector was awakened by sounds in the corridor outside his cell. Weariness and pain engulfed him. He did not lift himself up from the mattress, and for a moment the darkness and silence in which he now spent most of his time seemed limitless and eternal. It was the darkness of the near blind; the obstinate silence of stone. Then the latch was thrown and the door slid away. He flinched as the naked grey interior of his cell was illuminated by the harsh light of the corridor.

Sometimes when he was alone and the pain from the interrogations was not so bad, he stood and, stretching his body to its full length, pressed his fingers against the ceiling, which, like the walls and floor, was cool featureless concrete. In an attempt to exercise he had walked the length and breadth of his cell again and again and judged it to be six feet by ten feet, just a bit smaller than the kitchen of his family's fifth floor flat in the building on Rua Santa Maria. There were no windows. A weak spray of light entered through a crack between two bricks near the ceiling. The light came and went, seemingly at random. The only furniture was a lumpy straw-filled mattress that exuded the pungently sweet and faintly musty aroma of overripe breadfruit. The door was metal and slid into place on a rail.

Two men entered. They grabbed his arms and pulled him from the mattress, standing him upright. One cuffed his hands behind his back while the other placed a hood over his head. They worked efficiently and in silence. Hector could hear the distant echo of steps, conversational voices, and the metallic clatter of other latches and other doors.

His shoes had been taken when he first arrived and his bare feet ached from the cold of the grimy concrete floor.

The first time they had come for him, Hector had stared into the faces of the men and been beaten for his impudence. The second time he had asked where he was being taken and for an answer had received another beating, the effects of which he could still feel in his lower back and legs. Today he kept his eyes down. He would say nothing until addressed.

The two men smelled of sweat and exertion. Hector wondered when last they had been outside. It did not occur to him to wonder what time of day it was. In the absence of daylight he had lost the ability to mark the passage of minutes, hours, and days. The initial shock of emerging into consciousness and not knowing what day it was or if it was morning or midnight had stolen the breath out of his throat. How long was it since he'd been thrown into the back of a van and brought here with a hood over his head and his arms and legs in shackles? Weeks? Months? He could not even begin to guess. He envisioned himself afloat on a limitless ocean of time. It stretched in all directions. It had no bottom, no horizon. The very notion of an hour or a week—something as simple and consoling as a fragment of time with a beginning and an end—had become meaningless. Events, when they occurred, took place within a vacuum: they came either before or after one another but did not happen on Tuesday morning or Saturday afternoon, or on the third Sunday in the month of February. These terms meant nothing. By locking him up in darkness and isolation, they had robbed him of the vocabulary of time—it was like being robbed of life itself because life was lived in days and weeks and months, and these concepts were no longer within his grasp. Much of his time he spent sleeping. When he was awake he waited for them to come, because they always came, sooner or later. But the question of when they would come held no meaning.

His left leg throbbed. The muscles from his calf up to his thigh tingled. During one of his beatings he had fallen and been kicked with more savageness than usual. All this time later the pain persisted. He had exercised and massaged the tenderness from his leg, but it always came back. He had learned it was not wise to arouse their anger by limping or appearing unsteady on his feet.

They released his arms and he stood without support. But once they were in the corridor he had trouble moving as quickly as they seemed to want him too. Someone prodded him from behind. Still, no words were spoken.

In the corridor, which he had never seen, the quality of sound changed. Hector pictured a cavernous space with a high vaulted ceiling. It was cooler than in the cell, where the air was dense and moist. At the worst moments the substance he drew into his lungs seemed to expand and coalesce as it descended his windpipe. But if he put his face next to the crack where the door met the jamb, he could feel the faint but steady movement of cooler air and hear the distant echo of footfalls and voices. Sometimes, when the moisture in the air clung to his face like a damp cloth, he pulled the mattress over to the door and lay until sleep offered a welcome release. But because they came without warning, he felt safer when the mattress was at the back of the cell, away from the door.

They stopped at the end of the corridor. Someone opened a door. He heard the key in the lock, the deafening snap as the bolt retracted. In the silence that followed, the buzzing in his ears that was left over from the explosion seemed to leap forward. With a hand steady on his back, Hector passed through the opening. Now it was cool and the air he breathed almost seemed sweet, as if it had originated out of doors. The quality of the sound changed again, seemed to move closer on all sides. He detected the reverberant hum of electricity, the hiss of water in pipes. They ascended nine wooden steps, turned, and ascended another nine steps. After being taken this way precisely twenty-eight times, the route was imprinted on his memory. He had counted the number of steps from his cell to the door of the interrogation room, and it rarely varied by even a single one. The regularity of the routine was not only predictable but comforting. He wondered if his captors ever thought of it this way.

Early in his imprisonment he had cried until exhaustion swept over him and he slept. But at some point—a long time ago it now seemed—the absurd futility of these tears that were costing him so much anguish and effort struck him as an obvious and embarrassing fact, and he had not cried since. With the relief that came from removing himself from everything and everyone he cared for he had even managed once or twice to laugh. Later it came to him that his previous life had receded into the vagueness of rumour and innuendo. Supposedly he had been alive for almost eighteen years. But the things that had happened to him had occurred in locations so remote in time and space that he could hardly conceive of them being real. Like everything else that existed in the world beyond his cell, the past meant nothing. Whenever he found himself dwelling on thoughts of his family, Claudia or Francisco, or of Nadia, he would watch the images roll by as if a film were playing in his head. But when he'd had enough he switched it off without a flicker of regret. It was as if he were dreaming another person's dreams and recalling another person's memories.

They were nearing the interrogation room. This was where he had been beaten. This was where the same questions about the explosion came at him again and again, and which he had answered again and again in the same way. The stucco walls of this room were painted a rosy shade of pink. It had windows, but the blinds were always drawn. The lights were dim. Each time he was seated in a tubular metal office chair. The hood would be yanked from his head. Someone would remove the handcuffs and he would be cuffed again to the arms of the chair, always in the same way. The chair was placed at a wide table where three military officers sat across from him. Sometimes his chair was pushed right up against the table, sometimes it was further back. He didn't know how he preferred it. The officer in the middle of the three was always the same: a tall thin man with a drooping moustache and swarthy skin wearing a military cap. His eyes were small and close together and his infrequent smile revealed large, tobacco-stained teeth. The two who accompanied him often changed. They were young and old — on two occasions female — but they all had the same coldness in their eyes that offered no hope of mercy. The man in the middle did most of the talking. Hector had grown to expect certain things in these sessions. The man lectured, laughed, barked insults, hurled accusations. He once spoke for a long time about "foreign elements." He could send Hector back to his cell after only a few minutes, or order a beating for no reason. Once, Hector had been told to stand in the corner of the room while holding his bound hands above his head. The three at the table had watched him for a few moments, then stood and filed out of the room. The armed guard who was always present remained. When Hector lowered his hands the guard pointed his gun at him, so Hector moved his hands back to the raised position. A while later the guard changed, but he was not allowed to move. The room darkened as night came on, and still he stood in the corner, the muscles of his raised arms screaming with pain. Hours later his bladder was full and he could hold it no longer. The urine briefly warmed his feet but cooled quickly. They made him stand all night, and in the morning the same three officers entered the room and resumed their places at the table. Hector was invited to sit in his chair.

"Do you have anything new to tell us?" the man with the moustache asked.

Hector shook his head. His limbs ached. His mouth was parched. He was sweating.

"That is too bad," the man said.

On that occasion they made him stand for another twenty-four hours before returning him to his cell.

Expecting to be taken once again into the interrogation room, Hector slowed his steps. But one of the guards poked him in the back with his gun and growled, "Keep moving!" Instantly his thoughts were in disarray. A spasm of panic gripped the muscles of his abdomen. In that room he would at least have known what to expect. The questions, the mocking, the beatings had become almost a ritual; almost a comfort.

Now he was moving into a new place where anything could happen. And in his time here he had learned, among other things, that the unknown was to be respected and feared.

From the bus station in Envigado he had been transported with dozens of others to a small hospital where a tent erected in the parking lot housed a temporary triage centre. Since he could walk without help, he was not immediately taken before a doctor. Instead, a young woman with a brusque manner and wearing a blue-and-white striped shirt shone a penlight into his eyes and took his pulse—all in a few seconds. He watched her lips as she spoke, but the explosion had damaged his hearing and made her voice sound like she was talking through a pillow. She shook her head and seemed cross at his inability to understand what she was saying. But he could not help it. The ringing in his ears made him feel as if his head were immersed in water. She led him and a few others to the grass at the edge of the parking lot and indicated they should sit.

The hospital or clinic was a two-storey whitewashed building with two rows of square windows. It faced a busy main street. Cars and vans with flashing lights sped past. Across from the grass was a strip of storefronts. The sidewalk was lined with curious bystanders, gawking and pointing. He had not been there long when an army truck arrived filled with the wounded; then, moments later, another. Soldiers helped or carried the injured into the tent or into the hospital or sat them on the grass, according to the instructions of the doctors. The dead were carried away on stretchers and laid apart from the living at the far end of the parking lot. As Hector looked on, a truck pulled up and a crew of workers in blue overalls began erecting another tent. In a moment of panic, he instinctively looked around where he was sitting, but of course there was no sign of the canvas bag containing his belongings. He had lost everything. He had missed his bus. He did not have enough money to buy another ticket.

He would not be returning home anytime soon.

Without warning tears welled up in his eyes. He wiped them away, but they did not stop. They overflowed to his cheeks and dripped down his chin onto his shirt and pants. He gasped for air and lowered his head, covering his face with his hands while his body convulsed. He was not seriously injured, but every muscle in his body ached. He longed for sleep. Someone placed a hand on his shoulder and squeezed. Someone else thrust a handkerchief into his fingers. He blew his nose and handed it back. The high-pitched ringing in his ears pushed all other sounds deep into the background.

Doctors and nurses appeared from time to time, the brusque woman among them. They led people into the tent. He started counting the wounded, but became confused when it seemed he had counted the same people more than once, and so gave up. He saw people on crutches, a woman with a jagged gash across her cheek, a child with no apparent injuries lying inert on a green blanket, a man holding a bloody towel to his forehead and crying as a doctor spoke to him. Midway through the afternoon more soldiers arrived. They began questioning people. Hector tried to avoid thinking about the helplessness of his position, but all he had was the 950 pesetas Francisco had given him and the clothes he was wearing. If he was still here two or three days from now his money would be almost gone, even if he slept outside and bought only enough food to keep himself from starving. An image of the roll of bills that Federico had shown him emerged into his mind. He wondered if he would find any money if he returned to the bus station and scoured the ruins.

Above him clouds moved in and the sky turned dark. A man in a white hospital uniform came with a cart on wheels and distributed sandwiches and bottles of water. As the day wore on the group sitting on the grass became smaller. The air had cooled and the afternoon light was beginning to fade when the brusque woman came and indicated that he should follow her. She was wearing a white lab coat, but underneath this her blue-and-white striped shirt that Hector had thought so crisp and clean when he had first seen her was dirty and spattered with blood. Her face was pale and her eyes had a glassy look.

He followed her into the tent. She pulled back a curtain to reveal a metal table. She patted its top. The space was lit by a bare bulb suspended on a wire. He sat on the table and looked at her.

Hector watched her lips move.

"I can't hear you," he said, not sure how loudly he had spoken. His voice vibrated in his throat.

She pulled on rubber gloves, took an instrument, and looked into his ears, then had him take off his shirt. She checked him over, making him shiver when she touched him with her cold fingers. When she was done she took a pen and a pad of paper from her coat pocket and wrote, *You're lucky.*

Hector looked at her. He didn't feel lucky.

Then she wrote, *The soldiers will want to talk to you before you go.*

He asked, "Am I deaf?"

She shook her head and wrote, *It's temporary. In a week you will be fine.*

Hector nodded. He wasn't sure if he could expect anything from her, but because she seemed sympathetic he told her that he had lost everything he owned in the explosion, and that he had only a few pesetas and nowhere to go. His family was a thousand miles away in B——.

She said nothing, but with an earnest glance met his eyes. She had dark hair and dark eyebrows, and when he caught himself thinking she was very pretty he swallowed deeply and looked down, towards the pavement. Her expression was enigmatic. He was unable to tell if she wanted to help him or if she wished he would go away. Finally, he shrugged and let himself down from the table. He grabbed his shirt and pulled it on.

"Thank you," he said.

She wrote on the pad, *Come with me.*

She led him into the hospital, through the front entrance and past a harshly lit area where two women shared space at a wide desk. The furniture was old and the scarred linoleum floor was littered with discarded gauze, bandages, and plastic gloves and tubes. The air smelled soapy and bitter. Hector avoided looking at the people with bandaged limbs and heads lying on gurneys and occupying chairs in a waiting area. With languid circular motions, an old man mopped the floor. The woman took Hector down a hall and into an empty room with a table, a refrigerator, a few chairs, and a sink, where a fluorescent light fixture in the ceiling flickered disconcertingly. She went to a row of lockers and used a key hanging from a string around her neck to open one of them.

Hector felt hope bloom in his chest, though he had no idea what he was hoping for. ·

She rummaged through a purse. He watched as she drew paper bills from a wallet. Instantly his face grew warm and he looked away. He could not help feeling ashamed, though he had no choice but to accept whatever she offered.

She pressed the bills into his hand, her eyes telling him that the money was his. She took the pad and pen and wrote, *There might be somewhere for you to sleep.*

"Thank you," he said again. He pushed the money into his pocket without counting it.

They were in the hallway. At the very end she tapped on a wooden door before pushing it open. She flicked on the light to reveal a small room painted pale green with an old earth-coloured sofa against the wall. Across from the sofa a very old television sat on a low table. Draped across a pillow lying on the sofa was a single blanket, beige with frayed edges. In the corner a stack of cardboard boxes filled with something heavy were collapsing into one another.

Stay here, she wrote. *What is your name?*

"Hector," he said. "Hector Tomás."

I am Eva García Pérez, she wrote. *I will make sure you are not disturbed.*

"I . . ." he began, but then he stopped and shrugged when he realized he did not know what to say. He didn't know how to thank her.

From the doorway Eva began speaking, then, smiling and shaking her head, took the pad from her pocket and wrote, *Sleep. In the morning we will decide what to do.*

She pulled the door shut behind her.

Alone, Hector gazed at the closed door. He was suddenly overcome by drowsiness. As if his bones had dissolved, his body drooped. He felt like he hadn't slept in days.

Before turning out the light he emptied his pockets and counted his money: 1410 pesetas. It was enough for a bus ticket and some food. Assured that he could resume his journey, he allowed himself a smile and a moment of calm. Though suffering from exhaustion and hunger, he felt strong again. Then, as if afraid someone would come and take it from him, he quickly folded the money together and pushed it into the bottom of his pocket.

He kicked off his shoes, switched off the light, stretched out on the sofa and covered himself with the blanket. He would make it difficult for anyone to steal what he had by sleeping on the side where his money was. He had barely enough time to formulate this thought before he drifted into a soundless, tranquil state of unconsciousness.

But it seemed only minutes had passed when the light came on. Hector sat up and lifted his arm to shield his eyes from the glare. Eva stood in the open doorway. She said something.

Hector shook his head and shrugged questioningly. "What's wrong?"

Anger had deepened the furrow between her eyebrows. She pulled the pad from her pocket and wrote, then stepped into the room and held it in front of his face.

They are looking for you.

She regarded him sternly, her mouth twisted with disgust.

Hector shook his head. "Who?" he asked. "Why?"

I trusted you, she wrote.

Dread knotted every muscle in his body until he thought he would double over. Suddenly she hated him. He looked her in the eye, but could not endure the pain this caused. Cautiously he peered around her towards the doorway.

She wrote something else and with a contemptuous gesture dropped the pad into his lap. He read, *twenty-four people died.*

"I didn't do anything," he pleaded.

She was leaving. Hector thrust his feet into his shoes and followed her. She did not look back. He was going to pass her and escape out the front entrance when he remembered the soldiers in the parking lot. That's where she was going, to tell them he was here. But why? Why would they be interested in him? It came to him that the building would have a rear exit. He turned and fled past the room where he had been sleeping. Through another door he found a stairwell. Steps led up to the second floor and down to the basement. He chose the basement.

He pushed open a door. It was dark. He found a light switch but before flicking it on thought better of it. He groped forward, through darkness. When his leg struck something he lowered his hands and felt along the edge of a flat table. He moved and his arm knocked something that toppled to the floor before he could catch it. He stood still, straining to hear, but was surrounded by muffled silence. In frustration he slapped his ears until the pain forced tears into his eyes. But he was already crying. The tears had soaked his face and were flowing in a stream down his neck. Confusion, disbelief, and panic shot through him. He could not think. He seemed to be suffering from paralysis. Should he go forward or back? Maybe he should turn himself in. They would understand if he told them he was innocent. Until this moment he had not wondered about the source of the explosion, but now realized it had been a deliberate attack. Someone had set out to kill innocent people. How could she believe he would be involved with that? But of course, she did not know him. In her eyes he was a stranger who was capable of anything.

He was groping his way through darkness when the yellow walls of the room, its contents of boxes and assorted furniture, leapt abruptly into sight. He heard nothing but imagined voices ordering him to keep still. He raised his arms. In the movies when people surrendered they linked their hands behind their head. He did this, and in seconds felt a strong hand gripping his shoulder and forcing him to his knees. He was pushed all the way down until his face was pressed against the cold concrete floor. Something cold and hard touched his neck. Hector winced when someone stepped on him and drove the heel of a boot into his ribs.

He was cuffed and hauled to his feet. Hands gripped his arms. The room was full of soldiers, triumph animating their young faces. But they grew solemn when an older man with a moustache, wearing a dark green uniform and a beret, entered the room. The man locked a steely gaze on Hector and calmly approached through the maze of boxes and furniture. He was speaking. Hector breathed rapidly but did not make a move. He knew they would have no patience if he tried to explain his deafness. The man continued to speak until his face was only inches from Hector's. His breath smelled strongly of garlic. The man smiled, and Hector noticed the single gold *colmillo,* the radiant eyetooth, gleaming beside a row of stained incisors. The man raised his hand and lightly patted Hector's cheek. Hector tensed in preparation for the blow. But the man turned quickly on his heel and Hector was propelled forward, across the room, up the stairs, and out into the night.

TWENTY-FOUR

They left the interrogation room behind. The pain in his abdomen sharpened suddenly. He stumbled, nearly fell. One of the guards laughed. In defiance of the pain and the laughter, he held himself upright and stepped more quickly, almost outpacing his escorts. Then they stopped and he was shoved through a doorway. Hands gripped his shoulders.

"Over here," he heard someone say. The voice was casual.

He was moved across the room, his feet almost lifted from the floor. They turned him so his back was pressed against the wall.

"On your knees."

Hector carefully lowered himself to a squatting position before dropping his knees to the floor. His joints ached. His body felt like a raw wound.

He heard the scrape of table legs.

The hood was pulled from his head. The light striking his eyes ignited a blazing pain that penetrated to the back of his skull. Even with his eyelids squeezed shut the orange glare of light shining through the flesh of his eyelids was dazzling. He lowered his head to avoid the light, but the pain did not diminish.

"I'm sorry," the voice said. Then, more resolutely, "Turn off those lights."

The glare vanished. Hector held his head still, waiting for the pain to subside.

"You've been kept in one of the dark cells. My apologies. I wasn't told. You can open your eyes now. It shouldn't be so bad."

Hector kept his eyes shut as he struggled to make sense of what was happening. To be spoken to in this manner, as if someone in this place actually regretted causing him pain, was even more confusing than the other things that had been done to him. After all this time, why would they suddenly begin treating him as if he were human?

He lifted his head and opened one eye a crack. The only illumination came from a gooseneck desk lamp on a table at the far end of the room. A man in a tan military uniform stood over him. He was bald and clean-shaven. Fleshy jowls concealed his neck. His eyes were dark and small, like pinpricks. A smile spread across his face.

"This is good," he said, and with a sweeping motion of one hand seemed to indicate the room and all its contents. "You see? We mean no harm. We don't want to hurt anyone. It's just, you know, we have a job to do."

Hector opened his other eye. He stared upward, straight into the man's plump face. He pulled a breath into his lungs and held it for a moment before exhaling. Tears filled his eyes.

The man shrugged and all at once appeared solemn.

"I admit it is a burden, what we do. It's not easy. We work very hard. But you should not be afraid. Come. Let me help you."

He took Hector's arm and gently lifted him to his feet. Hector did not resist but also did not take his eyes from the man standing before him.

Again, the man smiled. When he spoke, his voice was just above a murmur.

"I must apologize for the conduct of my colleagues. I suspect you have been subjected to the crudest sort of interrogation techniques. They think a big stick and a loud voice are all you need to get things done. These people know nothing. You will be glad to learn that we do things differently here. This is my room. I am in charge."

He stepped back and, with his fat hands folded together, surveyed Hector up and down.

"You look like you are in good health."

Hector let his weight rest against the wall. Should he admit to being in pain? Should he admit his fears and hope for the best? He let his glance wander. The room was long and narrow. It was warm and there were no windows. A lone guard occupied a position beside the closed door at the far end. Next to the guard was the table bearing the lamp; next to this, a single tubular metal chair.

"I was," he said. "Now, I don't know."

"But they have been feeding you. What do they give you?"

"Soup," Hector said, speaking without enthusiasm of the bowls of vinegary broth with tiny bones and white doughy lumps floating in it that were placed in his cell, along with a plastic bucket in which he was instructed to shit and piss. He did not know what motivated him to keep eating, or even breathing. The filth of his surroundings often made him think of killing himself, but his confusion was such that he did not even know if he had lost all hope. What, he wondered, were the signs? He had not been allowed to wash since coming here, and was sickened by the stench of his body and by the clothes he wore, which were the same ones he had put on the morning he and Francisco had set out for Envigado for the last time. His hair had grown long, stringy and greasy; his sparse beard itched. When he was unable to sleep, visions of a skeletal version of himself prostrate on the floor of his cell, being prodded by a concerned soldier's boot, formed in his head. Though he did not know if it was within his power to make them suffer for his death, he daydreamed longingly about the clean simplicity and romance of starving himself. But whenever the door of his cell was drawn back and the bowl appeared, and the sour brackish aroma entered his nostrils, he would fall hungrily upon the bowl and not stop eating until the last repulsive morsel was gone. If there was bread he would soak up the dregs. Afterward he suffered the guilt of someone who, by satisfying the primitive needs of the flesh, has sacrificed an ideal or broken a promise.

"And how often do you eat? Once a day? Twice a day?"

Hector looked down, away from the man's unremitting scrutiny, his bright eager eyes.

"I don't know."

In the brief silence that followed, the man's heavy breaths wheezed in and out of his lungs. There were no other sounds.

"Do they beat you?"

Hector nodded.

"Why do you think they do this? Why do they beat you?"

Against his will Hector raised his eyes to meet those of his inquisitor, who smiled in the satisfied manner of someone who has caught another person in a lie. Hector did not relish thinking about his situation or speculating upon the reasons why his tormentors treated him the way they did. He knew from the questions he had been asked that he was suspected of having played a part in the bombing at the Envigado bus station. But he also knew these suspicions had no basis in fact. And because he had protested his innocence every time he had been questioned and had not yet been released, he could only guess that the reason he was still being held had nothing to do with the bombing.

"I don't know," he said.

The man's smile broadened. "I'm sure you know more than you think you do. It is one of the tragedies of the human condition that our memory is porous, like the nets they use to catch fish. It captures and retains some things, but others escape. You see something, but because it means nothing to you at the time, your mind allows it to slip by. It is only later that the true significance of this detail is revealed. But by that time, it is too late for you to make sense of it. You forget. We all forget. It is my job—the job of all of us here—to help you to remember."

For a few moments the man continued to smile but did not speak. He stepped back, moved to one side, and, as if arranging a camera shot, briefly regarded Hector from this angle. Then he shifted slightly and observed Hector from a different angle. Hector looked past him, towards the array of tools spread out on a long table and next to this a simple metal bed frame with no mattress. The rest of the room's contents were lost in shadow.

"Forgive me for staring," the man said as he set out walking from one end of the room to the other. "I am trying to observe something. You see, we will become intimate, you and I. Like the closest of friends. And I want to know as much as I can about the person I am expected to spend my time with. You are very young. Almost a boy, though I can see you are a man. Your strength is formidable. You have some bruises, but these will fade. You have adapted well to your new surroundings. This is not normally how it goes. For example, young men miss their lovers and will do anything to see them again. This is to be expected. People are vulnerable in ways they don't realize. There are countless weaknesses we can exploit in order to reach our objectives. For instance, you were put into a cell with no lights or windows because someone thought you might be afraid of the dark." He shrugged. "Sometimes, I admit, we are wrong about specifics. But we are never wrong about our reasons for doing the things we do."

Moving his eyes but not his head, Hector watched as the man circled the room, pausing here and there as he closed in on him. His immediate fears receded for a moment as hope stirred within him. Compared to the guards and officers who had beaten him, he could not help but regard this man—with his portly physique, his curiously precise enunciation of each word he spoke, and his prissy mannerisms and gestures—as something of a buffoon.

"In this room we will conduct a number of lessons." As he spoke, the man gestured with his hands as if he were delivering a lecture. "So it will help if you regard our time together as training. I call them lessons because over the coming weeks and months you will learn many things about yourself. Hopefully, I will learn things as well. And my employers too—I mustn't forget them."

The man had made a complete circuit of the room and now stood before Hector with his hands behind his back, smiling broadly as if he'd touched upon a point of great interest. The room seemed to have grown warmer, and in the dim light Hector could see the beads of perspiration that stood out on the man's upper lip. Hope fell away and his fears returned as the man tilted his head and continued to smile.

"Forgive me. I have been doing all of the talking. Is there anything you would like to say, or ask?"

The question caught him off guard, but Hector spoke quickly.

"How long have I been here?"

"I assume you mean how long have you been a guest of this establishment and not how long have you been here with me." The man chortled under his breath. "I'm sorry. It's my little joke. I understand perfectly what you mean. I'm afraid I have no idea. I only had the pleasure of making your acquaintance today. I can tell you, however, that the crime of which you stand accused occurred about six weeks ago."

Hector's knees suddenly threatened to fold beneath him. It felt as if the earth had crumbled beneath his feet. He shuddered and would have collapsed had the man not gripped him tightly by the arm.

"It is strange, isn't it, how the mind plays tricks on us. You were expecting me to say it had been months or maybe even a year since the incident at the bus terminal? No. I'm afraid I must disappoint you on that score. But still, six weeks is a long time when you're being held in a place like this, and I'm speaking from experience. Come. We'll sit you down."

As he helped Hector across the room, he motioned towards the guard, who turned the chair out from the table. Hector sat heavily but remained hunched forward. His arms, still cuffed together behind him, made it impossible to lean back. He had imagined himself strong, but now he had to fight off both tears and despair. This world made even less sense than he had thought. He also felt numb, as if he'd been told that everyone of his acquaintance was dead and everything he had ever owned destroyed. His gaze fell languidly upon the scuffed floorboards, on the man's feet in shiny black army boots, the laces tied with meticulous criss-cross precision. Upon his own dirty bare feet.

"My employers are curious about many things, but none of these are of the least importance to me. I will not be questioning you. You can say as much or as little as you want. I do not care. My role is not to persuade you to talk to me but to suggest to you that you would be doing yourself a favour by talking to my colleagues."

Hector shook his head. "Please, I've already told them I don't know anything. I met him for the first time that day. I don't know what was in the box. It had nothing to do with me."

"And yet, he was in the process of purchasing a ticket for Villa Real when the bomb went off."

Hector said nothing. He lifted his head. The man was scowling.

"You must understand why my employers are confused. They have in their custody two boys—or, if you prefer, young men—who say they had nothing to do with a disaster that claimed twenty-four innocent lives. Yet, one, who was in possession of a considerable sum of money, was seen placing a mysterious box on the bus that exploded, and the other was seen in his company. Someone heard him say to you, 'You are my friend.' He was buying a ticket for a destination that you already had a ticket for. One could conclude from this that you were travelling together."

"I lost my ticket. He was buying a new one for me."

"So you say. But you had a ticket for Villa Real in your pocket at the time of your arrest."

"I—" Hector shook his head. Tears streamed down his face. "I found it on the floor. Someone stepped on it."

"So why did you allow your friend to waste his money on another ticket?"

"There was no time—"

"And you still haven't explained why a complete stranger would go to the expense and trouble of buying you a bus ticket."

Hector gazed into the fat man's expressionless face. How could he convince these people he was innocent when everything that had happened to him, and was still happening to him, was so far beyond his comprehension? He felt as if he had stumbled across a border and into a country where words he had used all his life to make himself understood carried unfamiliar, contradictory meanings.

"I don't know why he bought it," Hector said. "He had a lot of money and he told me he wanted to. If you ask him he'll tell you."

The man's expression did not change. He stood over Hector without speaking.

Shifting in his seat, Hector added, "He told me that someone had given him the money to put the box on that bus."

The man raised his eyebrows and quickly turned. For a moment he paced back and forth and appeared deep in thought.

"You were not careful," he said as he paced. "An employee spotted you at the bus terminal before, a number of times." He punctuated his words with a raised finger. "But you only bought a ticket on the day of the explosion. The man who saw you on those other occasions told the police, and they confronted you."

Hector nodded.

With a raspy sigh the man stopped moving. He turned. The light from the lamp tinted his features with a wan yellow glow.

"When that man was killed by your bomb the police lost a very good witness." He glanced sidelong at Hector. "You are very fortunate."

"It wasn't my bomb."

Hector stared at his inquisitor, who was smiling again.

"You have made such claims before. But none of this interests me. Obviously I am familiar with your case. But today, we will begin again. You are Hector. I am Dimitri. I am not from here. I learned my trade in Greece, where my home is. I came to this country because I offered my services and was accepted. I miss my home, but I like to travel and see other places. There is no better way to experience a country than to work there. You learn the language and meet the people. It is a gift you will use for the rest of your life. I highly recommend it."

Hector remained silent. He was still unsure if this man posed a greater or lesser danger than those he already faced.

"But enough pleasantries. You and I have work to do." Dimitri stepped quickly and in a second was standing behind the chair, out of Hector's sight. Hector turned towards a sound that was like the soft rustling of some sort of material. It reminded him of a package being unwrapped with great care in order to preserve the paper. His mother used to do this.

"It is time for your first lesson. I think you are ready."

With astonishing swiftness, something swooped before Hector's eyes and covered his head. His air was cut off by a plastic bag. He gasped and strained to stand up, but a strong arm had wrapped around him, pinning him to the spot. The inside of the bag fogged and grew warm as he fought to breathe. He could not move his arms, which were crushed between his body and the back of the chair. He kicked, but his feet connected with nothing. In only a few seconds he felt as if his head was being lifted from his neck. Pressure building in his lungs felt like hands inside him trying to rip his chest open. The pounding of his heart roared in his ears like detonations. He struggled using every part of his body, and all his remaining strength. The chair tipped over. He fell to the floor, but the arm held him fast and the plastic bag clung to his face as if it were a living creature. He lay on his back, conscious of the warmth of human contact: the arm that held him even more tightly, a soft thigh or belly on which his head reclined. His jaw moved up and down, but no sounds came from his mouth, no air entered his lungs. He could no longer feel his arms. When he tried to kick, his legs merely twitched. The razor edge of terror that had ripped through him in the first agonizing moments of suffocation had dulled. It came to him that life was seeping away and he felt contentment spread like warm liquid through his torso. As death approached, the arm that held him seemed protective, and he felt that he should not have struggled against it. He continued gazing upward, through the fogged plastic. The grinding rasping sounds he heard were his attempts to draw breath.

Then there was movement. On the other side of the plastic a distorted version of Dimitri floated into view. No longer fighting to breathe, Hector followed the other's progress across the room with dimming watery eyes. Dimitri stood over him and smiled. He seemed to be speaking. Then in a flash Dimitri's face was very close to Hector's. The sounds his words made were like the thud of heavy machinery. They reached Hector as if through a wall of concrete. Hector tried to listen and understand, but his attention was drawn to other figures crowding the room behind Dimitri:

his mother and father, Carlos and Julio, Dulciana, Cesara, Rosaria, and Helena, Nadia, Señor Volos, Claudia and Francisco. They were trying to speak to him, and he suddenly understood that they were dead and calling him to join them. They were all smiling, because once he passed into their ranks everything would be all right. He would never suffer pain or humiliation again. The Day of Judgment would come and go and leave them unscathed. The angels would guide them to the throne of the Almighty. Together they would bask in the eternal warmth of heaven. Others would celebrate their lives on *el día de los muertos,* and on that day they would rise and join the celebration, but for the rest of the year they would lie quietly in their graves, grateful for the lives they had lived. This thought gave him comfort. He welcomed the idea of passing from this life into the next and answered Dimitri's smile with one of his own. Then he sank into unconsciousness.

TWENTY-FIVE

The restraints cut into Hector's wrists. The hood covered his head. He stood very still, fighting dizziness. Weariness and pain occupied his body and obliterated all other feeling. He struggled to remain standing. Perhaps he had slept, but how could he have slept? He remembered entering a small, brightly lit, windowless room with white walls and being tied to a chair. Mariachi music played over loudspeakers, the same songs repeated again and again, the pulsing rhythms washing over him hour after hour. Then they had come for him and just like the other times he had been marched along the corridor. But he had lost his bearings and no longer had any idea where he was or where he had been.

They had pushed him through a doorway, and he stood with his back against the wall. He rested his weight on his one good leg and waited. There was new discomfort in his shoulder. This recalled his session with Dimitri. They had tried to smother him and somehow he had survived. But why? Why were they keeping him alive?

He tried to feel resentment, hatred, but could not summon even these. Instead, he felt depleted, like a vessel that has been emptied or a rag that has had the water wrung from it. He did not think about what was coming and tried to push visions of things that had already happened out of his mind. He could not rid himself of the idea that because of his claims of innocence everyone in his family had been murdered. Maybe he should have told them what they wanted to hear. Was it too late now to say this? That his family had been murdered made no sense, but none of this made sense and if it was true it meant he had no hope of being saved. Who would be looking for him? Who would be petitioning for his release? Nobody. Except Nadia. But he had left her without saying goodbye. She probably hated him. His life was here—this moment, and whatever was awaiting him.

His muscles tensed to the sound of furniture being dragged across the floor. He moved his foot one inch to the left and took solace from the sensation that the gritty surface of the floor left on his skin and from the fact that he had done something that his captors did not know about.

Without warning, hands grabbed his arms and swivelled him out from the wall. Someone was removing the straps which bound his wrists. The hood was yanked from his head. Dimitri stood only inches away. He smiled.

"My young friend, I am glad to see you are well."

The room was brightly lit by what seemed like spotlights. They cast their harsh glow from each corner and radiated the warmth of a summer day. Dimitri was not alone. There were three others standing with him. Hector lifted his hand to shield his eyes from the glare. He said nothing.

Dimitri cocked his head. "We will get started. First, you will disrobe."

Hector didn't move. He stared straight into the fat man's eyes, which were small and pale and receded in their sockets. He felt a prickling sensation in his chest. His upper body grew warm.

"Come, come. We have no time for this. Your second lesson won't start until you have removed your clothes. I'm sorry if it's embarrassing for you."

For a moment the sound of breathing was all that Hector could hear, both his and Dimitri's. But as he focused on these sounds, another emerged from the background and grew more distinct as he listened. It was faint and distant, so he couldn't be sure where it came from. Yet it was also unmistakable: screaming that gained volume and intensity with each second that passed.

Dimitri said, "You will take your clothes off."

Hector did nothing.

One of the others stepped forward, a burly guard in a khaki uniform, but halted when Dimitri raised his arm.

"No. He will do it himself."

Everything in Hector's recent experience told him to be careful, that anything could be a trap. Yet he stood before his chief tormentor unshackled. The man was within arm's reach. The temptation to grasp him by the throat and squeeze the life out of him was almost more than he could resist. But with his wounded body, what damage could he hope to inflict in the few seconds before the others descended upon him? His shoulder had been wrenched and twisted in their attempt to kill him. He was so exhausted that even as he concentrated his energies towards the moment when he would have locked his fingers around this man's stout neck, a fog descended and blunted his awareness of his surroundings. When full wakefulness returned, the throbbing in his shoulder and leg seemed to have intensified. He was dizzy, weak, hungry. He could barely stand up.

With his eyes on Dimitri, he pulled his shirt over his head, moving slowly because of the pain in his shoulder. He pulled his pants and under-wear down and stepped away from them. Naked, he stood as straight as he could and stared Dimitri in the eye. His neck grew warm.

Dimitri smiled. "Take these away," he ordered, and the burly guard quickly stepped forward to retrieve Hector's clothes. "You will not need them," Dimitri said to Hector.

Dimitri backed away. This appeared to be the signal for the other two guards to step up and take Hector by the arms.

"You look tired, my friend. I am afraid you are not getting enough sleep. Today we will let you lie down."

As Dimitri spoke the guards shuffled Hector across the room towards the bed frame that he had noticed during the previous session. It was dented and afflicted with lesion-like rust patches. Beneath it on the floor was a yellow plastic washbasin. Next to the bed frame, a black metal box about a foot square—fitted with dials and switches and a small hand crank—sat on a table. Two thick cables connected the box to the frame. A cascade of thinner wires flowed from the back of the box across the table to the floor.

"The *parrilla* is one of my favourite devices," Dimitri remarked. "I've seen it adapted in so many ways. Some surprise even me. Today you will discover its most popular use."

Lacking strength to resist, Hector allowed the guards to force him down and on his back. Using two pairs of handcuffs each, they bound him to the frame by his wrists and, with his legs spread wide apart, by the ankles. The cuffs clanked noisily against the frame and the uneven metal slats chafed and pinched his skin. Hector looked into the eyes of each guard as they fastened the cuffs but could see nothing in their blank depths that told him they were even capable of sympathy. The distant screaming gained urgency.

When the guards had completed their task, Dimitri bent over Hector and held one of the wires where he could see it.

"You see, on its end there is a small clamp. Once we attach these I don't think further explanation will be necessary."

Hector shut his eyes as the four men went to work. He heard laughter and felt himself shrink as fingers manipulated his penis and scrotum. A clamp pinched his foreskin and another bit into the skin covering his balls. They attached clamps to his nipples and earlobes, under his arms, between his toes, to one of his eyebrows, and to his upper lip. The pressure of the clamps brought tears into his eyes, which squeezed between his clenched eyelids and dripped down both sides of his head. His throat muscles tightened. The air seemed to coagulate in his lungs. His heart pumped wildly.

In a voice that lurched from his mouth between gasps, he said, "I'll say I did it. I'll say I blew up the bus and that I did it all by myself. Please. If I confess you don't have to do this."

Someone laughed.

Chuckling, Dimitri said, "Don't try to spoil our fun."

"Please." Hector's voice had become faint and strained. He shook his head and struggled weakly against the handcuffs. "Please."

"As you will see, the challenge is to create just the right charge. Too little and nothing happens. Too much and the subject is killed outright or permanently disfigured. You can open your eyes. There is nothing to be afraid of. We know what we are doing."

Hector clenched his teeth and tried to steady his breathing. He had not cried like this since he was a child throwing a tantrum over some imagined injustice. His chest heaved and a whine escaped from his throat. He was unable to suppress it. Tears had steamed from his eyes and soaked into his hair. Since arriving here he had prayed sporadically, but now in his mind he called out to God to spare him.

A hand slapped him hard across the face. Surprisingly, there was no pain. But the impact stunned him. Then the sensation of panic returned. His entire body was shaking. The handcuffs rattled against the bed frame.

"Do not disappoint me, Hector," Dimitri said. "Look at what we are doing. This is for your own good. We have all been where you are. It's the only way to learn."

Hector shook his head. The tears had stopped. His throat muscles throbbed from weeping. He coughed dryly. There were no other sounds. He opened his eyes.

The burly guard sat before the machine fingering some dials, his eyes alive with anticipation, his expression childlike. The tip of his tongue protruded from between his lips. But for a few scars in the region of his mouth, his skin was smooth. Hector took note of the fact that he was probably no older than himself.

"Lucas is our technician. He is an expert," Dimitri observed. He stood behind the younger man and watched the deft movement of his fingers with apparent admiration. For just a moment Dimitri's expression relaxed, and Hector detected something like pride in the smile that crept across his lips.

Lucas shifted the machine over to give Hector a better view of the front panel.

"These meters tell me what's happening," Lucas said, pointing towards two small glowing crescent-shaped windows. His voice was soft and surprisingly light in timbre, almost girlish. "Volts, amps. The red part is the danger area."

Dimitri nodded.

"It works like this."

Lucas turned the crank. This part of the operation was hidden from Hector's view, but he had no trouble imagining it. The mechanical whirring, like the sound of a coffee grinder, was accompanied by tingling that surged quickly towards a fiery sensation at each point where the wires made contact with his skin. His muscles seized and contracted as the bed frame seemed to dance beneath him. Searing pain spread throughout his body. It was like being boiled alive. His breathing halted. He could not distinguish his limbs. He was falling, floating, weightless.

"Wait just a minute."

Hector opened his eyes. His blood pulsed in his ears. His skin grew numb as the pain faded. He opened his mouth to speak but could not utter a sound. Tears soaked his face, and it came as a surprise to discover that he could still cry, that there were still tears left to weep.

Dimitri retrieved something from another table. With one hand he forced Hector's jaws apart and inserted the object between his teeth. It was flat and made of plastic.

"Just a precaution," he said. He patted Hector's cheek and smiled the way a nurse might, to bring comfort to a suffering patient. "To keep you from biting off your tongue."

"Now?"

Dimitri nodded.

Lucas turned the crank. But for the merest fraction of a second Hector's attention was drawn to movement behind Dimitri. The two who had cuffed him to the bed frame stood with their backs against the far wall. He saw now that they were not guards. In their green tunics, which he had mistaken for uniforms, they looked like hospital workers. They leaned their heads together to exchange a remark. One smirked. As the whirring resumed he could not believe they were indifferent to what was happening. How could they stand by and do nothing? Would they care if he died? And then it came to him: they would clean up the mess once Dimitri and Lucas were finished.

Dimitri bent down and retrieved a bucket. Holding it in one hand, he looked Hector in the eye and raised the index finger of his other hand to his lips. Then he hefted the bucket and splashed the contents over Hector's body.

A torrent of pain surged through him. It was like claws, needles, cigarette burns. It felt as if his skin was being peeled inch by inch away from his flesh and his hair had erupted in flames. His body seemed to vaporize. The water had cooled him, but only briefly, and now it heated and turned to steam. He could not control any of his movements. His head flew back and his jaws clenched around the object in his mouth. His muscles stiffened. Spasms shot through his arms and legs. The cuffs rattled against the bed frame. And the frame itself lurched and jumped as the spasms grew more violent. A strange sound filled Hector's ears. Someone was groaning, "Unh, unh, unh," but the pain was too great and he was not aware of making any sounds himself. His eyes were closed but filled with a crimson radiance, a fiery glow, like an infinite shimmering sunset. Red permeated his brain and filled his thoughts. "Unh, unh, unh," the groaning continued, and from some distant place other voices reached him—voices shouting that he had to tell them everything, had to give himself over to them completely. He could smell shit and was aware that his bowels and bladder of their own volition had emptied themselves. More water flowed over him, cooling him for one impossible second before the temperature rose to boiling. He knew nothing. His head was empty. He knew nothing but they didn't believe him. It didn't matter what he said, they would do these things anyway, because he was here and could do nothing about it. If only he could die, they would not be able to reach him. That was the only way. And then suddenly he found his voice and screamed—but this was because the cranking had stopped. He opened his eyes. For some reason he was still breathing. Dimitri stood over him. Lucas sat at the table. He wanted to ask if they would kill him, but their eyes were on him and Hector was suddenly afraid that if he spoke he would be subjected to even more excruciating torment. Then Lucas and Dimitri looked at each other. An invisible signal passed between them and Lucas began turning the crank. Dimitri held the bucket. Hector shook his head but couldn't speak. He bit down on the thing in his mouth as the pain surged upward and carried him with it. His head flew back. His aching limbs wrenched against the restraints. They had penetrated his skin and stripped away the muscle. Now they were tormenting his bones. He had nothing left. A voice he didn't recognize was chanting, "Unh, unh, unh." Then, like the overturned bucket, his head was empty. He saw nothing. Heard nothing. The pain radiated from deep inside him. It embraced him. It obliterated his world, his past, his soul. All that was left was pain. Nothing but pain.

TWENTY-SIX

He was awake again. In the darkness he lay absolutely still, breathing softly. Gradually it dawned on him that he was not in his cell. It was a different kind of space. He sensed this, though he could not say how. Perhaps the murmurs and groans of the building echoed in an unfamiliar way. Perhaps the air blanketing his naked body had a strange texture. In the end it didn't matter. It simply was.

He'd had no dreams that he could recall. No images came into his head. And though he had no sensation of crying, his eyes ran with tears. An occasional twinge of pain or hunger shot through him. But these passed quickly, and the sensations they left behind remained vague or distant, like an echo, or like the face of someone he knew he should recognize but did not. He searched inwardly, but his mind groped through a vacancy of thought. Who he was, where he'd come from—these were things he reached for with difficulty.

Finally, after many hours, the two small windows set high in the wall began to admit a dim wash of sallow morning light. He lay flat on what appeared to be a bed. But, raising himself, he realized it was a simple straw pallet on the floor. All the surfaces of the room—walls, ceiling, floor—were covered in grimy white tiles. In the centre of the floor was a drain hole. A few bugs scuttled back and forth.

The air reeked of sewer.

He felt chilled through and strained to remember the last time he had worn clothes. Each movement set fire to his joints. Exhausted, he lay back, careful not to make a sound. The room was small but had a high angled ceiling which held both shadow and light in equal measure. For a long while he pondered this.

Someone must have brought him to this room and left him. He thought of his previous cell, where he had been confined in darkness between interrogations. How many times had he sat handcuffed to a chair with three faces staring at him from the other side of a broad table? How many times had the man with the swarthy skin and drooping moustache barked the same questions at him? How many times had he been knocked to the floor and beaten unconscious? He remembered that he had tried to keep a count of these and other things: the number of steps between his cell and the interrogation room, the number of bones in the fish soup. At the time these numbers had seemed weighty with meaning. Now he could not think why he had bothered to count anything.

For reasons that escaped him, he was still alive. Why hadn't they killed him? They could have destroyed all evidence of his existence long ago. But if they wanted him dead, surely he would be dead. That meant they wanted him alive.

His mind drifted to thoughts of food and how nice it would be to eat something. Maybe they were watching him starve, just to see how long it would take. But he was no longer that hungry. Food was not a craving, just an idle wish. Something must have happened inside him. His body was shutting down. Perhaps if he refused food and water he would be dead soon and it would be his own doing. Was that what they wanted?

He pulled himself up. He had always taken his body for granted and was never surprised by how easily he met each and every challenge he'd set himself, to be stronger, faster, more nimble than everyone else. Now he was shocked by how skinny he'd become and his flimsy graceless movements. His limbs lacked substance; the bones seemed too close to the surface. His ribs stood out. In school books and on television he had seen photographs of African starvation victims and prisoners released from Nazi concentration camps, and now he envisioned himself like this: haunted sunken eyes, scrawny arms and legs, knobby knees and elbows. He turned over and knelt on the mattress. His penis flopped uselessly between his legs. A memory of adolescent lust and burning sexual arousal set off a buzzing in his head, how he had gripped himself in the night, his brain filled with visions of Nadia—the softness of her skin, the scent of her hair—how he had longed for her touch.

Tears dribbled from his eyes. He swiped at them with the back of his hand and licked them. The salt on his tongue stirred something alive within him. He placed one hand flat on his chest and followed the laboured drumbeat of his heart. His empty stomach moaned.

He stood, swaying on trembling legs, maintaining his balance with effort. This was not a cell. A single door bisected the wall to his left. There were no other details, just the tile, which covered every surface, and the drain hole ringed by brownish stains. A sensation of wet beneath his feet. Insects, a few dead, some still moving.

Then he saw them: beneath the windows, positioned to hold chains that would restrain an adult's raised arms, two ringbolts stood out from the wall.

He moved quickly. The door—whatever promise it held—drew him closer. Surely it was a trap. But he could not stop himself. Standing slightly ajar, it beckoned. He pulled it open.

The room beyond the door had no windows and was pungent with rot. In the near darkness he recognized the shape of an overturned chair. Weak light gleamed on rounded metal surfaces. The floor near his feet was strewn with scraps of paper, odd pieces of building rubble: hunks of wood or brick or concrete—it was impossible to tell. The far wall was veiled in darkness.

He threw the door back and ventured further in, stepping with care. The stench embraced him and stung his eyes. His misgivings were strong, but he understood with a prisoner's instinct that he would not be permitted to roam further than they wanted him to.

A piece of torn cloth under his foot was the sleeve of a shirt that at one time could have been white. He unfolded the lid of a cardboard box and found truncated lengths of chain, twisted shards of metal, all of it coated with rust. In the corner next to this: coils of heavy twine.

Hector turned. His heart accelerated when he saw, at the far end of the room, dimly illuminated by the morning light seeping in from the tiled room, a seated figure hunched over a table. He tensed and waited. But there were no movements. All was silent. This, then, was what he was meant to find. He crept closer. The figure did not move.

It was a man: he could tell that much from the breadth of the back and shoulders and the remnants of beard on the face. A gaping wound had carved out a hollow where one eye and most of the forehead had been. Matted with dried blood, the man's hair was dark and flowed in a braid down the length of his back. The remaining eye was closed but the mouth hung open, as if in the midst of asking a question: *Why?*

Hector recoiled. The reek of death swelled to fill the space around him, seemed to hum in his ears and slither over his feet like a living thing. His attention was drawn by squirming movements within the head wound. A twinge of nausea doubled him over but then passed so quickly that afterward he thought he had imagined it. On the table before him lay the man's last meal: food on a plate. A spoon to eat it with. He almost swooned as saliva surged into his mouth, a torrent that was trickling between his lips before he could stop it. His brain conjured objections—moral, hygienic, cautionary—but was silenced by a painful clamour in his guts. He lifted the plate and spoon from the table and backed slowly away from the body. A Mapuche Indian. Who was he? Why had he been brought here and murdered? But the questions faded from his mind the instant they formed. In his previous life he might have cared.

He retreated to the tiled room and shut the door. Holding his breath, his eyes closed against what the plate held, he brought the spoon to his lips, pushed it into his mouth, licked it clean, and swallowed. Some vestige of reason told him to eat slowly, that his weakened stomach would rebel if asked to process too much too quickly. Between spoonfuls he rested, five, maybe ten minutes, squatting on the pallet, back against the wall, his eyes shut tight. His stomach groaned as it went to work on the first solid nourishment he had consumed in many days. The pasty food was reminiscent of mashed beans. Some firmer bits he chewed with great care. It could be anything. But he would not open his eyes. He would not look. Instead, he imagined fat kernels of corn, chunks of grilled beef, searing hot peppers, an ice-cold beer. Tears poured down his face.

Was it bad luck to eat a dead man's meal?

But he did not want to know the answer to that question.

TWENTY-SEVEN

He had been moved to another cell. It was small and square and absolutely empty. There was nothing to lie on but the floor, which was covered with grit and small stones. Creatures with many legs explored his body. There were too many for him to swat away, so he curled himself into a ball, his hands covering his eyes and nose. Things crawled through his hair, which remained unwashed and uncut. His only relief was to scratch. He scratched until blood flowed. He breathed with difficulty. Mucus poured in a steady stream from his nose and congealed in the hairs on his upper lip and chin. Over many days the damp had seeped into every orifice of his body and now seemed as much a part of him as the thoughts in his head. He slept, but was awakened often by the extreme discomfort of the cold unyielding concrete against his skin. Every muscle ached.

He was afraid that his mind was failing. In waking dreams he saw and felt things that were not there: Nadia leaning over him, playfully brushing her lips against his, Señor Volos smoking a cigarette, the lean, taut body of his brother Carlos illuminated by moonlight, his mother bustling about preparing a banquet for the entire family, his father holding Jorgé by the hand and gazing sternly down at him. His father's eyes were ringed with mascara.

The cell had a single tiny window high in the wall, and they came for him with the first of the morning light, pulling him from where he lay huddled on the damp floor.

They did not bind his hands or cover his head. As he moved Hector was conscious of the weariness in his bones and the blazing irritation of his scalp. Two young soldiers marched with him as he limped along a

187

dark barren corridor. From elsewhere he heard whimpering, voices crying out, occasional bursts of laughter. A soldier sitting at a desk paused in the act of writing to watch him pass by. He had grown insensitive to being the only naked one among many clothed people. Given a bucket and told to urinate, it didn't matter if he was alone or in a hallway full of people, he did so without question or hesitation. Nearby, more laugher rang out and echoed the length of the corridor.

In a room off another corridor they sat him at a table. Someone entered and placed a steaming bowl of beans and rice and a glass of water before him. There was no spoon so he ate with his hands. To his surprise he was hungry, and was disappointed to see how quickly the bowl and the glass emptied. Resigned, he tipped the bowl up to his mouth, licked the last of the juice from his dirty fingers. Finally, he wiped his wet fingers on his chest.

He pushed the hair away from his eyes and raised his head. The two soldiers responded by positioning their hands on their guns. One observed him with an empty expression, his lips barely parted; the other glanced away. Hector stared back at them and scratched his scalp, scratched and scratched until his eyes watered. Then, at a signal from someone he couldn't see, he was told to stand. His hands were manacled behind his back.

They descended several flights of stairs, passed through several doorways, and walked the length of another narrow dimly lit corridor. There were no windows, and when the last door slammed shut behind them the silence was absolute. Again there was grit and moisture beneath his feet. Hector did not think about where he was being taken and noted only that the air was warm, damp, foetid. He walked just ahead of the two soldiers. But when the corridor ended at a small wooden door in a stone wall, he understood that something different was about to happen.

One of the soldiers knocked and the door was opened from the outside. They passed through and Hector was suddenly staggering from a barrage of sensations that were at the same time familiar and impossibly remote. He had the impression of entering a vast covered space—a tent or auditorium. But it was tree branches meeting overhead that formed his ceiling. Beneath his feet a dirt and stone trail wide enough for a single vehicle had been worn into the forest floor. He flipped the hair from his eyes and raised his head to look back at the building he had just exited, but stumbled forward when he was pushed from behind. Trees grew tall to either side. Insects buzzed. Birds twittered. The scent of pine mingled with a rich, complex, subterranean odour, like bog or swamp. Here and there the earth was hidden beneath thickets of ferns. He drew the warm moist air into his lungs and sensed, fleetingly, the strength such air could give him were he to breathe it every day. Glancing upward, he observed through gaps in the foliage a grey sky swarming with clouds. Everything bore traces of recent rainfall. He let his gaze wander. The undergrowth was lush, chaotic, exploding with tender new shoots. A thought formed clumsily and irrationally in his head: here was his chance, to slip in amongst the trees and disappear. If he moved quickly he would take them by surprise. They wore heavy thick-soled boots and carried guns, but he was naked, his body slimmed and hardened by privation. He could easily squeeze between trees and past brambles that would snag their clothes. Would they even bother to pursue him? He had not been asked a single question for days, weeks, months—he didn't know how long. He was of no use to them. What reason could they have for keeping him locked up?

Then it was too late. A hand was on his shoulder, another on his arm. He was forced into the centre of the trail as it curved and sloped gradually upward. Hector heard voices before they rounded the last bend. Then he and the two soldiers emerged into a clearing, where a group of uniformed men lingered, their boots concealed by knee-high grass. Among them Hector recognized the man with the drooping moustache who had led the interrogation sessions, whose name he had learned was Commander Ruivivar. The man's booming voice returned to him, along with the accusations, ridicule, and threats that he had listened to day after day. He shuddered suddenly with shame at his nakedness as cooler breezes swept down from the hill and caressed his exposed skin. Tears leapt into his eyes and he was nearly overcome by faintness. His steps faltered, but he was steadied and propelled forward by the hand on his arm.

Ruivivar turned when their approach was brought to his attention. With one hand he gestured imperiously towards another soldier, who marched quickly down the path.

"My young friend, would you like a cigarette?"

Hector heard Ruivivar's question at the same moment that his eyes met those of the soldier who took charge of him. Distracted by the depth and beauty of the boy's eyes, he found he could not speak. In the pale light of day the boy's unblemished skin was smooth like the creamiest *café con leche* and his irises a luminous shade of aquamarine. Hector had never seen such colour in a person's eyes. The pupils seemed to float within depthless turquoise pools. The upper lip, adorned with pubescent beginnings of a moustache, seemed about to speak, but in the end held still. The spell was broken when the boy glanced away, but he briefly returned a stricken gaze to Hector's face, letting it rest there before tugging on Hector's arm. Transfixed, Hector allowed himself to be led to the crown of the hill, where the others waited.

"Are you deaf, boy? We have enough cigarettes to go around."

"I don't—" But his mind went blank when he noticed that all the soldiers, save for the Commander, cradled rifles in their arms. Most of the group stood regarding him with a kind of haughty disdain, as if his presence was for them a great inconvenience. Two were examining their weapons' barrels and checking sightlines by taking aim towards the line of trees at the horizon. Hector's throat tightened as he sensed the approach of a fate he had failed to anticipate. His brain threw off its mantle of fatigue. Suddenly he was struggling to absorb a profusion of sensory detail, all of it incandescent with meaning. He had never been so aware in his life. Trivialities leapt out at him: the tight weave of the cloth of the soldiers' uniforms, the clicking of rifles being readied for firing, the angled pillars of golden light penetrating the cloud cover, the cool leafy forest smells, minor variations of colour among countless blades of grass, tiny pink and lavender flowers dotting the field. The expression on each soldier's face was something he would never forget. His trembling body cycled between hot and cold; his knees, weakened, threatened to buckle. But he also found unexpected comfort, even pleasure, in the gentle warmth of the boy's hand on his arm.

Ruivivar turned towards Hector and casually thrust a cigarette between his lips.

"Light this, will you?"

The boy dropped Hector's arm and lit a match, which he held up to the cigarette.

"You will not tell us your secrets. So this is how it ends."

"I didn't do anything," Hector said, allowing the cigarette to drop from his mouth. Through the hair falling over his eyes he met and held those of the other. The robust timbre of his own voice surprised him.

The Commander smiled, revealing the row of tobacco-stained teeth with which Hector was already familiar.

"We have your friend's confession."

"He's lying."

Ruivivar gazed upon Hector with an expression of amused contempt before turning away. "Pick that up," he said.

The boy with the aquamarine eyes held the cigarette to Hector's mouth. He parted his lips to receive it. Again their eyes met. Hector felt a strange calm—like warm summer rain—descend over him.

"Do not fool yourself into believing we take care of the likes of you with a firing squad. Such extravagance would be wasteful. In cases like this one bullet will do."

Ruivivar had turned again and now approached Hector with a pistol in his raised hand. Hector noticed that the Commander was wearing black leather gloves.

"Hector Tomás, do you believe in God?"

Hector felt the boy's hand squeeze his arm. He was unable to move or speak.

"If you do not, now would be a good time to start."

He clenched his lips around the cigarette and struggled to fill his head with some final thoughts, but his mind remained steadfastly vacant.

"On your knees. You, back off."

The boy gripped his arm long enough to help Hector lower himself. Then he was gone.

Hector raised his eyes as the muzzle of the gun grazed his forehead. Still holding the cigarette, his lips formed words of which he was only remotely conscious. *Damos vuelta a usted para la protección, madre santa del dios,* he whispered. *Escuche nuestros rezos y ayúdenos en nuestras necesidades. Excepto nosotros de cada Virgen del peligro, gloriosa y bendecida.* He felt neither fear nor sadness, only numbness and mild shock. Life had turned against him. It came down to a bullet in the brain. It hardly seemed to matter, so many others had died ignoble, agonizing deaths. Hector observed the morning light reflected in the shaft of the gun—beyond it the gloved hand and extended arm. His executioner's expression was lost in shadow. Hector closed his eyes.

The echo of the gun's discharge rang in his ears and ricocheted across distant hills. Beneath the reverberation he was dimly aware of laughter and voices. Somehow he was lying on the ground, his shoulder nudging the earth. The stiff grass scratched his skin. A hand tugged his arm and without ceremony dragged him to his feet.

"You can thank Dimitri for preserving your life. He thinks you'll make a fine soldier. Don't disappoint him." Then, to someone else, "Clean him up. Get him some clothes."

He stumbled over soggy terrain and was steadied by the firm hand gripping his arm. Suddenly he was on his knees. The beans he had eaten surged up his gorge and sprang in a torrent from his mouth. For a moment he hovered, coughing and trembling, over the steaming puddle before allowing himself once again to be pulled to his feet. Exhaustion had returned. His limbs quivered from the effort of placing one foot in front of the other.

The morning had turned bright. Ahead, the gap in the line of trees opened to reveal the trail he had followed to get here. He shuffled forward drunkenly, his hands bound behind him, his footing uncertain, his back bent as if under the weight of a heavy load. His throat burned and he coughed again and again, trying to dislodge something. No hands touched him. His vision cloudy, his eyes aimed downward, all he could make out were a few feet of rock-strewn earth and the boots of the soldiers walking beside him. As the sun broke through the clouds he stumbled, fell, and bloodied his knee on loose stone. Someone yanked him up and with a violent push sent him lurching forward. Then a gentle hand took his arm and steered him down the path.

He wept, for he did not know if he had cheated death or if death had cheated him.

TWENTY-EIGHT

White light flooded the room. The tiles were smeared with blood. The smell he had thought was sewer was actually the reek of death.

"With this simple act the process will be complete. I've done all I can. What happens next is up to you."

Hector tilted his head in the direction of the voice telling him he could live. His chest swelled as he drew in a series of deep breaths through his mouth. Sweat dripped from his brow. He lacked stamina because of his torments and had just finished kicking and beating someone who was smaller than him and whose attempts to fight back were comically half-hearted and girlish. The boy, Federico, lay writhing on the floor.

"I understand these choices are hard. I would not want to see you die like your friend. It's unfortunate but it sometimes comes to this. We try to be fair in all things."

Hector let his gaze rest on the dying boy. In his mind he had returned often to the bus station and wondered what might have been had that encounter never taken place. But that was a long time ago. Federico's moans and whimpers filled Hector with loathing. Blood spurted from the boy's nose; his emaciated body was mottled with welts and bruises. His hair was dirty and matted, just as Hector's had been before they had shaved his head and applied salve to his wounds. He was naked, as Hector had been before being given the plain grey shirt and trousers and black boots issued to new recruits.

"We all have choices to make in this life. God asks a lot of us. Some of us are not up to the task. You, Hector—you have proven there is no challenge you cannot face."

Hector relaxed his fists and massaged the bloodstained knuckles of his right hand. He did not take his eyes off Federico and yet in his mind he could see Dimitri roving from corner to corner behind him, pacing back and forth like a caged animal, or a condemned prisoner. But Hector was not afraid. His life had taken a dramatic turn. He had been clothed and fed. His wounds were healing. When he went to sleep tonight he would be warm and dry. He had no intention of dying. The time to be afraid was in the past.

"I will tell you a secret. Commander Ruivivar is impressed. You survived when men twice your age would have given up. That day on the hill, you didn't beg for your life. You were ready to accept your fate, like a true soldier. He said to me afterward, that's when he understood you were going to be useful to us."

Hector moved his head in a barely perceptible nod. Dimitri had taught him many things in a short time. For the months of his captivity he had been confused and afraid. He'd craved an obvious course of action, some way to make them stop, either by killing him or setting him free. Now he knew what he had to do. Federico was the only thing standing in the way of freedom. The choice was not difficult.

"People are ruled by a personal morality, a private code of conduct. I am not against this. But it is unwise to rely on yourself for everything. Just look how easily we are tricked and led astray! The ancient Greeks understood. They knew that the story of human civilization is one of bloodshed and tragedy. We look back now and see that nations fall because people cannot make themselves do what is necessary. They forget that on our own we can only know so much and see so far. In times of anarchy when it is impossible to tell your friend from your enemy, we have to submit to a higher authority. I think you know this."

Federico was quiet. He held one hand over his nose, trying to staunch the flow of blood, and he was breathing through his mouth. His exhausted gaze wandered upward and met Hector's, his eyes moist and rimmed in red. When Hector was shown into the tiled room he had not immediately recognized him, the boy was so thin. But as recognition came it was accompanied by feelings that rushed one upon the other so rapidly and with such violence they almost brought Hector to his knees. The first of these was wonder, for he had assumed without being told that Federico was dead. The second was a visceral abhorrence so powerful it made his hands tremble and set off a thunderous hammering in his brain. It took a few moments, but what finally dawned on him was that a world in which Federico existed was something he could neither comprehend nor tolerate.

Before he knew what he was doing he had grabbed Federico's hair with one hand and was punching him with the other. The boy yelped and twisted, trying to shield himself from the blows. In seconds his nose was gushing blood, and still Hector pounded him without mercy. When Federico slipped in the blood pool and fell to the floor, Hector continued the beating with his feet. Only when he felt himself beginning to grow light-headed and out of breath did Hector pull back and cast a dispassionate eye upon Federico lying curled up on his side, bloody and bawling.

Dimitri, sensing the moment was right, ceased drifting about and stood beside Hector. He didn't like this room, though he understood it was necessary. It was too stark. The bare tile, harsh light, and empty space left him feeling exposed. The bugs made his skin crawl. He preferred the clutter of the torture room.

"Technically," he said, speaking in a low voice and glancing down at the bleeding, moaning Federico, "you are still a prisoner. Anything can happen."

Hector turned. Dimitri met his eyes and was astonished by the shrewd and level gaze with which Hector regarded him. This was better than he had anticipated. After everything he had suffered, Hector Tomás had not been seduced by false hope nor become a sadistic maniac. He was passionate but did not lack self-control. It was a triumph to rival what he had earlier accomplished with Lucas, who had also arrived here from some stinking outpost without the least notion of what life held in store for him. Dimitri swelled with pride. A twinge of admiration for this boy, who had endured months of training masquerading as ill-treatment and yet somehow gained both strength and confidence, tugged at his throat. For a moment he felt teary. Rogue desires flooded his brain, followed by the familiar stirring in his groin. He smiled. He had witnessed Hector naked and bleeding and screaming for mercy. At the sight of the electrodes Hector had grovelled and wept and raved like an animal caught in a snare. But early in their acquaintance Dimitri had spotted in Hector a quality of majestic self-possession, almost an awareness—perhaps a belief—that the things being done to him were necessary for a higher purpose. Instantly Dimitri understood that Hector was among the select and would survive. It was a great relief to be able to make his recommendation to Ruivivar and do it truthfully, because otherwise Hector would have been marched into the forest as so many others had been and treated to a bullet in the brain. At this moment his beautiful body would be mouldering in a mass grave. He had saved the boy's life and basked in the glory of this. But it was also a cause for regret because, not privy to how those in the upper echelons of power made their decisions, Dimitri had no idea where Hector might be assigned. If he were sent away the loss would be great. But, known to be of a lustful as well as sentimental turn of mind, Dimitri had no say in the matter.

But it was so tempting to gaze at him. Dressed and in full possession of his physical and mental self, Hector Tomás was a commanding presence and by far the most alluring of his pupils. In the last few weeks, while tutoring him in the intricate—and intimate—art of persuasion, he had watched Hector gain back the weight he had lost. Still a boy, but on the cusp of manhood. Dimitri licked his lips. Before drawing the knife from his back pocket he allowed his hand to roam along Hector's shoulder to his neck. He caressed the smooth skin above the collar. Hector did not flinch or pull away as Dimitri feared he might.

"You will learn to love pain," he said, taking Hector's hand and placing the knife flat in his bloodstained palm. It was a steel hunting knife of Swiss origin sheathed in black leather that Dimitri, in anticipation of this moment, had purchased at his own expense in the town of Chiachi, ten miles away.

Hector's expression as he gazed at the gift was difficult to read, but Dimitri believed he saw gratitude lurking in the softly tentative upturn of the lips.

"Thank you," Hector said. "I—"

"Please, don't say another word." He had restrained himself to this point. But the moment was too important. He approached Hector, placed a hand on either side of his head, looked into his eyes, and kissed him on both cheeks.

"You will use this wisely, I know," he said, turning quickly and pretending to scratch the side of his face as he wiped away a tear. "I pray you remain with us."

The two men—for with this gesture Dimitri felt he had done everything in his power to usher Hector into the blessed state of manhood—separated and exchanged a lengthy gaze of fellowship and complicity.

"I will leave you now to complete your task," he said, glancing one last time at the unfortunate Federico, who had dragged himself into a corner. A persistent whine issued from the boy's smashed mouth. His leg appeared to be broken. His face and chest were covered with blood. Dimitri's lip curled with distaste.

He knocked lightly and the heavy door was pulled opened. He stepped through, but glanced over his shoulder in time to see Hector advancing on the doomed boy, the unsheathed knife in his hand.

TWENTY-NINE

Enrique checked the press of his suit in the full-length mirror that hung on the back of his office door. In a short time he would be meeting with Nadia Wladanski and he wanted to look his best. This morning he had settled on an Irish wool blend dyed a sober dark grey with an ivory pinstripe to give it a hint of dash. These days he was more conscious than ever of what it took to make himself presentable. After a security checkpoint was installed at the end of the street the cleaning service where he had taken his clothes for half his life had shut down for good. Now Enrique cleaned and ironed and mended his clothes himself, but at least it was one aspect of his life that had not gone completely to pot. For a variety of reasons he still prided himself on his appearance and spent an hour or more each morning preparing for the outside world that each day became more nightmarish and menacing.

He returned to his desk and sat down and took another sip from the cup of coffee he had purchased on his walk to the campus that morning. His head buzzed with nervous energy in anticipation of his meeting with Nadia, but there was no way to deny that he was exhausted. Sporadic gunfire had once again ripped through the night, interrupting his already fractured sleep. Very early that morning, while it was still dark, he had sat staring out the bedroom window, which provided a semi-obstructed view of the military checkpoint at the corner where Rua Santa Maria met Avenida Independencia. There were not many cars, but every vehicle that came along was stopped. Every driver was questioned. Finally Enrique had dozed off in the chair, waking a couple of hours later with a crick in his neck and drool seeping from the corner of his mouth.

For the first months of the power share the citizens of B—— enjoyed relative peace. For them, the trouble was elsewhere. Seeing little evidence of insurgency or a rebel presence in their own back yard, people questioned the official line. Soldiers and guns and identity checks were constant irritants and, given that nothing appeared to be going on, seemed unreasonable and excessive. As the weeks passed people grew edgy and combative. But the army had its supporters, and almost every night in the city's bars and *tavernas* disagreements erupted over the military presence. More often than not these led to fistfights that spilled into the street. Then spring came, and as the weather grew warm the rebels stepped up their offensive, bombing train lines and blockading highways. Suddenly the movement of goods throughout the whole country slowed to a trickle. From north to south, empty store shelves stayed that way through one whole month and into the next. Panic led to protests, riots, and looting. Miraculously B—— remained immune to the unrest, and its citizens, watching the reports of violence on television, shook their heads and clucked their tongues at the senseless rage of their compatriots. Then the war changed, and when the fighting moved north, B—— got the worst of it. A series of bloody rebel attacks shocked everyone and accomplished what the government could not by silencing the voices of dissent. Night after night army artillery rained down upon rebel positions in the hills.

At the Archives, it was a rare morning that staff complaints over the straitened circumstances of life in B—— grew loud enough to reach Enrique through the door of his office—and even if they had he would have closed his ears against them. In the building where he worked, which also housed the library and some faculty offices, Enrique heard little talk of the army and the new powers it held. Few were willing to risk drawing the attention of the military officials who freely roamed the campus. The University of B——, already distrusted by the military and regarded as a hotbed of radical sentiment and a sanctuary for rebel sympathizers, had come under scrutiny in the early days after the takeover, and remained open only after student protests had been quashed and a command post established in the main administration building. A colonel had moved in with an entourage of armed subordinates, forcing the president into a leaky windowless storage room in the basement where broken and rusted furniture was kept. Snap inspections and random searches took place any time day or night. Enrique had no idea if the searches were yielding damning evidence, but one day while returning to his office after lunch, he had witnessed a well-known professor of economic history being hustled out of the building by a group of armed thugs—handcuffed, his nose bloodied—and unceremoniously pitched into the back of a black unmarked van. In the stairwells and washrooms of the building, one still heard grumblings about injustice and the tyranny of force. But this was the sort of talk that placed anyone within earshot under suspicion. Those foolish enough to voice such opinions out in the open, even in a whisper, were shunned by those who did not share their views or who were simply afraid and wanted to stay out of trouble.

Under such circumstances Enrique had no regrets about sending his family to Puerto Varas. Their safety was worth any price. But he had not been able to adapt to the silence that now swamped the flat in an enervating murk, a dense and heavy stillness so absolute he sometimes thought he was going deaf. Even the tension of the office was preferable to this. He'd never imagined he could hunger for the steely edge of Lucinda's tongue (which had kept him ever on the alert, a snide rejoinder ready on his lips) or mark longingly the absence of his daughters' chatter, which he had so often railed against. After Hector's sudden (but necessary) departure and Dulciana's marriage to Roberto, Julio, at least, had grown to prefer silent, solitary amusements, until last year when he had taken it into his head to emulate some scruffy American troubadour and enrolled for after-school guitar lessons. Having lost so much, Enrique had not had the heart to dissuade him, and he'd breathed a sigh of relief as he watched the guitar being loaded into the train—knowing that in a day or two it would be a thousand miles away. But only a week ago, as he sat in his armchair reading, there had been a moment when Enrique found himself close to tears, an absurd ache gripping his heart at the memory of his youngest son's inept plucking and tuneless crooning.

It was true that he was lonely. But just because the world was full of brutes and thugs, and people disappeared without a trace, and the simple act of shutting your front door behind you had become an act fraught with risk, this was no reason for him to let his sartorial standards decline. If anything, he had redoubled his efforts and appeared in his office spiffier and more stylish than in the past. As a supervisor, he wanted his staff to know that he was not afraid, that it was business as usual, that he would provide a buttress if need be. It was the least he could do for them since, truth be told, he did very little that could be regarded as work. And today he was lunching with young Nadia Wladanski, whose passions needed reigning in and yet whose charms were undeniable. Out of nowhere she had called him and asked to meet. Suddenly his sagging spirits were buoyed. Perhaps she had news. Or maybe she just wanted to talk. It didn't matter. Here, at long last, was something to anticipate and relish. So today of all days he had every reason to keep up appearances.

It was time to go. He closed the door to his office and jiggled the knob to make sure it was locked. Once the elevator had let him out in the lobby, he put on his gloves and sunglasses. He checked his appearance again, in a section of mirrored glass near the main exit: he had dressed as any man would who was going to be spending time with an attractive young woman over lunch. The glasses, he decided, completed the picture. He looked distinguished enough to be meeting with diplomats.

It was a crisp autumn day. He had left himself plenty of time and had no need to rush. As he walked past the stately buildings of the university he kept his head down, avoiding the glances of soldiers patrolling the campus. He knew that luck was the only reason he had not attracted their interest.

With his research at a standstill and yet cursed with a brain that could not be quieted, Enrique's fears for his family's well-being became the intellectual fuel that kept him going from one day to the next. After everything, he still looked forward to walking to and from the university, but as he walked all sorts of calamities and accidents sprang fully formed from his lively imagination and played themselves out in his mind. On top of the countless mundane mishaps that can take a life prematurely (car crashes, falling down the stairs, food poisoning) his worries were magnified by an escalating civil conflict in which rebel raids and military reprisals were daily occurrences. He said to himself, "Don't be a fool. This is what it is like to be a parent in dangerous times." But for him the dangers were not hypothetical. He could not leave behind the tangible losses he had suffered or the burden of unanswered questions that accompanied him everywhere he went. The photograph in his wallet—the last one of the whole family together—was creased and worn thin from excessive handling. He refused to give up hope that someday he would discover what fate had befallen Carlos. Hector's absence was easier to accept, for he considered Hector out of harm's way. But a turning point came with the Envigado bus station bombing, which claimed the lives of twenty-four innocent people. Like many of his countrymen, Enrique Tomás would never forget where he was and what he was doing at the moment he learned of that hideous tragedy.

News of the attack galvanized a nation already reeling from a currency crisis and still trying to adjust to the unwelcome sight of armed soldiers on every street corner. As terrorist attacks go, it was regarded as crude and senseless. But as the damage was assessed and the death toll counted, it became apparent that the country was grappling with an enemy that operated completely in the shadows, that could claim within its ranks the expertise needed to plan elaborate acts of terror, and possessed a sinister capacity to set these plans into motion. Early press reports called the Envigado bombing craven and inhuman. Later, even while the dead were being buried, Enrique shuddered with revulsion when he heard a report describing it as "bold but reckless." All agreed, however, that at every stage of its planning and execution, the goal was to kill as many people as possible. It made front-page news and condemnation poured in from around the world. Reserves were mobilized and a new influx of soldiers swarmed the streets of every city in the country. Special units rounded up hundreds of people whose activities and connections placed them under suspicion. A strict curfew was imposed.

For Enrique, the bombing was too close to home. Claudia and Francisco's farm was remote and isolated, but he knew that Francisco brought his produce to the Envigado market on Saturday, and Claudia had written that Hector had become like Francisco's right arm. Images flooded his mind: of Hector swept up in a stampede as panic gripped all of Envigado and people fled for their lives; of Hector prone on a hospital gurney, bloodied and unconscious; of Hector's inert form being zipped into a vinyl body bag. For most of that afternoon, while muddled and conflicting reports spewed from the radio, he paced the flat, smoked an entire package of Derby king-size cigarettes, and a hundred times picked up the telephone and a hundred times put it down. He wanted information on Hector but didn't know who to call, and again and again he cursed Francisco for waging his absurd and futile battle against modern technology. The country's inefficient and primitive *Telefonica* system was poleaxed by the crisis, and when he tried to call Lucinda in Puerto Varas the lines were so clogged he couldn't get through. By early evening he knew that Lucinda would have worked herself into a frenzy. The pressure in his skull was building. He was hanging on by a thread. Maybe Hector had been able to reach her in Puerto Varas. But he knew nothing for sure. His isolation was so complete he might as well have been on the moon. It was getting dark and the phones were still not working. Going out and walking around the block would ease the pressure, but what if someone was trying to get through to him? How could he not be here when Hector called? Or what if it was someone else trying to call, what if Hector was not all right? One thing was clear. He had to confirm the thing he feared most: that Hector had been in the town at the time of the bombing. But how was he to do this?

Finally, a dial tone. He had the phone in his hand. He would call Lucinda right this minute. He would assure her that he was doing everything possible to find out if Hector was all right. But he still had to do think of how he was going to say this.

Then someone was pounding on the door. Who could it be?

The poor waiflike creature stood in the hall in blue jeans and an oversize hand-knitted sweater. Tears streamed down her face. Her hair was going every which way. "Is Hector all right?" she cried as she rushed at him. She banged her fists against his chest. "What do you know that you're not telling me?" Then she collapsed, weeping, in his arms.

The memory of Nadia Wladanski's slender body crushed against his own more substantial one was not just pleasurable; it was significant because it was the only time in their acquaintance that she had lost herself to him completely, and he still cherished the dizzying rush of power that had swept over him as her weeping intensified and the heat and animal scent of her skin rose into his nostrils. Since that day they had met several times but, to his regret, never embraced. Poised and calm, never again had she been as helplessly reliant on his good graces. Ridiculously, he often dreamed of that moment and entertained a furtive hope that it might be repeated.

On the day of the bombing, Enrique's dithering had threatened to make a bad situation worse. However, much as Lucinda's had on the day of the mock interview, Nadia's arrival rescued him from the ineptness that always seemed to plague him at times of crisis. Until he opened the door to her (someone had taken pity and let her into the building), he had been unable to act. The situation was too extreme and the questions whirling about in his mind too numerous. He had no idea where to start. But when he had calmed her, helped dry her eyes, and explained the situation, Nadia suggested in a quivering voice that surely someone living nearby Claudia and Francisco's farm would own a telephone. He gazed at her in amazement. Why had *he* not thought of this? Enrique recalled the bundle of Claudia's letters in his dresser drawer. Looking through these, he found references to a woman named Carissa Villégas. The name came up again and again. Carissa—Claudia's friend and great comfort—had taken her here, Carissa had taken her there. In one letter Claudia boasted that Carissa and her husband owned a resort. Nadia was able to make a series of phone calls, at the end of which he found himself speaking to this very Carissa. As he pleaded with Carissa to find out from Claudia if Hector had been anywhere near the blast, his eyes insisted on straying in Nadia's direction.

Because Nadia was exquisite in her torment. While he talked, she hugged a pillow and rocked back and forth on the sofa, tears staining her face. It troubled and perplexed him, how she had grown. Her lips and cheeks had filled out, but her features retained an exquisite delicacy. In seconds his heart was reaching out to her. Where were the girl's parents? Why was *he* her last resort? In the meantime Carissa said hardly a word and seemed annoyed by his request (What *had* Claudia told her about him?). She was busy, the resort was full. All these people were making plans to leave the country. Later. She would do it later. *Bitch!* he almost spat into the phone, *If only you could see the pain you're causing.* But he choked back his irritation and assumed the tone of frosty restraint he used when negotiating his way through thorny issues at work, angling the instrument away from his ear slightly so she would catch Nadia's sobs. Finally, with a noisy exhalation, Carissa relented. She would drop everything and go to the farm right now.

They spent the evening and well into the night in the shared agony of awaiting Carissa's return call. Given the circumstances, the time was—for him—filled with an improbable union of bliss and anguish. In his memory, every second they were together carried special significance, and afterward played and replayed itself in his mind with the shimmering clarity of a fully experienced moment. Months later he could recall every word that had come out of her mouth, silent looks and gestures, the way her eyes danced when she smiled. He often thought fondly of the way her hair fell across her forehead, and that darling flutter of the wrist that seemed to be a nervous tick.

One moment she would be pouting like a little girl, and the next he would catch her regarding him in a manner that suggested womanly self-possession. Unaccountably, from their previous meetings (that regrettable encounter at the café with Jorgé, the two or three times she'd brought him letters she wanted passed along to Hector; and then there was that day only a few months ago when he'd taken her to the theatre café and tried to console her) he had retained an image of a spindly teenager with ringlets in a schoolgirl dress, all knees and elbows. But the creature who burst in on him the afternoon of the Envigado bombing had blossomed into a lovely young woman. A confusion of emotion swept over him as he realized how swiftly and profoundly time had altered her. He could offer comfort, yes, but was it proper for him to hold her in his arms? She was not his daughter. And yet, easily enough, she could be. He wanted to cancel out her pain. He wanted her to smile. He wanted her to eat something. But beneath the paternal instincts lurked something less admirable, something monstrous and grubby that he hardly dared acknowledge.

The hours passed and the apartment grew warm. She pulled off her sweater and socks and leaned back dejectedly with a soft moan against the arm of the sofa, her head resting on her hand, completely unaware of the effect her bare feet and slender T-shirt-clad body had on him. He averted his eyes.

For a long time they were silent. Unable to bear the reports of mounting casualties, he had switched off the radio. Then, unaccountably, she was crying, and he had no choice but to go to her and wrap his arms around her. "There, there," he murmured foolishly, feeling her heat. She clung to him. With great effort he turned his mind to his daughters, to Lucinda, a thousand miles away, no doubt crying just like this. But he was aware of his hands and the proximity of Nadia's flesh.

Then, like a revelation, the events of the day reaffirmed themselves in his consciousness, and he was shamed by these crude inclinations that too often shut down his intellect and left him salivating like an animal. He held his breath, determined not to defile their budding friendship with imaginary glimpses of her peeling off her undergarments. But the instant he let down his guard the very image he sought to avoid bobbed into view. He willed his mind blank. He knew that she would leave as soon as they received word that Hector was safe. With luck he would never see her again. But in a minute he was wondering, when *would* he see her again? In his head he concocted scenario after scenario that would bring them together.

He panicked whenever their dialogue grew desultory and her gaze drifted towards the window. In his desperation not to be a bore, he scoured his reserves of useless knowledge for topics that would interest her. When they had exhausted these and also spoken at length of Hector, her family and their struggles, the weather, he asked her about herself, what she did for fun, and was delighted with the peals of disbelieving laughter that issued forth when he revealed complete ignorance of popular movie stars and musicians. She reeled off the names, and he hadn't a clue. How could he not know who this one was, or that one? He revelled in her, relieved that they could put aside their grief for a few moments. He enjoyed being chided by her and found that by exaggerating his disdain of modern music and motion pictures, the reward was the thrill of hearing her laugh.

But when they grew quiet, her reason for being there would creep up on him, and his anxieties would return. Noticing her colour rise at any mention of the army or politics, he deflected her attempts to steer the talk in that direction.

In the midst of their vigil neither of them wanted to leave the flat and risk missing the call, so as the evening drifted towards night he allowed her to contrive a meal for them out of a few slices of stale bread, a jar of pickles, and a tin of corned beef.

By the time the phone rang it was very late. In a clipped voice, Carissa informed him that she had been to the farm. Claudia was clearly upset by what had happened and would not let her inside, so she had not seen Hector for herself, but Claudia had repeated over and over that everything was fine. Everything was fine. Enrique should not worry.

Enrique rang a taxi for Nadia, but he was on the phone with Lucinda when she left to go home, with only minutes to spare before the curfew would take effect. They had embraced lightly at the good news, and while he savoured the contact he did not have the heart to watch her go and only waved over his shoulder when she called goodbye from the entryway.

Now, strolling to his rendezvous with Nadia Wladanski, it had been four and a half months since the Envigado bombing. Strangely, with all the unrest, Enrique had attained a plateau of serenity. For the moment he felt settled and at peace. Lucinda and the children remained in Puerto Varas, where regular contact assured him they were safe. A pause of several weeks in Claudia's correspondence had caused him some concern. He had expected mail service to suffer disruptions, but when a month passed with no word he began to worry. If Claudia's letters were not getting through, then his own were probably going astray as well, along with the money enclosed with them. Or maybe she and Francisco were having second thoughts about the arrangement. Maybe Hector had become a burden they were unwilling to bear. For a few weeks he sent nothing at all as he waited to hear from her. Then it occurred to him, with travel more dangerous than ever before, he did not want Hector attempting the trip home. If Claudia was under the impression that he had abruptly terminated their arrangement, which she might be since he had not written, she might send Hector on his way. Finally, as a last resort, he had written a letter apologizing for the lapse in correspondence and offering to double the amount he sent each month. A time went by before she countered asking for triple, which he agreed to, and ever since then her letters had arrived weekly, letters that went on and on, brimming with lavish and improbable praise for Hector. She rambled, groping, he imagined, for something new to say, filling page after page with mundane details that were of no interest, repeating things she'd no doubt forgotten had been reported in earlier letters. He already knew the boy was an expert goatherd, carpenter, and baker's assistant—he didn't need to hear it again; and surely Hector had not added weaver and stonemason to his list of accomplishments. Soon he gave up trying to read them all the way through. He put it down to old age. They were simple country people, his aunt and uncle, superstitious, devout, trustworthy. It was just her way of giving him something for his money. And though the money was significant, he considered it a small price to pay to provide a safe haven for a boy who, left to his own devices, didn't know how to stay out of trouble.

In B—— the dusk-to-dawn curfew was still in effect but, for whatever reason, people seemed to enjoy greater latitude in their movements about town. There was just one thing troubling him at the moment: maybe it was his overactive imagination, but had more soldiers been deployed in the city, and were they really as young and frightened as they seemed?

On the other hand, anyone on the outside looking in would think the situation had improved. The highways and railways damaged in the insurgency had been repaired. Shops were lavishly stocked with goods. People walking in the street joked and laughed. For the time being the rebels had backed off from the grand symbolic gesture and instead seemed content to cause the army occasional minor irritation: a random sniper attack, an ambushed supply convoy. Enrique had to admit that there were lots of things worse than having one's sleep interrupted by occasional gunfire.

In the last several months he and Nadia had developed the kind of rapport that occasionally evolves between siblings who are separated by a vast difference in age. Maybe they were not intimate. Maybe they did not exchange secrets. But they shared a mutual concern, and this brought them together on occasions when they had no one else to talk to. Undeniably, he enjoyed being with her and had flattered himself with the whimsical notion that people who saw them together might think they were lovers. Not only did he groom himself carefully on these occasions, but after the first time so did she, for his benefit (he imagined) putting aside the tawdry attire of the modern student—ragged jeans, flat shoes, tights with holes in them, reams of jangling costume jewellery—and dressing herself tastefully in a blouse, skirt, and, the last time, even fashionable high-heeled boots. To his delight she had become adept in the use of makeup. He imagined her borrowing her older sister's things and, seeing himself as an inspiration to her, even entertained the idea of a shopping expedition so she could have some things of her own.

But recently he'd noticed a subtle change in her demeanour towards him. A quality of disdainful coolness had crept into her manner that, when he caught sight of it, made his neck prickle where the collar chafed his skin. A few times he had noticed her smiling as he spoke, when she thought perhaps he wasn't looking, not in silent agreement but as if he were saying no more and no less than what she might expect of someone of his age and temperament. He'd made a comment about young men with long hair who couldn't keep their opinions to themselves, who went on underground radio stations spewing inflammatory rhetoric about human rights and insulting the generals. Maybe he was risking her friendship, but he would not hide the contempt he felt for people so stupid they hurled provocations at a military regime that already needed no justification to make everyone's lives more difficult than they already were. He did not enjoy living under military occupation any more than the next person, but causing trouble would solve nothing and probably make it worse. "You might as well protest the sun and the moon and the stars," he'd said, and she'd diverted her gaze and seemed to roll her eyes. For a moment neither of them spoke, and then she made an apparently innocent remark about someone at school, a girl whose boyfriend had received his conscription notice. But in his struggle to ignore a gesture he could not help but find insulting, he'd hardly heard her. It seemed to imply a kind of ironic distance had opened up between them, which he found both frightening and repulsive. It was as if she'd been sitting in judgment of him all along, and now that all the evidence was in had delivered a verdict that was not in his favour. They'd parted amicably, but the gesture replayed itself in his mind afterward and had haunted him ever since. Did she take him seriously, or was he a distraction, a way to kill time when she had nothing else to do? Did she talk about him with her other friends?

During the weeks that followed he wavered back and forth between a desperate longing to hold her close, and a desire to push her away towards whatever fate awaited her. He wanted to never hear from her again, and he wanted her with him always. He understood of course that she would tire of him sooner or later, and hoped that when this happened she would continue with her studies and perhaps accompany her sister to America. But to lose her to a band of renegades with crazy notions and no regard for their own safety would be excruciating, like a stake through his heart. So when Nadia phoned and asked to see him, he could not help but anticipate the meeting with his customary excitement tempered with dread. He knew her family was suffering, but in her voice he detected more than the usual signs of stress and exhaustion. It was as if the youth were being drained out of her. He wanted to see her immediately, but because she was so adamant he agreed to the time and place she suggested, which was a week hence in the tiny bistro near the train station. Yes, he said, he knew it. But it was an odd choice, and he wondered silently, why there? What was wrong with their usual place? But he went along with it. She seemed on edge, and he thought that if he pressed her with questions she would back out and he might never see her again. Afterward he wondered when he had become so dependent on her, fearing her disdain, in thrall of her choices. How had he become so vulnerable?

T he train station was heavily patrolled, and the restaurant catered to a mix of military types and civilians. In the French style, the tables were small and round, fashioned out of wrought iron with glass tops. At such a table two could share a snack but risked bumping elbows with every move. The weather was pleasantly cool and yet warm enough at mid-day to allow for outside dining, but she was not at one of tables on the sidewalk. Enrique threaded his way between these and entered the building, removing his sunglasses as the doors swung shut behind him.

At first he did not recognize her, and then momentarily found himself doubting it was her. She was seated at the very back, dressed sedately, in sober dusky shades. Unlike him, she had kept her sunglasses on, and as he watched she sipped pink liquid from a martini glass. *That is not a girl,* was the thought that crossed his mind, as he dismissed the possibility that this woman was eighteen-year-old Nadia Wladanski. But she had said she would be here when he arrived. Not many of the tables were occupied, and he counted only two other women in the place, neither of whom resembled the girl he knew in any respect whatsoever.

She smiled when he came up to her and stood so he could kiss her cheek. She wore a stylish suit, with a short pleated skirt, black nylons, ankle-high black leather boots with spike heels. A pair of black leather gloves lay folded neatly together on the table. He removed his coat and hung it from the hook on the wall next to their table. A glass ashtray held two recently stubbed-out cigarette butts, their filters circled with red lipstick. Most alarmingly, the long girlish hair had been cut so short it barely covered her ears. Her exposed neck distressed him in ways he would not have been able to explain to anyone, including himself.

"I surprised you, didn't I?"

212

"You surprise me Nadia, always," Enrique declared. He sat down and looked at her.

Nadia cupped her hand and spread her fingers in a gesture of presentation. "Don't you like the new me?"

"Nadia, who are you? What have you become?"

"I'm disappointed. I thought you would like it. I was bored with myself. I wanted a change. It was time for the hair to go. Nothing would satisfy me until I had it all cut off."

She seems so cool, he thought, and then realized it was calculated, artificial, deliberately and excessively dramatic. It had to be a game. Well, he would play along.

Without warning the waiter was at his side. Enrique accepted the menu but did not take his eyes from her.

"What are you drinking?"

"Oh, this is just a Shirley Temple."

"How about a real drink? I'm going to have one."

He tried to read her response, but the sunglasses hid her expression from him. Perhaps she would see now that he had no intention of backing down from the challenge she posed.

"Order something for me," she said, smiling and tilting her head slightly.

"Take this away." He indicated the martini glass. "And bring two vodka tonics. Lemon with mine."

He looked at her.

"Mine too," Nadia said, hesitating only briefly.

"And for lunch?"

Enrique's faint hope of sharing a pleasant meal with an attractive young woman was fast eroding. Before Nadia could speak he dropped the menu on the table and snapped, "We'll decide later."

"Mademoiselle?"

"I said we'll decide later."

Enrique turned to confront the man, who was young and sported a closely cropped moustache. The white frilly shirt and undersized black vest did nothing for him. The man gave a respectful nod in Enrique's direction, and it dawned on him that he had been afraid up until now. But he was afraid no longer.

"Please just bring our drinks. We'll decide on food in a few minutes."

The man took the martini glass half filled with pink froth and left.

"I'm sorry, Nadia. I hope you're not famished. I'll call him back if you like."

"No, it's all right. He was being a bit pushy."

Enrique smiled, though he didn't understand what she meant. The man had behaved impeccably.

"I hope you don't think I'm being rude," he said, forging onward, "but do you think you could take off those ridiculous glasses? I'd like to be able to see your eyes."

He noticed then, in the smile that came and went and came again, that he had finally succeeded in flustering her. He had attained the upper hand. In that brief moment, she didn't know what to do.

She reached into her purse, which sat on the floor, and retrieved a glasses case.

"It's too dark in here anyway," she said, removing the glasses and putting them away. She took the opportunity to drop the gloves into the purse as well. When she was done she folded her hands on the table and looked him full in the face. "Is this all right?"

Her eyes, heavily but not garishly made up, were beautiful. She could have been twenty-five or older. She looked nothing like the girl he had spent an afternoon with four and a half months ago. He might not have known her if he'd passed her in the street.

"Yes," he said. "Thank you."

The waiter brought their drinks and silently placed them on the table. Enrique lifted his glass and clinked it against hers before taking a sip. Nadia squeezed the lemon wedge and with an expectant gaze watched the juice flow into the glass. Then she stirred the drink around with the plastic stick.

"Now," he began, "I want you to tell me what's going on with you."

"I don't know what you mean."

"Oh, come on. The clothes, the hair. You can't afford any of this. I can't imagine what your parents think."

"My parents don't think anything."

Suddenly afraid for her, he reached across the table and took her hand. "Are they all right?" he asked. "Your father's not sick is he?"

"They're fine, as far as I know. I've left home."

She removed her hand from his and lifted the drink. He watched her take a long sip. When she put it down, the rim of the glass was smudged with lipstick. In an instant he saw his advantage slip away.

"Why? What happened?"

In response she reached into her purse again and retrieved a package of cigarettes. The unhurried coolness was back. She observed him closely as she tipped a cigarette out of the package and placed it between her lips. Without thinking he took his lighter from his pocket and lit the cigarette for her.

"Nothing happened. I just can't live that life anymore."

"It's the only life you have. Everything else is a dream."

"No. That life doesn't exist anymore. You're dreaming if you think it does."

He lifted his glass and was surprised to find it empty. The constriction in his throat made it difficult to speak, but somehow he managed to say, "My God, Nadia, what have you done?"

She leaned across the table and lowered her voice. "I've done the only thing I can do and still live with myself. I'm going help get this country out of the hands of tyrants."

She was serious. He was suddenly very warm. He had to think.

"Is it too late to get you out of this mess? Is there anything I can do? You can live with me. I'll keep you safe. If you want me to, I'll try to get you out of the country—"

She leaned back. There was no change in her expression.

"I'll have the soup," she said.

"And you sir?"

He hadn't noticed the waiter return. The restaurant had filled up. Two soldiers were settling into their seats at the next table, within earshot. It occurred to him that he had to get her out of here.

"I'll have another drink. And . . . oh, how about the spinach salad?" He had no intention of eating anything.

"Very good."

For a moment they looked at each other across the table. Enrique turned away and covered his anguish by lighting a cigarette for himself. His hands were trembling. When he lifted his gaze she was still staring at him, posed with the hand holding the cigarette beside her face, the elbow resting in the palm of the other hand. She was not smiling.

"They arrested my mother and my father," she said.

He nodded. It was obvious that something had happened. He should have expected this.

"They came in the middle of the night and smashed the door down. My father's so worn out he couldn't do anything to stop them. He didn't put up a fight or resist them at all, but they beat him anyway. They dragged him outside and threw him into a van. My mother . . . they didn't want my mother. They only wanted him. But she went after them and made so much noise they threw her into the van too. I screamed and screamed, but they paid no attention. Poor Magda was hiding under the bed. She wet herself."

Enrique asked, though he knew there was no answer, "Why would they do this?"

She gave a little shrug. "Because my father comes from Poland. Because he talks with an accent and doesn't know the language like he should. Because we live in a house with an odd number. Because the grass is green. Because it rained on Tuesday. I don't know."

Enrique allowed his glance to veer in the direction of the two soldiers at the next table. They were chatting and joking. With their hair neatly trimmed and their broad shoulders and the clean cut of their uniforms, he would not have been disappointed to see one of his own daughters holding the arm of either of them.

He started as if out of a reverie when the waiter appeared and placed the drink on the table in front of him.

"It wasn't them," she said.

"What?"

Her eyes flitted briefly in the direction of the soldiers. "Boys like these would never do the things that were done to us. The men who arrested my father were no different than criminals. Trained kidnappers. They were dressed in black and carried clubs and automatic weapons. The van was black and had no markings. They weren't soldiers."

And in Enrique's mind the night of his eldest son's arrest played itself through yet again, when men matching the same description had burst into the flat and taken Carlos away.

"Onion soup," the man said, setting the bowl on the table before Nadia. "And spinach salad." He set the plate down. "Would either of you like freshly ground pepper?"

Nadia continued to gaze at Enrique, making no response to the question and no move towards the food.

"Thank you, no," Enrique said, answering for both of them. "But I'll have another drink."

The man gave a quick nod and was gone.

"Nadia, is there anything I can do?"

"Anyway, it's not like I was recruited or pressured into doing something I didn't want to do, if that's what you're worried about. I went looking and found someone who could help me become part of the . . . cause, or whatever you want to call it."

He nodded. Resignation and weariness swept over him and for a moment he thought he would topple off the chair. "Where's your sister?"

Nadia tapped the ash off the end of the cigarette. "With a friend."

He nodded again, understanding. "What about Carmel and . . . ?"

"Raoul. His security pass was revoked. I don't know what happened. I've lost contact with them."

"Is there any chance—" He almost couldn't ask the question, but then pressed on. "Is there a chance your parents will be released soon?"

Suddenly the drink was before him on the table. He hadn't noticed its arrival. Numbed, he lifted it dutifully to his lips.

"We don't know where they are. We don't know why they were taken. We don't know who did it. No one will tell us anything."

He didn't nod this time. He had the feeling she was observing him again, looking for weaknesses. Well, he had plenty of those.

He lifted his fork. Nadia stubbed out her cigarette and lit another.

"Please, Nadia. You have to eat. Let me do this for you if I can't do anything else."

But it was like she hadn't heard. She made no move towards her lunch. Instead, she tilted her head and took a drag on the cigarette and let her gaze fall somewhere beyond his right shoulder. He poked around in the salad but couldn't bring himself to put any of it into his mouth. For several minutes they were silent. Words and phrases from nearby conversations caught his ear: babies, the local soccer league, somebody's birthday, the price of a loaf of bread. Then, suddenly, his glass was empty. He set it down and shook his head to think a world filled with such banalities could unleash its horrors in totally unexpected ways.

"If you need a place to stay—" But he knew it was pointless.

"I'll tell you something," she began. He felt the coolness of her manner sucking the marrow from his bones. It was like he had never known her. How could he have imagined he had? "I shouldn't tell you anything because it will only upset you. But I owe you this much." She leaned forward again and lowered her voice. "There's so much going on they're probably not watching you right now. But your turn will come. Everyone at the university is under suspicion. I know you think there's nothing about you that could interest them. But it's part of what they do. They let you think you're safe. Why would they be interested in you? For one thing when Carlos disappeared you made inquiries. There's a police file on that. The other thing is you have property. Anyone with property is of interest. And anyone who works with books, anyone who teaches, anyone in a position to influence the minds of young people is of interest. You're my friend, Enrique, and I love you, but you are already in danger. At some point they will get to you. You're just what they're looking for. You have to save yourself before it's too late."

The turmoil of his emotions at that moment was so great that he was surprised to find himself standing, dumbly gazing around. Her words—incomprehensible as they were—struck him like a slap in the face. He felt old and out of his depth. Nothing made sense any more. It was as if he'd awakened to find himself a character in a film. Surely she was wrong, or at the very least exaggerating. Looking at her gazing up at him he understood now—too late—that he had known without being told that she loved him. He had been waiting, hoping that she would say it and spare him the humiliation of saying it first, but he'd known it all along.

He straightened his tie, cleared his throat, and sat down.

"My God, Nadia. You must know I love you too. I don't care about myself. I want to find some way to save you. That's all I want."

He tried to snatch her hand but she pulled away from him.

"Don't be so dramatic," she said, with a hint of irritation in her voice that had not been there before. "You make a display in public and we're both in trouble."

Like a chastened youngster he fidgeted in his chair and peeked from side to side to see if anyone had noticed.

"How do you know all this?" he asked in a near whisper.

"It doesn't matter. What you need to know is that every moment you spend ignoring what I just told you brings you closer to being arrested. People deceive themselves with wishful thinking. Things are much worse than it looks on the surface. You have to accept that and start making plans. Only, you can't do anything that will tip them off. Act normally. Go to work. Take a walk. Talk to people. But at the same time make whatever arrangements you have to."

He nodded in a distracted fashion, not accepting a word of it, but unwilling to dismiss her advice altogether.

Then, with a swift glance over his shoulder, he was gripped by a sudden comprehension.

He leaned across the table and almost spat the words into her face. "We're being watched right now, aren't we?" Inexplicably, he was angry with her. He didn't know if she was deliberately trying to mislead him, but he was sure she was not being completely honest. "Your friends are here keeping an eye on things. Which ones are they?"

He was in the process of turning to get a better look at the occupants of the room when she gripped his wrist and dug her fingernails into his flesh. The pain brought tears to his eyes and quieted him instantly.

Her lips were next to his ear. The warmth of her breath caressed him as she enunciated each word with care.

"If you do what I think you're about to, then I am gone from your life. You will never see me again. Never. Is that what you want?" There was a pause. "Now calm yourself and turn around."

He followed her instructions and sat looking at the top of the table for what seemed like several minutes. At one point he grew conscious of the waiter drifting in and out of his field of vision and imagined that the man's curiosity would certainly be aroused by two people ordering food and not touching it.

"I'm sorry," he said finally. "You have to forgive me. This is all so strange to me."

He looked up and was disappointed to see that she had put the sunglasses back on. But it was precisely what he deserved and he gave a slight nod as if to indicate he understood where this rebuke had come from.

"We should leave," she said.

He nodded again and reached for his coat. Estimating the cost of the wasted meal and the drinks, he pulled some bills from his wallet and left them on the table. Nadia stood. Her jacket had been hanging next to his, and he removed it from the hook and helped her put it on. Her skirt was shorter than it had seemed at first glance while she'd been sitting, and he noticed the two soldiers looking her up and down as she stepped from behind the table, teetering slightly on the spike heels of her boots. The clothes were sophisticated in a trashy kind of way. He had no doubt they were also expensive.

When they were outside she took his arm and directed their steps away from the university, towards the shopping district. The sun hung almost directly overhead and hurt his eyes, but he didn't want to disrupt his delight at holding her arm in order to retrieve his sunglasses.

"Where are we going?" he asked.

"I'm not sure," she said. "That sort of depends on you."

"You'll let me know when we get there?" he asked, steadying his steps with difficulty and trying to sound calm, though his heart thundered and the first paroxysms of a pulsing headache were blossoming at the base of his neck. The alcohol had wreaked some sort of damage to his muscle control centres and set off a commotion of bleating and buzzing in his ears.

She smiled up at him. "Of course."

They walked in silence for a few minutes. Enrique was tempted to glance around to see if they were being followed but did not want to spark another incident and risk having her repudiate him in public and walk away, never to return, though he expected this would happen before too long in any case. Instead, he searched the reflections of people in the windows of the office buildings as they approached and passed in an attempt to catch a glimpse of any pursuers.

"There's something else I have to tell you," she said as they crossed a street where some workers were repairing the tarmac. A few soldiers stood around, watching. Enrique noticed again that her clothes and the way she walked captured their attention. "Well, two things, actually."

He kept his mouth shut and waited for her to go on.

"I know you're looking at me like I'm a different person. But I'm not. Not really. I have to dress this way because of what we're doing. My job is to gain the trust of people, to make them think I'm something that I'm not. I have to play a part to get them to open up. Once they believe I am who I say I am, then I can get my hands on the things we need."

"What kinds of things do you have to do?"

He felt her looking at him.

"I have to do whatever it takes."

He tried to keep a grip on himself, but he was weak to begin with and the drinks had weakened him further. He felt a tear escape from his eye and dribble down his face.

"I don't think I have the strength to hear any more of this—"

"You're stronger than you think," she broke in. "We all are. One of these days you'll surprise yourself."

They walked on. As they approached an intersection between two office towers, he swallowed the saliva that had been building in his throat and, looking at her, said, "Nadia, would you do me a great favour and hold my hand?"

She presented him with a friendly smile and gave him her hand, which he gripped, but not too firmly. As she had completely defied his expectations to this point, he did not put any store in her ready assent to his whim. He knew it meant nothing. His only wish now was that they were not wearing gloves so he could feel the cool elasticity of her skin and experience the supple flexing of her young muscles and the pulsing of her blood.

Eventually they came to a small stone-faced building and she steered them inside. The structure—square and nondescript in every way—seemed neither new nor old. It appeared to house the offices of a delivery company, a credit union, and an assortment of notaries and lawyers. Before opening the door of the credit union, she took off her glasses and said, "My name is Angelica. You are my Uncle Marco. You're visiting from Puerto Varas."

She stared at him and raised her eyebrows. After a moment he nodded and they went inside.

It was no different from a small branch of any bank, with teller stations, employees in cubicles flipping through stacks of papers and tapping away, either at typewriters or at the keyboards of those newfangled computer machines that some of the science people were using on campus. The privileged few had offices with windows fitted with blinds. The only feature he noticed that might distinguish this establishment from others of its kind was that all the people waiting in the line and being served were either dressed in one variation or another of standard-issue military dress or else had a definite military bearing about them.

Nadia waved to a young man in one of the cubicles. Immediately he stood and came out through a latched part of the counter to meet them. Enrique flushed as the fellow pulled Nadia to him and kissed her on the lips. For just a second his anger blinded him, but this passed as quickly as a summer breeze, and he was calm once more. It was nothing, really. The world had just taken on a further aspect of strangeness and left him another step behind, trying to catch up.

"Did you have a good lunch?"

"Wonderful," Nadia gushed. Her manner had changed completely. Once again she was a schoolgirl. A schoolgirl who had raided her older sister's wardrobe.

"Uncle, this is Steven. He's second in command here."

Smiling sheepishly, Steven glanced down at his feet and quickly up again. He was young, but not thin, not handsome, not a match for Nadia. He was dressed in a white short-sleeved shirt and a sober dark blue tie. His fleshy jowls were clean-shaven and he looked (if it were possible to look so) painfully naïve. He was like a piece of clay waiting to be moulded into shape.

Enrique took Steven's hand and shook it in a pantomime of affection.

"I finally get to meet the famous Steven," he said, smiling. "Angelica has told me so much about you. You have made her very happy. I'm glad to see her so happy."

A flush crept up both sides of Steven's chubby neck. "Thank you. I'm not, actually, second-in-command. I'm the comptroller. I'm in charge of finances. I have to make sure we have enough cash on hand to cover all the transactions." He gave an irresolute shrug. "But if everything goes well there's a chance I might be manager someday."

Enrique detected a slight inflection in the young man's speech, which betrayed his origins as American. Other than this minor flaw, his Spanish was impeccable.

"And how is it in Puerto Varas these days? Angelica says you have not seen much military activity."

Enrique smiled, not missing a beat. "We're off the map. It's a relief. I just hope it lasts."

Steven cinched his brows together in an attempt to look thoughtful. Enrique almost burst out laughing to think of this lummox courting his Nadia.

"I'm sorry my schedule is so tight I can't stay, but it wouldn't do for me to interrupt your work any more than necessary. I wouldn't be able to forgive myself if I put your promotion at risk."

"Thank you, sir," Steven said in all seriousness, thrusting his hand in Enrique's direction once again. "It was a real pleasure to meet you."

They shook hands for a second time. Enrique gripped the soft flesh tightly, succumbing to a momentary pang of sympathy for this ignorant young man, obviously the dupe in some swindle.

"We'll meet again, I'm sure. My dear?"

"Give me a minute please, Uncle." Nadia smiled while taking Steven's hand into hers and drawing him aside.

Enrique inclined his head and stepped towards the door, moving around the line of soldiers waiting to conduct their business. He watched the intimate conversation between the two young people take place from a distance of twenty feet or so, screened by a wall of potted plants, but even from here the young man's infatuation was plain to see. He nodded repeatedly, taking instructions, spoke a few words, nodded again as Nadia corrected him.

Nadia, his beautiful Nadia, held this grotesque young man's heart in the palm of her hand. What would he give to be present when she returned its pulverized remains to her lover?

In a minute they were outside again. He drew out his sunglasses and put them on. Checking his watch he saw that it was nearly two o'clock.

"Where to now?" he asked.

"One more stop," she said, businesslike. She reached into her purse, pulled out a lipstick, and touched herself up using the window of the credit union as a mirror. "Do you want a coffee or something first?"

He shrugged. "Why not?"

He thrust his hands into his pockets as she led him down the street and around a corner.

"Do you have any feelings for him?"

Nadia's only response was to step up her pace.

After crossing at an intersection and turning down yet another street she said, "We'll have to go in here. I told him I was taking you back to your hotel. I can't have him surprising us over a *café con leche*."

"So, do you? Have feelings for him?"

She stopped walking and released a sigh. "What do you want me to say? He's a tool, like a screwdriver, and I'm learning to use it. It's what I have to do so the people I work for can get the things they need."

"But it's not fair. It's not right."

223

She astonished him by slapping him in the chest. And again. The impact forced him to take a step backward.

"Don't you tell me what's right and what's fair! I saw what happens to people who stay out of trouble and do everything they're supposed to do. My parents lived in this country for eighteen years and followed all the rules. Maybe I wasn't born here, but I belong here. I'm no different from you, and they treat me like I have no right to ask questions when someone kidnaps my parents. I went to the police for help and they turned me out on the street. They said if I didn't go away they'd throw me in jail."

Afraid to try to take her into his arms, he could only gaze at her.

"I don't want to do this! Can't you see? I don't want to. I just want to live my life. But they made me like this! When they told me I'd be arrested for asking what happened to my parents, I couldn't stay the way I was. *They* did this to me! I didn't want it to happen. But they didn't give me any choice."

He felt rooted to the spot. He reached out one hand to touch her but she whirled away.

"Please, Nadia!"

She turned on him again.

"Don't call me that! She's gone. My name is Angelica." She grasped his arm in the same place where she had dug her nails in earlier and squeezed. He winced from the pain but didn't pull his arm away. "Say it! Say my name! Say it!"

The dull throb of his headache—steady, unrelenting—was making him nauseous. With difficulty he focused on her face, her mouth, which was not beautiful when twisted in anger. He could only guess at the depths of her anguish, the desperation and stark misery that had forced her to these extremes. His own family, at least, was as safe as was possible in these dismal times.

"Angelica," he said weakly. "My dear girl."

They exchanged another glance. Now that the tables had turned he struggled with the urgency of trying to calm her in order not to attract any more attention than they already had. She released his arm but he quickly grabbed her hand and squeezed. She did not pull away and after a few seconds returned the pressure.

He found the coffee establishment, sat her at a table away from the other customers, and went to the counter to purchase two cups of coffee.

When he returned, the sunglasses were gone and she was dabbing at her eyes with a napkin.

"God, I'm a mess."

"You're doing things nobody your age, or any age for that matter, should have to contemplate, even in their worst nightmares. No wonder you're upset."

"I'm doing what I have to do." She pried the plastic top off the paper cup.

"You said you didn't have a choice. I know that. But I don't think that's quite true. I'm your other choice. You should have come to me first, but since you didn't I can still help you find a way out. I can make some inquiries. You wouldn't expect it, I know. But I'm not helpless. I can do things. You'd be surprised."

She was shaking her head. "I'm sorry, but you have no idea what you're up against." One after one, she tore open four packets of sugar and emptied them into the coffee. A kind of weariness had crept into her manner that he found almost as alarming as the cold detachment he'd witnessed earlier.

"But I have to ask that you never get me to do anything like that again. Imagine, posing as your uncle. Your games are beginning to wear thin. What am I supposed to do if I bump into him on the street?" He shook his head and sipped his coffee. "That young man, I feel sorry for him. He's the one who doesn't know what he's up against."

One hand stirred the drink with the wooden stick; the other, with her elbow propped on the table, supported her chin. She stared at him as if she'd heard it all before.

"Listen, Enrique," she said. "And please listen to everything I say. I've made a lot of mistakes in the last little while, and one of them was getting you to meet me for lunch. But now that it's happened, I have to let you know that you're implicated."

She paused to take a sip of coffee.

He stared at her. What was she saying?

"I'm going to do some things. They're against the law. Maybe I'll get away with it and maybe I won't. But Steven will be the one who gets in trouble because when the money disappears, the trail will lead back to him. He authorizes the transfer of cash. If it works out the way we hope, I'll be in another province with a new name by the time he figures out what I've done, and he won't be able to convince anyone that he didn't do it all by himself. But he's not stupid and he will remember things. Everything I've told him about myself—about Angelica Petrona—is false. But he will remember me. And he'll remember my uncle from Puerto Varas."

Enrique felt a cavity yawn open in his gut. Suddenly his hands were trembling. Thinking he was going to drop the cup, he set the coffee on the table. He was trembling all over.

"You're telling me . . ."

"I didn't want to do it, but I wanted them to trust me, to take me in, so I could do some good. I told them everything about myself. I didn't hold anything back because you can't have secrets, and when they heard about Hector being sent away, and that I was keeping in touch with him through you, they came up with the idea that bringing you to Steven's office would make Angelica Petrona more convincing. They needed him to see a member of my family, someone older and respectable, and there was nobody else who could do it. You're not involved in anything, but the others are all living underground, and they don't look the part. There was nobody else I could approach. It seemed like a good idea, and I thought, what's the harm? But then it came to me, about Steven remembering afterward, and I said it was too dangerous and that I wouldn't get you involved. I would risk my own life, but not yours. By then I was deep inside, and you know, once you're inside you can never leave. If you try, they hunt you down, and if that doesn't work they leak your identity to the police. You might as well be dead. I wasn't at that stage, nowhere near it. All I had were some reservations about how they wanted to do this. But they said if I refused to use you the way they wanted, then I would never see you again. They would send me somewhere else and set me up for another job, but I could never come back here."

"But what about when this is over. You could come back then. It's not going to last forever."

She nodded. "But this is war. None of us can be sure of anything."

The silence between them stretched to a minute or two before she ventured an upward glance and in a small voice said, "I'm so sorry. It was selfish of me. I should have just let you go . . ."

Their hands were linked across the table. Enrique struggled with the notion that, however unwittingly, he had taken part in a crime. Still, though, a crime that hadn't yet taken place.

"But," he began, and then he faltered. Everything was whirling around in his head. One moment he thought he saw it clearly. The next, the facts were hidden beneath a jumble of conflicting details. But then, why waste energy trying to think this through? How could he be sure she was telling the truth, even now?

"They didn't want me to warn you. So, here I am." She gave him a rueful smile. "Here I am making another mistake, going against a direct order. They said it would be better if you didn't have time to think up a story if the police came looking for you. But I had to tell you so much of it anyway, just to get you to go in there and shake hands with him, I thought I might as well tell you the rest."

"How long is this thing going to take?" he asked, appalled by the tremor in his voice. "With Steven. And . . . uh—the money."

"A couple of weeks. Three at the most. I have to work quickly, but I have to get his confidence too. Make it so he doesn't suspect anything."

"Are you in physical danger? I mean, for your life, if this doesn't work?"

"I have a way out," she said, not looking at him now. "There's a plan to get me out of here if something goes wrong. I have to give a signal, and then I can be a hundred miles away in a couple of hours."

She let go of his hand, and he realized that her grip had been firm and strong. "I'm too valuable to them to let me go to waste. You can see why. I can be sixteen. I can be thirty if I have to. I can get men to do things for me. My looks might be enough to keep me alive, but I'll have to earn it."

Enrique shook his head. "Nadia," he sighed. "You're just a child."

She didn't respond to this. After a moment she straightened herself in the chair and said, "We have to go. The banks close at three."

He checked his watch and gave her an enquiring look. "Forty-five minutes."

"You're going to hate me," she said. "And I won't blame you. I hope you can remember me the way I was, before all this." She took a deep breath and brushed a few strands of hair back from her forehead. "I told them everything about myself, and everything I could remember about everyone I know. They need every piece of information they can get, because you can never tell when something's going to give you an advantage. I told them . . ." She exhaled and at once seemed resigned, trapped, infinitely weary. "I told them about the first time we met. That day when Hector brought me to the café and you were there with that boy."

Enrique felt his temperature rise. Sweat trickled between his shoulders. "Jorgé," he said through lips that were suddenly parched.

Nadia nodded. "Yes. I told them everything I could remember about where the place was, what the street looked like, the church where Hector and I sat on the wall, and the boy himself. I said you had your face all made up with rouge and kohl, and that I almost passed out from the heat. I didn't say it to humiliate you. But it is how we met. I didn't want to know about that part of your life. It doesn't mean a thing to me. People are the way they are. But they took the information and then, it was like the next day, they showed me a photograph, and it was the boy, Jorgé. Only he was covered in cuts and bruises. It was all written down in some report, how someone had attacked him. You never told me, but that's how I found out why you sent Hector away. To keep him from being arrested. It made sense to me then. But they asked more and more questions about you, where you live and where you work. I think . . . I think they sent someone to follow you, to make sure I was telling the truth. Oh, God. I'm sorry. I betrayed you. You were good to me, and look what I've done. They want money. If you don't give them money, they're going to hand it all over to the university. The photographs. Everything they have. They've even spoken to the boy's parents, and they know you. They remember you."

Enrique sat absolutely still gazing at her. She avoided eye contact. She sat slumped in her chair, twisting her fingers together on the table. Now that she'd admitted handing him over to her friends, she appeared to be suffering genuine torment.

His voice, when at last he spoke, was level, drained of feeling. "And how do I know you're telling me the truth? What proof can you give me that will persuade me to empty my bank account?"

She reached into her purse and retrieved a small square envelope. She slid it across the table towards him. Reluctantly, he took it up and lifted the flap. Inside were several photographs. He recognized Jorgé's parents, that lascivious pair of cretins, caught in a snapshot speaking with a younger man across a long table in a room with whitewashed walls. Spread over the table between them was a scattering of shots of himself, probably taken as he walked to work. Another photo, just of him, had been taken in the lobby of the Archives building. Still another showed the interior of his office, which was, he'd always thought, locked whenever he wasn't there. The last had been taken inside the flat. It showed a newspaper lying on the hallway table, beside his mother's Tiffany lamp. Alarmingly, his keys were there as well, next to the newspaper. He had been in the flat when the picture was taken but had heard nothing, noticed nothing.

"How much?" He tried to expunge all feeling for her as she lifted her gaze. Coldly, he met her eyes. "How much, my dear Angelica, to make this go away?"

"Forty thousand. They want forty thousand."

He nodded. "And if I don't give it to you, they will—essentially—ruin my life and the life of my family."

She continued to look at him, but remained silent and completely still.

He let the photos drop from his hand and stood. "Collect your things, my dear. We have to make a withdrawal."

He didn't wait for her and strode quickly out of the coffee shop and into the sunlight. Somehow it was a relief to slip out from beneath her gaze, and for these few seconds he breathed more easily. But she quickly caught up with him and fell into step by his side. He did not acknowledge her and they did not touch. It occurred to him, as they went along, that, though to a frightening degree his own destiny had been taken out of his hands, she had presented him with an equally powerful instrument with which he could destroy her, simply by returning to the credit union and repeating to Steven everything that she had told him. Just passing by the front window of the building would compromise her operation if Steven happened to be looking out and at that moment spotted them together, at a time when he expected them, or him at any rate, to be somewhere else. But once again he allowed some vestige of tenderness for Nadia Wladanski to overwhelm his desire for revenge against Angelica Petrona, and at a crucial juncture he veered left instead of right and went down the street behind the row of buildings that included the credit union.

The branch of the National Banque where he conducted the majority of his dealings was located between his home and the university. But, as a hedge against bank failures and following an example of prudence set by his father, he had spread his business around and maintained active accounts at a variety of locations. Lucinda was ignorant of most of these, necessarily so because he would use this money to pay for the illicit recreations that had now, at long last, landed him in hot water. But it also meant that he could raid one of these accounts today and still leave plenty in the coffers for Lucinda and the children should anything happen to him.

The route he took meant that they retraced their steps past the bistro and the train station and along the broad boulevard of Avenida de la Universidad. Occasionally he checked to see if Nadia was still at his side, and slowed down once or twice so she could catch up. Neither of them had spoken.

It was not until he was actually within sight of two of the banks he dealt with that he made his choice. He crossed the street and went up the steps of a sandstone Greek revival structure.

"Are you coming in?"

"I'm supposed to stay with you, to watch what you're doing."

He almost laughed. "I see. No monkey business then."

He held the door for her and they went inside.

He had chosen this bank as much for the high vaulted ceilings, inlaid granite walls and floors, marble columns, and plush furniture as for the account he kept here, which he estimated would be holding in excess of 200,000 pesetas. He stole a glance at her. To the uninitiated the interior space would be intimidating. Surely, he thought, nothing tawdry or indecorous could happen in these hallowed environs. Surely she would keep her mouth shut and not make a scene in an attempt to extort even more.

"I know you're supposed to keep an eye on me," he said. "But, all things considered, I think I can speed things along if I take care of this myself."

They stopped. She removed her glasses and looked up at him.

"They know me here. My request is going to be highly unusual. I'm sure the transaction will go more smoothly if I'm alone when I explain why I want the money."

"If you try anything . . ." She paused and looked away, surveying the massive space, buzzing with activity, in which she stood. "I have to report back. If I don't . . . if something happens to me, everything I showed you will go to the university and the police."

Enrique inclined his head slightly in acknowledgement of the threat.

"I'll just sit over here then," she said, indicating a dark green leather sofa at the centre of a waiting area: several imposing pieces of furniture resting on an intricately patterned Turkish carpet.

"Thank you," he said.

He approached the receptionist and in a moment was being shown into the office of Bourque, the branch manager.

"It's been a while," Bourque said brusquely as they shook hands and Enrique took a seat in a high-backed armchair. Bourque's office was lined with dark wood shelves holding row upon row of leather-bound books, though Bourque had once admitted he never read anything more demanding than the newspaper. Bourque himself looked vaguely antique, with his round spectacles, thick grey moustache, and bristly grey hair cropped in a flat-top manner that Enrique always found incongruously Teutonic.

Enrique gave his instructions and Bourque wrote everything down.

"Fifty thousand is a lot, my friend. Are you sure you need it all at once?"

"Lucinda is with the children in Puerto Varas," he explained. "I don't want them relying on the charity of her brother. I'll bring this for her when I visit, probably next week."

"Heh, just don't wager it on the horses," Bourque joked.

Enrique smiled thinly. All he wanted was to dispense with the pleasantries and get this business over with.

"I'll be right back."

Bourque exited through a panel between two sets of bookshelves that silently eased open at the touch of his finger. Enrique had always envisioned that during a robbery, Bourque would make his escape through this otherwise undetectable opening in the wall that led to a secret passageway and end up in the catacombs at the other end of town.

As soon as Bourque was gone, Enrique stood and, pulling the other door slightly ajar, peered into the cavernous public expanse of the bank. He had been fully prepared to see Nadia deep in conversation with some long-haired lout in torn jeans and a leather jacket. But she sat alone, as he'd left her, perched ridiculously on that gigantic sofa, her hands clasped together, looking up from time to time with a timorous glance, as if expecting that at any moment someone would come along and challenge her right to be there. One thing she'd said was true. Her beauty was her ticket. If she was able to perfect the art of changing her appearance to suit the occasion, it would ensure her survival. Maybe he was worrying needlessly on her behalf. To look at her now, if not for the clothes you would think she was a little girl whose parents had forgotten all about her.

He shut the door quickly. He felt his heart melting, opening towards her again. He had to toughen himself against the kind of cheap sentiment to which he knew he was susceptible. Her beauty made it far too easy to fall into that trap. He could see why her colleagues had decided she was too valuable a commodity to use once and discard. That face would pierce a hundred hearts before she was finished.

He resumed his seat and in a moment Bourque returned with the cash and some forms. Enrique signed in each place his friend indicated. Then, in a ritual he had enacted many times in the past, he counted the bills as Bourque looked on. Everything was in order. He palmed 10,000 pesetas off the top, which he thrust into his pants pocket, and left the remainder in the unmarked brown envelope, which he slipped into the pocket of his coat.

"One other thing," he said, after he and Bourque had exchanged a final handshake and Enrique prepared to leave.

"Yes, my good friend."

"I'm here today with my niece," he said, not knowing what he was getting at until the words were already out of his mouth. "I've been showing her around the campus. Her name is Angelica Petrona. She's waiting outside in the foyer. Would you like to meet her?"

Bourque looked perplexed for only a moment. He would realize that with no siblings, Enrique would have no nieces or nephews on the Tomás side. But what of Lucinda's family?

Enrique watched the last lingering doubt subside.

"I'd be honoured," Bourque said as they stepped out of the office. "Petrona is an unusual name, don't you think?"

"Her mother is Lucinda's sister. The fellow she married is . . . well, I'm not sure what he is."

The two men shared a polite chuckle.

Nadia stood when she saw them approaching. Enrique watched as confusion swept over her and her eyes darted back and forth between them. She reached into her purse, for the sunglasses Enrique guessed, but couldn't come up with them quickly enough.

"My dear, this is Señor Bourque, the manager of the bank and a very powerful friend indeed."

"It's an exquisite pleasure to meet you, Angelica." He held out his hand and Nadia took it. "Your uncle does me great credit by exaggerating my importance. But I can still welcome you to my humble establishment."

"Thank you," Nadia mumbled.

"Petrona. The name is not a common one. Could you indulge my curiosity and tell me where it comes from?"

Again, Nadia's gaze flitted several times between Enrique and Bourque in the space of no more than a few seconds.

"It's Polish," she said without emotion. "My father is from Poland."

"There, you see?" Enrique said, tapping his head with one finger. "I knew that, but I couldn't remember."

The men laughed. Enrique felt her gaze drill into him.

"Uncle . . ."

"One other thing," Enrique said, talking over her. "Where are you with that security system? There were going to be cameras and everything?"

"Oh, that was finished long ago," Bourque stated blandly. "The cameras cover all the angles. The only private places are the washrooms and some offices. We're all being recorded. Say hello, Angelica."

Bourque waved towards a cylindrical-shaped piece of apparatus bolted to the ceiling, at the crown of a marble column, about thirty feet above where Nadia had been sitting for the last fifteen minutes. Enrique watched as her gaze shifted briefly in that direction and quickly down towards the floor. Her hand was trembling when she pulled the glasses from her purse and put them on.

"Uncle, my appointment . . ."

"Yes, you're right." He shook hands with Bourque. "Thank you for everything."

In a minute they had passed through the outer lobby and were on the street again.

He stopped at the bottom of the steps to await her instructions, but Nadia made no move. So Enrique turned right. When they were two blocks further on, a final left turn would bring them to Rua Santa Maria and within a short walk of his apartment building. Nadia strode in silence by his side as they passed the boarded-up storefronts and dilapidated rooming houses that had become prevalent in this corner of the city. Enrique didn't bother to ask what the plan was.

"You . . ." she began, but she didn't go on.

233

"I hope you're not going to say it was mean of me to trick you," he commented, trying to sound composed as he extracted a handkerchief from an inner pocket. To his surprise his heart was thudding and the perspiration collected on his brow as fast as he could wipe it off.

"It was unnecessary," she said in a voice that betrayed nothing by way of emotion.

"Maybe from your point of view. But I'm sure Señor Bourque will never forget my niece Angelica. And if your beautiful face ever fades from his memory, he can always watch the tapes."

She looked up at him now, her mouth set in a line, her expression behind the glasses inscrutable. "Did you at least get the money?"

"Yes," he said. "I got the money."

She paused and glanced around, taking in their dubious surroundings, searching perhaps for a suitable venue in which to make the exchange. Approaching them on the sidewalk was a cluster of boisterous children wearing blue Catholic school uniforms and carrying book bags. Up ahead was a bus stop where several people, young and old, stood waiting. A taxi cruised slowly in their direction, the driver apparently looking for an address. A woman, half-heartedly sweeping the front steps of a building across the street, seemed to be taking note of all these movements. Somewhere out of sight someone was revving a car engine. Enrique glanced at his watch. It was approaching three-thirty.

"Let's go in here," Nadia said, indicating a narrow lane between a small brick apartment building and a rundown four-floor domestic walk-up. The passage was cluttered with bags of trash and littered with empty beer bottles, crushed cardboard boxes, and sticks of broken lumber.

Enrique had wanted this over with and behind him. But as he followed her into the alley and past the bags of garbage, he could find no comfort in the inevitable finale: that once the transaction was complete and they went their separate ways, the possibility that he would ever see her again was remote at best. He had loved her so dearly, and she had done a terrible thing to him. But, really, what harm had she done? He would survive as he always did, by filling his days and making sure his family was provided for if it was ever his fate to be one of those who disappeared. But despite her warning, he was still not convinced the police or the army or the men who had abducted her parents—whoever they were—would be remotely interested in him. He was a failed intellectual whose lifelong passion for

234

ideas had led him into a dead end and abandoned him there. As far as his life was concerned, the tragedy had taken place years ago; anything she or anyone else did to him from this point on was meaningless.

On the other hand, she was young and beautiful and motivated by righteous indignation to do good things. If she acted wisely and didn't let her emotions get the better of her, she could help the country recover from this time of darkness. But instead she was throwing it all away.

She turned and confronted him for the final time. They faced each other in shadow. The air was chilly. The sun's rays would never reach far into this narrow space.

He removed his sunglasses, as much to show her his distress as to get a better look at her. He folded them and slipped them into his pocket. Then he reached across to her and removed the glasses from her face. If she was surprised by this she did not show it. He folded these as well and tucked them into her purse, which was open at the top. Then he removed his gloves and put them away. She did not react when he reached out and cupped her cheek in his hand. For a moment he stroked her face, let his hand drop down to her neck, moved it back up to her face. He brushed her hair with his fingers, traced the line of her eyebrows.

"Look at you," he said.

He knew she would never sufficiently harden her heart to survive in the world she had chosen, and so was not surprised when she closed her eyes and a few tears rolled down her cheek. He reached behind her head and drew her towards him, angling her face upward while lowering his own. She complied and for an instant he imagined their lips meeting. But even he could not blind himself to the grotesque obscenity of this, and at the last moment simply gathered her to him. To his surprise, she wrapped her arms around him and let herself fall forward so that he stumbled and his back struck the wall. With childish desperation she clung to him, pressing her face against his chest as she wept. His shirt grew damp with her tears. The heat of her breath warmed his skin. She rested her weight against him and he had to slip his hand down her back in order to hold her more securely. He imagined then that at a word from him she would renounce this ludicrous campaign and let herself be steered away from the path of self-destruction. In his fantasy she followed him to some remote mountain town, where they made a life together as father and daughter. But at the same time he could not resist the spell she cast, unwittingly or not, with her all too womanly flesh, her flawless skin, her heat, her passion and energy, which swept him up in a struggle against primal urges and brute appetites. Stricken by lust and shame, he fed hungrily on the vigour of her youthful body and briefly sensed the revival of his own dry carcass.

Then it was over and she pulled away. He watched as she adjusted her clothes and swiped at the tears that streaked her face. The purse lay toppled on the ground, its contents spilled over a small radius.

"I can't be doing this," she said, glancing about her with a vague expression of bewilderment.

"I had no intention—"

"It doesn't matter," she said, crouching to gather her things.

"It does."

She looked up at him. "We have to finish this."

"Why?"

She stood and straightened her skirt. She did not respond.

"Why, Nadia, does it have to be like this? I only want you to have another way out."

"It will never work," she said.

"Why?"

"Because I've made my choice."

Enrique hesitated before saying, "So, you're determined to ruin your life."

"I'm determined," she said in a tight, level voice, "to do something that needs to be done."

"You're—"

"Don't question me!" she raged. "Don't tell me what to do! Don't say another word! Don't you dare say another word!"

She put the glasses on again, and Enrique knew he had seen her eyes for the last time.

"I'm only—"

"Give me the money."

He pulled the envelope from his coat pocket but stopped short of handing it over.

"The photographs," he said.

She shrugged and took the envelope from her purse.

"You realize," she said as they made the exchange, "this doesn't mean they're through with you. Jorgé's parents are still waiting to tell their story.

That's probably enough to keep you quiet about the credit union. But I don't know how many other photos are out there or who's been told to follow you. All I know is that the next time they come looking for money or something else, I won't be the messenger."

Enrique paused only briefly before giving a perfunctory nod and thrusting the envelope into his pocket without checking its contents. He had not, in fact, thought the situation through to that point, but what she said made perfect sense. Why put a cash cow out to pasture?

"Please, Nadia, give me another moment of your time."

She had started to walk away and had her back to him.

"Why?" she asked over her shoulder. "What now?"

He drew what felt like half of the extra 10,000 pesetas from his pants pocket.

"You have to take this and put it somewhere safe, somewhere these people you're involved with won't find it. Think of it as insurance. You can buy yourself a train ticket to anywhere and be gone."

She seemed to regard with suspicion the contents of the hand extended towards her. But after a few seconds she took the money and without a word put it into her purse. She started walking away again.

"One other thing."

She stopped. "Yes," she said over her shoulder, half turned in his direction, at the end of her patience.

"I'm going to write a note to Señor Bourque, telling him that Angelica, my niece, might come by from time to time when she's in need of funds. He will be instructed to give you whatever you want, no questions asked."

He could see this had some effect on her, despite the stony façade she was at pains to uphold. She swallowed thickly.

Her lips seemed to form the words "Thank you." Then she turned and walked away, unsteady on her spike heels as she wove a path around the trash bags and empty bottles. He watched her exit the alleyway and turn left. When she was gone he collapsed against the wall, slumped to the ground, and wept.

THIRTY

Because of the curfew Enrique had not been venturing far during the evening hours. Sometimes he took a short stroll after dinner, to help ease whatever food he'd ingested pass from his stomach into his bowels. Within walking distance of 53 Rua Santa Maria were a couple of taverns and a public garden that had actually been cleaned up since the military gained power because it commemorated the victories of a naval commander (famous at the time) during one of the wars of independence. He sometimes stopped at one or the other of the taverns for a drink and some teasing banter with the bartender. But he found these places depressing because the music was dreary, the décor archaic, the furniture shabby, and the stools and tables were occupied by the same lonely old souls night after night, people whose lives had reached a nadir of sorts, and he didn't like to think of himself in such hopeless company.

That night he had no plans for any kind of activity. He'd gone back to the flat and sat in his favourite armchair. An hour later it was getting dark and he had not moved a muscle. The encounter with Nadia had left him in such a state that he didn't know what to do or where to go. A tavern was an option, but the thought of maintaining a sociable façade was odious, even in one of those dingy places where standards of social interaction were low. He had not returned to the office for that very reason. Backed into a corner by someone who wanted to talk business, his frustration could boil over. He might say anything. What if he slandered the generals? If Nadia's intention had been to shatter his calm, she could not have done a better job. He did not trust himself to behave rationally. But at the same time, he knew that he should have returned to the office, if only to sit behind his desk and give the impression that all was normal.

Though he had struggled to dismiss it at the time, he could not put Nadia's warning out of his head. This was a regime that feared independent and creative thinking. It made perfect sense that all university staff would come under suspicion.

Finally, he got up and switched on all the lights in the flat. He went from room to room, looking for proof that his privacy had been violated. There was nothing. They'd left no evidence of their intrusion. But how many times had they been in here? Had someone let them in? Had they forced the door open without breaking it? He went out to the entryway and studied the doorknob and bolt lock mechanism for damage or signs of tampering, but he could detect no traces of any such thing.

He went into the kitchen. Every aspect of his life was compromised. He had no secrets. He opened a bottle of Cabernet and poured some into a glass. He had made a decision. He would get drunk and lose himself in an alcoholic stupor. For one night he would forget everything that was troubling him.

But a few hours later, as the last drops of red wine dribbled from the second bottle into his glass, he understood that there was no escape from the demons that Nadia had unleashed. He would be targeted, once, twice, a hundred times. He would suffer for his indiscretions. Alcohol might cushion the blow, but it could not hold off the inevitable.

It was late, but he pulled on his coat and went downstairs. He needed some air. He needed a plan of action. Money had always been his way out, but his reserves had been greatly reduced. Nadia was right. He had to start making arrangements for his escape, but slowly and discretely, in a way that did not draw the attention of the police or anyone else. Do nothing out of the ordinary. Go to work. Meet people. Go for a walk. But very soon he would close up the flat and join his family in Puerto Varas.

The air was still and cool. Walking up the street towards the public garden he did not see another soul. His steps produced a hollow echo that rattled off the buildings on either side. Perhaps he was tempting fate, but not long ago he had been out later than this, absolutely alone, and no one had bothered him. The curfew was in effect, but people still had to live their lives. He reached the end of Rua Santa Maria. From here the view was less obstructed by tall buildings and he could see all the way to the western horizon. There were bright flashes in the hills, brilliant pools of illumination which glowed for just an instant before being snuffed out. As he watched, Enrique became aware of the frequency and abundance of these flashes, and of the distant rumble that accompanied them, the soft irregular detonation of artillery. He lowered his gaze and walked on.

A few minutes later he turned and went through the gate and into the public garden. After midnight it was empty and would provide a tranquil setting for a brief stroll. Then he would return home, no harm done. His heels made a brushing sound against the brick path, and it was so quiet he could hear the rubbing of his coat against his trousers. The park was rectangular in shape, with tiered gardens and some benches. Steps led from one level down to the next, until one reached the bottom, where in the middle of a bed of tulips and begonias a brass plaque was affixed to a concrete stand. At a leisurely pace it would take no more than three minutes to walk around the perimeter.

He thrust his hands into his pockets and tried to empty his mind.

Then he heard something and turned. There were three of them, and, as Nadia had said, they were dressed in black. One cradled a sort of gun on a short strap at shoulder level.

The man closest to him reached out a gloved hand.

"Come with us, please."

Instinctively he turned and thought to run. But something came down hard on his head, then his shoulder. Something hit his leg and his knee exploded with pain as he fell to the ground. He lay there not moving, and still the blows descended. He heard voices cursing. A boot landed heavily on his hand and he cried out. Then he was lifted swiftly to his feet and held in place as the first man delivered one punch after another, not to his face, but to his abdomen. All the various pains melded into one, and he was barely conscious of being dragged out of the park and heaved into the back of a waiting vehicle. The door was slammed behind him. He lay still on a gritty corrugated metal surface and heard other doors being opened and closed. He tried to raise himself, but his limbs were battered and sore and could not support his weight. When, to the abrupt squeal of tires, they pulled away from the curb, he was thrown in the direction of the movement and rolled painfully on his side. Nobody spoke. The only utterances were his groans and dry brittle coughs. He wished he could be unconscious, to be spared the agony of wondering what was in store. But fate was not even so kind as that. And as the van in which he was captive hurtled through the night, down the uneven roads of the provincial capital of B——, Enrique Tomás began to suspect that his selfish existence of useless dreams and squandered opportunity was soon to come to an end.

THIRTY-ONE

Sitting in darkness with her back to the wall, behind the pieces of broken furniture screening her from the staircase, Nadia knew that dawn had arrived and with it an intensification of the search being conducted by the combined forces of the military and the police. Yesterday they had made it back to the house on Calle de Vasquez to retrieve their things. But afterward, because of the roadblocks and increased patrols, they had made it only as far as this building in the industrial district. Step-by-step they would make it out of the city, but for now would have to stay put, at least until nightfall. Where they would go when darkness came, she had no idea. But she was beginning to think their only option was to split up.

Beside her, Krista was asleep. The girl's head was slumped against Nadia's shoulder. She was older than Nadia by at least two years, but she seemed younger. When Krista moaned, Nadia stroked her hair. A loaded pistol lay on the floor within arm's reach. Upstairs, Gustavo was keeping watch. Before it got too light one of them would have to go out and get food and water. She would volunteer, but she knew that Gustavo would insist on doing it himself.

None of this would have happened if she had listened to Enrique and followed his advice. Or maybe it would have happened anyway. Certainly the assassination would have gone ahead. That had been their object all along, as she discovered afterward, and they would have found a way to do it with or without her help. The supposed plan to steal money from the credit union had been a cover and had helped ensure her participation and that of others who might have balked at the taking of a life. When they proposed it to her, it sounded like an initiation, a way for her to get her feet wet and at the same time make a small contribution to the cause. It also fed her belief that she would not be involved in any major actions until she'd had success with some lesser task. Once they saw she could be trusted, once they saw what she was capable of, she would be given greater responsibility.

But, as it turned out, there were no lesser tasks. As the new recruit, they had naturally placed her in the category of those from whom the mission's true objective was withheld. The risks, after all, were enormous; the statement they were making one that would be heard throughout the country and probably beyond. Obviously, they doubted the strength of her convictions. Perhaps they had also thought the strain of knowing what was at stake would make it impossible for her to perform her role effectively. Maybe they thought she would be stricken by conscience and reveal everything to the authorities. As it was, she was not the only one who had been kept in the dark. Gustavo, Ruben, and Edmond had known. But Krista, Imelda, and Adriano, all of whom had been members of the cell for months, had not.

And if she *had* known that the real plan was to kill a man . . . well, what would she have done?

She had not reached any of her decisions lightly. But once she had seen Magda safely into the home of her friend Carola Castillo, knowing that the Castillos were planning to escape to America, it seemed her ties with the outside world had been severed. If she was going to join the resistance and help topple the regime that was behind her parents' disappearance, now was the time to do it. In her last conversation with Carmel—the very same day Magda was taken in by the Castillos—she said bluntly that because of what was happening, she intended to drop out of sight for a while. She told Carmel the name of the family that had taken Magda and said her goodbyes. She did not cry, because she believed that she would meet with her sisters again, just as she believed she would someday be reunited with her parents.

She had not seen Hector's father for a few weeks but did not contact him because whenever she was with him, the urge to make a complete confession of every little trouble that was on her mind was almost too strong for her to resist. He was such a sympathetic listener. He spoke so

movingly and drew his thoughts from such a deep wellspring of experience and reason. So far, she had not unburdened her soul to him, but
she was afraid that on this occasion her needs were extreme. If she made
even oblique reference to what she was planning to do, not only would he
attempt to talk her out of it, he might even succeed. Many fears and reservations still plagued her. The tasks facing her would be daunting even if
she knew of some way to connect with the rebels, let alone join forces with
them. But her problem was compounded because she had no idea where
to start. So she could easily see that if she allowed him to tell her, in all
the different ways he was able to say it, that she was powerless and helpless and asking too much of herself, then she could very well be persuaded
to do nothing. She decided it would be best to meet with him afterward,
when it would be too late for his arguments to make any difference.

Her school had not been immune to the effects of the conflict. Some of
the older boys had been called up into the army, and at least two teachers,
who taught geography and civics, had disappeared. She knew of the boy
whose father was a journalist. The entire family had vanished and their
house had been vandalized and spray-painted with slogans, and blood
had been smeared on the walls. She had never gone to look, but Hector
had told her about it. Another time, she heard that overnight someone had
painted the word *Libertad* in huge letters on the wall inside the school's
main entrance. By the time she came to see, the men had already painted
over it. She never knew if the story was true or not, but the fresh coat of
paint seemed to say that it was. Other acts of vandalism took place, and
on one occasion the chemistry lab was ransacked. When soldiers began
patrolling the hallways, the students were told that there had been a threat
of a rebel attack. It could happen anywhere, at any time. So the soldiers
stayed, keeping watch over the change of classes like armed school mon-
itors. The vandalism stopped. And as the months passed, she became
used to seeing soldiers in the hallways as she went from one class to the
next. But even to her, with her limited knowledge of such things, a rebel
attack on her school seemed unlikely. Other schools, she heard, were not
similarly guarded. Why theirs?

After her parents were taken, she and Magda went to school only a
few more times. She wanted to keep up appearances. She didn't want to
become an object of pity in anybody's eyes. She thought they could carry
on, just the two of them. But Magda could not be consoled and for a day

or two refused to leave her bedroom. Very soon it became impossible for Nadia to convince herself that everything was going to be all right, and she couldn't concentrate on the schoolwork anyway. She began to worry about money. Sometimes in the past, usually after several glasses of vodka, her father had told them he had money stashed away in a closet, saying that it would be enough to get by for a while if something happened. But when she and Magda found the cookie tin where the money was supposed to be, the coins and notes turned out to be worthless Polish *złotych*.

Nadia spoke to Carmel on the phone every day, and every day they ended up sharing tears instead of comfort. Carmel had been older when the family came over from Poland, and though she spoke fluent Spanish, she had never completely lost her Polish accent. She didn't know if she was being watched or not, she said, but on the same day their parents were arrested, Raoul's identity pass had been revoked and he couldn't leave the base until it was returned. Carmel had been working as a typist in one of the offices, but a few weeks ago her job was given to someone else, and she had been assigned to the kitchen. She could help by sending money. But they couldn't leave, and Nadia and Magda could not come there.

Through Carola the Castillos had learned about the arrest of Nadia and Magda's parents, and finally Nadia gave in to the pressure and let them take Magda into their home. They gave Nadia information she would need to reach them once they had gone to America. They wanted Nadia to come as well, but she said she had things she had to do, though she promised to follow later. She phoned Carmel, told her where Magda was, and said she was going to disappear for a while.

She had made her decision.

But the next day, alone, filled with doubts and new fears, she looked around the empty house where she had grown up and decided to call Carmel one last time, for a final conversation between sisters, to gather strength for the step she was about to take. The only greeting at the other end of the line was the raspy pulsating signal indicating the number had been disconnected.

She had thought it through and decided that the presence of soldiers in the hallways of her school indicated that this was where she would make her first contact with opponents of the regime. She had, of course, heard the same stories and rumours as everyone else, about who had painted *Libertad* on the wall of the main hallway and led the raid on the chemistry lab: a boy named Acevedo Torres, who carried with him a reputation as a troublemaker and a thief. But along with this reputation, which had kept Nadia out of his way for all the years they had been attending the same school (she had never exchanged even a single word with him), was talk that he knew the people who had shot out the window of the police station on Avenida Independencia, set off a bomb down the street from the Interior Ministry offices, and done other things to disrupt civil order. It was Acevedo Torres who had been first to the house on Avenida de Suarez, where the journalist's family no longer lived, to look at the wreckage of furniture and the blood-smeared walls. She had no way of knowing if any of the things that people said about him were true (maybe he had made it all up in order to seem tough), but she had nowhere else to turn.

The day after losing contact with Carmel she waited for Torres outside the school. She had bought the sunglasses and put them on, even though it was cloudy. After careful consideration, she had selected one of the work outfits that Carmel had left behind that she had worn when meeting Enrique, and touched up her face sedately and with care. She thought if she could gain a few years in his eyes she would gain credibility as well.

She was lucky that he was alone when he came out, because sometimes he was surrounded by friends. He looked around when he stepped outside, and she saw that a car was waiting for him. A couple of men sat in the front seat. He was walking quickly towards it.

She hurried over and was able to situate herself so that he would have to step around her. He tried to do this, but she moved to one side to stay in his path. He just looked at her. His expression beneath a pair of thick black eyebrows was not friendly. He said nothing. Her heart pounded.

"I want to help," she said, not knowing if this was right or wrong, if it would raise suspicions or allay them. "I . . . I need to do something."

In an instant his eyes had surveyed her from top to bottom, and he seemed to have made an assessment. She could see that, though he might have wasted his school years defying authority and doing everything he could to avoid learning, he was not stupid.

He looked past her towards the car. He smiled, but at the same time seemed bored. Then he recited some numbers.

"What?"

"Did you get that?"

She shook her head.

"Listen." And he recited the numbers again. "Wait until after nine o'clock and go to a pay phone and call that number. Don't write it down."

"I'm—"

"I know who you are. Just do what I say."

He slipped by her and got into the car. Before the door closed she thought she heard him say *amiga* to the others in the front seat. He was laughing, and soon the others were laughing too. The one on the passenger side in front craned his neck to get a better look at her.

The car drove off.

She walked home, and for the next five hours visualized the number written on a piece of paper in order to keep it in her head.

At the appointed time, in defiance of the curfew and dressed all in black, she left the house and, keeping to side streets, walked to Areos Park, where she remembered there was a row of payphones beside the playground, out of sight of the main roads. The streets were deserted except for a few stray dogs that paid no attention to her. Along the way her resolve nearly failed; she wavered back and forth a hundred times in her convictions. What was she doing? How would getting involved with these people help her parents? She should be with Magda, waiting to escape to America. As Enrique had said to her, once this was over she could get involved in the clean-up and demand justice for those who had been persecuted. But if she ended up in jail now, she would be no use to anyone, including herself.

Finally she was within sight of the phones. She held her breath. She did not want her voice shaking when she made the call.

It was picked up halfway through the first ring. A man's voice spoke. "Who is this?"

"Nadia Wladanski."

"11 Carretera de la Coruña tomorrow at six."

He hung up.

His terse manner made it seem like she had done something wrong, and for a moment her throat tingled and tears welled up in her eyes. But as she hung up the phone she knew that she had passed the first test. The new life she had chosen for herself was beginning.

She heard treads on the stairs and reached for the gun. But it was Gustavo.

"I'm going to get us some food," he said, coming over to the corner of the room where she and Krista sat on the floor behind a wall of broken cabinets and desks. The building had at one time housed some sort of business that had failed, but for whatever reason had remained vacant. She had learned that shortly after their formation, her group had been given a list and map of many such buildings in the city, annotated with information about which window or door would give most easily if it were prodded from the outside, and what they could expect to find once they'd gotten in. One of them—Edmond, she supposed—had pared this list down to the buildings nearest their base of operation on Calle de Vasquez. Nadia didn't know where the others had gone or even if they were still alive. By design or simple luck, she and Krista and Gustavo had ended up here.

"I'll go," Krista said. "You get some rest."

The morning light was peeking through the cracks around the plywood panels that had been nailed over the basement windows. Gustavo's tall, slim figure towered above them. On her first day on the inside, Nadia had identified him as the gentle one among the leaders, a pleasing foil to Edmond's ruthless competence and often sour abruptness and Ruben's mistrustful irritability. She had been attracted to him immediately and imagined that maybe he would protect her. But then one time she saw him looking at Krista, and she knew at once that he was in love with her.

"I know a neighbourhood around here," he said, squatting down to their level. In his hand was a small pistol. He handled it so casually, it was as if he'd never been without it. "There are a couple of people who might help me."

"It's not safe," Nadia said. "With all the police out there. They'll be watching your friends. Why don't you wait?"

"It's never going to be safe, and I'd rather do it now," he said. "The police have been out all night. Even they have to stop for breakfast." He looked at Nadia. "I didn't say they were friends, Angelica." Then he added, "I might be a few hours. If I'm not back by the time it starts getting dark, get out of here."

Nadia could see Krista's gaze follow him as he retreated into the shadows and disappeared up the stairs. She didn't hear him leave the building.

Nadia got to her feet. "I'll go keep watch," she said.

"I'll come with you," Krista volunteered.

"You don't have to."

"I don't want to be alone," she said, without hesitation and without shame.

In the semi-darkness the two young women looked at each other. A few days ago such an admission would have been unthinkable. Nadia knew that the situation called for courage and resilience and an unquestioning fidelity to the larger cause. But the traumatic and unexpected events of the last twenty-four hours had descended upon her—upon all of them—like a crack of thunder from a clear blue sky. When she'd caught the look of shock and then of pure terror on Steven's face in that last moment of his life, even though she didn't like him, she could not help reaching out to him with her heart. One day later the fear in his eyes was still with her, and would remain with her, she suspected, for the rest of her life

"I don't want to be alone either," she said.

THIRTY-TWO

As instructed, she had arrived at 11 Carretera de la Coruña at six o'clock the following evening. It was a street of houses where, it seemed, ordinary people lived. She heard a mother calling to her children. Then a baby crying. A dog barking. Number eleven was a derelict bungalow. It looked abandoned. She knocked on the door anyway and stood waiting for several minutes. Not sure what to wear, she had reverted to loose-fitting jeans, baggy sweater and flat shoes, but left the jewellery behind. She wore no makeup. She had also decided against burdening herself with a purse and carried her identity card and money clipped together in her pocket.

Thinking she had misunderstood or that they had decided they weren't interested in her after all (but firm in her resolve to call the number Torres had given her again), she returned down the little dirt pathway to the street and began quickly retracing her steps to the bus stop, worried now that if she didn't hurry she would soon be in danger of violating curfew.

Then a car turned along the street, coming towards her. Suddenly it veered to the wrong side and braked with a screech. A man jumped out of the back and grabbed her arm. He said nothing as he dragged her towards the car.

Before she could even cry out, she was in the back seat and a hood had been pulled over her head.

A voice spoke to her through the hood. "Don't say a word."

The man held her arm the entire ride, which was neither long nor short. She sat very still, gasping for breath through the hood, which smelled of cigarettes. They turned down one street, then another, and soon they had made so many turns she had no idea where they were.

When they stopped, she was taken out of the car—not roughly, but the hand on her arm continued to hold her in a grip that forced her to move quickly. They walked over gravel, then concrete, went through a door and into a building, and down some steps. She had begun to choke as fear took hold of her, but held her breath to keep the tears at bay. Even if they were going to kill her, she did not want them to see she was afraid.

They brought her into a room and left her standing. She heard the scrape of chair legs against the concrete floor. A voice said, "Lift your arms and hold still." She did as she was told, and then, humiliatingly, there were hands on her body, under her sweater, on her breasts. She understood that this was necessary and clenched her teeth, forcing herself not to squirm. Then they were done. She was pushed into a chair and the hood was pulled from her head. It was the basement room of an abandoned building, cluttered with pieces of machinery, odd lengths of pipe, planks of wood, a coil of wire on a table, papers and crumpled cardboard boxes strewn all over. Several small rectangular windows set high in the wall near the ceiling had been painted over with black paint. There were three young men in the room with her: two standing facing her, the other, taller than the other two, moving around from behind her with the hood in his hand. The three of them eyed her unsmilingly in the quivering spray of yellow light that came from two oil lamps sitting on a desk. The room was damp and smelled musty.

When the first one spoke, she recognized his voice from the telephone call.

"Who are you?"

"Nadia Wladanski." It was a struggle to keep her voice steady. She swiped strands of hair away from her face and out of her mouth.

"What do you want with us?"

"I want to help," she said, wondering now if that was good enough. "I want to make a difference."

The other shorter man demanded, "Why?"

She turned to face him.

"My parents did nothing wrong and they were arrested. I . . . I can't sit by and let it happen to someone else. I can't let these things happen."

The two who later became known to her as Edmond and Ruben did not take their eyes from her, and there was nothing in their gaze to comfort her. The taller man seemed more composed.

That was not the end of it. She had no idea how long it took, but hour after hour the questions came at her in a relentless inquisition. They asked about her political and religious beliefs, about every aspect of her life, every member of her family, every friend she'd ever had, places she'd been, where she bought her clothes, her groceries, what she ate. They asked about her teachers, her dentist, her family doctor ("We never had one," she'd said). They seemed very interested in Carmel and Raoul and his position at the naval base in San Sebastián. Questions about Hector and Enrique and that day at the café with Jorgé took more than an hour. She said things she never intended to say, gave away secrets she knew were precious to other people.

They asked her the same questions over again using different words.

They had made her empty her pockets, and at one point Ruben and Edmond took her identity card and left her alone with Gustavo. He gave her water and a wet cloth so she could wipe her face. But she was so exhausted she was unable to stop the flow of tears, even when the urge to cry had passed.

"All this is necessary," he told her.

"I know," she said.

"We have to take every precaution. I'm sorry."

"What happens," she asked, "if I don't make it? If you don't want me?"

Gustavo sat on the edge of the desk.

"Truthfully? If there's any reason to think you're working against us, we will kill you." He paused as she stared at him with her wet eyes. "But if we simply decide we can't use you, then we'll blindfold you again and leave you somewhere, and you will make your way back to where you came from."

Nadia, in her weakened state, moaned, "I don't want to die."

"None of us want to die," he said, and she detected a note of irritation in his voice. "But if we're not willing to risk everything then we're of no use. You've already said you want to make a difference. How can you make a difference and not risk everything? It's impossible."

"I know all your names," she said, startled to realize this and admitting to it as if to some transgression.

He laughed. "We don't use our real names. And neither will you, if you become one of us."

"I know what you look like," she insisted, as if this, finally, would make him see the folly of letting her live.

He approached and lowered himself, placing one knee on the ground and bringing his face to a level with hers, inviting her to make note of every scar, every blemish. He was clean-shaven and beneath a mop of curly hair were a pair of deeply set green eyes and a large nose. With their expression of absolute calm, the features spoke of an easy-going nature and a sophisticated intelligence.

"And we know what you look like," he said, taking the cloth from her and dabbing at her fresh tears, his tone hinting at compassion even if his words did not. "We know where you live. We know everything about you. You will not be permitted to harm our cause."

She could not help it. She wrapped her arms around his neck and leaned against him, her cheek resting on his shoulder. The tangy smell of his skin and sweat was potent, intoxicating, and she was reminded of clinging to her father when she was a little girl and so tired her eyes were drooping shut, but didn't want to go to bed. Gustavo remained still for a few moments, but didn't wrap his arms around her; didn't touch her at all. Finally, he extricated himself and stood looking down. "If the police arrest you," he said, "what we are doing here will seem like child's play. Are you sure you're strong enough?"

The answer that leapt into her mind was, *Of course not*. But she held her tongue.

In a while, Ruben and Edmond returned. Gustavo left, and the interrogation resumed.

After more hours than she could count, it seemed to be over. They worked in shifts, refreshed themselves with rest; they had smoked and brought out food and eaten it in front of her. She had been granted no respite except to go to the bathroom. She was dizzy and nauseous after having had nothing to eat and very little to drink. Afterward she was led from the building and put into a car, though her recollection of this was dreamlike, as if it happened to somebody else. When she awoke, she was in a small room with no windows, curled up on an old sofa and covered by a wool blanket. The sofa and blanket smelled of cigarettes. And, in fact, on a table next to the sofa was a glass ashtray filled with crushed butts. She had never smoked in her life, but inexplicably she found herself craving a cigarette. She didn't know where she was or what day it was, and when she saw by her watch that it was three o'clock, she realized she didn't know if it was day or night.

"**W**hy did you join?" Krista asked.

The broken windows did not keep out the cool morning air rolling down from the mountains, and they sat huddled together for warmth on a waiting room bench, in a room that at one time had been someone's office, on the building's sixth floor. Cloaked in dust, a lone pen and some paperclips lay scattered on the surface of the desk. A few framed prints hung askew on the walls, which had been spray-painted with gang-affiliated graffiti. From the corner where Gustavo had positioned the bench, they had views out two windows, one facing west, towards the city centre and, beyond that, the ocean (for the moment veiled in fog), the other looking towards the northbound highway, which appeared as a flat stretch of pitted tarmac for about half a mile before curving east into the hills.

Nadia thought for a moment before answering. As part of her rite of passage (when she had ceased being Nadia Wladanski and assumed her new identity as Angelica Petrona), she had been cautioned against making friends within the group. In their world, Ruben lectured her, there are many periods of inactivity, and the temptation to tell secrets and make confidences can become very strong. But for a group such as theirs, personal affiliations were not simply pointless and counterproductive, they could be actively destructive. Imagine, Edmond said to her, that you tell Krista that you are worried about your sister Carmel, whose husband is assigned to the navel base at San Sebastián. If Krista is arrested and questioned under torture about her confederates, that fact might be the one thing she remembers about you. Your slip of the tongue could put your entire family in even greater danger than they already are.

"I had no choice," she said, Edmond's words echoing in her head. "Everyone is gone. My whole family is gone."

She glanced at Krista. The girl's eyes were a soft hazy blue, almost grey. Her skin was not pale like Nadia's but had a creamy texture and was lightly bronzed. Her hair, cut short and barely covering her ears, was the colour of dirty straw.

Nadia asked her, "And why did you join?"

"To be close to Gustavo," she said without hesitation, looking down for a moment and then up again to meet Nadia's eyes. "It seemed like a wonderful adventure. I thought, I'm really going to do something. You know? It was romantic and dangerous. After what happened I knew I wasn't going to be able to keep him from doing it. So I made him promise, after he was inside, to let me know what to do, and I would join him. Since I would come after him, it would look like we didn't know each other."

"I knew that he was in love with you," Nadia said. "I saw him looking at you. But I couldn't tell if you shared . . . if you felt what he felt. I thought he fell in love with you after you joined."

"I didn't know if he would be able do it. You know, give me a way to come to him. But after a few weeks he sent a message, and I made the contacts. He and Edmond and Ruben were the leaders. He was already one of the leaders, in only a few weeks! I couldn't believe it. They questioned me like I'm sure they questioned you. I don't know how I got through it. I thought they were going to kill me. And I didn't know . . . Would he stand up for me? I made a silly mistake, because when they asked me the name of my boyfriend, I said . . . well, I said Gustavo's real name. It just came out. Just his first name. I realized, and then gave a different second name, which was the last name of a boy from school I used to go with."

Nadia looked at the young woman sitting beside her on the bench, hugging her knees and chewing her bottom lip. Krista's skills as a costume and makeup artist had turned out to be very useful to the group. But she was mousy and tentative and, as Nadia was discovering, needy. Since the assassination and through all that had happened since, she had grown even more vague and childlike. No wonder Gustavo didn't want her going out looking for food. She had refused to lay a finger on the gun, which sat on Nadia's side of the bench. Nadia had begun to think she was a bit touched and didn't understand the gravity of their situation.

"It was hard because we had to pretend we didn't know each other. I had to watch him do things . . . hurt people. But, you know, this is bigger than any of us. You do what you have to do."

"What about your family?" Nadia ventured, probing deeper. "Did you say anything about what you were planning?"

"My father is a doctor and Gustavo was studying medicine, so they were great friends. My parents went into mourning when he disappeared. They assumed he had been arrested or kidnapped. I acted my part, which was not hard because I was sad to be separated from him. But, no, I knew that I couldn't tell them what I was going to do. Gustavo and I were living together. I stayed with my parents for a while after he went away, and then I went back to the apartment. When I was getting ready to leave for the last time, I turned over the tables and chairs and threw the desk drawers on the floor and scattered things all over the place, to make it look like someone had come searching for something. It was sad not to be able to say goodbye."

Nadia lowered her eyes. After her interrogation, and once she had been accepted into the group, she had been allowed a final visit to the house to retrieve things she would need. Everything had to fit into a single canvas shopping bag. Ruben drove her to the street and let her off down from the house. She did not even have to give directions. He knew exactly where to go.

"What did you mean when you said, about Gustavo joining the group, 'after what happened' you weren't going to be able to stop him?"

"That was . . . In the hospital he saw a lot of things, but one night when he was working in emergency, two boys came in, he said, supporting each other because they both had injured legs. They were no more than fourteen or fifteen and they were terrified. They wouldn't tell him their names or anything about what had happened. He said that what he took out of their wounds were bits of twisted metal, like from an explosion. But, he said, there had been no reports of any bomb attacks that night. Anyway, he said, he cleaned them up and was letting them rest on benches in the corridor when these soldiers came in demanding to know where these boys were. They had their names and photographs, so there was no mistaking. They took the boys away, and one of the soldiers came up to Gustavo and told him to forget he'd ever seen them. The next day, one of the nurses told him to go to the morgue. The two boys were there and they had both been shot in the head."

Krista gazed in her vague fashion out the window beside her, towards the city.

"After that, all he could talk about was putting an end to the brutality."

Nadia turned to look out the other window. There was a smattering of rain and a bit of wind. The sky was a steely grey and there were very few cars on the road. Her gaze followed the straight half mile of highway out to where it turned and rose into the hills, and then in her mind she went beyond this. The vast distances into which her imagination took her seemed to imply that they would escape, that rescue was close at hand. How could it not happen? Beyond the city was a huge world that would take them in, feed, clothe, and shelter them, allow them to shed their current identities and assume new ones, and turn them out transformed and no longer fugitives. Her parents would be released, Carmel and Raoul would call from San Sebastián saying they were all right, Hector would return home, and they would all get on a boat together and sail away to join Magda in America.

"God, I need a cigarette," Krista murmured. "I wish . . . I really wish I had a cigarette."

Nadia wiped a tear from her eye. "Me too," she said.

The group lived together under one roof in the house on Calle de Vasquez. Their movements were strictly controlled. Only the group leaders, Edmond, Ruben, and Gustavo, came and went freely. Adriano, whose technical skills seemed to bestow upon him a special status within the organization, was often gone for days at a time. But Nadia, Krista, and Imelda lived as virtual prisoners, performing the tasks assigned to them and only setting foot outside on the order of one of the leaders.

The day after Nadia retrieved her things from her family's house, they were brought together for a meeting. Edmond, Ruben, and Gustavo presided. Nadia sat beside Krista and Imelda on a tattered sofa, but there were no introductions, though she soon learned that Krista was good with hair and makeup and a skilled seamstress, and Imelda was a thief and a forger. Gustavo explained that they had been assigned the task of stealing money from a financial institution. They needed to take a significant prize that would make a difference to their operations. Adriano then stepped forward and unrolled a large square paper on the table: a building plan. The credit union served a twofold purpose: it housed large sums of cash on a daily basis and a lot of military personnel took their business there. A major theft would disrupt military activity and erode confidence.

Because of her beauty, Nadia was assigned the role of the girlfriend. It would be her job to seduce a vulnerable male employee, who had already been targeted. Once her allure had made him dependent on her, and once she had gained his confidence and he had lowered his guard and become lazy and trusting and given her access to his life, she would gather whatever useful information she could find and plant other information that would incriminate him in the theft. Eventually, once the foundation for his guilt had been laid, they would force him to turn over his security clearance codes.

Ruben said she would probably have to have sex with him and asked if that would bother her. No, she said, feeling the blood rise to her cheeks, but holding her head up high so maybe they wouldn't see her embarrassment.

"They've been looking for someone like you," Krista confided afterward as she was cutting Nadia's hair. The next day they would receive more specific information on how the operation would unfold, but Krista was told to begin preparing Nadia for her role immediately

"What do you mean?" Nadia asked, though she knew perfectly well what Krista meant.

"Someone to be the tart," she said. "Someone who paints her face and puts on a short skirt, then crosses her legs and watches the men fall all over themselves trying to get to her. Don't think for a minute they didn't have that in mind from the beginning. I mean, just look at you."

She put the mirror into her hand, and when Nadia saw the girl with the short black hair and exposed neck gazing back at her, she wondered who on earth it could be.

THIRTY-THREE

She had been afraid that the "target" would be some ancient lecher with fingers like claws and cheese-smelling breath. But these anxieties eased when Edmond showed her the photographs of Steven Downing. He was young and paunchy around his middle—certainly not as handsome as Hector. With his soft skin and close-set eyes, he struck her as neither formidable nor very intelligent, but she would have no problem sharing a meal with him or even holding his hand. That he was American would make her job easier. She had never known an American and would have no difficulty asking questions about the place he came from. So even if she wasn't interested in him as a friend or lover, she wouldn't have to pretend about being interested in his home country.

They had been following him and knew where encounters could take place that would have the appearance of happy accidents and not arouse suspicion. So as a first step, over a period of several days, she crossed his path at a delicatessen (she made sure he noticed her by standing close to him at the counter), a newspaper kiosk, and on the street outside the credit union. The first time she only smiled at him. The second time he spoke to her (saving her the trouble of creating a pretext for talking to him) in a nervously familiar fashion, about the coincidence of having seen her only a couple of days before. The third time they both laughed and he asked if she would meet him for coffee.

Krista was kept busy altering clothes that Imelda stole so that they'd fit Nadia's slim build, but other aspects of Nadia's story fell more easily into place, and soon the persona of Angelica Petrona was complete. On the strength of an expertly forged student ID, she told Steven she was beginning her studies in economics at the university and had gotten a part-time position as a researcher for one of her professors. A "professor" was standing by to verify this if need be. They had access to an apartment close to the university if Steven ever asked to see where she lived, but Edmond instructed her to discourage or delay for as long as possible any glimpses into her private life since the idea was for her to get inside his life.

The immediate problem, Edmond had explained at their next group meeting, was her family. Because of her pale European colouring, no one in the group could pose as a brother or sister. But to make a convincing case for Angelica Petrona they needed a relative, preferably an older man with some appearance of dignity and an air of authority. Edmond looked at Nadia and said that this was where they would bring in her friend Enrique Tomás.

Astonished, Nadia had stood and objected to Enrique's involvement. What made them think he would cooperate? She had already told them, during her interrogation, that he had no patience with the resistance or rebel activities. He called it "dangerous nonsense" and got angry with her whenever she spoke of these things sympathetically. But Edmond reminded her that while being questioned she'd also said she believed he would do anything for her. Was that a lie? If it was, she'd better tell them now.

"Besides," Ruben had added, looking at her coldly. "He is vulnerable."

She sat down and the meeting continued.

Without her knowledge they had been watching him. The photographs of Enrique and his office had been taken immediately after her interrogation, and they had since tracked down Jorgé's parents and shown them Enrique's picture. Adriano had forced his way into the Tomás flat and taken the hallway photo of the newspaper and the lamp. The stage was largely set. Nadia was to phone and ask him to join her for lunch at the bistro next to the train station, where the streets at midday were busy and anyone observing the encounter would be shielded by the crowd.

Maybe, she had thought as the details were revealed, he will do this for her and then just walk away. But then it came to her that Steven would remember him. She would be gone—secure in a new town with a new identity—but Enrique would still be here. She said again she couldn't place him in that kind of danger, he had been so kind to her. But they would not be moved. They said if she continued to object to the plan, they would pull her out of the current operation and send her somewhere else. She would never see him again. And her refusal to comply with their wishes would put her at risk within the organization. They would have to question her loyalty and her motives. Edmond's next words stayed with her: "When you joined us you placed your entire life and everyone in it at our disposal. It's too late to pick and choose. It's either this life or no life."

Finally, her eyes were completely open. "Yes," she said. "You're right. I'm sorry."

The night before the lunch date Nadia was called in for a private conference with Edmond, Ruben and Gustavo. They were all smoking. Gustavo lit a cigarette for her, as he would for any colleague.

"You will tell him only what you have to in order to get him to cooperate," Edmond began. "We will be watching closely. If we believe you're being threatened, you will see one of us approach and you will leave him immediately. We will also be watching him afterward, to see what he does with what you have told him. We will kill him if his actions become suspicious."

"He won't do anything to hurt me," Nadia said, horrified. She was certain of this, and yet understood the necessity to plan as if the worst was inevitable.

"Regardless, you are responsible for him. If he is something to you, you will see to it that his actions don't make it necessary for us to eliminate him. His life will be in your hands."

"I have to tell him that he's in danger because he works at the university. Maybe he'll see reason and leave the city."

"If you like. He probably won't believe you."

"I don't—"

Gustavo broke in. "Angelica, please understand that he has done this to himself. It is not your fault that we are in a position to exploit his foolish actions to extort money from him. He is your responsibility, true, but only as far as our needs are concerned. Once you leave him, what he does next is his decision." He drew on the cigarette and went on. "All of us have left behind another life. It's a huge sacrifice. What you are going to do tomorrow will be difficult because you are going to mix your old life with your new life. This is unusual, and was the subject of debate at higher levels of our organization. But the benefits outweigh the risks, and you will be doing us a great service. The money is needed as a short-term measure."

She nodded.

Ruben added, "Maybe it will comfort you to know that the next time we approach him for money, you won't be involved."

She sharpened her gaze, but any protest she might have formulated did not even coalesce as phrases in her mind.

"You can't allow yourself to be weak," Gustavo observed. "Sentiment and affection have no place in our world and can get you killed. After this is done and we get you away from here, you can put your old life behind you for good."

She turned to him. The look in his eyes that time she'd caught him gazing at Krista had been, unmistakably, one of heartsick longing. It had lasted for no more than a second or two, but she knew that for those few moments, sentiment and affection had been the only things on his mind. She saw now that he was faking. They were all faking.

"I'm ready," she said, and she stubbed out her cigarette.

Around noon Gustavo returned with a grocery bag full of sandwiches wrapped in waxed paper, fruit, bottled water, and cigarettes. He pulled a chair over to the bench and stayed with them while they ate, but he didn't say anything. Nadia saw Krista peeking at him from time to time, and she must have recognized that he was upset because she did not ask any questions.

Finally, after the food was gone and they were all smoking, he said, "Major Downing is dead. Our mission is accomplished."

Nadia did not feel it was her place to speak. Krista also remained silent.

"Unfortunately, Edmond is dead as well. Ruben is missing. We can only presume he's dead or in custody."

The previous evening, after they'd hidden themselves in the building, Gustavo had explained that from the outset the target had been Steven's father. The plan had been to get to him through his son. It had not been necessary for her and Krista to know this in order to perform their tasks.

Finally, Krista asked, "What's going to happen to us?"

"I've been told to stay put and await further instructions."

Nadia watched him in profile as he smoked his cigarette. She was struck, not for the first time, by his distinguished features and stately bearing. Everything about him commanded respect.

"But," he said after a moment, "I don't know if that's a good idea."

The meeting with Enrique had done two things for Nadia. It had taught her that if she did not soon gain complete control of her emotions she would not survive, and it had demonstrated her value to the group in obvious and quantifiable terms.

It had also made her wonder how closely they were watching her. Had they seen her ranting at Enrique on the sidewalk near the coffee shop, in full view of at least a dozen other pedestrians? Had they noticed them arguing in the bistro, and Enrique's agitation when he rose to his feet? Had they been watching when she and Enrique embraced in the alley-way? Had they seen her snatch the money out of his hand before walking away? When she turned over the 40,000 pesetas to Edmond, he did not thank her, but he also did not ask for the rest. Were they waiting to see if she would offer it up voluntarily?

The room she shared with Krista and Imelda was not large to begin with and was crowded by the three small beds that almost completely filled the space. Her options for concealment were limited. She had brought a sweater, jeans, and sneakers from the house, but the rest of the clothes she wore did not belong to her and could be taken away at any time. She had not been permitted to bring anything of a personal nature that could lead the police back to Nadia Wladanski. In the end, she divided the money (6,700 pesetas) into two rolls and pushed one into the toe of each sneaker.

Over the following weeks, as her relationship with Steven Downing progressed through stages of friendship towards intimacy, she suppressed thoughts of Nadia and through sheer will compelled herself into the role of Angelica, who had no brothers or sisters, whose parents were dead, who was taking economics at the university and working part-time for Professor Quintana, and whose Uncle Marco lived in Puerto Varas. When she was with Steven, the clothes helped her to become Angelica, and there were times when she found herself enjoying the performance because the clothes and makeup were such fun to wear. At the house on

Calle de Vasquez she helped Krista with the mending and sewing and tried to not think about anything.

Steven himself was shy and courteous and did not force himself on her. Her first time in his apartment, before going out to a movie, they kissed once, lightly, because that seemed to be all he wanted to do. The second time, they kissed on his sofa. She had unbuttoned his shirt and helped him take it off. But he seemed unwilling to take the encounter beyond this, and she did not push it. One evening he confessed that he was so unsure of himself around women that he was afraid that if they ever ended up in bed together she would laugh at his clumsiness. He had two older sisters whose friends used to come to the house and some-times they flirted with him, but he knew it was only to embarrass him. They whispered in his ear about things that girls liked to do. They said they were trying to help him, but he always assumed they were mak-ing fun of him. He did not want to lose Angelica by moving too slowly, but he also did not want to make a fool of himself by doing something stupid.

Nadia found him charming, if a bit childish, and could not believe that he was twenty-five, seven years older than her.

She told him she was in no hurry.

To her surprise, Edmond and Gustavo did not seem troubled that Steven was content to let the relationship evolve slowly.

"Give the poor guy a chance," Edmond said. "He'll make his move before long. Then you can make yours."

Gustavo laughed at this.

But Ruben did not laugh. He glanced at her sullenly and then looked quickly away.

There was something wrong, but she didn't know what it was. Per-haps Ruben suspected her of deception, because he seemed displeased with her all the time. The only thing she could think of was that he knew about the money Enrique had given her and wanted to confront her with this knowledge, but the others wouldn't let him. One afternoon she was helping Krista at the sewing table, and Ruben stopped in the doorway. He didn't say anything, just stared at them, his expression dour and unsettling. Nadia shuddered and pretended she hadn't noticed. After he went away, Krista whispered, "He gives me the creeps."

That night she was awoken by raised voices. She recognized Ruben's staccato shouts and Edmond's angry muttering, and then Gustavo's softer tone of conciliation during the pauses.

Then, quite suddenly, everything was fine again. At their meetings, when Ruben spoke, it was in a normal voice. He smiled more often than before, and he was pleasant to her. He no longer seemed suspicious.

And she thought that maybe she had imagined the whole episode, that whatever had been troubling him had nothing to do with her.

One day shortly after this, Steven said, "My parents will be here on the weekend. I want you to meet them."

He had told her only that his father's company had a contract and was doing some work for the government. She had not asked for more information because it didn't seem relevant.

When she reported Steven's invitation to Gustavo, Edmond, and Ruben, it raised only passing interest. "Find out what you can," Edmond said to her. "Let us know when and where it will happen. We will probably want to observe in case anything comes out of it that we can use later on."

Steven's parents were staying at the downtown Hilton, one of only a handful of hotels still open for business two years after the military assumed power. Many of the material aspects of life had remained unchanged since the takeover. Some, despite occasional commodity shortages, sudden price increases, and the instability of the currency on international markets, had actually improved. But you can't force people to visit a country if they don't want to, and tourism had dropped off significantly.

She was to meet Steven's parents on Sunday morning, over breakfast. His father had business meetings most of the afternoon and that evening they were having dinner with friends. She was, in a way, looking forward to it. They were Americans, and so they would be interesting. If they were anything like Steven, they would be polite and respectful. If she had truly been interested in their son as a mate, she would have been nervous. But since she felt nothing for him other than as a means to an end, it didn't really matter if they liked her or not. All she wanted was to enjoy the meal and let them see enough of Angelica Petrona to be comfortable with the fact that she was going out with their son.

It seemed strange that when she was readying herself to leave the house on Calle de Vasquez, Gustavo, Edmond, and Ruben were all absent. It would be the first time since the operation began that she received no last-minute instructions on her way out the door, regardless of whether she needed them or not. She hoped she had not done something wrong. She hoped they were not losing faith in her. Edmond had reminded her the other day that laying a foundation took time. But it had been three weeks since her first conversation with Steven, and she felt that, if their movement was in such dire need of the money, more progress could have been made.

She left the house by the side door, as she always did, and walked to the rear and along the carriageway between the two rows of houses that backed against each other. Her first point of contact with the street was always several doors away, in one direction or the other, from their headquarters.

Summer was approaching. It was a fine clear day, the warmest in a week. Krista had provided her with a new outfit, a light sweater to go with pants and a jacket, all within a brown-beige range of colours. She liked Krista despite her dreaminess, admired her handiwork with a needle and thread and her proficiency with the sewing machine. Nadia had never mastered the art of mending and had grown used to the jokes told within the Wladanski household about her hems coming unravelled and buttons falling off.

She smiled at the memory, but when she felt her throat tighten and tears welling up in her eyes she clenched her jaw and banished all thoughts of her family from her mind.

It was a twenty-minute walk to the city centre, and soon the hotel was in sight.

She strode through the sliding doors and into the lobby. She had become used to walking into places like this, places where Nadia Wladanski would never have ventured. Women looked her up and down, frowning in appraisal, men smiled and held doors open for her. The clothes, the makeup, and the hair made the difference. Even at the bank with Enrique, as uncomfortable as she'd been, people had looked at her and assumed she belonged. She was approaching the main desk when she saw Steven coming towards her from the direction of the hotel restaurant. He was wearing slacks, a jacket, and a shirt and tie.

"You look terrific," he said and kissed her on the lips.

"So do you," she said, and they both laughed, but his smile did not linger on his face and she guessed that he had reason to be nervous.

"We can go in. They'll be down in a few minutes."

As the waitress was showing them to the table, she asked, "Do you always wear a tie to have breakfast with your parents?"

He shrugged. "My dad's a bit of a stickler. But no, he wouldn't have cared. I just thought it would make an impression, you know, if both of us looked good for them. You always dress so nicely."

They sat down. The waitress filled their cups with coffee and left them alone.

"Have you ever thought," Steven began, and she could tell he had been thinking about something because his neck flushed and the colour rose unbecomingly into his cheeks. "Have you ever thought about going to school in the States?"

"What?" She laughed because the idea seemed crazy.

"I don't mean anytime soon, necessarily. But just, you know, someday."

She stirred some milk into her coffee. "I hadn't thought of that, no," she said. "But I guess, maybe. My English isn't very good."

"That doesn't matter," he said. "You're smart. You can learn."

"I'm just starting," she said, and looked down, made suddenly shy by what he seemed to be implying.

"I know," he said. "But in a couple of years my dad's contract here will run out and we'll probably move back home. I know we just started seeing each other. Maybe I'm out of line. I don't want to assume anything. But if you don't have any family here but your uncle, what would stop you from coming with us?"

She looked at him. Her smile fell away when, over his shoulder, she saw a man in a white jacket carrying dishes to the buffet table against the wall. From the back he seemed familiar, and when he turned she saw that it was Edmond.

"Uh . . . I'm—"

Steven touched her hand.

"I shouldn't have said anything. I'm sorry. Me and my big mouth. I guess I do want to know though, if . . . if the chance came your way, would you consider living in the States. But it's just an idea: something that came to me right after you said you were taking economics. You can study that anywhere. Anyway," he said, "it doesn't matter."

"No, no." She touched his wrist. "I will. I'll think about it." And she gave him an encouraging nod.

The waitress was leading another couple towards their table. Nadia glanced around. Edmond was gone.

She stood and found her hand tightly gripped by a beefy man with dark hair flecked with grey, a ruddy complexion. He was wearing a dark brown turtleneck sweater and jacket, and he was stocky but obviously in good physical condition. Steven's mother was chunky and had a swirl of blond hair piled on top of her head. She wore a dark blue short-sleeved sweater and matching slacks and had an elegant floral-patterned wrap draped over her shoulder. Steven's parents were not tall; his mother was shorter than Nadia, and when they shook hands, she tugged on Nadia's arm until Nadia bent down in order to receive a kiss on the cheek.

"You look sweet, my dear," Steven's mother gushed. "You shouldn't have gone to all that trouble just for us."

"She can go to as much trouble as she wants," Steven's father huffed, taking his seat.

Steven introduced them as Thomas and Sharon Downing, originally from Pittsburgh and now living in Encino, California.

"Please, call me Sharon," Steven's mother said, bestowing a lavish smile upon Nadia.

"They call me Major Tom," his father joked. "You know that song . . . ?"

Nadia tried to catch all that was being said, but her attention was divided. She had just noticed the two men in black suits who had accompanied Steven's parents into the dining room and who now took seats at the next table. She had spotted Edmond again, stationed next to the buffet table, but now he was gone. The dining room was quickly filling with hotel guests and others arriving for breakfast. The noise level rose. Their waitress poured coffee for the Major and his wife, topped up hers and Steven's, and took their food orders.

"Petrona . . . That's an unusual name, isn't it, for these parts?" the Major was asking.

"My father came over here from Poland," Nadia explained.

"And what did he do?"

"Landscaping," Nadia said. "Groundskeeping. He knew plants. He was a gardener."

"But still . . . why did he come to this country?" the Major persisted. "It's an odd choice. Don't you think?" He paused as Nadia gazed at him.

270

"So, Steven says you're taking economics?"

"Tom," his wife interjected. "Give the poor girl a chance to breathe." She turned to Nadia. "Angelica, my dear, my husband is an inveterate fact-checker. Everything has to be explained."

"I don't mind," Nadia said. "Everyone asks the same questions."

"It's the military background," he said. "Can't seem to shake it. Thirty years in the service will do that to you."

"The service?"

"You're wondering about my friends here," Tom said, jerking his thumb towards the next table, where the two young men in suits were stationed. They would have heard the Major's comment but did not acknowledge it. Instead, their eyes constantly roamed the room, making a continual survey of its occupants and contents.

Free now to observe them more closely, Nadia turned and immediately noticed the table where they were sitting was completely empty. There was not even a knife and fork.

"I spent years doing that, keeping watch and starving while some bigwig bozo got tanked and overfed with presidents and prime ministers." He grunted. "Now I'm the bigwig bozo."

Nadia was overcome by curiosity. "What do you do?"

"My company," he said, "provides security services for the government."

She nodded. Somewhere in her mind, a connection was forged.

"Steven will come to work for me eventually," the Major continued. "But he's not the type for surveillance work, and I wouldn't want him out in the field anyway. He'll do the finances, keep the books."

"Yeah," Steven said. "I'm not really cut out for that cloak and dagger stuff."

The waitress was placing their meals in front of them. Nadia was not hungry but had ordered a single fried egg with bacon and toast. Steven had pancakes. His father's plate was heaped with scrambled eggs and brown sausages, and Sharon had soft-boiled eggs on an English muffin. Each of them also received a side dish of fruit salad.

As they were eating, Tom and Steven chatted and Sharon engaged Nadia in a conversation about clothes and where she did her shopping. She admitted that as a student she had very little money and explained that she bought all of her outfits used and altered them herself.

One of the surveillance men stood and walked towards the entrance of the restaurant. Sharon was fingering Nadia's jacket.

"But the stitching is superb," she said, plainly amazed. "And that lining. You'd swear it was brand new."

"Thank you," Nadia said.

Sharon asked her another question, then another. In between, Nadia tried to remain attuned to the back and forth movements in the room around her.

"What's the matter, dear?" Sharon asked. "You look like you've seen a ghost."

Nadia picked up her knife, which had clanked against her plate when it slipped out of her hand. She had seen Ruben cross in front of her, wearing a busboy's outfit. And there was no mistaking Gustavo, dressed in a suit, standing just inside the entrance of the dining room.

She shook her head and smiled. "I'm just clumsy sometimes."

"You must be exhausted, with your schedule. All those classes, and you work too, Steven says."

"Yes. I'm—"

The surveillance man had leaned over and was speaking directly into the Major's ear. The Major's expression grew solemn.

Sharon lowered her voice, leaned in closer towards Nadia and touched her hand. "You must take care of yourself, Angelica. Steven let himself get terribly run down when he was going to college. And he didn't eat properly." She smiled. "He's very taken with you. I hope that once the semester is over you can visit us in California. We'll be going there in a few weeks for the summer. Steven will come up for his vacation."

Nadia looked hopelessly into the older woman's eyes. At this moment there was nothing she would rather do more than accompany this generous, warm-hearted family to their home in California, to America.

Major Downing dropped his napkin on the table and pushed his chair back.

Nadia looked up in time to see Gustavo, still standing near the entrance, with a gun in his hand. He raised it and, as if in a silent movie, the surveillance man next to him crumpled and fell to the floor.

The other surveillance man had pulled a gun out and was taking aim. Then he toppled forward. The gun flew into the air.

Nadia was conscious of screaming all around her. People were running in every direction. Suddenly she could not see Gustavo or Edmond anywhere. When she tried to get to her feet, thinking to get a better view of what was happening, she found that Steven's mother was holding her hand in a vice-like grip.

Words were coming at her from all directions. There were so many she couldn't understand them. The Major was pulling on Steven's arm, trying to get him to move. She felt eerily calm, as if nestled safely in the eye of a storm. The voices washed over her, incomprehensible. The thought came to her that once this was over, they would resume their breakfast. Ruben, in the busboy's uniform, was approaching their table. In his eyes was a crazed, purposeful look. He marched up to them. Somehow, he had a gun in his hand that she had not noticed. He took aim at the Major and pulled the trigger. The Major raised his hands, then, as if in pantomime, fell backward in his chair. Ruben turned and took aim at Sharon Downing, who sat beside Nadia with a look of innocent wonder on her face, her mouth wide open but silent. He pulled the trigger. A bright red wound opened on her forehead as she toppled over and fell to the floor. Then Ruben turned to Steven, who was not looking at him but at Nadia. Steven's face was speckled with blood and held an expression of bafflement that, as Nadia watched, contorted into fear and then terror. He reached across the table towards her, but she did not move, and when it seemed he was going to stand up Ruben fired the shot. Steven's head snapped backward, his eyes went dead, and he fell where she couldn't see him, leaving behind a spray of bloody debris across the top of the table.

With Steven gone Nadia had a nearly unobstructed view of the room. People were climbing over one another and crowding towards the exit. Then she turned and saw that Ruben had taken aim at her. She sat motionless, uncomprehending, transfixed by events that were still unfolding around her. Some remote part of her brain seemed to be urging her to take action, but she felt untroubled and safely removed from it all, as if she had been lifted out of her body and was observing everything from a great distance. Then, as she gazed at him, his expression softened and he lowered the gun. He said something that she did not hear, came to her, grabbed her arm and pulled her out of the chair.

She offered no resistance. She could not think. Her brain seemed paralyzed. He shoved her forward, propelled her through a swinging door and into the kitchen. People scattered, removed themselves from her path, or else dropped to the floor and huddled there, shielding themselves with their arms. Then there was another door and a set of stairs. At the bottom, they went through a door and into a corridor.

Here it was quiet. As if plugs had been removed from her ears, she could hear their steps and Ruben's noisy breathing.

He paused and seemed to listen. "Do you hear that?" he asked.

But she could hear nothing except his voice. She looked down and saw blood on his uniform.

He pulled her back the way they had come and took her through the door again. The space under the stairs was used for storage. He knelt and banged at the lock with the gun barrel until it gave. Then he flung back the doors.

"Get in there," he said, rising to his feet. He slid the gun into his waistband.

But she clung to him. She didn't know what to do.

"Get in!" he urged, prying her fingers one by one from his arm until she had to let him go. He pressed on her shoulder and forced her into a sitting position, then helped her slide over and into the space.

"I'll put the lock back on. It will look like it hasn't been opened. Stay here until I come back for you."

He closed her in. A bit of light filtered through the cracks between the doors and the jamb. There were scraping noises on the other side, then silence.

She sat still. Her breathing seemed very loud. She moved her leg, but bumped something, which knocked against something else with a hollow sound. She went still again. Images flashed through her mind—of Gustavo's upraised hand with the gun in it, of the surveillance man sliding to the floor, of Ruben approaching their table, of the Major, Sharon, and Steven each falling away from her field of vision the instant Ruben's gun went off. Strangely, she had no recollection of hearing shots fired. Suddenly Steven's face was before her eyes. She raised her hands to push it away, but it stayed fixed in place. A sound that seemed hardly human emerged from between her lips. "No," she protested, and moved her leg again, bumping something else that fell with a clatter. She became dimly aware that her hands were wet and sticky. Maybe she had been crying, but her eyes felt dry. It was like something had spilled on her.

She felt hot and cold at the same time. A wave of fatigue, like fever-induced weakness, rolled over her. As if drowning, she began gasping for air. She couldn't stay in this space.

She pushed at the doors, and, when they didn't give, swivelled her leg around and kicked. The door swung open. The broken lock skittered across the floor.

She crawled out and went through the stairwell door and into the corridor where she and Ruben had stood while he decided what to do. There were doors to other rooms on either side. But she didn't trust any of them. She heard voices. She had to find a way out.

Her legs were like rubber. Supporting herself with her hands against the walls, she crept along until she saw, at the very end, a glass door leading outside. As she watched a figure ran by, then another going in the opposite direction, then several people wandered past. She turned to look for another way out and saw smears of blood along the wall behind her, leading right up to where she stood. She looked at her hands, which were crusted with blood, then down at her blood-spattered clothes. She touched her face, her hair. It was all over her. The panic that had made it impossible to breathe when she was trapped in the space beneath the stairs, but which had released its grip once she was free, came hurtling back, and without warning her breakfast surged up her throat and splashed onto the floor at her feet. She staggered backward as her stomach contracted again, and then again. When the heaving stopped and she could stand upright she turned and groped along the wall, found the door, and was outside. Gasping, she fell to her knees on the grass next to the driveway that led to the parking lot behind the hotel. The glare of the sun attacked her and she was nearly blinded. She raised her hand to shield her eyes just as a figure emerged from the same door she had just come through. The person stopped and stood above her, blocking out the light. A couple of seconds passed before she recognized it as Gustavo.

"It's you," was all she could say.

He pulled her to her feet and shoved something at her. Her purse.

"We have to get out of here."

He took her hand. She went with him, grateful—as she had been to Ruben—that he was saving her the torment of deciding what to do next.

The parking lot was a crosshatch of cars blocking each other's way. The whole world seemed transformed into a cacophony of people yelling, horns blaring, and sirens wailing. Gustavo dragged her in a zigzag path through the maze of stationary cars. In a few seconds they had left the parking lot and were walking quickly along a footpath through a grassy area with trees and benches. The few people here stood gazing with concern in the direction of the hotel. A couple tried to stop them to ask what had happened, but Gustavo brushed by them. Others backed away when they saw the blood on Nadia's clothes. They left the path and went down a hill. Below them was a chain-link fence and on the other side, train tracks. Gustavo lifted a flap that had been cut in the twisted metal strands. She crawled through and he followed.

He took her by the arm and pulled her after him up the steep incline on the other side of the tracks. Here were streets, trees, houses, parked cars: a residential area. Three children skipping on the sidewalk paused in their play and stared at them.

They had left the children behind them when she found her voice and asked, "What happened?"

He did not respond immediately. When he did all he said was, "No questions."

They walked side by side for a short distance. She felt strength returning to her legs. Then he turned a corner and crossed to where a motorcycle was parked.

"Get on."

They sped through the streets. Nadia clung to him, her eyes squeezed shut, the side of her face pressed against his back.

Gustavo ditched the motorcycle behind an abandoned house several streets from Calle de Vasquez and they walked the rest of the way, using side lanes and, finally, the carriageway. He barely acknowledged her and stayed several steps ahead. Watching him an abrupt realization startled her: when she envisioned him in the hotel dining room with the gun in his hand, he was wearing a suit. But now he was wearing jeans and a plain shirt. Had she been mistaken? Surely it was important. She should notice such things. Her life could depend on it.

She stumbled along behind him. The way he was ignoring her made her think he was displeased, but with how the mission had gone or with her specifically? She couldn't tell and wasn't going to ask.

Her fractured mind had begun piecing together the events of the last half hour. She understood that Steven and his parents were dead. The reason for this eluded her, though she guessed that the Major's contract with the government had something to do with it. Two phrases that often surfaced during their group's meetings were "strategic act" and "symbolic act." She assumed that the murder of this family of Americans was a symbolic act.

When they got to the house, Krista cried out when she saw Nadia covered with blood.

"Oh my God! What happened?"

Gustavo was abrupt. "We have to get out of here. Don't ask anything. The less you know the better. Take what you need and leave. Remember your escape routes." He turned to Krista. "Get her cleaned up. We're leaving in five minutes."

Krista took Nadia upstairs.

"They shot them all," Nadia said, quickly stripping and discarding the bloody outfit on the bathroom floor. "In the middle of the restaurant. In the middle of all those people." She had not cried to this point, but as she spoke she began to tremble and the tears flowed down her cheeks. Krista had taken a cloth and with shaking hands was trying to wipe the blood and other matter from her face and hair. In the bedroom a few minutes later, Nadia pulled on the sweater and jeans she'd brought with her from her family's house, and pushed her feet into the sneakers where Enrique's money was hidden.

"I don't understand," Krista said. "Why kill innocent people?"

Nadia did not look at her. "I've told you all I know. I don't know how innocent they were."

The only thing Nadia took from the purse was the ID card under the name Angelica Petrona. Her old card had never been returned.

They were downstairs in time to exchange farewells, which Nadia had expected since the evacuation plan called for everyone to leave separately along different predetermined routes. But Imelda and Adriano had gone already. Gustavo said to her and Krista, "We'll go together." And Nadia felt palpable relief that, once again, the need for her to decide what to do had been taken out of her hands.

They doubled back to the motorcycle and she and Krista climbed on behind Gustavo. He drove slowly, avoiding main streets. Several times he pulled into a driveway or a parking lot behind a building and went off on foot to scout what was ahead.

In a couple of hours they had passed beyond the core business and residential districts and into the industrial outskirts. This part of the city was filled with factories and office buildings, many of which had been abandoned when the military took power, but which were now being reoccupied as normal economic activity resumed. Massive trucks rocketed along the road in both directions, filling the air with exhaust fumes and the guttural snarl of their engines. Not far away was the main arterial highway that all vehicles followed in and out of the city.

Gustavo cut the engine and they walked along a narrow passageway to the rear of a dark, apparently empty, six-floor office block barricaded behind a chain-link fence. Nobody spoke. Without trouble he located the break in the fence, and they passed through, taking the motorcycle with them. They wheeled it into a wooden shed and concealed it behind some garbage bags. Then, without any hesitation, as if he'd been here only the day before, Gustavo approached one of the basement windows and lifted away the board that covered it.

Once inside, he drew a gun from his back pocket and gestured for them to stay in the basement while he checked the upper floors. When he returned he had another gun. He tried to give it to Krista.

"No," she said. "I won't. Give it to her."

"Don't be an idiot," he said. "We can't afford to be squeamish."

She crossed her arms.

Reluctantly, it seemed to Nadia, he handed the gun to her. There had been no time for training with weapons. The weight of it astounded her.

"Just keep it close by. I pray to God you won't need it."

She nodded.

"Stay down here," he said. "Go behind that pile of stuff over there. I'll be back soon. I have to check where the roadblocks are. If we can get out of town tonight, we'll go."

They did as he said and waited in the shadows for his return. They were silent for lengthy stretches, during which the only sounds were trucks roaring along the street outside. As the afternoon slipped away, these became less frequent. The light filtering through the crevices where the boards did not quite fit the windows began to dim. In the darkness,

Krista reached for Nadia's hand. Nadia felt it would be cruel to pull away.

Soon Gustavo returned with news that a complete blockade of the city was in effect. They would have to stay where they were for the night.

THIRTY-FOUR

The food had rejuvenated Nadia briefly, but after several hours in the otherwise silent sixth-floor office where she and Krista and Gustavo continued their vigil—the patter of rain lulling her and wrapped in an almost hypnotic embrace by exhaustion—she was finding it increasingly difficult to keep herself upright on the bench.

Finally, she snapped awake to the sound of Gustavo's voice. He had his hand on her shoulder.

"There's a sofa in one of the rooms up here," he was saying. "Go lie down. Nothing's going to happen for a while."

She didn't protest.

The room was cool because of the broken windows, and there was nothing for her to use to cover herself, but she fell instantly into a depthless slumber that, for the time she remained there, admitted no visions, no nightmares.

She awoke in darkness to the sound of voices. Rain was still falling, but not as hard as before. She pulled herself up and reached for the gun, but remembered she had left it in the other room.

It was Krista and Gustavo. They were arguing.

"I don't know who you are any more."

"Don't say that. We all have to do things—"

"You're a doctor, not a murderer! You give life, you don't take it."

"I have," he cried in a pained voice. "I have taken lives."

"When it serves a purpose. This serves no purpose."

They were quiet for a moment. Nadia got to her feet.

"I never should have gotten you involved."

"I helped you," Krista said.

In her mind, Nadia envisioned the scene between the lovers, Krista crying and pleading: a spoiled child; Gustavo standing above her, calmly placating. But a difference in both their voices ruined the image. Krista's voice was firm, decisive, wholly adult. Gustavo sounded lost.

She crept down the hall.

"You needed me. I made a difference. I made the same sacrifice you did. And so did she. She made the same sacrifice." There was a pause. "If you do this it will destroy you."

Nadia reached the doorway and watched for a moment before stepping into the room. Gustavo, slumped with one hand holding his head, sat staring at the floor. Krista stood facing him.

"There," Krista said when she saw her. "There she is. Are you going to tell her or will I?"

Gustavo directed a glance towards Nadia but quickly turned away as if he could not bear to look at her.

"You were . . ." he began, speaking over his shoulder. He paused and rubbed his face with his hand. He turned. "Ruben was supposed to kill you along with the Downings."

Nadia just stared at him. What was he saying?

"You were considered expendable—"

"Who did?" Krista demanded.

He looked at her and then back at Nadia. "We considered you expendable. A loose end. We thought if the police found your body at the restaurant along with the Downings they'd waste time trying to find out who you were."

"And you agreed to this," Krista insisted, pushing him to admit it.

He nodded. "It didn't come from us," he added. "It wasn't my decision, or Edmond's or Ruben's. It came from higher up. They were looking for a way to make a high-profile hit. There were many names on the list, but they settled on Downing because of his son. You came into the group just as the plan was taking shape. They decided to use you as a lure. We could never get hold of Downing's schedule. He never travelled or stayed at a hotel under his own name. But he had business dealings here. With you on the inside with the son, they felt contact would be made at some point."

The strength had gone from her legs. Nadia sank to the floor and leaned her head against the wall.

"Ruben went along with it at first, but then he started saying it made more sense to keep you alive so we could use you again. He said it was a waste to kill you. To tell the truth, I think he was in love with you. He argued with us about it and dreamed up other operations that you could be part of. But he seemed to come around when we pointed out that you were the public face of this operation. All of the son's friends and colleagues would remember you. Even if we moved you to another location, we could never use you again. It would be too dangerous."

Nadia noticed one of the guns in his hand.

"He said he would do it. He convinced all of us. Anyway, he didn't, and now it's even worse, because you were there, at the table with them. The people at the restaurant will remember you. So not only can we not use you again, now you're a liability. You're a danger to anyone who comes into contact with you."

"But," Nadia asked, locating a detail that seemed to point in another direction, "you brought my purse. I thought—"

"That I was covering for you? Helping you get away?" Gustavo shook his head. "Taking the purse was part of the plan. It would make it more difficult for the police to figure out who you were. When the crowd rushed for the exit I lost sight of what Ruben was doing. But when I got to the table and saw you weren't there, I knew something had gone wrong." He shrugged. "I took the purse because it was what I was supposed to do."

He looked at Nadia and then quickly away.

"I didn't know . . . if I found you somewhere while I was leaving the building, if I would be able to kill you or not. Then, outside, with people all around . . . And I didn't have the gun any more."

"He was going to go in there while you were asleep and shoot you in the back of the head," Krista said.

Gustavo looked down. His suffering was palpable, a fourth presence in the room. The lines on his face were those of a much older man. Nadia almost felt sorry for him.

"We—Krista and I—we have to go and meet them. They'll give us new IDs and get us away from here. When I told them what happened and that you were alive, all they said was 'She's supposed to be dead. Complete the mission as planned.'"

"But he's not going to kill you," Krista said. "If he was that sort of person he would have just gone in there and done it. He told me what they wanted him to do because he knew I would stop him."

With his free hand Gustavo covered his eyes. He bent forward and rested his elbows on his knees. The gun dangled from his fingers. Krista grabbed the other gun from the bench.

"You have to get out of here now."

Nadia watched her approach. She shook her head. "I don't—"

"Get up," Krista ordered. "And take this." She pressed the gun into Nadia's hand.

"Wait," Gustavo said. He remained seated and did not look at her. "The ID card. Angelica Petrona. I need you to give me that."

Nadia reached into her pocket.

"But I have nothing else—"

"If they catch you with it," he said, "I don't want to think about what they'll do to you."

She gave the card to Krista. Their eyes met. Krista looked away.

"Don't go back to the house," Gustavo advised. "They've probably found it by now. Your family's house . . . Maybe it's being watched . . . I don't know."

"He'll tell them he carried out the order and that we got rid of the body."

The weight of the gun was like some dead thing in her hand. Slowly she inserted it into her pocket. "I don't have anywhere to go," she said.

"I think he's right," Krista said as she went to Gustavo and stood beside him. "I think Ruben fell in love with you. That's what saved you. So remember, you have that to fall back on. It might save you again."

"Nadia, your only hope is to get as far away from here as possible," Gustavo said, looking at her. It had been so long since anyone had used her real name. "Please be careful."

"Go!" Krista urged.

Wiping her eyes, Nadia turned and ran.

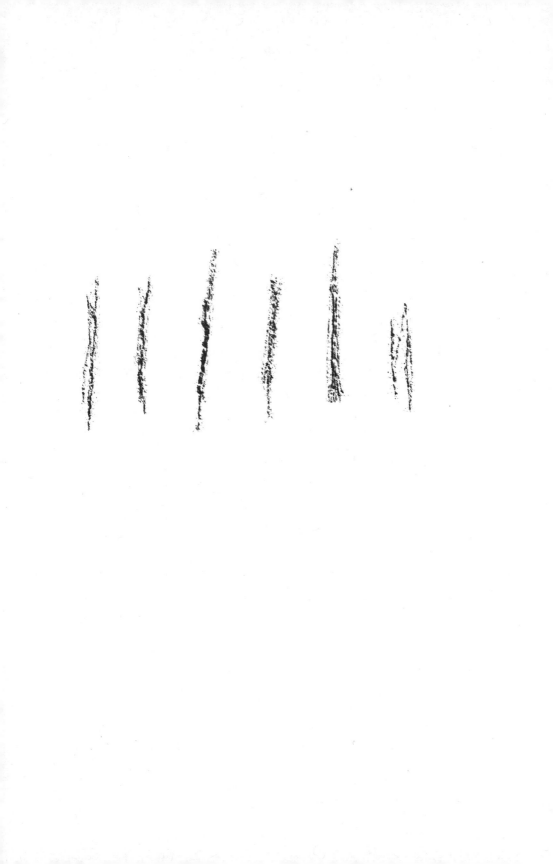

THIRTY-FIVE

"It's her, sir. I'm sure of it. That's the face in the picture."

Could it be?

"It's her all right, just look—"

"Quiet," Corporal Christopher Montoya snapped. "Let me think."

The young man held the paper towards him—a grainy copy of a surveillance photograph of Angelica Petrona with her hand in her hair —but Montoya ignored it. He'd already spent more time than he cared to admit studying the original. Instead, he inspected the tiny emaciated figure hunched over the table on the other side of the one-way glass. The hair had been haphazardly cut—hacked off close to the scalp in some places but left longer in others—making it look like the job had been done in a great hurry in the dark with a pair of dull scissors. She wore a black T-shirt with some sort of logo on it, baggy jeans, a pair of running shoes. The feminine aspects of her body were veiled beneath the clothing. If her intention was to fool a casual observer into thinking she was a teenage boy, she had succeeded.

He stepped away from the other man a few paces, changing the angle of his view. She had not moved since Montoya entered the room, holding her gaze steadily downward and her hands out of sight beneath the table. Her expression was blank, utterly devoid of emotion. She did not seem to be afraid, but how was that possible? During five minutes of close observation he had not seen her so much as shift in the chair, twitch, or even blink. He wondered if she was holding her breath as well. Undoubtedly it was a façade, a coping tactic. He'd seen it before: the self-induced trance—achieved by slowing blood flow and brain activity —an ancient Mapuche trick to fool enemies into thinking they were dead. Terrorists had their own form of training. They were all familiar with ways to resist interrogation, knew how to endure the most intricate and invasive modes of questioning. But for a moment all he could do was marvel at the absolute stillness, the apparent calm in which she resided.

Was it really true that Angelica Petrona had been in custody for the better part of two weeks without his knowledge?

"Exactly when was she arrested?"

The other man opened the folder and consulted the single sheet of paper. "Seven p.m. on April twenty-third."

Montoya nodded. That was four days after the hotel murders.

"And she hasn't said anything?" Montoya ventured, glancing at him. The young man wore the standard army issue khaki pants and boots and a sleeveless T-shirt. His shoulders were thick from weight training. Bristly black stubble covered his head. He would be twenty, twenty-one at the most.

"According to her sheet she was interrogated the night she was brought in. But it was the same time the protests were starting, and the place was filling up. She wouldn't say anything so they sent her over to women's detention. That's where my unit is stationed."

"Identification?"

"Nothing. That's why she was picked up."

"Where was this?"

"The train station. She was trying to buy a ticket. But since she had no ID they wouldn't sell her one."

Montoya glanced again at the younger man.

"What's your name, Private?"

"Jiménez, sir. Juan Miguel Jiménez."

"Who's your squadron leader?"

"I haven't been assigned, sir."

Montoya nodded. "You're right, Private. Her resemblance to the girl in the photo may be superficial, but it's undeniable."

The young soldier shifted his weight from one foot to the other. The slightest trace of a smile flashed across his lips, then vanished.

"The transfer. What reason did you give?"

"I put her down for further interrogation."

"Based on . . . ?"

"She was seen talking to other prisoners, in a secret kind of way, sir. As if trying to make some sort of deal—"

"But really . . ."

"Really, sir, I didn't see her talking to anyone. She kept apart from them."

"You didn't want to claim to have identified a fugitive? Take the credit?"

"No. Because, sir, what if I was wrong?"

"Yes," Montoya agreed. "Precisely."

"But I don't think I'm wrong, sir. Especially now, looking at her like this."

During this exchange Montoya continued to study the subject. She still had not moved. "What else did you see?"

"Sir?"

"Anything I can use when I question her?"

"I don't think so. She stayed away from the others. Never spoke to anyone."

"Did anyone try to speak to her?"

"Once. A woman offered her a cigarette. She walked away without taking it."

Montoya nodded.

"This is all outside the barracks, sir, where I do my patrol. I was never inside. I can't say what happened inside."

"Of course."

The two men fell silent and observed the prisoner. Then, alarmingly, Montoya's confidence wavered. Something made him doubt he was looking at Angelica Petrona after all. This person was a child: spindly and unsophisticated. He sharpened his gaze and focused on her features, her eyes and lips. He was so familiar with them. His doubts fled as hope and then certainty rushed to take their place. Yes. It had to be her.

He spoke abruptly. "I want to thank you, Private Jiménez, for bringing this to my attention and for coming in during your off-duty hours."

"It's no problem, sir." Jiménez handed him the folder. "I'm glad to help."

"We'll take it from here, but I'll be in touch."

"Thank you, sir."

They shook hands. Jiménez saluted and was gone.

To his surprise, Montoya found he was sweating. It was the anticipation. He had to calm down before stepping into the interrogation room. He felt confident of a positive outcome, but there were so many ways this could go wrong.

He picked up the phone and punched in the number of his own office. His personal assistant, Marcel, answered.

"I want every scrap of evidence on the hotel murders brought to Interrogation One. Right now. I'll be along in a few minutes."

Then he left to inform Major Sandoval, his direct superior, of the latest developments.

THIRTY-SIX

His heart was thudding when he opened the door of Interrogation One. He approached the table and let the stack of files drop from his arms. It landed with a hollow thump, like a small detonation. A few sheets of paper fluttered to the floor. As if deaf, the girl did not react.

He studied her across the table for a moment, and then he went and stood close to her, looking down at the top of her head. He forced himself to stand there longer than he would have chosen to, thinking that if his proximity made her uncomfortable, she would shift or squirm an inch or two away from him. From this perspective, he could see that despite the unkempt hair and the ill-fitting clothes, she appeared clean, even healthy, in a general sense. Still, clinging to her was a raw, pungent human smell of unwashed skin and stale urine. He raised one hand and, as if measuring the height of something or testing for heat, held it a couple of inches above her head. She did not move.

He drew a breath and returned to the other side of the table. He sat down.

"I am Corporal Christopher Montoya. I am going to ask you questions and you would be well-advised to answer them."

No response.

"Please, look at me."

She did not move.

"I said look at me."

Nothing.

Montoya raised his arms and brought the flat of both hands down —two, three, four, five times—with such force that the table shook and more papers spilled to the floor.

"LOOK AT ME! LOOK AT ME! I TOLD YOU TO LOOK AT ME!"

Slowly, as if wearying of a childish game that had gone on too long, she raised her head and turned a pair of dull, unreadable eyes towards him.

Montoya resumed his calm demeanour. "Thank you," he said, glancing over his shoulder towards the two-way mirror. "The witnesses will note that the prisoner can hear me."

"Now," he began, businesslike, searching for his rhythm. He selected a few photographs from a folder. "You will confirm for me that you are the person who, for the last several months, has been using the name 'Angelica Petrona' while acting as a covert operative for a terrorist cell."

He pushed the photographs across the table. When she did not move, he leaned forward in order to arrange them in two neat rows before her. The array included photos of her (with long hair) and Enrique together at the café outside the Arroyo Salas Theatre, of her wearing a short skirt, black tights, and spike heel shoes while walking the city streets with Enrique, and a couple of her alone in similarly chic outfits standing before shop windows. Also included was the close-up of her with her hand in her hair that had been distributed to the police and other security units.

"You will notice that we have been observing you for quite some time. You came to our attention when you were spotted in the company of this man—" Montoya indicated Enrique—"whose two sons have been arrested because of subversive activity. He has since been arrested as well."

He watched her gaze flicker briefly over the photographs. In vain he awaited a response to the news concerning Enrique and his sons—shock or indignation or horror—that would allow him a toehold on her state of mind. Instead, her expression remained blank. At this point, if he were asked for a single word to describe her, he would have to admit she seemed bored.

Once she'd completed a quick survey of the photographs, she raised her eyes and again met his.

He felt stymied suddenly, handicapped by the distance between them. He lifted his chair and moved it so that the corner of the table was all that separated them.

Maintaining eye contact, he gently tapped the scarred tabletop. He was not angry—he would never become angry. But his curiosity was growing by the minute.

"Place your hands up here, please."

She did as he asked, laying her hands flat, palm down on the table. The ethereal thinness of her bare arms seemed to him a silent rebuke. Her hands were small, delicate, entirely feminine.

He lifted her left hand and began to study it, the way a doctor might. He turned it over, stroked the skin of the palm and the underside of her small fingers. Examined closely, he found she was not clean at all. Trace amounts of dirt were embedded in the creases of her skin, and there were dark smears up and down her arms. He let his own fingers caress the tiny wrist and wander a few inches up the arm and then all the way to the elbow. Rubbing the inner joint with his thumb, he detected no bruises or scars, as he might have were she a drug addict. He laid the left hand down in its original position and took up the right, turning it this way and that, examining the skin and lightly pressing on the soft tissue beneath. What could he conclude from this? The knuckles of both hands had suffered recent abrasions. The nails of all her fingers had been gnawed to the quick. She was nervous and afraid and at some point in the last week or so had been compelled to defend herself. None of this was surprising.

He leaned forward, situating his face just inches from hers. Her gaze was steady. Her eyes did not deviate from his. Yet her expression remained blank, impenetrable. When he sat back, he continued to hold her by the wrist. It was extraordinary how she surrendered to this gratuitous manipulation of her flesh. She offered up her limbs willingly, it seemed, helping the process along. Perhaps she was conserving her energy, saving her strength for the real struggle, which might not begin for hours yet. But it would be agony to wait that long. He wanted to wear her down and grind away at her resistance. He wanted to hear her voice pleading *No more!* He wanted to see her brush away tears. These desires were strong, but he knew how to practice patience. Patience was the key to the art of interrogation. Patience was a formidable weapon.

He placed her right hand back on the table. When he looked again into her eyes he thought he saw something in them that was challenging and scornful, as if his inquiries to this point had amused her. But, like a lightning flash, it vanished almost before his brain had registered it. Her eyes suddenly went vacant, as empty of expression as those of a child's doll. She had gone somewhere and left him behind.

Where, he wondered with a strange mixture of longing and envy, had she taken herself?

Now he lifted the photograph of Angelica Petrona with her hand in her hair and held it up so that he could more easily compare the girl with the image.

"I don't think I need to tell you that you are in a great deal of trouble," he commented. "The people you are involved with are criminals of the most despicable sort. It's going to take our country years to recover from the damage they've caused."

The face of the girl in front of him was bare of makeup and had lost enough flesh to qualify as "gaunt," but the attempt to alter her appearance had gone no further than the crudely executed haircut. She would never be able to disguise her nose or her eyes. She could do nothing about those lips. Only death would rob the skin of that glow. He reached forward—again, she did not flinch at the approach of his hand—and brushed away the hair that concealed the gracefully rounded forehead and low hairline. The features of the girl in the photograph were distinctive and memorable, her beauty both subtle and tantalizing. For weeks the girl seated before him had been carrying a burden of exhaustion, hunger, and fear, but it had left her physical splendour intact. There could be little doubt that she was the same person as the girl in the photograph.

"You do not seem inclined to speak," Montoya said, "but I guarantee that in a short while, you will be speaking only too freely."

He gathered the photos into a stack and shuffled them into a folder.

"Angelica Petrona," he said, gazing at her. "Or should I call you Nadia? Nadia Wladanski."

Once again, the revelation elicited no response. Her eyes, though turned towards him, remained dull and unfocused.

"I will tell you a story then. Once upon a time there was a little girl named Nadia who lived in Warsaw, Poland. Her father worked for the Communist Party; his name was Tadeusz. Tadeusz was always regarded as a loyal party member because he followed all the rules and never complained. But one day the officials to whom he reported became suspicious and began watching him. He was a clerk working in the offices of the local Communist Party chapter and had access to sensitive documents. Somehow information from these documents was finding its way into the hands of Poland's enemies. When the officials discovered Tadeusz in the act passing copies of documents to a British agent, he was given an opportunity to redeem himself by working as a double agent against the British. Instead, like a coward he fled and moved his family far far away, to the other side of the world. Here, he took menial jobs and did everything he could to avoid attracting the attention of people who might go looking and find out about the terrible things he had done. Over the years, he and his wife—whose name was Alicja—raised three beautiful daughters, Carmel, Nadia, and Magda, and lived a quiet life. Eventually, however, someone put two and two together. Tadeusz was arrested and is awaiting extradition to Poland."

He smiled.

"Isn't that a nice story?" He reached for yet another file and flipped it open. "I just have to remind myself of some details. Oh, yes, the oldest daughter, Carmel, married Raoul Martínez Valdez, who had joined the navy right out of school. They are both being held under suspicion of espionage. The middle daughter, Nadia, is being questioned regarding her involvement in the murders of Major Thomas Downing and his wife and son. Magda, the youngest, has unfortunately disappeared. Presumed dead."

He let his gaze settle on Nadia's face.

"The Wladanskis were such a nice family, and look what happened to them. Who would have thought it possible?"

He waited.

"What I need from you is simple," he said, "and you are going to give it to me." Montoya closed the file and exchanged it for a much thicker one from the stack of documents.

"I want to know everything about the murder of Major Downing. I want the names of your accomplices, I want the location of your headquarters, and I want to know what these people are planning, what their next target is. If you are prepared to give me this information, I can make inquiries into Carmel's whereabouts and see what I can do about getting her released. I can look into your father's situation as well, though I can't promise anything because that's in the hands of the Diplomatic Corps."

He waited for a response. There was none.

"What is it with you people? Have you been brainwashed? Are you really going to sacrifice your sister and her husband for some absurd ideal? Does your family mean so little to you? I suppose you've been told all kinds of lies. They must make us out to be monsters. They probably said we breathe fire and walk on all fours. And you believed them."

He folded his hands on the table and stared at her, watching for any adjustment in her manner or posture. Her expression did not change. This went on for a minute, then two, then five. From the outset, his duty had been to test the limits of her endurance, and there were many ways to do this, but at the same time she seemed to be testing his. Ten minutes. He continued deliberately to stare, mimicking her: holding himself expressionless, motionless. Now he was curious. How long could he put up with it? The seat was not comfortable, but he had endured much worse and for longer periods.

He stared at her. How he had longed to meet her, how he had fantasized about her, about this moment. It had been particularly satisfying to follow the trail she had left behind. Interviews with Downing junior's coworkers at the credit union had yielded some very useful information. Downing junior had boasted about her to anyone who would listen. In the weeks following the murders everyone who was detained and questioned was shown her photo. Finally a lead: someone brought in from that school where all the trouble was admitted to knowing her. Within an hour they were forcing their way into her family's home. Here Montoya found photographs, belongings, a whole history. He went from room to room, amazed and somewhat awestruck to think that he was walking in spaces where she had spent years of her life, touching things with which she had been intimate. Nadia Wladanski began to take on human dimensions before his eyes. Afterward he did his research, discovered the truth about her father, and all the while the fantasies became more frequent. And now he sat across the table from her.

Maybe he was a bit overwhelmed, to think that the object of what had become a passion—almost an obsession—was here, within easy reach. Was he disappointed? He had imagined a young woman, defiant, haughty. And instead, here was this child—and yet, with a woman's face. He stared. How long could this go on? He had lost track of time, lost touch with his surroundings. His buttocks were growing numb. A tingling sensation had crept from the base of his spine up to his neck. Her beauty was truly mesmerizing. It would be easy to lose yourself to the delicate symmetry of her features, the paleness of her skin, the dark radiant pools of her eyes.

And of course there was also her youth, her frailty, her helplessness. Was this what she was counting on? That he would feel sorry for her?

He stood and stretched, flexing the muscles in his back, which had grown stiff from sitting for so long. He observed her from above.

"I know how you get men to do things for you," he said evenly. "You paint your face and put on your fashionable clothes, and they are taken in by your charms. It would be easy for you. All you have to do is smile. I'm sure you thought you could get away with anything. Young Mr. Downing couldn't have presented much of a challenge. If it's any consolation, he was completely infatuated. His friends said he talked about you incessantly. Did you know he was making plans? He wanted to take you with him back to America. But he wasn't sure he could convince you to go. He said he didn't deserve you."

As he spoke he opened the thick folder, selected a series of photographs, and placed them one by one on the table in front of her.

"And I suppose in a manner of speaking he was right. He didn't deserve you. He didn't have any idea who you really were or what you are capable of. But you and I, Nadia. We know. Don't we?" He lowered his voice. "We know exactly what you are capable of."

The photos were from the hotel dining room on the day of the murders and showed the victims from a variety angles. Three were close-ups of the Major, Steven, and Sharon Downing. All three had their eyes and mouths open and gaping wounds in their foreheads. Their faces and hair were drenched with blood. The top of Steven's head was blown away. Another photo showed the table where they had been eating, the cloth, the scattered remnants of pancake, sausage, cut fruit, the utensils spattered with blood and other matter, and beyond this the disorder of the hastily vacated dining room. Other photos showed each member of the Downing family from a perspective distant enough to capture the upended furniture and the grotesque positioning of the bodies where they had fallen. Two final shots were of the splayed corpses of the surveillance men.

"Look at these, Nadia. Five people died that day, and for what? I ask you. For what?"

As her eyes darted over the photos, he stepped casually to his left and took up a position behind her. He was calm. He observed her in the mirror. For just a second her mouth dropped open and she appeared shaken by the images in front of her, but then she turned her head and looked away. Her jaw clamped shut, all expression drained out of her face. While she held this pose he leaned over and reached past her shoulder, and with his fingers straightened a couple of the photos. As he pulled back he deliberately brushed her arm with his hand. She did not flinch.

"I find it hard to look at those too, Nadia. It's difficult for normal people like you and me to conceive of the murderous impulse that causes these things to happen. But I have to ask that you look at them. I need you to look at them."

She remained as she was, with her empty face turned away from the photos, her gaze diverted towards an empty corner of the room.

He leaned over and whispered into her ear. "You're of no use to me, you know, if you don't tell me anything."

Montoya glanced up and caught his own reflection in the mirror, standing behind the seated girl. As if on cue, Nadia raised her head. Their eyes met in the mirror. For a moment he glared sternly at her reflection. When he smiled, Nadia looked away.

"I think, my dear," he said in a casual tone, "I will have to *insist* that you look at those photographs."

Montoya waited for a few seconds before placing his right hand on the back of her neck. He tightened his grip until he felt the first tensing of her muscles in response. Then he brought his other hand around and grasped a handful of her hair. He heard her gasp from the shock of sudden pain. She groped for his fingers, clutching at them, trying to pull them away, but her strength was no match for his. He quickly forced her so far forward that she was bent over with her eyes directly above the photo array.

"Look! This is the handiwork of your friends. You should be proud, Nadia. Why do you turn away?"

She continued to strain against his grasp. Something between a whine and a groan issued from her throat.

"The Downings had as much right to enjoy life as you, and your accomplices blew their brains out. You helped kill these people. The law says it's the same as pulling the trigger yourself."

He held her firmly in place. Finally she gave up the struggle. But instead of slackening his grip he tightened it. Slowly, he pushed her down until her cheek was pressed against the table.

He leaned over and spoke into her ear.

"This is the kind of mess they call me in to clean up. You terrorists keep me far too busy. I can't be everywhere. But when I heard about the tragedy at the hotel, I asked to have it assigned to me. The savagery of the attack was inhuman. My God, you should have seen the blood. You wouldn't believe how much blood there was."

He pressed down, pushing her face against the table.

"But actually you would believe it, because you were there, weren't you? A number of people saw you eating with the Downings before the shooting started. You were very cool, smiling and laughing. You were having a wonderful time, and all the while you knew what was coming. None of this is a surprise. You know exactly how much blood there was."

She was now, unmistakably, weeping. He released her.

It was a moment or two before she moved, raising her head slowly. When she was upright she touched the side of her face and felt along her jawline. She wiped away some tears. He was encouraged to see her hand was trembling.

Montoya gathered the photographs together. A few were wet. He returned them to the thick folder.

"Who fired the first shot?" he asked. He sat across from her and clasped his hands together on the table. She looked at him. The blankness she had adopted before was gone. With her lips slightly parted, the glance she cast him was watchful, guarded.

"This suspect was wearing a suit. He had curly hair. He was tall, clean-shaven, about twenty-six, twenty-seven."

He stared at her. Nadia did not move and remained silent.

"You know, when you don't say anything, the only reasonable conclusion is that you are refusing to cooperate. I assure you I will put that in my report. But if you don't know the answer, that's another thing." He shrugged. "Maybe, on the day of the killings, that was the first time you saw this man. It could be that you weren't important enough to be told certain things. I can understand that. There's a hierarchy, even among criminals. But I have to admit that right now, it looks like you're protecting your terrorist friends and that you are intimate with their plans. I can only assume that you are choosing to withhold what you know. Somehow, I have to persuade you to share this information with me. And if I can't do that, then all I can say is I hope God has mercy on your soul, because when you leave this room, the people who take you away will not."

He paused.

"Maybe you're thinking someone's going to break down the door and save you. But it's just me, Nadia. I'm your last chance. And if I can't get the information I need, then there's no reason for me to keep you around. So I'll ask you again. The man who fired the first shot. What is his name?"

Montoya opened the file again and retrieved a small envelope. He drew out a couple of photographs. From the corner of his eye he saw her lips move.

"What did you say? I'm sorry, I didn't hear you."

In a small voice, hardly more than a whisper, she said, "I don't know what his name is."

Montoya nodded.

"That's all right then. That's all right. I don't believe you. But this is a start."

He laid the two photographs from the envelope on the table in front of her.

"Maybe you can tell me the names of these two."

Her eyes seemed to gravitate reluctantly towards the images of the two men, both obviously dead. Edmond's eyes were closed, his lolling tongue visible in his mouth, his dark hair sticking out every which way, the collar of his shirt askew. There were spatters of blood on the floor around him, but none on his face. The photo was too brightly lit and slightly out of focus. In contrast, Ruben lay serenely on a gleaming metal surface, his hair neatly combed, his eyes and mouth closed.

"This one—" Montoya tapped the photo of Edmond—"was discovered discarding his bloody clothes in the staff washroom. Even though it's more dangerous, it's always best to take these people alive so you can interrogate them. But it seems he foolishly tried to shoot his way out against half a dozen officers from the tactical unit. Or maybe he knew it was up for him and chose this way to commit suicide. We'll never know."

Montoya rested his elbow on the table and propped his chin in his hand. At the same time he kept his eyes on the photos.

"The other one," he went on, "was discovered hiding in the basement in a storage closet under the stairs. He might have eluded capture, except that someone noticed the lock had been broken off. He fired a bullet through the door, wounding one of our team. We opened fire on him and he was hit by at least ten bullets. Miraculously, he survived and was taken to hospital. But he died while they were treating his wounds."

Now he looked at her. Her hands lay lightly on the table, the fingers of each touching the photographs. She breathed slowly through her mouth. There was something wistful in her gaze, but he saw rigidity there as well—her jaw muscles flexing—as if she were engaged in an internal debate. He waited a full minute, then two.

"Amazingly," he said, observing her and continuing the narrative, "other than their dead bodies, these two young men did not leave a trace of themselves behind. I probably shouldn't be telling you this, but it's fascinating in itself, and I suppose you already know. Their fingerprints are not on record. Nobody recognizes them from their photos. It's as if they never existed."

He paused.

"So Nadia, I'm hoping you can shed some light on their identities."

Without looking at Montoya she said, "I don't know their names."

"But, Nadia—and this is crucial—they *were* part of the group you belong to. Maybe, for the sake of discussion, let's suppose that you don't know their *real* names. But you knew them. You worked with them, made plans, discussed strategy. They went by some alias or other, the way you went by Angelica Petrona."

She bowed her head and said nothing.

"The other suspect—the man who fired the first shot, whose name you don't know either—he has disappeared. He's like a ghost. I could almost believe he never existed, except for the carnage he left behind and the blood-spattered suit recovered from a trash bin in the washroom on the second floor of the hotel—and the testimony of witnesses who saw him in the dining room just before the murders took place."

He kept his eyes on her.

"It interests me that he seems to have escaped completely. Somehow he got past the checkpoints and out of the city. By now he's hiding somewhere in the countryside, probably raising a toast to his criminal friends. While you're here being questioned for the first of what I guarantee will be many, many times."

He paused.

"How did that happen, Nadia? How is it that he was transported to safety while you were left to fend for yourself?"

With these last words she seemed to bend slightly, as if a weight had been placed on her shoulders. She seemed reduced, physically smaller, if that were possible. But she deserved no sympathy and he felt none. Her exhaustion, her half-starved state, her pallor and preternatural thinness—none of it impressed him. She had probably done it to herself and was playing the role that suited her appearance. It was part of her survival strategy. But he had thrown her off balance and pushed her to the edge. She looked different now than when he had entered the room. She sat hunched over, her head tilted forward, and peered at him through eyes angled upward. It was a defensive posture he had seen before, in suspects who were near the breaking point. She couldn't be faking that. Again and again, she wiped her face with the back of her hand.

"Names, Nadia. I need names."

She turned to the photos and pointed with the index finger of her right hand.

"Edmond," she said. Again there were tears. She used her left hand to wipe her eyes and her nose. "Ruben. The other one told me his name was Gustavo."

Montoya nodded.

"Were there others?"

She licked her lips and nodded. The tears were flowing more freely now, but she didn't bother to wipe them away.

"Two other girls, Imelda and Krista. A young man named Adriano. There were other men too—" her voice caught and she struggled for a moment to speak. "Sorry," she said and noisily cleared her throat. "Other men who came and went. They weren't part of our group. I was never told who they were."

"Would you be able to identify these people if you saw them again in photographs?"

She nodded.

"Good," he said. "We'll get to that."

He slid the photos of Edmond and Ruben from beneath her fingers and returned them to the folder.

"Now that you've found your voice, I'll ask you a question. You don't have to answer right away, but please think about it."

She had assumed the hunched posture. Her eyes were turned in his direction.

"This is what I want you to think about, Nadia. How do you suppose I came by your real name?"

301

Her only response was to wet her lips with her tongue.

"It's not something I could have plucked out of thin air. Someone had to tell me."

As he spoke, he inserted his fingers into the stack of documents and selected yet another folder, one that was less than a quarter of an inch thick.

"I know you're tired. You'll have a chance to rest. You might even get something to eat. But surely it's occurred to you to wonder how I know all these things about you and your family."

He let the contents of the folder—about a dozen photographs—spill onto the table. These depicted the interior of a house, apparently comfortable if not luxurious: a tiny kitchen, an unpretentious living room, bedrooms. The interior of closets with clothes on hangers. Mementos on shelves, pictures on walls. A crucifix. The domestic kitsch and clutter spoke eloquently of the ordinariness of the lives lived within these walls.

Her eyes widened and she clapped one hand over her mouth. As she sorted through the photos where they lay scattered on the table, she wept openly. One at a time she picked them up, holding each for a few seconds before her eyes. With her other hand she wiped ineffectually at the tears streaming down her face.

Montoya let her have a moment, watching her all the while. Several times her fingers fumbled and seemed unable to grasp the edge of the photo. He noticed that her hand was trembling so violently she was having trouble getting it to do what she wanted. At the end, when she was finished with the last photo, she let it slip from her fingers. She covered her face with her hands and leaned forward over the table.

When, a minute or two later, she faced him again there was something different in her aspect, a look of almost feral wariness combined with shock or bewilderment, as if she couldn't comprehend what was happening.

"If there is any chance you still believe that you have to protect these people, remember: they did not protect you."

She hesitated before speaking.

"I don't know what to do," she said, wiping her face again.

"Cooperate," Montoya stated sharply. "It's your only choice."

"Will you . . ." she began, but had to stop to swallow. "Will you really help my parents?"

"I will, Nadia," he said. "Depending on what you tell me. I promise I will do what I can for them."

She glanced away and gave a slight nod, then met his eyes again. "But I don't know anything. They didn't tell me anything."

"Let *me* determine if what you have to say is important. You just talk. I'll do the rest."

Her hand was on her face.

"Oh, God," she moaned. "Oh, God. I can't. They'll kill me."

He reached across the table and took her by the wrist.

"What choice do you have?"

He held her until she looked at him again. She did not try to pull away.

"Do you have any idea how much trouble you're in?"

He dropped her arm. She moved her trembling hands to her lap and stared at them dumbly.

"I don't think you do," he said.

She did not move.

"Nadia, your situation is complicated. What do you know about the man you murdered? Major Downing."

Still looking at her hands, she shrugged. "He was Steven's father. Steven said his company did things for the government."

"You never asked what these things he did for the government were?"

She shook her head.

"Nadia, look at me please." He waited until she had raised her head and turned to face him. "Sometimes a government needs help from outside. As you know, we're at war. Our government hired Major Downing to help purchase weapons. Downing had connections with the American military and, through them, a network of arms suppliers around the world. I'm sure even his wife and son didn't know what he really did. He might have said he was a security advisor. But the fact is that Major Downing used his connections to help our government hire military strategists and buy equipment. He was an important man, Nadia. He performed a sensitive function and operated in secrecy. He also made a lot of money for a lot of people. But he was reckless and apparently thought he was beyond the reach of those who wished to harm him. He would have known that simply being American was enough to make him and his family a target. So it's hard to understand why he disregarded the warnings. But my investigation shows that he travelled all over the country without taking any precautions for his own safety, beyond what was forced upon him by whoever he was working for. When he travelled alone he did so under a false name. But when his wife was with him, they used their real names. It was stupid, considering what he was here for. He made it very easy for you to kill him."

"I—" She raised her hands in a gesture of hopelessness and shook her head.

"Nadia, the Americans are very interested in this investigation. They want to question you themselves. I might be able to hold them off, but only if you tell me everything."

She stared at him. Montoya met her eyes, her blank look.

He brought his fist down on the table.

"You are *not* as ignorant as you say you are!" he bellowed.

She raised her hands as if to protect herself. Her mouth dropped open and tears sprung into her eyes.

He pointed a finger at her. "You're playing a dangerous game. And it's not going to end well."

Montoya stood. She followed his movements and seemed to shrink at his approach. She hunched and drew her arms in protectively as he came and stood beside her.

"The more you claim ignorance, the worse it gets for you. It's clear you were in on the planning. The Americans think so. I think so."

He gazed down at the tiny quivering figure. After interrogating her for nearly two hours it was not, in fact, clear to him what she knew and what she didn't know. She had stymied him with her silence. She had given away very little with the few words she had uttered. She had been well schooled in the art of resistance. But he would break her, and soon. Her whole body was drooping. There was a new fear in her eyes. She did not have much strength left.

"Maybe now you can see the enormity of your crime. I wonder though if you have any idea what's going to happen to you. What do you think happens to murderers?"

A small gasp escaped her throat when he pinched the muscle at the top of her back, between her neck and shoulder.

"I hope you remember this," he said. He squeezed and heard her breath catch. "If I can cause you this much pain with two fingers, just imagine what our American friends will do with a roomful of equipment and a team of inquisitors."

Conscious of the warmth and tender pliability of her flesh, he tightened his grip. She moaned in protest and tried to wriggle away from him. As he increased the pressure, the sound emerging from her throat rose in pitch, and still he squeezed harder, digging his fingertips into the muscle. She rocked violently from side to side in an attempt to shake him off, then tried to rise to her feet. He bent down and wrapped his free arm around her, tightening his embrace as she struggled. His lips grazed her hair.

"I don't know anything!" she screamed between sobs. She shook her head, grabbed his wrist, clawed at his hand. "I don't know anything! I don't know anything! Why won't you believe me?"

He squeezed harder. She shrieked from the pain and tried to jerk her body back and forth. He held her in place. The chair, bolted to the floor, did not move.

Then, taking her under the arms, he lifted her from the chair and gave her a shove. She hit the wall and went down. For a moment she lay still, coughing and weeping. She bent forward, supporting herself on one elbow, rubbing her shoulder with her other hand. When he took a step towards her she crawled into the corner and brought her knees up.

Montoya could smell her sour sweaty heat, the dizzying animal odours emanating from the unwashed crevices of her body. But because he knew what was in store for her, he felt twinges of empathy disturb his calm. He told himself it was like a chunk of ice melting in his gut, no more and no less than what he might feel for an animal bleeding by the side of the road. He did not often question women, but when he did they were young, like Nadia. Before coming in here he had worried that he might start looking upon her as human. That was where the danger lay. Because she was crying, because she was miserable, because she was young, fragile and beautiful, because she was going to die, all of these facts called out for him to cast a merciful eye upon her case.

He glanced briefly towards the mirror, then back at Nadia. Suddenly a wave of contempt swept over him that, in its rawness and purity, made his head spin. Without warning he kicked the wall just above where she lay. She screamed and raised her hands in front of her face. She pressed herself deeper into the corner. He kicked the wall again, his boot leaving black scuff marks. He was panting. His indifference had indeed been compromised.

He turned his back on her. She knew their real names, as surely as she knew her own. She knew the next target. He was certain of it. But that didn't matter. She had given him nothing. And he could do nothing for her if she would not help herself. It was out of his hands.

"I'm sorry, Nadia," he said. He began gathering up the files and papers. "Maybe I gave you the impression that I was your friend. You have to realize that nothing could be further from the truth. There's information I need. You can provide it. It's as simple as that. If you help me, then I can help you. But if you give me nothing, you get nothing in return."

Weighed down with documents, he turned to look at her. Nadia had raised herself to a sitting position. Her small face was wet, contorted, pale. She did not look at him. She made no sounds as she wiped at her tears with a trembling hand. Her eyes, glazed and vacant, stared at the nothingness a foot or two in front of her face.

"Nadia, it's not too late. If you talk, I will help you. Let me help you."

It had come out as a plea, which he had not intended. What was wrong with him? There was nothing special about her. Nadia Wladanski was just another subject. He could respect her courage, but not her stupidity. It was time for him to move on.

So why was there bitter phlegm at the back of his throat? She would talk. If not to him, then to someone else. He'd softened her up. Once she got started she would not be able to stop. That was the beauty of it. One way or another, they would get the information they needed.

"There is only so much I can do," he muttered, directing the words towards the floor. "You've given me no choice. I have to hand the job over to someone with expertise in more advanced methods of persuasion."

He rapped his knuckles on the door. He had to get out of here. He was tired. His hand was shaking. Lately he had not been sleeping well.

The door was unlatched from the outside. He opened it and paused on the threshold.

"Goodbye, Nadia," he said.

Beneath an attenuated silence, he heard a faint quivering rasp as she drew a breath.

Without looking back he bowed his head and let the door swing shut behind him.

THIRTY-SEVEN

Hector sat motionless in the back of the open truck. His breath clouded in the chill night air, which smelled of earth damp from the rain that had fallen lately. His leg pressed hard against the leg of Rudolfo, the soldier next to him, one of the low-level commanders who had helped plan the mission. His every muscle was tensed, but he was not afraid. His mind was clear, focused on the task ahead. They were to approach the farmhouse from the east because sounds carry and tonight a breeze was drawing the scent of the sea inland from the west. It was a dark night with no moon, and infrared night-vision goggles would give them a lethal advantage over the enemy. They had been driving for an hour. Their destination lay miles beyond the town limits, high in the hills, where dense pine forest concealed innumerable dangers. Experience had taught that. Death assumes its disguise casually—like a girl slipping on a summer dress—and lurks in even the most benign settings. An advance team had scoured the route they were taking and declared it safe, but nothing was guaranteed. Hector kept his head down, eyes to the floor. Squad leader Josquin sat up front with the driver. While heading out on a mission the men were not supposed to talk, but from time to time he heard a murmured voice followed by thin laughter that sounded like it escaped from between clenched teeth. Strained attempts at humour. A couple of the men were smoking, though this also was not allowed on missions.

The message had been often repeated. He heard it in his sleep, recited it when he showered, when he ate: *Trust nothing. The enemy is everywhere and shows no mercy to those who fall into their hands.* Nobody would be safe until every rebel in the country lay dead with a bullet in the brain. The army was performing a noble service and every day received the highest praise from the President. Progress was being made on all fronts. They were beating back the rebel forces. Soon—very soon—victory would be declared.

Hector was not afraid. Tonight's mission was vital and precautions had been taken to ensure its success. Scouts had reported that the farmhouse—the focus of the morning's assault—was headquarters for the largest rebel faction in Valdivia Province. This was the group that had launched raids on the army's regional munitions depot, bombed buses and office buildings, and often rendered the highways and railroads leading into Chiachi, and as far north as Envigado, treacherous and impassable. The Americans had provided high-resolution satellite photos showing suspicious activity in the vicinity of the camp where the farmhouse was situated. Earlier in the evening Hector's squad had assembled in the mess hall, which had been equipped with a projector and screen. Seated on a folding chair he listened, with other members of his squad along with a smattering of commanders and upper-level strategists, to Josquin describe the lay of the land and how to reach the farmhouse from the road. He showed them the pictures and a detailed drawing of the camp. "This is their command centre," Josquin emphasized with a confident smile, tapping the screen with a pointer. He ran his hand over his shaved head before resuming. "They won't give it up without a fight. But we are ready. Surprise is our most potent weapon. We can cripple them if we take them by surprise. We'll have enough information to wipe out their operation in Valdivia." He paused significantly as his gaze passed over the faces of his men. "It's an honour to be given this assignment," he said, still smiling. "Our leaders have placed their faith in us. We have it within our power to make our country safe again."

Josquin's words echoed in Hector's brain as the unescorted transport truck laboured up the slopes and groaned around hairpin bends. Seated in the back, he held himself still and shut his eyes as the truck bumped over the road's stony surface. His mind was at ease, free of doubt. Today, he would gladly give his life for the success of the mission. They all felt this way. They were like brothers. The flame of camaraderie burned brightly within each one of them.

Hector was one of ten soldiers dressed in black. On a strap slung over his shoulder was his American-supplied M16. In his hand he held the black balaclava that he would pull over his head after they had received their final orders and before they dispersed into the night to execute their mission. In a sheath strapped to his leg was Dimitri's gift, the Swiss hunting knife, sharpened, cleaned, and gleaming. A second truck carrying another ten soldiers had already discharged its cargo at the base of the hill. At this very moment those men were sweeping silently through the forest from a position just to the north, neutralizing the enemy as they advanced slowly up the hill towards the camp, clearing the way for the truck carrying Hector and his comrades, who would make the final assault.

Months ago, when all this began, he'd been often confused and sometimes repulsed by the things he was told to do, even while he was doing them. But at night, in the barracks where they slept, when they talked in hushed voices, he learned that one did not ask questions. He was new, and none of the others seemed troubled by the often brutal nature of their assignments. As his faith in his unit grew and his craving to understand their purpose weakened, he was able to quash his doubts. If they were ordered to do something that left bloodstains in the dust, it was for reasons that he, a humble foot soldier, was not privileged to know. They were doing good work. If someone died, it was never in vain. He was sure of that now.

And yet, paradoxically, he was sure of only one other thing: he did not believe the rebels were animals. For Hector Tomás still believed that his brother Carlos was among their number, and Carlos would never do the things of which the rebels stood accused. It was impossible, and yet . . . how could he quarrel with the destruction the rebels caused? He had witnessed the carnage. The Envigado bombing was just one instance. He had seen the results of car bombs, the twisted metal, body parts on the sidewalk. In his own unit a night patrol had been ambushed, everyone killed. His own barracks had come under attack. Many soldiers had died, boys called into service because the country needed everyone to contribute. Now they lay mouldering in their graves. Some had left the unit. He didn't know it was possible, to just leave. Where did they go? Back to their families? Did they take up their old jobs? How could they live with the secrets they took with them? He had thought of doing the same, but he had nowhere to go. His family was gone. So, dutifully, he strapped on the gun and did what he was told. He broke down doors and fired into the dark, hoping for the best. In Chiachi, daylight patrols took him into the streets, where young girls in flowered dresses lowered their eyes and scurried out of his way, and punks in tight T-shirts pretended not to be scared. But fear was everywhere. You could see it, smell it, taste it. And until the rebels were gone, there would be no escaping it.

What would his brother think if he could see him today? Would he laugh and slap him on the back and tell him he was doing a fine job?

On his first mission, his squad had arrested a journalist, smashing down the door of his apartment and yanking him out of his bed in the middle of the night. Hector had a grip on the prisoner's arm when another of his team silenced the man's screaming wife with a rifle butt to the side of her head. As if her bones had become like *jalea,* she crumpled to the floor. Then they took the man, bound and gagged, down the stairs and out to a waiting van, and delivered him, as ordered, to a detention centre. When the man's broken body was found on a desolate strip of road far outside of town, in a hill region where soldiers were not welcome, with a gunshot wound in the back of the head, the newspaper report blamed the rebels. A few weeks later they raided the local radio station. They cleared everyone out and destroyed all the equipment before setting the place on fire. Again, the rebels were blamed. These things needed to be done, he was told, to discourage the spread of rebel propaganda. But suddenly there were people marching in the street, raising placards and shouting for justice and an end to the fighting—ordinary people—and he was given a metal shield and a club and told to impose order on the chaos.

And so, like a wound that would not heal, the doubts returned.

But these were not the kind of thoughts he wanted filling his head in the last minutes before a mission. He closed his eyes and pushed them out of reach as if they were some material temptation he had sworn to renounce. Later. He would indulge later, after they were done. He thought again of the campaign they were waging, to rid the country of an enemy that stopped at nothing to promote its vicious agenda. He looked up. Across from him sat the youngest soldier in the squad, Alejandro Navarro, the boy with the aquamarine eyes who had saved him that day on the hill, when he'd stared death in the face and survived. Their bond was immutable, for all time—like love, but stronger, deeper than love. And

310

all at once the blood coursing through his veins was making his every muscle like iron. An adrenaline rush. It was insane how strong he was. He was dangerous. He could do anything.

Today he would make his country safe or die trying.

THIRTY-EIGHT

It was a rare and curious thing, Major Armand Eduardo Garcia-Figueroa reflected, to be called back into service after all this time. Out of the blue his good friend, Major Jesús Arriaga Sandoval, had called from the headquarters in B—— and told him to pull his uniform out of the closet and dust it off. The urgency in his friend's voice demanded full attention.

"I need something done," Sandoval said, skipping the preliminaries, "and you're just the man to do it."

The shrill summons of the phone had startled Armand and his wife, Elena, out of their languid early morning routine. It was not quite seven. The sky was clear. The sun had just crept out from behind the rolling hills and distant mountain peaks of the eastern horizon. In Chiachi town these days, though it was still summer, early in the day the air was often crisp with the first hints of autumn. Elena had been on the veranda, spooning bone meal into her potted tomato plants. Seated at the kitchen table reading the reports in the early edition, Armand had been drinking the dark smoky Guatemalan coffee he favoured and (against his wife's protests) eating bread crusts fried in bacon fat. So early, and yet the time was already slipping out of his grasp. He had not shaved yet and was wearing a sleeveless T-shirt and a pair of old trousers. This morning he had no plans. This afternoon he had no plans. Some days, to his shame, he slouched around looking like a *vagabundo* (Elena's word), avoiding her glances and her *tsk-tsk-tsk* and hoping that no one paid them a surprise visit. The threadbare slippers he wore, which should have been discarded long ago but which he could not bear to part with, had been a gift from Emilio José.

Elena answered on the first ring and with an adamant gesture beckoned him to the phone.

"I'm old and discredited," Armand had countered, lowering his voice. He looked down at himself. His paunch had flourished. He had to lean forward to get the merest glimpse of the slippers. He tried to suck in his stomach, but it did no good. "I have no energy for these things. I don't see how I can be of use to you."

"You sell yourself short," Sandoval commented brusquely, brushing aside his friend's objections. "Whether you know it or not, you are still connected. For thirty years you inspired the most passionate loyalty in everyone who served under you. A brotherhood grew up around you. You didn't even know about it. Discredited or not, people trust you. And besides, what I need done does not have to go through official channels. In fact, it's better if it didn't."

Major Armand Figueroa thought this over for a moment. What Sandoval said was true. His career had been notable for the number of his protégés who had gone on to stellar careers of their own. A few had shot up through the ranks at breakneck speed. Among them were majors, generals, even a diplomat or two. His own squeaky clean image had remained unblemished until a fatal instance of poor judgment landed him before a disciplinary tribunal. He had accepted a retirement package rather than subject his family to the humiliation of a guilty verdict.

But a brotherhood? Surely that was an exaggeration.

"And, Armand," Sandoval continued, his tone less gruff. "I wouldn't be calling if this weren't important."

"I don't know," Figueroa equivocated. "I just don't know." He sighed. "I've been out too long. Why should I get involved now? You're going to have to give me some details."

During a brief pause Figueroa heard the rustling of paper and the sounds of a heavy man with stiff bones having difficulty adjusting the position of his body. His noisy expulsion of breath sounded like something between a cough and a sigh. "My friend, are you listening?"

"Yes."

"So, what does your newspaper say this morning?"

"Eh . . . ?"

"Tell me. What headlines catch your eye this morning?"

"Um . . . just a minute."

He retrieved the paper from the table and brought it over to the telephone.

"Let me see . . . 'Rebel Stronghold Captured.' 'Army Recovers Stolen
Supply Truck.' 'Student Leaders Express Support for Campus Occupation.' 'Power Failure Blamed on Sabotage.'"

"And what do you make of all that?" Sandoval asked.

"Um . . ." Figueroa shrugged. Catching the sardonic tone in which
the question had been posed, he sensed that his friend was both amused
and annoyed.

"We're making great progress, eh?" Sandoval declaimed in a robust
voice. "These rebels, they're on the run. Their backs are to the wall. A few
more weeks, and the struggle will be over. Commendations and medals
all around."

"So it appears," Armand muttered. "It's all very encouraging."

"It's also complete *mierda*," Sandoval snorted. "*Mierda* of the smelli-
est variety. Well, most of it anyway. Usually they toss in something that's
true, just to give the whole load a whiff of credibility. They taught us well,
my friend. 'Leavening lies with a bit of truth helps it to go down easier.'
You'd think the people would know better, but it seems they want to
believe what we tell them. They want the reports to be true. For peace of
mind they can ignore the reek. The business about the power failure—
I can vouch for that. But the rest of it . . ."

"You mean . . . ?"

"We're no further ahead than we were months ago. That supply truck
was actually a munitions truck, a whole convoy in fact. Nothing was
recovered. No rebel stronghold was captured. And the students . . . they
would be kicking us off the campuses this very moment if we hadn't
locked up all their leaders. No, I tell you, it's bad and it's getting worse."

"I see," Figueroa mused, nodding and lowering his voice to a whisper
as he scanned the paper for anything else that seemed suspect. The same
thing had happened during the Aguaria dictatorship. He cast a quick
glance over his shoulder to see if Elena was within earshot. "So, I imagine
the radio and the television . . . ?"

"The same."

"Are you telling me we are losing the battle?" Figueroa shook his head.
"It cannot be true. I won't accept it."

There was a brief silence during which the two men listened to each other's breathing across the line. Figueroa passed a hand over his head. The chill of despair was creeping up his spine. Incompetence. Corruption.

"So, my good friend, tell me." he said finally. "What do you want me to do?"

"Ah, yes. I will get to the point. I need you to find someone and deliver him to me."

Figueroa nodded. "This person, this someone . . . he is lost?"

"Again . . ." Sandoval expelled a rush of air. "Well, you must know, it's not so simple. This is the army. Nothing is simple. What's happened is this. We are in with the Americans. These Yankees. Bah! This much I'm sure you know already. We are in with them. Too deeply. We should have known better, but there it is. Or, maybe I should say it this way: the President is in with them. He has become their *marioneta*. They fiddle with the strings and he dances. But this doesn't matter. The fact is that we have allowed them too much influence over our operations. The President doesn't fart without their say-so. And if they cut us loose, then look out. We all go down. But it's a complicated situation because they don't want us to fail, and, you know, we don't want to fail either. We want our country back. So far, the way things have been going has been of benefit to everyone. It's a mutual situation. Everyone has been doing well, if you get my meaning. So it does us no good to . . . ahem . . . give them the boot or stop cooperating. It makes no sense politically or strategically. To speak plainly, right now we need them more than they need us. And anyway, they're not going anywhere. The threat has been made, not in so many words. But it's gotten around that if we don't clean up our mess very soon, they will move in and clean it up for us. They want to protect their interests in this region. The rebels here, they have factions in other countries. So it's not just us. If we go down, the whole region tumbles into anarchy. The stability of the continent hangs by a thread. This is serious business."

"I see," Figueroa murmured. Gripped by his friend's words, with his fingernails he attacked a prickling itchy patch under his arm.

"No, Armand, excuse me, but you don't see. Not yet. In a minute I will make myself clear. But first, forgive me. My throat . . ."

Figueroa waited while the background was filled with a series of deep baritone hacking sounds and phlegmy whoops.

After a minute Sandoval returned to the phone. "Oh, my. I'm sorry. So, several things have happened. You know, I expect, about this American who was murdered, this Major Downing. Massacred along with his family and bodyguards in one of the hotels downtown here."

"Yes," Figueroa responded simply. "I read about that."

"Nasty business. The newspapers only know that he was a military advisor. But he was also an arms dealer, a valuable asset and a good friend to those in our government who cleared the way for him to do as he pleased. A very good friend, if you get my meaning. Many people were sorry to see him slaughtered like a pig and die in a pool of his own blood."

"Were you sorry to see him slaughtered like a pig?" Figueroa asked sternly.

Sandoval sighed.

"A fair question, my friend. But, no. No. I was not in any position to be sorry when Major Downing met his cruel fate."

"That's good, Jesús Arriaga. For the sake of your soul, I'm very glad to hear that."

"Yes, well. Anyway, as you can imagine, this event did not put smiles on many American Yankee faces. And not just the murder itself, which was messy and inconvenient. They don't like it when these things get into their newspapers. An American citizen murdered on our soil! People started asking, what's going on down there that this could happen? All of a sudden, the eyes of the world are on us. So we have that. And as you and I well know, when it comes to controlling the rabble it's best to make them disappear. That's how it's always been. Then, afterwards, you know, subtle threats to keep the family in line. Someone follows the daughter home from school. A dead rat on the doorstep. But something happened. I don't know where or when. It seems people aren't afraid any more. Maybe we overdid it. It got too easy. If someone became a nuisance, make them disappear. It doesn't frighten them off like it used to. So these protesters, these relatives of the ones who have gone missing, they're making so much noise, it's hard on the ears. And we can't arrest them. Some of them maybe, but not all of them. It's impossible. And this, too, is in the American newspapers, all this hogwash about justice and human rights. Bah! Don't get me started. It seems even their president is having a hard time pretending he doesn't know what's going on. Nosy journalists asking questions, making phone calls, and in America they can't just throw them into jail. So we have been told if it becomes a nightmare for them, it's going to be a nightmare for us. That, as the Americans say, is the bottom line. It seems, my friend, that we are not just printing *mierda,* we have stepped in it too."

"Our sins coming back to haunt us then?" Figueroa offered speculatively.

"Yes, yes, you could say that. Anyway, thank you, Armand, for your patience. It does me good to get this off my chest. It seems these days I talk more and more and do less and less. I feel like an old man. I'm like my grandfather, who told the same story day after day, about the rabbits in the back yard. I think I should retire. But at the moment it doesn't make sense. Not now. It's an ugly business but I have to see it through to the end. When this is over . . ."

There was a brief pause.

"Ahem! To get to the particulars, the fighting's been pretty intense up here. The murder of Major Downing was just the most brazen act of terrorism out of many. We've been pounding their positions; it's been relentless. There are roadblocks. The curfew is strictly enforced. But they're still getting into the city and setting off bombs and causing every sort of havoc you can imagine. So, anyway, I have a young squad commander, Montoya—you'll hear of him again, he's on the rise—competent, ambitious, maybe a bit too sure of himself. But that's a good thing. He's been a great asset. He's close to solving the Downing murder. We have one of the perpetrators in custody. Montoya's convinced she knows more than she's saying."

There was a brief pause.

"So, this girl . . . not much more than a child, it's outrageous, but the Americans are very interested in her, as you can imagine. Montoya thinks he can get her to talk. It's absolutely crucial for our credibility that we get the information out of her that we need. We have to do this on our own. More importantly, we have to be seen to do it. Downing may have been pushy and arrogant—a real *hijo de perra* by all accounts—but he died on our soil. The President has done all the bootlicking we can reasonably ask of him. These Americans treat us like idiots. So to show them we're not, we have to get answers."

"So this girl is the key?" Figueroa asked. "How can you be sure?"

"It's beyond doubt. That much is a certainty. There's witness testimony and other factors at work here that you don't have to concern yourself with. The main thing is that so far we've held the Americans off, but we can't do that forever. Once they get their hands on her, we'll never see her again and they'll take charge of the investigation. A great opportunity will be lost. What's more, the president wants this done now. So time, my friend, is of the essence."

"And my role is . . . ?"

"Your role, my friend, is to find her boyfriend and bring him to B——so that we can use him to get her to talk. I don't think I need to elaborate further on how that will be done."

Figueroa discovered many questions rushing to the tip of his tongue. "Is he in Chiachi, or some town around here? If you know where he is, why don't you just have him picked up?"

Sandoval chuckled ruefully. "Oh, my dear friend, if only it was that simple.

"The Americans have infiltrated our operation at every level. I could put the word out, but they would get wind of it in five minutes, and once they discover these inquiries are linked to the Downing murders, there will be no stopping them. I'll be forced to hand over everything I have and everything that Montoya has extracted from the girl, as well as the girl herself, this Nadia. Granted, this isn't much. But at the moment it's more than they have, and we want to keep it that way."

"So," Figueroa said, "I understand the need for secrecy. But can you even tell me where he is? And, if I find him, how am I supposed to get him to come with me? Or do I just take him into custody and have him shipped to B—— on the first train heading north?"

"Well, Armand, this is the difficulty. I didn't mention yet that he's a soldier. Not an ordinary soldier, mind you. Paramilitary. Goon squad. Officially he isn't on the payroll. He's nowhere. So you can imagine it's not been easy to piece together information concerning his whereabouts. I've had to be very circumspect in my inquiries. But what I gather is that he's been injured, and when this happens they have places where they send these boys to recover. I know what you're thinking. But I'm not naïve. I know these units are out there doing a job that needs to be done, but a lot of the men serving in these extra-military units are not regular recruits. They might be foreign mercenaries, but just as often they are people who have been arrested and held on suspicion of some criminal activity or other. The interrogation process for these detainees is particularly rigorous. It's like what we used to call brainwashing in the old days. If they come through it, and they seem more or less healthy and stable, they can be put to good use. But what's most interesting is that the army has no record of arrest or detention. Officially these people don't exist, either as prisoners or as soldiers. They're ghosts. If the family insists on forcing the issue, the army can truthfully say that since there's no official record, they have to assume that little José ran off to the hills to fight with his rebel friends. All the while, though, little José has been sent into combat to bolster his country's security interests."

Figueroa nodded. Of course, he had heard the tales and rumours as well, and, as seemed prudent at the time, turned a deaf ear. It was none of his concern. But now his curiosity was piqued. "So," he asked, "what's to stop little José from contacting his family and telling them he's just fine?"

"Huh! That's part of the training process. It can take months, you know. They have to be absolutely sure of the subject's loyalty. You get my meaning. There can be no chance of a security breach. That's why some don't make it. For the ones that do, their unit becomes their family. The recruiters will have gathered intelligence on the subject's background, falsifying and inventing to convince him he's been abandoned, or his family is dead or that they've left the country. Sometimes the subject is ready to accept a new station in life and the more elaborate steps are not needed. I don't imagine they go to any great expense. It could be as simple as drawing up a letter with a forged signature or rigging a phone line. Remember, the regime these people serve is ruthless. It demands unquestioning submission. These men are little better than robots. But they get the job done, and it's a job that you or I couldn't do and wouldn't want to do."

For just a moment Figueroa held his tongue. Was he prepared to commit to this task? Who was this boy? Was he dangerous? *Un asesino?* What would Elena say when he told her he was going back to work? She would probably be glad he'd found a way to occupy his time.

"How long do I have to find him?" he asked, stepping into it.

"A few days, no more. The Americans are getting impatient. If we don't give them something very soon this will be taken out of my hands."

A pause.

"Can I ask you a question?"

"Of course! Anything."

Figueroa glanced over his shoulder. He was alone. From the living room he heard the drone of the television—the morning newscast. Lowering his voice, he said, "You're not asking me to do something that could take me away from my Elena, are you? I'm everything to her. After Emilio José, she couldn't survive on her own."

Sandoval let out a breath. Figueroa heard the tapping of a pen or pencil on a wooden desktop.

"Armand, I won't lie to you. I have taken precautions, but this is a tricky business. If the wrong people get wind of what we're doing, there will be consequences. But I believe those consequences will land more heavily on me, and of course since you are acting on my request, I can insist that you were my unwitting errand boy. Even now, can you claim to know the whole story? No, you can't. I am keeping certain details from you, for your protection; for my protection too, I must admit."

Pointlessly, Figueroa nodded.

"I am grateful, my friend," Sandoval said, his tone grave. "Truly grateful. Your country treated you shabbily, but I knew I could count on you."

"Well then," Figueroa said. "What now? When do I get the information I need to get started?"

Sandoval emitted a breathy guffaw.

"I have a confession, my friend. I know you so well, despite all the years since we've raised a glass of illegal *aguardiente* together. Perhaps one day soon, we will do just that. But I knew you would accept the challenge that I am offering. Everything you require to take our project forward is already written out. Go to the *cuartel general* in Chiachi. The Secretary owes me favours. He can be trusted. In his office there is an envelope with your name on it, sealed with my official imprint. Inside you will find money for travel and whatever other expenses you run into, along with another sealed envelope containing your instructions and a letter of introduction. There should have been no reason for anyone to interfere with this package, but examine it carefully. I have confidence in your trained eye. If there are signs of tampering, leave it behind. Don't take it. It means I'm being watched more closely than I thought. But if the condition of the envelope does not arouse suspicion, then review the instructions and burn it. Immediately. Can you promise me that you will burn it?"

"Yes, yes. Of course. Don't worry. I will burn it."

"Good. Thank you." Sandoval sighed. "Armand, I am sorry to put you in this position. I am burdening you with something that is not your problem. But I have nowhere else to turn."

"You don't have to apologize. I am happy to do this. As I'm sure you knew I would be. Am I so very predictable in all things?"

"In this, maybe. I can't say about all things. You will have to ask Elena about that. But I knew, when I told you how important this is, your sense of duty would take over. You are that kind of man. Still, after all these years, ready for anything."

There was silence across the line.

"Another thing, it would be best if you do not take a weapon with you. Since you're retired they won't let you carry it into a government building. You'd have to check it when you go in and pick it up when you leave. They might even confiscate it. It will only slow you down. So best to leave it home."

"Thank you for the warning."

"I pray nothing will happen to make you regret this."

More silence.

"So," Sandoval resumed, and then hesitated. He cleared his throat. "I think you will agree it would be for the best if, for now, there is no more contact between us. If you do not take the envelope, the Secretary will let me know. If I do not hear from him, I will assume you are conducting your search. Now, my friend, do you have any questions?"

"Just one thing."

"Yes?"

"What is the boy's name? Can you tell me that much?"

"His name," Sandoval intoned, "is Hector Tomás."

THIRTY-NINE

The truck climbed to the top of the hill and rounded the last corner. The camp was apparently not visible from the road, so they drove straight through darkness that had no limit and no boundary. The driver had cut the lights and the truck moved very slowly, rattling through one hole after another and kicking up a ruckus.

Eventually they arrived at the rendezvous point where they were to meet the soldiers approaching the camp on foot. Hector did not see them, but instead heard the hushed impact of boots treading the stony earth, a hasty murmur of greetings. Anxious to get started, Josquin jumped from the truck and marched around to the back. He motioned for the men to get out. In an instant Hector was on the ground, mustering into formation with the others. They lined up, shoulder to shoulder. Alejandro stood beside him, ramrod straight, and he wished—not for the first time, probably not the last—that it was within his power to take the boy by the hand and lead him away from here, away from the danger and the killing. They all listened as Josquin spoke while the soldier who had driven the truck distributed the infrared goggles. His voice, hardly rising above the night murmurs of bugs and blind burrowing beasts, still conveyed the urgency and importance of their assignment. The camp consisted of four buildings. Reconnaissance had reported that three of these were supply huts, so they were to focus their assault on the large central house. One group would approach from the front. Hector and Alejandro were with the group that would approach from the rear. They were to make no noise until they were breaking down the front and back doors, which would happen in a coordinated fashion. Remember, contain the enemy with your weapons, your bodies, your voices. Make them think there are hundreds of you. Those who cooperate will be spared, those who resist will be neutralized. No exceptions. Another group will wait in the forest to capture or eliminate those trying to escape on foot or through tunnels.

Then they were on their way.

Alejandro sprinted ahead and Hector followed, his swift steps in the undergrowth creating that delicate whisper that could be anything: a flutter of night wings, a gentle breeze stirring tree limbs into lazy motion.

It was a dark, silent wood-frame house fronted by a raised veranda, a bungalow in style but enlarged by additions to left and right. Its sharply pitched roof, tidy expanse of lawn, little storage shed or *bodega,* and neatly stacked woodpile gave the impression of normalcy. Behind the house: a second smaller outbuilding. Possibly a latrine. At the back of the house, steps led up directly off the grass to another veranda and a set of wooden double doors. His trained eye caught other details and dismissed them as part of the ruse: at the far edge of the lawn there was a toy truck, a sandbox, a swing set. The field in back of the house had been cleared and orderly rows of some crop had been planted, poles to hold the plants upright off the earth. It had been done conscientiously, with careful planning and dedicated industry.

He went up the steps, off the grass. Another of the team was approaching the door. On the veranda Hector's foot nudged something and he looked down. A plastic doll with bleached hair wearing a frilly dress stared at him with its dead eyes. But with his gun at the ready and his heart thumping so hard he could count the beats, with Alejandro at his side and Josquin's instructions echoing in his head, this was no time to question the task that lay before him. The moment had arrived. He couldn't pause for even a second to consider a doll with bleached hair and what it might mean.

Then the smashed door lay in splintered fragments, and he was rushing behind Alejandro into the house.

He was in a kitchen, until that moment tidy and ordinary. The house echoed with shouts, shoulders smashing through hollow doors, the crash of objects being broken and overturned. Screams. As the team rushed through the kitchen and swarmed into the hallway, Hector touched Alejandro's arm and nodded towards a door. Alejandro aimed his weapon and Hector went to the door and pulled it open. Wooden steps led down into a basement. Somewhere in the house gunshots were followed by high-pitched shrieks and cries. Hector vaulted down the four steps, Ale-jandro close behind him. Stooping to accommodate the low ceiling, they made a quick circuit of the cramped space. In one corner cardboard boxes were piled one atop the other; in another, a stack of kindling; in the cen-tre, a wood-burning furnace. One wall was taken up by racks filled with bottles of wine. Nearby, against the wall, three barrel-shaped objects stood side-by-side. Hector crept across the room to examine them. Each had a spout on the front and a numbered dial or gauge protruding from the top. Alejandro joined him as he tapped one and gently rocked it, then did the same with the other two. Plastic tanks of some sort, all of them empty. He looked at Alejandro and shook his head.

None of this was threatening.

They returned to the bottom of the steps in time to see a ghostly shape flit past the open door above them.

Alejandro leapt to the top of the basement stairs and rushed into the kitchen. Hector emerged from the basement in time to see his friend lift his gun. Through the gaping hole where the back door had been, Hector saw the shape vanish down the steps from the veranda just as Alejandro pulled the trigger and fired half a dozen rounds. They waited for two, three seconds but heard nothing, saw no further movement. The house was quiet except for the heavy tread of soldiers' boots. The occasional shout. They went out to the veranda and looked down. Through his goggles, fuzzily, Hector saw the small figure splayed on the grass.

He stared at the motionless body, his heart galloping, conscious of Ale-jandro at his side. He wanted to touch the boy's arm, but held still. They did not look at each other. Then, silently, Alejandro turned and walked back through the kitchen, towards the front of the house. Hector followed.

It had been no more than three minutes since they'd forced their way into the house, but the raid was complete. In the living room some lights had been turned on. Hector stopped in the kitchen doorway and removed the goggles and balaclava. In the living room several from his unit, Alejandro among them, stood with their guns trained on a man and a woman. The two were kneeling with their hands bound behind them, their heads bent as if in prayer. They had been gagged and blind-folded. The man wore striped pyjama bottoms and had a hairy chest. He was bloody about the mouth. The woman had on a gauzy nightgown, beneath which she was naked. She was weeping and her face was wet with tears. Otherwise they were silent. In the front hallway Josquin stood consulting with Rudolfo. They seemed to avoid looking at each other as they took turns grimly surveying the chaos of the room, the overturned furniture, the bullet-riddled walls. Josquin, his scalp shiny with sweat, pulled out his walkie-talkie and spat a few abrupt commands, then grimaced in response to the blast of static that was delivered back to him. In a minute a couple of men arrived through the front door with equipment they would use to sweep the house for explosives.

Hector's attention was drawn to the sound of childish sniffling. He turned and saw two boys and a girl sitting perched on an antique-style sofa, their bare feet dangling inches off the floor. The girl had blonde hair and sat between the two boys, who were much smaller than her. One boy wore powder-blue pyjamas imprinted with images of spacemen. The other wore yellow pyjamas bearing images of cowboys on horseback, which Hector recognized with a start because his brother Julio had pyjamas exactly like them. The girl's satiny pyjamas were a pastel shade of lavender with a delicate vertical stripe. He guessed that none of them was older than ten. Like their parents, all three had been gagged and blindfolded and had their hands bound behind them.

He was not called upon to do anything, but mechanically, like the others in his unit, assumed the standard position, with his gun aimed towards the kneeling couple. In response to a voice, Rudolfo and Josquin disappeared into the kitchen. He heard muttering, rapid steps. Furtively, he looked towards Alejandro but could not catch the boy's eye. From all around him came sounds of men treading heavily throughout the house as they carried out the search. There were more voices, urgent whispers. Then the deafening crackle of the walkie-talkie, a blade slashing the night air. It drowned out anything else that was said.

Their search complete, the men exited through the front door. Several minutes passed. From the kitchen came the sound of shuffling feet, but otherwise a stifling silence had descended upon the house. Hector strained to hear words that would tell him what was going on, but there was nothing. In the absence of further orders, they maintained their position, their guns trained on the kneeling couple. Every few minutes he would remember, with an abrupt lurching of his heart, the shots that Alejandro had fired, the small figure lying in the grass, before shutting it out of his mind. The woman still wept, but more quietly. The children had stopped sniffling. For a few minutes Hector had welcomed the distraction of watching the girl wriggle and squirm and finally settle against the padded upright back of the sofa. The boys, who had been leaning for support on her shoulders, now had their heads resting in her lap. He wondered, briefly concerned, if she was comfortable. Some of the men who had been standing longer than Hector flexed stiffening muscles. There were murmurs, shifting limbs. Someone farted, lightly. The woman had lowered her body so her legs were curled beneath her and her head was resting against the arm of a chair. Her brown hair fell in all directions, and with her movements the hem of her nightgown had hitched up revealing the white skin of her thighs. Startled, Hector momentarily looked away from the prisoners and met anxious glances among the other soldiers. Quickly he lowered his eyes. Someone cleared his throat. The unease permeating the room—the sense that something had gone horribly wrong—grew stronger and more overt with each passing moment. Nobody said a word. Eventually, through the open front door, came the day's first birdsong. Soon the eastern horizon would begin to glow with morning light.

Many more minutes went by before Hector grew aware of a distant rumble, an engine. A vehicle was approaching through the forest.

Rudolfo and Josquin re-emerged from the kitchen. Glancing up, Hector noticed on both of them the same strain about the eyes, the same grim set of the mouth. They did not speak, did not glance into the living room as they strode down the hall and out the front door.

The sound of the vehicle grew louder until it pulled up and crunched to a stop on the dirt and gravel driveway in front of the house. Hector heard doors open and slam. Raised voices, Rudolfo's and Josquin's among them.

There was a series of terse exchanges and then the voices fell silent. Hector heard a procession of heavy steps approach the house. He focused on tightening his hold on the gun and, though his arms ached, keeping it steady. His stomach clenched involuntarily.

Rudolfo and Josquin stood with the other men in the hallway. Hector, his blood quickening, did not allow his gaze to stray from the prisoners, but nonetheless sensed the men regarding the scene in the living room soberly and with some degree of annoyance. One of the men sighed, an impatient, exasperated sound.

"Through here," Josquin said, and led the others into the kitchen.

Hector heard heavy treads on the back veranda. Again, but through their eyes this time, he saw the figure on the grass.

"*Mierda!*"

Steps. The voices trailed off. Hector strained to hear, but the silence that descended was absolute. He flexed his neck, lifted his eyes and scanned the room, which was filling with rosy morning light. A strange sort of fear, like warm liquid, was spreading upward from his gut. His eyes met Alejandro's and held the boy's taut gaze. They both looked down at the same moment.

After some minutes car doors slammed. The engine growled and the vehicle sped away.

Josquin and Rudolfo entered the house again through the front door.

Rudolfo strode into the living room. Hector had been the last to enter the room, and was now the first Rudolfo came to. Without speaking, he touched Hector's arm and indicated with a quick gesture that he go to Josquin, who was standing sullenly by, the revolver in his hand pointed towards the floor. Hector immediately lowered his gun and went into the hallway. Rudolfo did the same with three other soldiers standing within easy reach. They joined Hector and formed a line, the four of them standing stiffly at attention behind Josquin, who did not acknowledge their presence.

"The rest of you," Rudolfo said in a strained voice, his tone more a suggestion than a command, "back to the truck. Hurry!"

The others lowered their weapons and filed out, the hollow drumming of their boots against the floor at odds with the ethereal tranquility of the breaking day. Hector tried again to meet Alejandro's eye. But the boy only glanced at him as he fell in behind the others and left through the opening where the front door had once stood. Rudolfo followed them out.

When they were gone, Josquin said dully, turning away and not looking at the group of four, "Take the prisoners." He drifted listlessly into the kitchen.

Hector and the three others went into the living room and helped the two adults and three children to their feet. Hector took the man gently by the arm and lifted him from the kneeling position he'd assumed hours earlier. The man staggered on his cramped legs and Hector steadied him with a firm hand on each shoulder. The man moaned through the gag.

Hector noticed spreading bruises and deep cuts around his jaw. The man's face was wet with tears that had leaked from beneath the blindfold.

"Come on," he murmured, trying to seem kind.

The sound of the woman's weeping was steady, interrupted only when she coughed through the gag. The girl was quiet. The boys sniffled and moaned. As they were being led away, Hector saw that both boys had wet their pyjamas. The sofa bore stains where they had been sitting.

They followed Josquin through the opening where the back door had been and down the veranda steps. In the dim morning light, Hector was relieved to see the figure was gone, and was briefly convinced he'd imagined it. But then he passed a bloody stain, a glistening crimson pool that had spread over the grass in an almost perfect arc from where the figure's head would have rested.

All at once the scene became frightening in its clarity. Josquin moving through the grass with a swaggering gait, the woman shivering, stepping gingerly, naked beneath her nightgown, all dignity forfeited. The children: the girl walking unhesitatingly, her head held high, the boys shuffling, small bare feet wet in the dewy grass. The soldiers in their black uniforms, their bulky vests, their hands on the prisoners. The man at Hector's side, neck bent in mournful resignation. They were almost under the shadow of the mountains and the morning air was soft, clean, pleasantly fragrant of pine and raw earth. How many times had he filled his lungs with this life-giving draught? How many of his days had begun with such promise? He felt anger then, with this family that had so foolishly blundered into the path that his unit was following as they tried to do their work. Josquin and Rudolfo would not lead them wrong. He had to have faith. How could he have doubted the righteousness of their actions, the essential decency of their cause? He regarded the prisoners sternly and tightened his grip on the man's arm. He gathered phlegm from the back of his throat and spat it out. It was so unfair, to be called upon to do this. It should not have happened. If only the family had gone somewhere. How could they not have known, and been prepared? That was it, then. They had. They'd tipped off the terrorists, who had vanished into the forest. But his resolution wavered when he looked at these people and saw that they were ordinary. None of this was their fault.

He reaffirmed his grip on the man's arm. The feel of living flesh was comforting. He was glad for the companionship.

In silence, like lambs, they followed Josquin across the grass, away from the house. Hector struggled to impose order upon his thoughts, which had scattered like seeds in the wind. There was a way to avert what was coming, to answer this riddle, but he failed to grasp it. Beside the orderly rows of plantings, which in the gathering morning light he could see were grape vines, they joined a concrete path and followed this for a few moments. The tiny perfect budding clusters of grapes were a chaste, pale green. At his feet he noticed a scattering of blood droplets on the concrete.

Francisco had tried growing grapes, but had never succeeded. Hector remembered the old man muttering, scowling at the blighted vines, which occupied a rectangle of exposed earth at the base of a hill, mute in their accusation of failure.

The path veered right, towards a wooden building, too big to be called a shed. The door was already open, the lights on.

They went into the building. Dominated by a gleaming metal vat, the space they entered had a high ceiling and was lit by rows of fluorescent lights. There was a churlish smell of spoilage, as if something had been left out to rot. Josquin was using his revolver to direct them forward, around the vat and towards the back. Trembling, and with a new weakness in his limbs, Hector concentrated on the man at his side, gripped the arm tighter, tried to imagine him a criminal, planting bombs, laughing as they went off. But instead, he saw himself shooting Josquin and then the other soldiers and helping the family escape.

Stunned, he stopped in his tracks. The man halted by his side.

Looking down, Hector noticed, here and there, the spattering of blood on the concrete floor.

His ears were suddenly filled with sounds of whining and muffled weeping. The man was crying openly, quivering, shaking his head and attempting to speak through the gag.

"Get moving!"

Josquin was standing in front of Hector and had issued the command in an irate whisper through clenched teeth. His nostrils flared. He gestured with the gun.

As if jolted out of a doze, Hector jerked the man's arm and pulled roughly, forcing him to move.

Following Josquin, Hector dragged the man down the cramped passage between the vat and the wall, to the back of the building. The others were already there. The three soldiers stood to one side, their weapons aimed at the prisoners. Hector felt a deepening dread at the sight of the three faces, the three pairs of eyes that glanced towards him in unison and then looked quickly away. The woman and children had been positioned on their knees a few feet from the wall, facing away from their executioners. Beside them, on her back, arms straight at her side, lay the body of a small girl in a white bloodstained nightshirt. Her pale features, bearing traces of blood and dirt, were still. Her hair was like a pool of gold on the floor. Her head was turned and her eyes stared vacantly. A dark wound gaped at the top of her skull. Her lips, parted slightly, seemed about to speak.

"Hurry," Josquin urged.

Hector shoved the man towards the wall, gripped his shoulder, and pressed down to force him to his knees. The man shuddered as he wept. The woman had stopped moving but was whispering lightly to herself. The two boys knelt, one on either side of her. They squirmed and whined, nestling close to her body as if they could burrow inside. The girl knelt with her head held up, perfectly still, apparently calm.

He backed away and was about to join the others when he noticed they were watching him. Each held his weapon at the ready, but they all seemed frozen to the spot.

He realized that he had been imagining a moment when he could walk away from this, slip into the forest and vanish, become a fugitive, maybe join the rebels if they would have him. But his former comrades would hunt him down. Slaughter him and leave his carcass to rot in the sun. There was, after all, no escape.

Josquin was nodding towards him. "He will do it," he said. "He will teach us how to do our duty."

Hector noticed Josquin's revolver, the finger on the trigger. He could refuse and be shot. At least it would be over.

"Now," Josquin added, gesturing again with his gun. "Now!"

Watching his squad leader, Hector raised his weapon, wrapped his hands around it, held it steady. He placed his finger on the trigger. He had embarked upon this mission with warm thoughts for his comrades, willing to sacrifice himself for the success and security of the squad. And here was his opportunity, though it wasn't the kind of sacrifice he had envisioned.

He tensed his body and tried to empty his mind. But before he could even wonder how he was going to make himself do this, the bullets were spraying from his weapon, the kickback of its pulsations wracking his body. The two adults and three children toppled forward from the kneeling position and were still. Seconds later, when it was over, Hector gazed blankly at what he had done. The room was quiet. The wall was speckled with bullet marks. At first he felt nothing, then became sensible of a balmy glow radiating outward from his chest. Josquin waded into the tangle of arms and legs, prodding the bodies with his boot. He extended his arm, steadied his gun, and shot the man in the head, then the woman. Hector flinched as the detonations boomed throughout the space in which he stood. Moist, sticky air entered his lungs and congealed into a hardened mass. Josquin aimed and shot the girl. He made a terse gesture and one of the other soldiers jumped forward and lifted the woman's lifeless body out of the way. Beneath her the two boys lay face down. Hector, his vision clouding, could not tell if they were still breathing. Josquin shot each in the head.

With mounting horror he watched the blood pool creeping from the bodies, reaching out to him across the smooth concrete floor. For a moment he observed its silent approach, the stark contrast of liquid red against the flat grey surface. He covered his eyes and turned, gagged, staggered, and supported himself with his hand against the wall. He was having difficulty moving his legs. He sank to his knees. He'd been hit. His own shots had come back at him, ricocheted off the wall. He was leaking blood. It was on his hands. It had soaked into his clothes.

"Get him out of here," he heard: Josquin's voice, tight with fury. Hands grabbed him under the arms and dragged him along the passage beside the vat. Barely conscious, he read words freshly scrawled in dripping black paint on the wall near the door of the building: *traidor, muerte a los espías*. Outside, the sky glowed. The house was in flames.

FORTY

Major Armand Figueroa followed his friend's instructions and ventured down to the *cuartel general* right after the phone conversation, or as soon as he could be sure the place was open. Elena insisted on sending his uniform out to be pressed, so for the morning errand he wore his old blue suit and plain black tie (this he retrieved from the back of the closet whenever an event came along requiring formal attire—weddings or funerals; sadly there were far more funerals these days than weddings). Chancing a peek at himself in the full-length mirror in the bedroom, he thought he looked like an aging insurance salesman down on his luck. But it would have to do.

He gave Elena a clipped synopsis of his task, revealing only that he was being asked to escort an injured soldier to B—— to reunite him with his family, that the situation was sensitive and that the whole thing was supposed to be a surprise, so it couldn't be done by regular military personnel. He presented it as an act of charity. A kindness.

"This is what they ask of you after all this time?" she chided, on her knees, brushing the lint from his pants with strokes far too vigorous for the job. "To do something for someone else when their debt to you has never been paid. And you say yes?"

"Ow! My dear, I understand everything you say. But don't work yourself into a state on my behalf. I'm happy to do this, as a favour for Jesús Arriaga."

"You do not owe him anything."

"By asking me to do this he's recognizing my talent and my years of service. He knows he can count on me. Besides, after this he will owe me! It could be the first step towards reinstatement and restitution. Please stop!" He took her by the arms, lifted her to her feet, and pried the brush out of her fingers. He tried to appear stern in a good-humoured sort of way, to put an end to her anxieties, and also buoyant and confident, to give her hope. "He said so himself," he added with a smile. A white lie that could do no harm.

"And you believe him?"

"He's a good friend. He defended me, you know, back then."

"So he says."

He sighed and set the brush down on the bureau. He regarded her dotingly. She was his strength, his bastion. The lines of her beautiful face, hardened by adversity, softened by age. There was fire in her yet; he could still be singed by it if he wasn't careful. Today she was hot to the touch.

"I can see you won't be moved, and I don't blame you for feeling this way. But I will do what he's asking of me, and maybe some good will come of it."

This seemed to settle the matter. She had been standing back from him with her arms folded, one eyebrow raised, lips pursed—as if she couldn't believe he would do something so stupid. It made him crazy when she looked at him like that. But with these words her shoulders slumped and she fell—willingly it seemed—into his arms.

"It's just . . . Armand, I don't want you to be disappointed again."

"I'm going into this expecting nothing. How can I be disappointed?"

"You and I, we always find a way to be disappointed."

"Please, Elena, don't think like that. It's a lark, a little vacation. Nothing more. A couple of days. I will pick up the young man and take him to B——— on the train, God willing, tonight. I'll be home tomorrow or maybe the next day, depending. I won't listen to any promises. I won't do anything else they ask of me, even if they get down on their knees and beg."

He pressed his mouth into her hair and kissed the top of her head. He did not want her to be afraid. "I will bring something back for you, a present—"

"No need, no need. Just come home."

Sandoval's contact at the *cuartel general,* the Interior Secretary, Adolfo Botaya Sanz, a tall angular man, possibly in his late thirties —not a speck of dust on his uniform but whose eyes wandered here

and there as if in his mind he struggled to reconcile a hundred war-
ring details—ushered him from the depths of a soft leather chair in the
reception area into his spacious but unadorned office with a degree of
deference he found embarrassing ("It's an honour to meet you sir!"—was
the man serious? A moron?). He presented the package and escorted him
into a small room off to the side which contained a tiny wooden desk
and chair. Here Sanz left him alone to peruse its contents. A moment
later there was a knock at the door, and following his brusque request to
"Enter," the receptionist who had earlier greeted him and alerted Sanz
to his presence came in and, with a smile, laid a cup of tea and a plate
of biscuits on the desk.

Sandoval's fear that the envelope might have been tampered with
appeared to be unfounded. The seal was intact. The money (more than
he would need, surely, unless there were bribes) was wrapped in brown
paper crisply folded and fastened with cellophane tape. This left the plain
white inner envelope. He slit it open with the silver letter opener that lay
on the desk. The envelope contained two pieces of paper.

Most Trusted Friend,

*I am happy you have made it this far because I have reason to believe I am
under surveillance. So, a small victory for us.*

*I will be brief. The object of your search is Hector Tomás. He is a soldier but
not regular army. He was recently injured in the service of his country and is
recuperating at a medical facility somewhere in the interior, outside Chiachi.
I am not privy to the name or location of this facility but I am confident you
will discover this and deliver the young man safely into our hands.*

*Secretary Sanz is ignorant of your purpose and wishes to remain so. However,
he is essential to your task because upon your request he will make a phone
call to a covert training complex and barracks, which lies about ten miles
away from where you are sitting.*

*From here you will be on your own. You will have to trust your instincts.
My inquiries have led me to the conclusion that Hector Tomás is known to
people at this centre, but, beyond that, information is hard to come by.*

I know you will not reveal the truth about why you are looking for him. This is crucial, if we are to keep the Americans in the dark. As the letter of introduction attests, you are acting on my authority. Nobody will question that.

Once you enter the training complex you will be off the grid, so to speak. Secretary Sanz will deny all knowledge of what you are up to.

I don't believe you will be in danger. However—you will think I am being paranoid, but, believe me, things have changed since you left the service, and not for the better—when we spoke, I was calling from a private line that I had installed at my own expense. Nobody knows about it, so for the moment we are safe. I give this number to no one. If you need to contact me, call my office and leave a number where you can be reached.

The people you will meet operate differently than we do, but they remain our colleagues. They have standards to uphold, as do we. Believe this to be true and you will come to no harm.

Your ever grateful friend and colleague,
Major Jesús Arriaga Vargas-Sandoval

PS: Burn this letter!

Office of Zonal Operations
Plaza Agustín Chacón 2770, B_____
(+562) 2185240

To Whom It May Concern:

The bearer of this letter is Major Armand Figueroa, retired. He is to bring Hector Tomás, a soldier, whose statement is needed for an internal inquiry, to the headquarters in B_____ and deliver him into my charge.

Major Figueroa is acting on behalf of this office and on the highest authority.
I expect his commands to be carried out without delay, without question,
and with all due respect.

The Office of Zonal Operations will provide any necessary clarification.

Major Jesús Arriaga Vargas-Sandoval
Chief of Zonal Operations

Sandoval's letter did not clear up all the questions their conversation had
raised. A few nagging doubts remained. But the secrecy, the clandestine
nature of the operation . . . ah, now that's what he had been missing: that
tingling sensation up and down his spine in anticipation of the hunt. He
returned the money and papers to the large outer envelope, folded it over,
and stuffed it into the inner pocket of his suit jacket. It was approaching
noon. Rather than delay the enterprise upon which he was embarking,
Figueroa told Secretary Sanz to make the call. Clandestine or not, how
complicated could it be to pick someone up and take them to B⎯ on
the train?

Having spoken very few words, and those in an unintelligible mumble,
Sanz returned the phone to its cradle.

"There will be a car here to pick you up in a couple of hours, Major.
You can wait downstairs."

With this the Secretary seemed to indicate their meeting was over.
But Figueroa did not feel like leaving right away. Instead, uninvited, he
lowered himself into the chair in front of the Secretary's desk and glanced
around. The office had a makeshift look to it: no furniture other than the
desk and chairs. Not even a rug. The only picture on the wall was the standard portrait of the President, who was also the head of the armed forces,
stiffly uncomfortable in full regalia. Two windows offered an oblique
perspective on the town's central plaza and, distantly, the spires of the
basilica. In the silence, the tap-tap-tap of the receptionist's typewriter
was discretely audible through the closed door.

"Can you tell me who you were talking to?"

In a seemingly habitual gesture unrelated to the question, one that
made him look somewhat like *el albatros,* Sanz lifted his chin and swivelled his head from side to side.

"A contact, nothing more."

Figueroa nodded. "Who is coming to pick me up?"

Sanz lifted his chin and shrugged. "I'm sure I don't know."

"Then who should I ask for when—"

Sanz raised his hand. "Major Figueroa, please. When Major Sandoval impressed upon me the importance of what you are doing, I did not question him. I did not ask for details. His assurances were enough. However—" he touched one hand to his chest—"I am out of it now. I delivered the package. I made the call." He shrugged again, but more elaborately than the first time. He lowered his voice. "He did not ask anything further of me and I cannot volunteer anything. My time is not my own. I'm sure you understand."

Sanz smiled weakly.

Figueroa leaned towards the desk, stretched out his hand. "I'll take one of your cards then, in case—"

Sanz moved quickly and snatched away the little wooden display stand and the stack of his official cards it held. For a moment he entertained a vision of them engaged in a childish tug of war.

"I'm sorry. I can't let you do that." Sanz shook his head. "I'm sorry."

With his hand suspended in midair and gazing in disbelief at his interlocutor, who, as Figueroa watched, deposited the cards into a drawer, Figueroa slowly settled back in his chair.

"What is this training centre? How come I don't know about it?"

Sanz clenched his hands together on the desk. The knuckles were white. "Major, forgive me. I'm merely being prudent. My position is a public one. I serve many masters. I can't be seen to ally myself with any faction or take sides in a dispute. I would be hopelessly compromised—"

"What do you mean, 'dispute'? What dispute?"

Sanz stared at him. "It appears I've overstated the matter," he said easily, showing Figueroa his open palms. "Forgive me." He breathed deeply and all at once appeared to grow reflective. "Major Sandoval is the reason I am where I am today. I help him out when I can. Unofficially. In this matter, I can deliver a package and make a phone call. It's not much to ask. But the Major is far removed from Chiachi. He doesn't understand how things work here. I don't know what he told you and I don't want to know. But I do know that I will be of no use to him if I lose my position."

Their eyes met.

337

Figueroa nodded. "I see."

"Major, your reputation precedes you. I was sincere when I said it was an honour. But I can do nothing more for you."

Sanz stood and extended his hand.

Figueroa stood as well.

"Mr. Secretary, I understand completely."

They shook hands.

"I will say this, however." Sanz smiled, then became sombre again. "I'm mixing metaphors, but no matter. You are wading into murky waters. I have no idea what lies at the end of this road you have chosen to follow. You've heard of the protests. You might know we are being pressured to appoint a civilian government and hold elections. This could happen sooner than anyone thinks. People are afraid. Suspicion is rampant. My advice is to watch your back."

Figueroa acknowledged this speech with a little nod. Then he said, "Thank you." He coughed. "Excuse me. Your candour is appreciated." He made to leave. Then, turning, "A couple of hours you said?"

Sanz had resumed his seat. "The car, yes. Downstairs. Someone will look for you in the waiting area. Say an hour and a half. Best to be a little bit early."

Figueroa nodded. "I am grateful. You've been very helpful."

Passing through the reception area, as sumptuous as Sanz's office was spartan, he stopped by the receptionist's desk. Above it hung the identical portrait of the President.

She paused in her typing and smiled up at him. "Yes, sir?"

"Thank you for the tea," he said.

"You're most welcome."

"Um." He touched his hands to the pockets of his jacket and assumed a look of absent-minded puzzlement.

"Is there anything else?"

"I'm sorry. The Secretary was going to give me one of his cards, but he forgot. I don't want to go back in there and bother him . . ."

"It's no trouble."

She opened a drawer and took out a card. Their fingers touched as she handed it to him.

He pocketed the card. On the way out the door he gave her a smile and a quick salute.

FORTY-ONE

Directly after his interview with Sanz, he took a taxi home and changed into his freshly pressed uniform. Elena made sandwiches, but he was not in a mood to eat and put one in his pocket for later. He had everything he needed: the money, the letter of introduction, cigarettes, and wanted only to relax for a few minutes, but she fussed and fussed, making him nervous, until finally he told her he had to leave, that he was going to be late. He understood her fears, and to some extent shared them, but he managed to remain calm and joked about the assignment before embracing her lightly on his way out the door.

For half an hour he shared the dour *cuartel general* waiting area with a worried looking elderly couple and a very thin young woman who was unable to control her two squabbling children. He paid them no heed as he tried to organize his thoughts. A private wearing ordinary green combat fatigues and cap arrived to pick him up. They saluted each other and he followed the young soldier out the front door of the building into the warm early afternoon and around back to the parking lot. It occurred to him that he had not known what mode of transport to expect, but the dirty blue Fiat with the dented grill that the soldier unlocked was not a possibility that had entered his mind.

Standing ramrod straight as he held open the door (Figueroa was apparently expected to sit in the back), the soldier did not look him in the eye.

They drove in silence for a few minutes and were waiting at a traffic light when Figueroa asked, "Where are we off to, then? This training complex . . ." He chuckled under his breath. "It's all very mysterious."

His eyes hidden behind sunglasses, the soldier did not acknowledge the question. It was as if he hadn't heard.

Figueroa waited a minute before trying again.

"Excuse me. Maybe you can tell me who to ask for when we get there."

The soldier regarded him briefly in the rear-view mirror. "I'm not at liberty to say, sir."

He recognized the approach to the south road leading out of town. They were picking up speed.

Figueroa leaned forward. "Private, what is your name?"

Again, the glance. "I'm not at liberty to say, sir."

The provocation was transparent. He almost raised his voice to demand an answer before deciding it would only antagonize the man, and he did not want his adventure to start on a sour note. He nodded and rested back against the seat, which, like his escort, had no give to it. Then he noticed there were no handles of any kind on either of the rear doors. His heart leapt into his throat. Thinking he was in error, he ran his fingers over the surface of the doors like a blind man, but the casing was smooth.

"Soldier, am I being abducted?"

A guarded glance, but no words.

"You're not really a private, are you?"

Silence. The soldier stared straight ahead, both hands on the wheel.

With a grunt he choked back a throaty surge of panic. His palms were sweating. This was no game. He tried to think what he should do, but his brain seemed to have stalled. He stared dumbly at the back of the man's head. The soldier seemed absolutely composed. How could he be sure his prisoner was unarmed? But he was trained. Of course he would know. Figueroa hunted through his pockets for something—anything—that could be used as a weapon, but all he came up with was the corned beef sandwich that Elena had prepared, warm and squishy now in its waxed paper wrapper.

They were approaching the junction with the south road when the soldier abruptly pulled the car off the tarmac and jerked to a stop. Figueroa craned his neck, searching for other vehicles. Maybe he could signal . . . ?

Something soft landed in his lap. He picked it up. Black cloth. A blindfold?

The soldier had removed his sunglasses. In the rear-view mirror Figueroa met the young man's expressionless gaze with one of his own that he hoped was intimidating. Then he realized his mouth was hanging open.

"You expect—?"

"Sir, we can't go any further until you put that on."

"This is absurd."

"I'm sorry, sir. The location is classified."

"And if I refuse?"

"My orders are to drive you back to Chiachi and drop you wherever it's convenient."

He fingered the cloth, which was thick and a bit bristly, like stiff burlap. He raised his arms and began wrapping it around his head, fumbling to tie it with fingers made clumsy by the fright he'd suffered. It fit snugly around his eyes, effectively blocking out the light. It was not uncomfortable. He made an adjustment so that a tiny gap allowed his right eye a view of the road through windshield.

"You could have said something earlier, you know. You could have given it to me back there, when I got in the—"

He'd raised his head and was checking the sightline when he saw through the chink the soldier's extended arm, the hand gripping the gun, its barrel no more than two inches from his face. His breath caught.

"Please make it secure, sir."

As fast as he could manage with shaking fingers that felt swollen like sausages, he folded down the edge of the blindfold, shutting out the last of the light. His body was saturated with perspiration. He lowered his arms, sat back and waited.

In a few seconds the car juddered into motion and swerved back on to the road. He didn't say another word.

Figueroa held his silence when, a short time later, after a series of twists and turns and a brief stop where his driver exchanged a few words with someone at what he assumed was a checkpoint, the car halted on a surface of loose stone. The engine was cut. The entire journey had taken twenty minutes.

"Sir, I'll ask that you leave the blindfold on."

The driver's door opened and closed. This was followed by measured steps crunching across the stony ground. The steps quickly faded into silence. He was only a soldier carrying out orders, but try as he might, Figueroa could not think kindly of his driver, though, he had to admit, the man's cool efficiency was admirable.

341

He waited for several minutes, straining to listen. The car's interior was too warm and the windows were closed tight. His legs were cramped. The heat amplified his discomfort. The temptation to remove the blindfold was strong, but perhaps he was being watched. He could hear nothing. It was almost as if the car were sitting abandoned in the forest, miles from anywhere. He tried to divert his thoughts away from the alarming images this brought to mind, but instead found himself leaning over a yawning pit full of rotting corpses. One of them was Elena!

He jerked awake with a yelp. How long had he been out? How could he have let himself drift off like that? Stupid! Stupid! He needed to stay alert. His life depended on it. But it was too hot. He needed air. My God, what was the holdup? Sandoval was going to hear about this!

He turned his head. What was that sound? What was it? Car tires on crushed stone. It stopped. Doors opened and closed.

"Hello?"

Nothing.

He thumped the window with his hand. Then again, and again.

"Who's out there?" he bawled. "Let me out of here!"

Without loosening the blindfold he reared up and manoeuvred his belly around the driver's seat, groped for the steering wheel and found the horn. He leaned his weight on it. The car emitted a devilish low-pitched snarl.

In a few seconds the rear door was opening.

"Major Figueroa—!"

"Get me out of here, idiot!"

He'd played the wrong card earlier. Altogether too amiable, too gracious, caring what they thought of him.

With this man's help he was soon standing on solid ground.

"I don't know how this happened . . ."

Figueroa didn't believe that for a second. These people don't miss a thing.

"I'm taking this off. Shoot me if you have to."

"Of course. Let me—"

Their hands reached for the blindfold at the same moment and collided. After some awkward fumbling, Figueroa gripped the cloth and yanked it off.

"What a business," he said, releasing a breath and squinting against the sun. He thrust the blindfold into the hand of the young man standing before him, a corporal in full uniform.

"Who are you?"

The young man gave him a formal salute, which Figueroa returned indifferently.

"Corporal Victor Torres, sir."

The corporal was short and seemed very young, too young for his rank, but then looks were deceiving. Figueroa reached into his pocket and pulled out the pack of cigarettes. He lit one and greedily sucked in the smoke, drawing it down into his lungs. Instantly the palpitations in his chest slowed and he was calmed by the narcotic embrace of the tobacco. He surveyed his surroundings. The Fiat was one of only half a dozen cars scattered through the lot, along with two personnel transport vehicles. He stood before a sprawling U-shaped building that extended away from him for a couple of hundred yards on the two long sides that faced each other. It was constructed of flat stone blocks, a mix of grey and sandy brown, and was three floors in height all the way around. The slanted roof was covered with terracotta tiles. The façade presented three uninterrupted rows of identical windows that, rather than admitting light into the rooms seemed eerily to conceal their contents and occupants and what was going on behind them. The inner portion of the U formed a grassy courtyard that was empty except for two strapping pine trees. Near where he stood, at the top of the left arm of the U, a pair of tall unmarked metal doors beneath a stone arch looked to be the main entrance to the building, though there was no sign, no plaque, nothing to identify them as such. Dense forest surrounded the building and the parking lot and stretched in all directions, blanketing the distant hills. At a far corner of the lot, a gap in the trees revealed the trail—hardly wide enough to be called a road—that they had followed to get here. Otherwise the place was buried, unreachable, "off the grid," as Sandoval had put it. There were no other people in sight. For just a moment a twinge of anxiety seized Figueroa's throat and he coughed through the cigarette smoke to alleviate it. A faint breeze stirred the dead air, causing a gentle rustling of branches in the tallest trees.

He knew Chiachi and the surrounding areas. The building was vaguely familiar. What function had it served before being commandeered as a training complex?

"Well?" he said gruffly. He took a last puff and tossed the half-smoked butt to the ground. He turned to Torres. "What now? Do you know why I'm here? I don't want this to take all day."

"No, certainly," Torres agreed cordially. "But you'll have to have a word with the Commander before we go any further."

He extended his arm in a gesture of invitation.

"This way, please."

They approached the building. Torres held the door open for him and Figueroa passed through silently. He was beginning to find the corporal's deferential manner grating; all the more so because he knew it was false.

A desk and chair sat unoccupied in an otherwise bare entryway dominated by a metal switchback staircase. The long corridor he had expected was sealed off behind windowless doors. The walls were whitewashed. Again, there were so signs.

"The Commander's office is on the third floor, I'm afraid."

Figueroa ignored the insinuation.

"Who is the commander of this facility?" he asked, making his speech seem effortless as he matched step for step the corporal's rapid ascent up the stairs.

"Commander Ruivivar, sir."

"Well," Figueroa murmured, fighting to conceal the note of strain creeping into his voice, "I don't expect I'll be taking much of the Commander's time."

Every muscle in his body was screaming when they got to the third floor. Figueroa thought he would double over with the pain, but instead stood outwardly serene by Torres' side listening to the pounding in his chest and struggling for breath while a guard unlocked the door. He followed as the corporal marched smartly down the long unadorned brightly lit corridor, the regular rhythm of their steps echoing throughout the hollow space. As the pain subsided he grew aware of voices. A young man and young woman, both in civilian clothes and each carrying a box filled with papers, emerged from an office and glanced sombrely at them as they went by. Torres did not acknowledge them. Figueroa kept his eyes straight ahead. The place seemed partly abandoned, as if people were in the process of moving out, and there was a hushed formality about it that reminded him of a funeral parlour.

344

"Here we are," Torres said with a smile. He opened an unmarked wooden door and stood aside as Figueroa entered. The room was plain and square except for a wide mirror built into one wall. In the centre was a broad wooden table with two metal chairs on either side. Where the windows should have been, a rectangular sheet of wood or wallboard had been affixed to the frame and painted the same drab grey-green as the walls.

"This is an interrogation room!" Figueroa spluttered. He turned. Torres remained in the doorway.

"I'm afraid it's the only room available for your meeting."

"What's wrong with the Commander's office?"

But as if a mask had fallen away, the man's affability vanished. His face became blank, unreadable, softened only by what looked like the merest flash of irritation. Once again Major Armand Figueroa realized, too late, that he had been duped.

Without another word, without even looking at him, Torres shut the door and was gone.

Figueroa went to the door and rattled the knob. It wouldn't turn. He pressed his ear to the cool reinforced metal surface, but its sheer density made it impossible for sound to penetrate.

He raised his arm and clenched his fist, but then decided against banging on the door. It would be futile anyway, not to mention humiliating. He took a seat at the table. As he expected, the chair was bolted to the floor. He drummed the fingers of one hand on the scarred surface of the table while the other reached for his cigarettes. He didn't know what to think. Where was the intuition that for years had guided him past the hazards and pitfalls of a career in military administration? Evidently it had abandoned him. Letting Sandoval talk him into doing this had been a mistake—he could see that now. He could only hope it had not been a fatal one. Earlier he had steeled himself for what might come—Sanz's warnings echoed in his head long after they had been delivered—but now it seemed the game was lost. It was lost the moment he got in the car, probably lost the moment he'd hung up the phone after agreeing to do this! They were too far ahead of him. Everything had been choreographed down to the last move, probably long before he got involved. They already knew how this was going to end. All that was left for him to do was watch the whole sorry episode play itself out.

So who was this boy he had been asked to bring back to B——? Was there something at work here that even Sandoval didn't know about?

Lighting another cigarette, he caught a whiff of meat gone sour and realized with a spasm of regret that Elena's sandwich was still in his pocket. He would see her again. They could send him packing with his tail between his legs, but they had no reason to harm him.

He smoked and waited, letting ash drop to the floor, conscious of the mirror and the probability that he was being observed.

He was on his third cigarette when the door opened. He had not heard it being unlocked.

A small man in a tan uniform bustled into the room carrying a slim sheaf of papers under his arm. He had sparse, sandy blond hair and wore wire-rimmed spectacles on a small nose.

"I'm sorry you have been kept waiting, Major," he said, placing the papers on the table and seating himself across from Figueroa. "I am Corporal Mendoza. How can I help you?"

Figueroa gazed with tired amusement at his new interrogator, whose thick lips were not smiling, and whose eyes, like Secretary Sanz's, darted here and there. Outwardly, he seemed benignly subservient, as innocuous as a schoolteacher. Trusting nothing his eyes told him, however, Figueroa let the cigarette fall to the floor and crushed it with his foot. Rather than speak, which seemed to bring only trouble, he reached into his jacket's inner pocket and retrieved Sandoval's letter. He leaned across the table and dropped it where Mendoza could reach it, and watched the other man's brow wrinkle in perplexity (no doubt feigned) as he picked it up and began to read.

Annoyingly, Mendoza was smiling when he laid the letter back down. He flattened it with his chubby hand.

"I'm afraid this is quite impossible."

"You know of this Hector Tomás then."

The slightest pause.

"I am familiar with the case."

"Which case is that?"

Again, a pause.

"I'm not at liberty to say."

"What are you at liberty to say?"

With one finger, as if it were distasteful to him, Mendoza slid the

346

letter a few inches away across the table, then folded his hands together and maintained a cryptic silence. Figueroa tried to ignore Mendoza's irksome little smile.

"I have my orders," Figueroa said after some moments of silence, glancing at the letter that lay untouched between them on the table. "And these are to bring Hector Tomás with me to B——. If this is impossible, as you say, then I wish you would tell me why."

Mendoza shrugged. "He's not here."

"I know that," Figueroa snapped.

Mendoza's eyes narrowed. Immediately Figueroa regretted having spoken with such unconsidered haste.

"What else do you know, Major?"

Figueroa sighed and admitted, "Only that he's receiving treatment for some injury he suffered in the line of duty."

Mendoza did not move or say anything. Figueroa almost squirmed beneath the other's meekly unnerving gaze but held himself still before it could happen.

"Can you confirm this?" Figueroa asked, to fill the silence. He had started sweating again.

Mendoza took up the papers he had brought with him and began sorting through them.

Suddenly, incongruously, it came to Figueroa that the building had once been a Catholic seminary and that a monastery was located somewhere on the grounds. How did he know this? He fought to purge his brain of this now useless information.

Mendoza was reading the paper he held in his hand. "Major," he said, his tone having turned patronizing. He gave Figueroa a brief glance as he laid one paper down and selected another from the stack. "I don't have to do that."

"As a courtesy, then."

"You are Major Armand Eduardo Garcia-Figueroa, retired, having served under General Batista in 10th Division, and most recently of the Bureau of Regional Security in Envigado?"

Figueroa sat up. "What is this? You know who I am. I'm not hiding anything."

"Just making sure, Major, before we proceed with the charges against you."

347

"Charges? What—?"

"Please, Major Figueroa, sit down and control yourself. I don't want to put you in restraints but I will if you give me no choice."

Their eyes met. Mendoza's expression hovered midway between a scowl and a smirk. Figueroa carefully lowered himself into the chair as Mendoza looked on. Somehow, without realizing he was doing so, he had taken up Sandoval's letter and was crumpling it in his hand. He stopped himself, folded it and returned it to his pocket.

"I don't understand . . ."

"Documents in our possession indicate that you willingly and knowingly altered the medical record of one Felix Duarte-Figueroa, your nephew, the son of your sister Sophia."

He stared at the top of the table and said nothing. It occurred to him to wonder if they were really stooping to this level.

"You added a forged doctor's memorandum to his file stating that he had experienced a bout of rheumatic fever as a child and had suffered damage to his heart. Your forgery, had it gone undetected, would have enabled the young man to avoid military service. Do you deny it?"

"There were—" He was going to say *extenuating circumstances,* explain that he had lost perspective, that his judgment was impaired, that he was insane with grief. But these people did not deserve an explanation. "No," he said. "I don't deny it."

"You realize that helping someone avoid military service is considered an act of treason. Execution can be by firing squad, or another method if you wish."

His sharpened gaze met Mendoza's inquisitive glance. "This is absurd."

"Oh, I assure you it's not. We're prepared to move forward."

"I was forced to retire. I was disgraced. The matter was concluded—"

"To whose satisfaction? There was no court martial. The tribunal was dissolved without delivering a verdict." Mendoza searched briefly before picking up another sheet. "Ah, yes. You received full pension." He peeked over the edge of the paper that had given him this information. "One could make quite a convincing argument that you were not punished for your actions."

"I was under stress!"

"That's so. Your son was killed, in action no less. My condolences. But it doesn't excuse what you did."

348

His hands were trembling. Not just one. Both of them. My God, he wasn't afraid, was he? Empty threats to make him back off. That's all this was. Still, he felt a swelling in his gut. Ghosts always come back to haunt. You can bet on it. He would explain his failure to Sandoval in those terms, tell him to find someone else.

"Of course, we will have to hold you until a trial date can be set. Maybe in a few months, when things settle down . . ."

"What do you want?"

"Or, we can conclude the interview right now and someone will drive you back to Chiachi."

Figueroa sat without moving. The swelling had risen from his stomach into his chest. His breathing was shallow and laboured. He struggled to relax, to ease the tension through force of will. He could only imagine what it would be like, to die with this odious little man by his side, holding his hand. He waited until the tightness passed and gave a small nod.

"Excellent!" Mendoza went to the door, which had been opened from the other side. "If you'll come this way . . ."

In a daze, Figueroa pulled himself up and as quickly as he could manage on legs weakened by the effects of shock, passed through the doorway, bristling at the touch of Mendoza's hand on his back ushering him along.

"The clerk will take you out," Mendoza's voice behind him was saying. He did not turn around. "I'll arrange transportation. It may take a few minutes."

The clerk was the young man Figueroa had noticed earlier with a box of files in his arms. The girl who had been with him was nowhere in sight.

"This way, sir."

Figueroa followed the young man along the empty corridor, which had fallen eerily silent. In the time he had been in that room, all activity had ceased. The place seemed abandoned. Where were the people?

When the young man opened the front door for him, he was grateful to see the light of day. His concept of time had been so warped by events that had altogether overtaken him that if it had been the middle of the night he would have thought nothing of it. But he would not be sorry to spend the evening with Elena and enjoy a home-cooked meal. He'd been an idiot to think he could help Sandoval find this boy.

"Are you quite all right, sir?"

He had lost his footing on the top step. The young man gripped his arm.

"Just a bit fatigued, thanks," he said. His head was spinning. "I'll rest here and get my bearings."

"Do you want some water?"

Seated on the concrete step beneath the full glare of the sun, fumbling through his pockets for his sunglasses (there was that sandwich again), he was conscious suddenly of the thirst clawing at the lining of his throat. It was making him weak.

"Yes," he croaked, "Please. If it's no trouble."

The young man returned a moment later with one of those paper cups dispensed by water coolers in doctors' waiting rooms. But it was brimful of cold water. As it slid down his parched throat the intensity of the relief momentarily robbed him of breath. Tears welled up in his eyes.

"I'm fine now, thank you."

"You're sure?"

"Yes, you've been most kind, but I think I can manage now."

Sitting alone on the steps of the building, the shame that should have swept over him at the failure of his mission stood in abeyance while he revelled in the decision to put an end to it. At the moment, he didn't know what he would tell Sandoval, but he would come up with something before making the fateful call. All he knew for sure was that he had no intention of spending a minute in jail over past mistakes. Elena was right. He didn't owe anything to anybody. The debt was all on their side. His curiosity about this Hector would have to remain unsatisfied, but he could live with that.

The parked vehicles sat where they'd been when he'd gone in. What on earth would he do if Mendoza sent the same driver to take him back to town in the Fiat?

The sun's heat embraced him. A slight movement of air stirred the limbs of the tallest trees, which whispered as they swayed back and forth. Otherwise it was so quiet he could hear the chirping of field crickets somewhere in the scrubby undergrowth at the edge of the parking lot. The air was scented with pine, mixed with something faintly rotten.

The memory had grown clearer. He'd been here before—sixty years ago at least. He'd been a boy. His mother's brother had studied at the seminary. It was run by the Franciscans. The whole family had driven out here to get him and take him home. There'd been a big party to celebrate his ordination. Uncle Juan Manuel. He stayed with them for a few weeks and then left for some island in the Pacific. They'd never seen him again.

He hadn't thought of his uncle in years.

Here in front, in the parking lot—only it wasn't a parking lot then: everything was greener—there'd been a fountain and a stone statue of St. Francis. Yes, he could almost see it standing in the grass, the saint surrounded by baby animals.

He pulled the glasses off and rubbed his eyes and face. He was fading again. My God, he was tired. What an ordeal. What a waste of time.

He was reaching for a cigarette when the growling of a small engine interrupted his thoughts. It was several seconds before the vehicle lurched into view from around the side of the building, behind him to his right. A Jeep with open sides. It rolled up to the steps and jerked to a stop.

The driver stared at him. He was coffee-complexioned with dark hair and the faint beginnings of a moustache and a bit of patchy stubble. His clothing was regulation, but neither his khaki shirt nor the dark under-shirt underneath were tucked into his pants. He was very thin, his hair tousled. Most startling were his eyes, which were the vivid blue-green of the tropical waters further north.

"You are looking for Hector Tomás?"

Figueroa, in the process of standing, halted his movements. What was this now? Another trick? He took the cigarette from his mouth and studied the young man sitting in the Jeep. He could easily deny having heard of Hector Tomás. He would be home in time for supper. But something . . . This young man—boy really, now that he could see him. Those eyes—fear lived in them.

"What if I am?"

The boy jerked his head. "Get in."

Figueroa didn't move. "Where—?"

"Hurry, please!" He lowered his voice. "You must help us!"

Figueroa lumbered down the steps and around to the other side of the Jeep. Clambering into the vehicle he thought, *What am I doing?* But he had hardly settled himself into the seat before the boy rammed the gas pedal and they sped away, the tires kicking up a spray of stone and dust in their wake.

FORTY-TWO

The boy swung the Jeep around another turn and Figueroa had to brace himself against the hot dashboard to avoid being jostled out of the vehicle. He shut one eye, peeked cautiously with the other, and held on. The back road they were following snaked and spiralled apparently at random. Then, with a grinding of tires on loose stone, the Jeep mounted a rise and emerged from the trees. Ahead of them lay a level stretch of paved road, pitted but flat beneath a canopy of branches. This, now, was easier going. He drew a hand across his brow and settled back into the seat. Sunlight slanted through the dense forest growth, throwing its dappled radiance across the tarmac. It was late afternoon. They passed a man and boy on a cart drawn by a donkey, and he saw that they had entered peasant country, the land of hulking gum trees, remote nature reserves, subsistence farming. This is where the Mapuche lived, proudly in their squalor. If they were to continue at this rate, in another hour they would arrive at the base of the mountains.

But all too soon the young soldier steered the Jeep abruptly from the flat main road onto a concealed secondary road, taking them back into the forest. Figueroa's misgivings returned. What had he gotten himself into? An image sprang into his head: of Elena at home, innocently awaiting his return, stirring a pot of *sopa de topinambur,* which, together with a slice of crusty bread and wedges of soft cheese, she would eat by herself for supper in front of the television, and his heart felt like it would burst. Years ago, in the time of the Aguaria dictatorship, these remote forests were used for disposal. Problems of every description were brought here, covered up and forgotten. Fresh out of the academy, his first assignment had been as attaché for General Ramos, one of the primary investigators looking into the atrocities of the Aguaria regime. He had accompanied the General as he conducted field visits, interviewed survivors, and coordinated the excavation of burial sites. Horrified by the evidence that emerged—of corruption so widespread it seemed the rule rather than the exception, and of the cruelties inflicted on prisoners by their guards—he had also been fascinated by the General's good-humoured tranquility, which Ramos maintained through endless legal wrangling and long stretches of idleness, and even through graphic and sordid testimony that left other people in tears. Many of the officials they approached had refused to cooperate. Some were detained trying to flee the country. Others committed suicide. Documents that had been promised mysteriously disappeared. There had been threats. He had thought all that business was in the past, but here he was again, poking his nose into some grubby corner, getting ready to expose another of the army's dirty little secrets. Apparently his rank and connections weren't enough to shield him from deplorable treatment. How had he let this happen? And he was dying for a cigarette! But he had to hold himself steady or he'd end up through the windshield. He shuddered inwardly. Ever since those early days forests had spooked him. A few friends and neighbours enjoyed hiking through protected areas and he heard them talk afterward of scents and wildlife and ancient trees and natural streams, the quality of forest light, how there was nothing like it on earth. But all he saw were graves. Everywhere, graves.

As they bounced along a rutted forest track, the notion crept into his mind that "Hector Tomás" was a code for something, and those foolish enough to utter the name were given the full scare treatment before being carted off to some ignominious fate. Everybody was in on the joke but him. Did Sandoval know? Without a doubt the Americans were behind it.

He'd had his own dealings with their friends from the north back in his days with General Ramos. Every time they peeled back a layer of bureaucracy to reveal the official corruption underneath, there was some shady deal with the Americans at the root of it all. Mineral rights traded for weapons. Permits for the construction of hotels on unspoiled seaside property issued on the spot, no-questions-asked. Parkland designations repealed to allow clear-cutting of old-growth rainforest (at least they'd been able to quash that at the planning stage). Without a doubt the Americans had preyed upon a dishonest and inept regime to further their own interests. But they covered their tracks well. The paper trail always ended too soon, the money could never be traced, solid proof was always missing. No, you couldn't beat the Americans when it came to half-truth and obfuscation.

Still, as the crow flies, they weren't that far yet from the training complex. He would ask the boy, ever so gently, to return him there. If that didn't work then he would walk the distance into town. He could do it. He'd received the same survival training as everyone else. The main road was not far. With a little luck he might be able to catch up with the donkey cart he'd seen, less than a mile back. If not, he would find shelter of some sort when it got dark. The important thing was not to panic. He wasn't going to starve. The dangers were minimal. If he had to he could avoid rebels and bandits. His training would see him through. He had to believe that.

Without warning, the boy stopped the Jeep and cut the engine.

The forest's silence engulfed them. It was like a wall separating them from the rest of the world. Only the tentative warble of birdsong disturbed it.

Figueroa held himself still and waited for what was coming. In a few seconds he heard whimpering.

Figueroa glanced warily at his companion. The boy sat motionless, gripping the steering wheel with both hands and staring straight ahead, his mouth set in a tight frown. As Figueroa watched, a few tears trickled down his face.

"Is something wrong?" He had to check himself from giving the young man's shoulder an encouraging squeeze.

"Please forgive me." The boy straightened and quickly wiped the moisture from his face.

"This is not your fault," he said, turning towards Figueroa. He tapped the side of his head with one finger. "It's me. I'm the crazy one, for bringing you here. My friends told me that someone was looking for Hector. They said what you look like. But I don't know if I can trust you. I don't even know who you are."

Without further comment the boy leapt from the Jeep and ran into the forest.

"But they're right! I'm looking for Hector Tomás!" Figueroa called. But the boy had vanished into the undergrowth. "I want to help—!" His voice trailed off.

Silence prevailed by the time he stepped out and felt earth, solidly reassuring, beneath his feet. He peered through the trees in the direction the boy had gone but could see nothing. What now? He regretted more than ever leaving his revolver at home. How was he supposed to defend himself? He turned around in a circle. Trees in every direction. The trail they had followed, or track, if it could even be called that, had been packed down by the passage of many wheels. It had to lead somewhere. That smell—he hated it—of something rotting: forest floor decay. He looked back in the Jeep. He hadn't seen the boy take the key, but it was gone. They had stopped beside a tall pine tree with deeply furrowed bark. An X had been carved into the trunk at eye level. Figueroa ran his fingers over the X. The bark was coarsely sharp where the cut had been made, and there were ants. He pulled his hand away.

Should he start walking?

Then he heard the crunch and rustle of someone running across the dry forest floor. The boy approached quickly through the trees, carrying something—heavy, by the look of it.

It was a duffel bag, army issue. As he came up to the Jeep he pulled a pistol from it. A Glock.

Figueroa raised his arms and moved backward until the tree stopped him from going further. So this was how it would end. His worst nightmare fulfilled: summary execution and a shallow grave in the pine forest. How could this be happening?

"I'm sorry. I have to be sure I can trust you." The boy dropped the bag and aimed the gun at him, gripping it with both hands. "Do something! Prove that I can trust you!"

"What can I do?" His voice was the merest croak. He was having trouble breathing again.

"What do you want with Hector?"

"I—"

So did Hector Tomás exist after all? Should he show the letter? Whatever was going on here was personal. The boy was terrified, and more for Hector's sake than for his own. Best to leave the army out of it.

"I have to take him to B——. It's for his own good. He'll be safe there."

The boy's expression softened but he did not lower the gun. "His family sent you?"

What to say? What to say? Did he mean Hector's family lives there?

In B——? "Yes."

"He talks about his family. He misses them. He has a girlfriend."

Oh God . . . Think! Something Sandoval said . . . The girl. Damn it, think! Think . . . ! Yes! "Nadia."

"Yes, he misses her."

"She misses him. She cries all the time, she misses him so much." Was that going too far?

"She never sent him any letters." Abruptly the boy's face twisted into a grimace. More tears. He spat out the next words. "How could she do that? She never wrote to him. Not even once."

What could he say? He didn't . . . "I don't know anything about that." He shook his head.

The boy shifted his weight from foot to foot. One arm hung at his side. The other, together with the hand that held the Glock, moved irresolutely up and down, waving the weapon in Figueroa's general direction rather than pointing it straight at him. Slowly Figueroa lowered his arms.

The boy slumped and, as if shamed, averted his face. "I'm sorry," he said. He wiped the tears away again and turned towards Figueroa, but did not raise the gun. "Who sent you? Was it his father?"

"Señor Tomás," Figueroa agreed robustly, stating the name with the false confidence of a seasoned charlatan. "Yes. We've known each other for years. We're good friends. He sent me to bring his son back."

The boy nodded. Figueroa sensed a breakthrough.

"They told him his family was gone."

Again, something Sandoval said, about how they make these soldiers compliant. "Gone?"

"Dead. Or maybe they went somewhere. Left the country. Nobody knows what happened to them."

"Lies," he said with some force. "I can assure you they're fine. Nadia is fine too. They want him to come home."

The boy stared at the ground. The gun dangled from his hand. Another silent nod. Oddly, the news of Hector's family did not seem to cheer him.

"Son, what's your name?"

The boy bent over and strained to lift the duffel bag from the ground where he'd dropped it. He set it in the back of the Jeep. Figueroa stepped away from the tree.

"Son, your name? My name is Armand. Armand Figueroa."

"Alejandro. Alejandro Navarro."

"I'm happy to meet you, Alejandro," he said. Masking apprehension with a confident smile, he strode around the Jeep. Alejandro stared blankly for a moment before inserting the Glock into the waist of his trousers and accepting Figueroa's outstretched hand in his. They shook, but Alejandro did not answer the smile and neglected to tighten his grip.

"I think you'll agree," Figueroa went on, speaking confidentially while holding Alejandro's diffident gaze. "That we both want what's best for Hector. I'd be grateful now if you took me to see him."

Alejandro withdrew his hand and half turned, showing Figueroa a slender profile. Seeming more contrite than ever, he nodded in abashed schoolboy fashion.

"I'm sorry I didn't trust you," he said. "But it's not been easy . . ."

Figueroa waved his hand. "No harm done."

Now that his tears had dried and he had calmed down, the green of Alejandro's eyes appeared dimmed. Without speaking he pulled the gun from his waist and thrust the other hand into his pocket and came up with the key for the Jeep. Figueroa wondered if his problem was lack of sleep. Seen up close, his skin had no sheen and seemed bloodless. There was a jerky rhythm to his movements, as if he was on the verge of nodding off and had to constantly rouse himself. Could he use the boy's fatigue to his advantage?

He felt fine but was trembling when he got around to the other side of the Jeep. Trying to climb in, his legs nearly gave out. He missed the step on his first try and had to scramble into the seat to avoid falling down. He held himself absolutely still and drew a single slow breath. Just a delayed reaction. Too many shocks in one day. Glancing over, he saw Alejandro leaning against the Jeep, one foot raised, using a stick to scrape dirt from of the treads of his boot. He was getting closer, but he could not let this boy see his fear. That would be the end. How close had he come to losing his life? If he was lucky he would never find out.

Before starting the engine, Alejandro slid the gun into the crevice beneath his seat. Figueroa noted this, while he made an elaborate show of searching his pockets for cigarettes, extracting one from the almost empty pack, and lighting it. He suspected the duffel bag was full of weapons.

Ultimately, he wanted to know what this was all about, where the burden of fear this boy carried with him had come from.

Using both hands to mask the trembling, he held the package of cigarettes towards Alejandro. The boy glanced at him. Suspicion lingered in his eyes.

Ignoring Figueroa's lighter, Alejandro took a cigarette and placed it, unlit, between his lips. He jerked the Jeep into gear, stepped lightly on the gas, and they continued on their way.

FORTY-THREE

Dear Nadia,

You know I am not good with words. I am sorry you never wrote to me even though I wrote to you. It was hard for me to write to you because I am not good with words. I don't know why you didn't write to me. Nobody wrote to me. The thing I did was not so bad. It was that boy we met at the café. I beat him up. I got so mad, thinking about him with my father. I know it was wrong, but I couldn't help it, and they sent me away so I wouldn't have to go to jail. It was not easy living at the farm but Aunt Claudia and Uncle Francisco were good to me. They made me work, especially Uncle Francisco. I said this in my other letters. I have been away for a long time, but I want to come home and when I get there I will visit you.

I think they are dead. My mother and father and Dulciana, and Cesara, and Rosaria, and Helena, and Julio. All dead. Do you know? Maybe Carlos is alive. I don't know.

I can't tell you everything that happened since my last letter. I am so tired. But I will try anyway.

I wanted to come home to see you but there was an explosion and I was hurt. This was in the bus station. They thought I did it so I was arrested. They said I was one of those people who blows things up. But I wasn't. They did things to me. They tied me up and put me in a room with loud music and wouldn't let me use the bathroom and put electricity over me *and gave me rotten food to eat. They put me under water and held me there. They put a bag over my head and asked me questions. I didn't know the answers. They were going to shoot me in the head once but they didn't. There was more that they did to me, I can't say what. Then they said they knew I didn't set off the bomb but they still wouldn't let me go. They said everyone was dead, my whole family, and then they said, well maybe they are dead, maybe they are alive, we don't know for sure, so I might as well stay while they looked for my family. I was allowed to telephone but nobody ever answered so maybe they were right that they were dead. I telephoned you too but there was no answer and then the number didn't work. I was alone at first like a prisoner but then I was with other people who I think had things done to them too but none of us talked about it. They gave us new clothes and I had my own bed. I made a friend. His name is Alejandro. We all had to work hard and dig holes in the ground one day and fill them the next day. The food was better. They made us fight each other with fists, for practice they said. They made us get lost in the woods and then find our way out. Then we did it at night when it was cold. Then we did it in the rain. It was for teamwork, they said, to help each other. I worked very hard. I did everything they said for me to do. It was not easy to do some of the things they wanted. After a long time they said I was a soldier and they gave me a gun. It was our job to arrest the ones who were blowing things up. We went out at night and arrested them, I don't know who most of them were. We stopped the trouble that was going on in the street with clubs. The people were angry and throwing rocks and other things but we made them go away. We were doing a good job. Then something terrible happened. I won't say what but I can't stop it going in my head. I see it every time I try to sleep. Nothing was the same after that. I was hurt and in the hospital, but Alejandro came and took me away to a different place. Now*

FORTY-FOUR

Hector felt his head nodding, his eyes growing heavy. He folded the paper into a little square and tucked it into his pocket along with the broken stub of pencil that he had found on the floor of the Jeep. The piece of paper had come from the garbage at the hospital.

The inside of the hut smelled like animals and soiled bedding. The old woman's mumbling rose and fell as she swayed from side to side over the fire. He could not understand what she was saying because her language was not his, but the rhythm was soothing. She picked up a stick and waved it over the pot she had set to boil: a leisurely back and forth motion. The stick had broad leaves tied to the end. It looked like a fan. Hector watched from where he lay on a low table next to the wall, in a dim corner of the only room in the wooden hut. The table was covered with a thin mattress that was stuffed with feathers or hair. In another corner of the room a goat stood next to a pile of straw, chewing and from time to time contemplating him with its vacant pinprick eyes. Hector didn't like the goat. He recalled Claudia's caution, about how a goat would eat the baby in its crib and the eyes right out of your head if you gave it the chance. Goats were the Devil's emissaries. He was glad it was tied to the wall with a thick hemp rope, but even this might not be enough because goats chew through anything.

Earlier he had dozed, but the dream of the dead family had woken him. Alejandro was not back yet so he had resumed his letter to Nadia. He was sorry now that he had complained to Alejandro about Nadia not writing to him. It had been months ago, at the start of their training, and he had been frightened and lonely, and the words had escaped from his mouth before he knew what he was saying. Afterward it seemed like the worst sort of betrayal. He didn't know Alejandro would react that way, spitting and cursing, calling her names. Later he had excused her and said how beautiful she was, how much he loved her. He talked of her often, but Alejandro always turned away and refused to hear. Once he asked if Alejandro had also had his heart broken, and the boy had barked a laugh and said, *Never,* looking at him, eyes radiant with hurt. Ever since that day on the hill when they had held the gun to his head and pulled the trigger, but somehow he had survived, Alejandro had been like his brother and seen him through the worst. And yet Hector feared—even loathed—the intimacy that had sprung up between them. They had comforted each other in ways he would rather not think about. That, too, seemed a betrayal. He was unsure of so many things, but he knew he would never again speak of Nadia in Alejandro's presence.

The hut was round and had a high thatched roof with a hole at the top so the smoke could escape. The furniture was roughly hewn from wood. Rows of mysterious containers were arrayed on shelves against the wall. He did not know the woman's name and did not know what she was doing. All he knew was that she was the wise woman, the Mapuche *machi.* Alejandro had said she would make him better.

The woman raised her other arm and wiggled the hand not holding the stick. Her voice was suddenly louder. Should he be scared? An image drifted into his mind of the ramshackle houses along the road leading into Envigado: smashed windows, falling down fences, garbage strewn everywhere, children playing in dirt, dogs with their ribs showing. On this road on the way to market, even when he couldn't see any people he knew that eyes were following his every move. The sensation that crept up his spine did not lie. Claudia and Francisco never spoke of the Mapuche, but Hector's father often fumed over stories in the newspaper, slapping the page and calling the Mapuche troublemakers. His mother agreed with this assessment, shaking her head and lamenting, "What's to be done?" Otherwise they pretended the Mapuche didn't exist. Until coming to the farm Hector had never troubled his mind about them one way or the other, even though the Mapuche were always there, on the streets of B____. He'd never wondered about their colourful costumes or the music they played or the potions they sold, or, like the man at the market who was beaten by the soldiers, the carvings they peddled to tourists. There were no Mapuches living in the apartment building on

Rua Santa Maria, no Mapuche children at his school. They were part of a visible world to which he was blind: familiar yet mysterious, close by but infinitely remote. In plain sight, they all but disappeared from view.

This passed through his mind in an instant. He thought again of the letter. What else could he tell Nadia? There was space on the paper for more words and he longed to share everything with her. But the effort of writing exhausted him.

Why was he here? Alejandro had said they were in danger. Dragged him out of bed in the middle of the night and got him dressed while no one was around. Took him outside and put him in the Jeep. They had driven miles and miles, through the forest, up into the hills. The others had gone missing—that was it—the ones who had been there when he killed that family. All of them had vanished. Because of what they knew, what they'd seen. Even Josquin.

So Alejandro had saved him again. But he felt strange. He saw Alejandro watching him sometimes. The look in his eyes . . . it was all wrong . . . Alejandro's hands on him.

The woman turned. Her lips moved. She had no teeth. She cradled a steaming clay cup in both hands. Her fingers were fleshy, the skin smooth, but her leathery face was almost as wrinkled as Aunt Claudia's. A few wisps of grey hair hung loose from the soiled red scarf that covered her head. He remembered now. He had watched her lift the lid off a box and empty dried bits and pieces of something into a pot. She poured water over it and set it on the fire. Now she wanted him to drink it.

"What is it?" He trusted her. He was not afraid.

"Will help you sleep," she said in halting Spanish. "*Maikoa.* Will help you sleep. Chase bad things away."

Her manner made him feel warm.

He had been hit by bullet fragments from his own gun. The vest had stopped most of them, but he had fired to get it over with, thinking of nothing, taking no precautions. He should have angled his gun down, but instead fired straight into the wall. He'd been wounded in both shoulders and the upper part of his chest. They had dressed his wounds at the hospital, but she had removed those dressings and replaced them with mossy stuff and wrapped everything tightly in bandages. He was still sore, but he raised himself and accepted the cup. He sniffed and sipped the thin brew. It was not tea. It was not soup. What then? Its perfume was flowery but not cloying. He nodded and sipped again, deeply. Less pleasant this time, it attacked the back of his tongue with herbal bitterness. But he choked it down. He would drink anything that promised to make the dream go away.

When he woke he did not know how much time had passed. The room glowed as if bronzed by the light of candles placed here and there on shelves. The flames flickered and danced and cast shape-shifting shadows on the rough wooden walls. It was night. He had been covered with a blanket. He propped himself on his elbows. Where the shrapnel had pierced him, his skin felt stretched tight. But the sting of his wounds seemed distant, a memory.

She was there, sitting at the table, tinkering with something in the quivering candlelight. The goat was beside her, off its tether. She heard him and turned.

Words came out of her mouth that he didn't understand.

He smiled and said, "Yes," hoping it was a sufficient answer. His head felt light and heavy at the same time and every muscle in his body was slack, hanging loosely from his bones. He realized that he had slept. The sweet and bitter potion she had given him had kept the dream away. He wanted more of it.

Grunting, she pulled herself to her feet. The goat skipped nimbly out of her way. He noticed for the first time the bulk of her. She was heavy and old, like Aunt Claudia. Tonight her body was cloaked in a long ochre dress with a pattern on it that looked like lizards. A short blue buttoned-up jacket covered her shoulders. Carvings made from bone—animal and human figures—dangled from a leather cord around her neck. Burnished brass hoops hung from her earlobes. The scarf held her hair tightly in place. She was smoking something that looked like a homemade cigarette. Several of these lay on the table in front of her along with the ingredients to make more. The air in the hut was spiced with the nutty, caramel fragrance.

Before he could say anything else she had opened the door and ventured into the night. She bellowed a few words that sounded like *Halla, halla!* The echo of her call was followed by silence. He looked at the goat, which had retreated to its corner. It stood chewing, regarded him smugly, as if it knew things he did not. He almost dozed off before he heard her voice again as she approached the hut, chattering happily. The door swung open. He had expected Alejandro, but behind her was an old man: not tall, with a belly that stuck out, a grey moustache, and a receding hairline. He held a jacket over his arm. The uniform was army and of rank. The man wore a startled look on his face and smiled unconvincingly. The smile revealed two rows of large yellow teeth. He nodded at the *machi* woman's words but the confusion in his eyes told Hector he didn't understand what she was saying.

"What's going on?" he said. "Where's Alejandro?"

Had they had been found out? He should have kept one of the guns! He tried to sit, but the potion had numbed him and slowed his movements. He felt no urgency to do anything. When he swivelled around and placed his feet on the earthen floor, his head spun and he almost fell over.

She gripped his shoulders and eased him back until he was lying flat on the mattress.

"*Amigo*," she whispered, her lips tickling his ear. She settled him and replaced the blanket. "No worry."

Hector watched her toothless mouth stretch into a grin. Beneath the smouldering fixity of her gaze and the quieting touch of her hand, the anxiety that had tightened his muscles melted away. Willingly, like a convalescing child, he took refuge in the cocoon of unthinking trust she wove around him.

He allowed his leaden eyes to fall shut and listened as a chair was dragged over to the bed. At the sound of creaking, he pictured the man sitting on it.

"Who are you?" he asked without opening his eyes. "What do you want?" The clearing of a throat.

"My name is Armand Figueroa. Hector, please listen. This is important. Your father sent me. I've come to take you home."

Instantly he was staring into the man's face and trying to pull himself up.

"My father—?" He grabbed the man's arm and pulled him closer.

"Hector, please listen—"

"My father is dead—"

"It's not true—"

"They're dead! My family is dead."

"My boy, it was all lies. They lied to you."

He stared uncomprehendingly into the man's eyes, the whites of which were tinted yellow and flecked with tiny veins. Reacting to the flickering candlelight the pupils shrank to pinpricks, almost disappeared, swelled grotesquely. He was smiling, but it was a different smile, nothing like the fearful one he had worn when he entered the hut. Like the *machi* woman, his manner was gentle, reassuring.

The goat emitted a bleat. The man glanced uneasily over his shoulder. "Nadia . . . ?"

He turned back to Hector.

"Yes. Nadia too. She's waiting for you. They all are. Your father asked me to find you. So here I am."

"But—"

"I know, I know . . . It's hard to believe. Alejandro told me that you haven't heard from them. Not for a long time. The fighting kept their letters from getting through." The man nodded and smiled wider.

Hector released the man's arm and sank back on the mattress. A few tears trickled down his face but he was hardly aware of them. "They're alive?"

"Just think what this means. You can go home."

"But . . ." He tried to remember. Hadn't there been proof that they were gone somewhere, or dead? They'd shown him a photograph of the empty apartment. He'd phoned, got no answer. Nadia's number had been disconnected. It didn't necessarily mean anything. But he'd assumed the worst, resigned himself to the emptiness of having nothing to go back to. It was easier that way.

"It made perfect sense for you to believe what you were told. You hadn't heard from them. And with all the fighting, the disruption of services—" The man shrugged. "Anything could have happened."

His heart galloped. A rush of blood to his head made him tremble. He would see Nadia again! The realization brought a fresh eruption of tears. Through wet eyes he tried to look at this man, Figueroa, sent by his father. Could it be true? All this time. He had tried with no success to force her from his mind, to bury those memories that brought him only torment: her beautiful eyes, her lips softly brushing his, the living perfume of her, his tender awareness of her slight, fragile body. He had failed to dismiss all hope of seeing her again. Instead, he had clutched it to his heart, even as it pushed him to the edge of despair while, feeling like one of the walking dead, he kept himself alive, did what he was told, watched over Alejandro. But she was waiting for him. All this time, she had been waiting.

"Tomorrow we can leave on the train. We'll be there in a couple of days."

He gripped the man's hand, but couldn't speak. He was crying, shivering as if cold.

Suddenly there was a commotion. Something fell to the floor. Figueroa dropped Hector's hand and jumped from the chair. The old woman pulled him by the arm and herded him, like an obstinate cow, towards the door.

"Hector, you should get some sleep . . ."

"You go now!" she said. "Go! Go!"

"I'll see you in the morn—"

The slam of the door echoed like a gunshot. She made an irate gesture with both hands and lumbered after the goat, which had something in its mouth. It scuttled out of her path, easily dodging her attempts to grab it. Whatever was in its mouth quickly disappeared and when it was done eating it retreated to its corner and did not resist as the woman tied it up.

Hector wiped his face and laid his head down, resting one arm across his eyes. He heard the woman slap her hands on the table. This was followed by the clatter of things being moved about. She was talking furiously, at him if not to him. Though he'd woken not long ago he was giddy with exhaustion. Could he sleep now? His mind was burning. He had been living with the certainty that his family was dead for so long it was hard to let it go. But why would the man lie? What would anyone gain from such a lie?

Tears continued to leak from his eyes. Absent-mindedly, he wiped them away.

He would see Alejandro in the morning and ask what he should do. But . . . He sat up. How had Figueroa come to be here? But then he relaxed. If Figueroa had spoken with Alejandro, then Alejandro must have brought him. It was the only explanation.

Should that trouble him? Or was it good? He couldn't think. He was so tired.

The woman leaned over, whispering, pressing on his shoulder to get him to lie flat. He did not feel the wounds at all. She was holding one of her cigarettes towards him and he took it. She had made the dream go away. He could trust her. The cigarette was fat and lumpy and it brought back a memory of the cigarettes he had assembled on the rooftop of the apartment building, using tobacco that Señor Volos had discarded and paper from his father's old books. The pigeons, the damp ocean air, the stories, the realization that Señor Volos was the loneliest man in the world all passed through his mind as the woman went over to the table and waddled back with another cigarette and a candle. She held the candle out. He placed the cigarette between his lips and leaned forward, igniting the tip with the candle flame and drinking in the smoke. He watched her light her own cigarette, puffing expertly. The tip glowed. The smoke tasted like hair and flesh on fire and burned all the way down. The swirling in his head picked up speed. He lay back and let himself go. He was floating. He weighed nothing at all. He drew on the cigarette, trusted the cigarette. New tears flooded his eyes, but he held the smoke in and didn't cough, not even once.

FORTY-FIVE

Outside the old woman's hut a great fear rose up inside him. Above him, the moon glowed behind a veil of churning cloud, brightening a small patch of sky. While spinning his tale in the old woman's hut he had been in control, but outside now he glanced around and felt a familiar panic rise into his throat. A thick, heavy darkness cloaked the hills between which the settlement was nestled. Unidentifiable sounds came at him from all directions, mutterings and the muted rustling of living things. There was that smell, like rotting vegetation. Corpses.

He jumped when he noticed a skinny dog sniffing his leg. It whimpered and turned two mournful black eyes towards him. He went to give it a kick but it leapt away, bared its teeth, snarled.

"*Bastardo!* You don't fool me." He made a clumsy feint towards it, shaking his fist.

The thing backed off.

He tried to calm his heart but could not. He had never been so far off the map in his life. When Alejandro parked at the edge of the settlement, Mapuche elders appeared from nowhere and gathered around the Jeep. As they frowned and pointed at him he sensed a mob. But all he could do was watch helplessly as Alejandro spoke to these people in their own language. Finally the boy struck some sort of deal, allowing him to stay. He couldn't do it though. The damp huts and smells and dank forest air made him feel like things were crawling under his skin. He had to get out of here. This was no place for a civilized man.

He stood outside the old woman's hut, quaking with indecision. It started to rain.

He tugged the collar of the jacket up around his neck and trotted down the path, starting at the sight of a Mapuche man who emerged like a phantom out of the darkness and passed him by without a sound.

There was that smell again. He couldn't shake it. Like a swamp. The whole place reeked.

He had to take control and to do that he needed a gun. But Alejandro was not letting down his guard. Apparently there was no trust between them after all. Changing from one moment to the next, the boy was giving him a pain in the head. He was never any good at puzzles. . .

Damn it, all these huts looked the same . . . Here. This was the one.

He opened the door, trying for quiet, but the hinges creaked. God, that shit smell! They had noses didn't they? How could they stand it?

The ghostly spray of light coming through the window allowed him to make out Alejandro's shape beneath the blanket, curled like a shrimp, hugging the duffel bag with both arms. His hair caught the light and returned a silver gleam; the adolescent stubble on his lip was just visible. The rain was falling harder now, drumming insistently on the roof. Thunder grumbled in the distance. He crept along until he located a stool he had seen earlier and sat down. Was Alejandro asleep or was this a state of semi-conscious watchfulness that his training allowed him to tap into? It hardly mattered. If he tried anything the boy's hands would be wrapped around his throat before his own hand got anywhere near the gun. It seemed strange to think of someone who cried so easily as a trained killer. But that's what paramilitary training would have made of him. Hector too. So the idea was foolish. Alejandro—stronger, more agile—would make short work of him in a physical contest.

The other bed invited him to lay down his weary bones. His body clamoured for rest, but there was no time. He rubbed his eyes. They had to get moving. The rain was pelting harder by the minute.

He went over to the bed and shook the boy's shoulder.

"Alejandro . . . ?"

Before Figueroa could let out a gasp, the boy's eyes snapped open. One hand was aiming the Glock straight into his face while the other gripped his arm so tightly it hurt.

"Woooa! It's me. Armand. Remember? It's all right. Take it easy, now. Take it easy."

He held himself still and waited.

It was a few seconds before awareness flickered in the boy's eyes. His grip relaxed. He lowered the gun. Figueroa smiled and nodded in a manner that he hoped was reassuring but which probably only made him look old and foolish and frightened.

"It's all right. Listen. We have to move. We have to get out of here."

Alejandro stared but made no response. The muted light of the moon shimmered across his eyes. For all the training that had turned him into a killing machine, there was something eternally fretful in his gaze, something that would never respond to the measured voice of reason.

"The rain. We have to leave before the rain makes it impossible."

He straightened and waited. Still the boy stared, wild-eyed. His look carried no hint of recognition. Why, oh why had he let Sandoval talk him into this?

"Alejandro, you asked me to help you. The only way I can do that is to get you away from here. It's not safe."

The boy shook his head. The tears were not visible, but they left a trail down his cheek that glistened in the moonlight.

Pretending not to look at the gun, Figueroa leaned over the bed and gripped Alejandro's shoulders.

"Listen to me! We have to get on that train. I came to take Hector home to his family, but it doesn't mean you can't come too."

"I don't . . . I can't lose him. He's all I have."

"You won't. You'll be together."

"He loves that girl."

"You don't know that. Just listen to me! The important thing is to be safe. You can deal with everything else later. As long as you're both safe—"

"I don't want to be safe without him."

"You won't be without him. You'll be together."

"You're lying! There's nothing for me there. Nothing!"

Alejandro tried to wrench free but Figueroa held on.

"Listen to me!" Roughly, he took the boy's damp face between his hands, but was stunned into silence when it seemed he was peering into the face of his son after Emilio José had hurt himself and Elena struggled to comfort the boy with murmurs and caresses, a sweet, and a bandage for his scraped elbow. The fantasy was vivid enough to rob his legs of strength and bring him down awkwardly to his knees next to the bed. Then Emilio José was gone, and it was the boy-soldier Alejandro Navarro staring at him, his eyes ablaze with anguish and terror. With fresh lies ready on his lips, Figueroa fought to contain his own tears.

"Alejandro, if you love Hector you will do this. As long as you remain here, whatever you're afraid of will be around every corner. But I can help you escape from this. You will be safe. You can start over. I don't know what Hector will do when we get there. But you'll be with him and maybe you will get the chance to stay with him. I can't promise you anything more than that. But if you stay here, you have no chance at all."

With his powerful arms Alejandro locked him in an embrace. Figueroa could feel the stiff metal of the Glock pressing into his back. With every sour breath he expelled, the air grew heavier. The clammy tartness of sweat and fear rose up around him and mingled with the pervasive smell of shit. He wrapped his arms around the weeping boy and held on.

"It's my fault," Alejandro moaned between sobs. "I shot the girl. All of this is my fault."

"Shhh. Shhh. It doesn't matter. It doesn't matter."

The lies were piling up, and he hated to lie, but he would not give in to despair. He had told the right stories, made the right promises. He had done everything necessary to avert an imminent threat. For all his self-doubt, when it became a question of survival, his instincts had kicked in after all. Now the end was in sight. Alejandro would drive them to the station. At six o'clock the train would leave, heading north, and he and Hector Tomás would be on it. But Alejandro—crucial to the completion of his mission but an obstacle to its success—was a problem. Security was tight. They would have to leave the weapons behind. What would this lovesick boy do if forced to choose between his guns and Hector? Would he give them up, try to smuggle them, make a scene? Who could tell?

After they got to B____ ... well, whatever happened then was out of his hands. He couldn't see much in store for Alejandro Navarro beyond arrest and detention. The army had its rules and for breaking them he would be punished. As for Hector Tomás, the assignment was to deliver him to Sandoval, and in a few hours that would be accomplished. He would return home to Elena and not give this misbegotten escapade another thought. His life could not accommodate more regrets, and he certainly had no reason to feel sorry for these boys. The army was not in the habit of transforming trained personnel into fugitives. Whatever they were running from, chances were they had brought it on themselves. He would delve no further into the matter. Let Sandoval get his hands dirty for once, if he had the stomach for it.

Someday—not today, but someday—he would weep for a country that never learned from its bloody past. He would weep because the excesses of the Aguaria regime had so quickly been forgotten. He would weep for his wife and son, and, yes, he would weep for the boy in his arms and for all the others held facedown in the muck by a governing hand that had vowed to lift and carry them forward. They were not a wicked people. So why were they made to suffer time and time again? Why, when prosperity was just around the corner . . . why did they turn against themselves? Why was their thirst for blood never quenched? Why were their leaders vicious and corrupt? What had they done to deserve such an unkind fate?

Emilio José had died a noble death, a useful death. Nothing could change that. The price was high, but the goal was worthy. It was his sole comfort. But Hector and Alejandro . . . what had they done that was noble? When the knock came and news of their deaths was delivered, what scraps of truth would their parents cling to?

As Alejandro wept, Figueroa raised his head and gazed out the window at the sodden night. The rain had eased to a patter, but he sensed it was just a lull. The real storm was yet to come. In his imagination he saw the forest track they had followed swamped with runoff, turning slimy, impossible to navigate. They had to get out of here, but there was still time. There was still a little time.

FORTY-SIX

"That's the train coming now, sir," Marcel said.

They exchanged a glance. Montoya extracted the cigarette from between his lips and held it with his thumb and forefinger. He cocked his head and listened. The distant rumble could be a train, or it might be the clamour of street traffic outside.

Then the loudspeaker crackled and a woman's voice spilled into the cavernous space announcing the arrival of the train from Villa Real.

Montoya gave Marcel a smirk and tossed his cigarette over the edge of the platform to the tracks. A set of binoculars dangled from a cord around his neck, and he steadied them with his free hand. His other hand held the portable transceiver. When he turned, the four soldiers he had selected for this assignment because of their advanced tactical and sniper training stood quickly to attention. The newest member of D-Squad was among them: Jimenez, the soldier who had spotted Nadia Wladanski at the women's detention centre. They were dressed formally, in black, with vests. All four carried transceivers. Two were armed with automatic weapons, two with rifles.

"Remember," he said, "keep the targets in range but no shots until we know what we're dealing with." He looked them up and down. It came to him again that he liked being in charge. It was intensely satisfying, giving people instructions, getting things done. He suppressed a smile and self-consciously adjusted his own vest. He and Marcel wore them as a precaution. "Take your positions."

The four saluted and sprinted away.

From separate vantage points these men would cast eyes over the entire station platform. Two would remain at ground level on platform four, nearest to the exit on the building's west side. Two would climb into the rafters and monitor the situation from metal gangways normally for use by the maintenance crew. He had given this operation a lot of thought; the planning had taken hours. But the operation had more than its share of unknowns and in considering these unknowns he had worked with Marcel, who had a good mind for strategy. Known factors included the location of the sleeper compartment that Figueroa had purchased, so they could be reasonably sure which car the three would emerge from when they left the train, though of course this was far from certain. Major Sandoval had arranged for service and security staff to be questioned at the train's main stops in Envigado and Villa Real, but none had reported seeing any passengers from that compartment other than the older gentleman. Public places were high risk, but Marcel had suggested not having the station evacuated and he had agreed based on two factors: an empty platform would alert Navarro that something was up, and they knew the train was full and B____ was a major destination, so when disembarkation began the platform was going to be crowded regardless of their efforts. If Navarro had managed to smuggle a gun on the train as Figueroa's message suggested, then it had to be a small calibre piece, which would have limited range but could be concealed easily on the body. Was Figueroa being held hostage? Both Navarro and Tomás were trained killers, covert ops, highly skilled and extremely dangerous. What was their frame of mind? What had Figueroa told Tomás and Navarro to get them on the train in the first place? What had he said to convince them that travelling more than a thousand miles from Chiachi to B____ would improve their chances of survival? What had he promised? What kind of reception were they expecting?

Yes, there were too many unknowns to pretend this was simply a matter of taking prisoners into custody.

For Hector Tomás it was a homecoming. So why wasn't Enrique Tomás here to greet his son? Montoya had miscalculated. He had instructed a couple of his top agents to pick up Enrique Tomás and give him a beating—as a reminder that he was being watched. Unfortunately things had gotten out of hand, and Enrique was now in a civilian hospital recovering from his injuries.

With his portable transceiver, Montoya tried to confirm with his men that they were in position but their voices were obliterated by the tremendous rumble of the train as it rolled into the station. He lifted the binoculars and surveyed every corner of the vaulted space, swinging his sights up and down, seeking visual contact. There they were, two on the ground near support pillars, two thirty feet in the air on gangways situated on the building's west side. The station had four platforms—the four sets of tracks entered from the south—but the other three were empty as the Villa Real train was the only arrival for the next hour or so.

Four men had seemed enough when they were discussing options and strategy and studying floor plans, but in the light of day the station's interior appeared enormous, and within it his men seemed puny, trivial, buzzing around like flies in the forest. How could they hope to control events unfolding in so vast a space? It had been his decision to exclude the local police. Extra eyes could be helpful, but you never knew what you were getting with men from the civic constabulary, who could be lazy and incompetent or skilled and efficient, but more likely an infuriating combination of all those qualities. In the end, he had instructed the supervisor responsible for the station's security to position his men near the exits and out of the way.

The crowd roamed about restlessly. He wished they would keep still and stop blocking his view. He lowered the binoculars. Lobera and another soldier were waiting outside in the van. Maybe he should call them in. But the soldier was driving and Lobera was his eyes and ears on the street. Neither were snipers. And it was crucial that someone remain with the van so that once the prisoners were secured they could get out of here immediately. The train was still inching forward, its brakes shrieking as it slowed. There was the hiss of escaping steam. Another announcement, but he couldn't make out the words. Pigeons flapping and fluttering above the tracks dropped shit and created a stir in the air. But the crowd had stopped milling now and stood watching the train crawl forward. He lifted the binoculars. He had a clear view. The people had stepped back. His men on the ground were in plain sight. The train had come to rest. No, it would be all right. It would be all right. Six would have overloaded the space and gotten in each other's way. Four was perfect. He had estimated correctly to begin with.

Someone was blowing a whistle. A conductor in uniform had climbed down from the engine car and was blowing his whistle. Its single strident note pierced the air.

The doors of cars all the way down the line were swinging open. Train staff emerged at intervals and began lowering mechanical steps to the platform.

He spoke into the transceiver. "Checking status."

"Alpha one. No visual."

"Alpha two. No visual."

A brief pause.

"Alpha four. No visual."

He waited.

"Checking status. Alpha three. Status please."

He waited.

"Checking status. Alpha three. Status please."

Alpha three. That was Garcia on the southwest gangway.

"Garcia, checking status. What's going on?"

Silence.

He took up the binoculars but couldn't find his man Garcia. The gangway was clear.

"Can you see Garcia?"

Marcel raised his binoculars.

"I can't see him. He's not there."

"Jesus Christ!"

Montoya spoke into the transceiver. "Alpha four. Jimenez, check Garcia's position."

There was a brief silence.

"No visual on Garcia."

"Shit! What's going on?"

"The door off the gangway is open."

Montoya looked at Marcel and held his gaze as he spoke.

"The door's open. What else do you see?"

Pause.

"The angle's too tight. The door's open a few inches. Someone on the ground could see it better than I can."

He lowered the transceiver.

"Get over there."

Marcel nodded and was gone.

"Alpha one, Alpha two, Alpha four, checking status."

People were pouring out of the train and others were rushing forward to greet them. In seconds the place was swarming. Voices rose and echoed around him. It was too noisy, too messy, too volatile. How could they enforce a plan in this mayhem? If Navarro didn't appear to be threatening violence, they were to follow the three outside, converge upon them and press them into the van, taking them by surprise before Navarro could access his weapon. However, since Navarro was expendable from a national security standpoint, if he was posing an obvious threat to others, no matter to whom, they would take him out, either from above or from the ground.

But something was wrong. Garcia was a good soldier. He wouldn't abandon his post.

Marcel was at his side.

"The door's standing open but there's no sign of Garcia."

Montoya nodded.

"This is Alpha four. I've got visual on Navarro. Heading west. Hands in pockets. He's alone. No visual on a weapon."

"Alpha four, confirm. The subject is alone?"

"Confirming the subject is alone."

"Alpha one, confirm sighting."

"This is Alpha one. Visual contact confirmed."

"Alpha one, Alpha two, isolate and detain the subject. Isolate and detain. Use force if he shows a weapon. We're on the train looking for the other two."

He pressed a button on the transceiver and switched to a second line.

"Lobera?"

"Here."

"Stand by. We have visual contact."

He nodded to Marcel. They drew their Glock 22 sidearms and set off.

The Garcia question aside, he felt in control again. The situation was evolving reasonably. Navarro's threat could be neutralized in the open field while he and Marcel removed the other two from the train.

"Alpha four, any visual on the others?"

There was no answer. He slowed and Marcel slowed beside him, but he motioned for him to go on.

"Alpha four, checking status."

Nothing. With the gun in one hand, he had to clip the transceiver back on his belt before he could lift the binoculars. It took a moment to focus. Jimenez was down, slumped on the gangway, his rifle dangling from the strap on his shoulder.

He didn't panic.

"Alpha one, Alpha two, there's a threat in the house. Alpha four is down. Take Navarro now and get him out of here . . ."

Then he heard the crack of a rifle shot. Screaming. People scattering. In an instant the exits were jammed. He couldn't see a thing.

"This is Alpha one. We have shots fired from above. There's a sniper. Repeat. Shots fired. Navarro is down. I repeat, the subject is down."

Montoya looked for movement on the gangway but someone fleeing the scene slammed into him. The transceiver went flying. He was on the floor.

He scrambled to his feet. Marcel was on the train by now. The transceiver. He went looking for it, found it by a trash bin.

"Alpha one. Alpha two. Status."

"This is Alpha one. Navarro's dead."

"Leave him. Clear the station. Get these people out of here."

He pressed the button and switched to the other line.

"Lobera!"

"Sir. What's happening?"

"Radio for backup. We have shots fired and men down. There's a sniper. There might be more than one. He shot Navarro so I assume he'll shoot the others if he gets a chance. We're keeping them on the train until it's safe to move them."

"Calling for backup."

He ran for the train and leapt through the open door of the engine car. The conductor was standing just inside, his mouth agape. His eyes widened at the sight of the gun in Montoya's hand.

"Stay here," Montoya snapped. "Don't go near the door."

He went down a narrow corridor that smelled greasily of combusted oil, and which at the back of the car opened up to a small murky space containing a table littered with filthy tools, a couple of chairs, and three standing lockers. He peered through the grimy window. Scattered across the station platform were dropped bags and other items left behind by people still rushing for the exits. His two men were helping a few of the slower moving ones. Navarro's prone body lay stretched out in the middle of the cavernous space, now almost completely vacated. He spoke into the transceiver.

"Status report. Alpha one? Alpha two?"

"This is Alpha one with Alpha two. West side street exit is secure. Heading to the north side—"

Montoya broke in.

"Use extreme caution. The sniper could be on the move. We don't know how many—"

A bullet ricocheted off the frame of the window and sprayed him with debris as it flew into the compartment. Montoya threw himself to the floor just as another pierced the window dead centre and punched through the metal door of a storage locker.

He rolled over. He wasn't hit. He groped for the gun and transceiver, found both, and got to his feet.

"Keep him busy!" he yelled into the transceiver. "I need cover!"

He burst through the door at the rear of the car, crossed the coupling, and pulled open the door of the next. This was upright day seating. He warned a couple of terrified porters on cleanup duty to get down and stay away from the windows facing west.

He could hear shots as he crossed from that car to the next, also day seating. There was nobody here. He thought of Garcia, the best long-distance shot in the squad. The operation could not be halted, but he should have called for backup the moment he'd lost sight of him. A matter of a few seconds, but it would have made a difference. Now one subject was down and he'd put the others and his own men at risk. What in God's name had gone wrong? Why had he not seen this possibility? What piece of information had he missed? The whole thing was a fiasco and he was responsible. Sandoval would have his head.

Hurrying down the centre aisle, he pressed the button on the transceiver that opened the line with Marcel.

"Talk to me. Where are you?"

Static. What was this now? Had he turned the thing off?

He stopped moving, gave it a shake and tried again.

"Marcel? Damn it! What's your status?"

Nothing.

"Shit!"

The next two cars were also day seating. The one after that was the dining car.

He stormed down the centre aisle and through the doors at the back.

Outside, in the station, the gun battle raged. In the dining car he found half a dozen train staff trapped by the gunfire. Most had taken refuge under tables, but two young women were standing helplessly in the aisle, frozen with fear.

"Get down," he yelled, gesturing with his gun.

He grabbed a young woman with long dark hair by the arm and forced her away from the window.

"What's happening?"

"Never mind. Just get down." He gestured to the other one, who was crying and holding her hands in the air. She was staring at his gun. "You too."

They crawled under a table and held each other.

"All of you!" he said. "Stay here and don't move until someone tells you it's safe."

He left them. The first of the sleeper cars was next. It was here that Figueroa had taken a compartment.

Before venturing from the dining car he switched the transceiver off and clipped it to his belt. He removed the binoculars from around his neck and set them on the nearest dining table. He held his gun in front of his face and pushed open the rear door. Distantly, from within the station, he heard a shot, then another: Alpha one and two were still occupied with the sniper. Backup might not arrive for another few minutes. He was on his own.

He opened the door of the sleeper car and stepped inside. Voices? It sounded like an argument. If there were staff hiding in one of the compartments it was unlikely they would be talking. He peeked around the corner into the corridor, which extended along the west-facing side of the train. A row of windows offered the sniper an unimpeded view of the interior and any movement within. The corridor was clear. The top and bottom window casings were at a level with the top of his head and his waist. He fell to a crouch and crept forward. The voices gained in volume, but he could not make out what was being said. Abruptly there was silence. All the compartment doors were shut. But he was too exposed. He had to find cover. He inched forward. Then, ten feet in front of him, a bullet exploded through a window and hit the inner wall. The glass—shatterproof—fractured but remained intact. Then, much closer, another bullet blasted through a window. Figueroa's compartment was two compartments away, but that was still another twenty feet. He reached up and pulled the latch on the door beside him, pushed it back, and rolled inside. The spring-loaded door swung shut but not before a bullet drilled through it a foot above his head.

He rolled away from the door and got to his feet. Another bullet pierced the door. Then another. With his heart straining against his ribs he fought to control his breathing. His muscles twitched. He pressed his back against the side wall and took in his surroundings. The compartment was messy and cramped: a single window behind a tattered curtain. Under the window a small table protruded from the wall. On either side of the table, upper and lower sleeping berths. The bedding was disturbed, beige blankets bunched up as if kicked aside in a rush.

The silence was punctuated by the sporadic plunk of bullets hitting the train.

He unclipped the transceiver from his waist and switched it on. He dialled back the volume.

"Lobera, where's our backup?"

"A minute out. What are your instructions?"

"Shut down that sniper and secure the building. Coordinate with Alpha one and two."

"Yes, sir."

"Marcel's not answering his radio. I think there's a situation in Figueroa's compartment. I'm going in."

"Sir, shouldn't you—?"

"There's no time."

He switched off the transceiver and clipped it to his belt. For a few seconds he remained still, adjusting his grip on the gun and breathing slowly through his mouth. If he had read the voices right, Figueroa was being threatened, but either didn't know or wouldn't tell where Tomás was.

He moved towards the door.

A pause in the gunfire. There were no other sounds.

Except . . .

He held his breath and stood motionless.

Breathing . . .

It stopped.

Someone was in here.

He knelt and peered beneath the berth furthest from the door. Wedged into the shallow space was a huddled body partly covered by a blanket. A pair of military style boots protruded from under the blanket.

He tightened his grip on the gun, kept his voice low.

"I'm a soldier. My name's Montoya. Who's there?"

No response. No movement.

"Tomás? Hector Tomás?"

There was a sound: a groan or a whimper.

"Show me your hands. Move slowly or I will shoot."

A pair of hands emerged from beneath the blanket, and with the movement the blanket fell away to reveal a young man's face: dark eyes, skin and hair, straggly growth of beard. The gaze did not waver and the eyes were defiant.

"Are you Hector Tomás?"

"Yes."

He angled the gun away. At that moment there was an eruption of gunfire that rose rapidly to a crescendo. The interior of the station reverberated with the discharge of automatic weapons. Backup had arrived.

"Stay there. Don't move."

"He lied."

Hector's voice cracked. The tone of despair chilled Montoya and rooted him to the spot.

"He said that my father had sent him and that my family was waiting for me to come home. But he was lying."

Montoya said nothing.

"I saw what they did to Alejandro. He's dead, isn't he?"

"Yes. I'm sorry."

"He knew it wasn't safe. When we stopped in Villa Real there were soldiers waiting. They took us from one train and put us on this one. Figueroa went to make a phone call and when he came back we could see that something was wrong. We decided we had to escape. I didn't want to hurt Major Figueroa, but we had no choice. When the train stopped Alejandro said that he would go first. I tried to stop him . . ."

The gunfire intensified.

"Stay here—"

"I'll never be safe."

"You will, if you do what I say."

"It doesn't matter. After what I've done, nothing matters."

"Don't worry about—"

"They're following me . . ."

"Just stay here."

Montoya was on his feet, through the door, and sprinting down the corridor to Figueroa's cabin. The gunfire within the station sputtered, stopped, sputtered again. Between shots he heard voices. Then it was silent.

He burst into Figueroa's cabin.

In the cabin, Marcel was standing over an older man, presumably the Major. Figueroa had drawn his legs up to protect his abdomen. His face was a bloody mess.

"Tomás is hiding. He won't tell me where."

Figueroa cried, "Stop him! He's going to kill all of us!"

Montoya extended his hand towards the door. "He's—" He paused. This was all wrong.

Marcel turned. "You know where Tomás is?!"

"What are you doing?" He noticed the transceiver clipped to Marcel's belt. "Why didn't you answer when I radioed?"

Marcel held a gun aimed at Figueroa, but it was a gun he had never seen before. A Beretta. It had a silencer. Marcel's foot connected with Figueroa's upper body one, two, three times, hard. When Montoya stepped forward, Marcel turned the gun on him. The old man raised his arms to shield himself, and Marcel gave him one last kick. Figueroa let out a yelp, groaned, and hugged himself.

Marcel turned, his face flushed from the exertion, his gun levelled at Montoya. His expression did not acknowledge any connection between them. His eyes were impenetrable. He was a different person. It was like a stranger had taken control of a familiar body.

Montoya stared. All he could find to say was, "They got the sniper."

"Tell me where Tomás is."

"It was you." He raised his gun. "You're the leak."

Marcel's hand was as steady as his gaze. He didn't seem to care that Montoya's gun was aimed at him. "Just tell me what I need to know and I'll be out of your way."

Montoya said nothing.

"I already checked the compartments along here. I couldn't have missed him. He must have doubled back and gone into one after I looked."

Ignoring Montoya's weapon, Marcel tried to brush by him. Montoya blocked his way. "I have to know why."

Marcel released a breath and shook his head. He gazed impassively into Montoya's eyes, only a few inches away. "Your orders don't matter anymore. Everything's changed."

Montoya didn't move.

"Don't you know anything? We're being watched. I'm being watched. You're being watched." He swung his arm in Figueroa's direction. "He's being watched. It's the way things are done. This shouldn't be a surprise. To you of all people."

"We need him alive. To make Nadia talk. You can't kill him."

"He's a security threat. There was a botched mission with civilian casualties. As long as he's alive there's a chance he'll talk about it, and that means criminal charges. We can't take the risk. And he's of no use to you anyway. She's gone. It's already happened. The order came down. Prisoners subject to special treatment have to be liquidated." Then, after a pause, "It was always going to happen this way."

He felt like he'd been punched. His focus drifted. He recovered in an instant, but it was too late. Marcel struck him with his gun, a savage blow to the side of the head. The impact and explosion of pain brought him down, and Marcel was past him and into the corridor. Some instinct compelled him to move, and he had flung himself across Figueroa's passive body when three shots punctured the door and hit the floor where he had fallen. Figueroa waved him away when he tried to check on him. He turned and approached the door. He unlatched it and pulled it ajar. Throbbing in his jaw and around his eye splintered his vision, but he saw Marcel enter the corridor from the next compartment over and turn towards where Tomás was hiding. Montoya pulled the door open and, still on the floor, braced himself in the doorway. He tightened his grip and took aim.

"Marcel, it's over. Drop it and turn around."

Without pausing in his movements, Marcel swivelled and raised the gun. Montoya fired three rapid shots, aiming outside the vest, aiming to kill. Marcel spun as the first bullet hit him in the shoulder. The next two pierced his neck. He crumpled and dropped to his knees. The gun was still in his hand and for a moment he struggled to raise it. But then his eyes turned glassy and he fell sideways. His shoulder slid down the wall and he came to rest on his back.

Montoya pushed himself up and staggered towards his fallen adversary, steadying himself with one hand against the wall. His other hand gripped the gun still aimed at Marcel. Standing over the body, he explored the head wound where Marcel had struck him and grimaced when his fingers came away wet. With his probing the throbbing swelled and a fierce shooting pain bore deep into his skull. He was suddenly battling weakness in his knees, and he shuddered as a wave of nausea passed over him. Then all he was aware of was the heat of anger and a gnawing sensation. Betrayal. His eyes were wet. The moisture overflowed and mingled with the blood on his face.

"Fuck."

He knelt and grabbed the gun out of Marcel's hand. He pitched it away. It clattered against the wall at the end of the corridor.

He looked at his dead friend. He had trusted and been deceived. Private conversations had been reported. Somewhere, everything was written down. There was probably more to this than he would ever know. Marcel had been with him for almost two years. Every case they had worked together was tainted. Where had it begun? Without preliminaries of any kind, Sandoval had called him in and presented him with a new assistant. At the time he had been perplexed, then grateful. But the instigation had come from higher up.

The finger-pointing would have to wait until later.

We're all being watched.

He brushed Marcel's face with the back of his hand. In death, his skin was cool and had acquired a papery sheen. Like any good soldier he had followed his orders to the letter, fully aware of the price he might be called upon to pay. Loyal to the end. No wonder he seemed at peace.

Montoya groped at his waist for the transceiver. It was gone.

He managed with difficulty to stand. Listing woozily against the window, he glimpsed some of the men from the backup unit heading in the direction of the train. Navarro lay where he had fallen but the body was covered by a sheet and standing over it were a medic and a regular soldier.

Tomás!

His vision blurred. He saw the world through a fog. He brought his hand up and cautiously explored the side of his head, but again the pain shot through him and almost brought him to his knees. In a second the nausea had passed. But when he turned, he stumbled against Marcel's body and had to grope for the wall to keep from falling. As he staggered towards the compartment where Tomás was hiding, his hand left a crooked smear of blood.

And Nadia! He would question her again, with Tomás where she could see him, someone holding a gun to his head or giving him a pounding each time she refused to answer. She'd talk. Oh yes, she'd talk.

But that wouldn't happen now, would it? Marcel had said she was gone. Liquidated.

He was in the compartment. How had that happened? He didn't remember opening the door.

His body felt heavy, weighted down and sluggish, as if he were moving underwater.

He knelt and peered beneath the berth. Tomás was not there. Was this the right one? Yes . . . there was the disarranged bedding, the same beige blankets, bunched up as he remembered. But there was fresh blood on the floor. It dripped and spattered as he watched. Where was it coming from?

The window!

He went to it. It hung loose in its frame. The top dangled on a hinge, the bottom was disengaged: an emergency exit.

All at once he could hardly lift his gun. He stared at it in his hand and tried to tighten his fingers around it. He fought to hold on, but some force was dragging it down. Then it became too much. He had to let go. Strangely, when it hit the floor, he didn't hear a thing.

Maybe he would ask Sandoval for some leave. What would be the harm? He'd take a week or two and put this behind him. Come back a new man—

His arms and legs tingled. He felt cold. He had to sit down. Just for a minute.

Someone was leaning over him, shining a light into his eyes.

"It's Corporal Montoya! He's alive! We need a medic in here!"

Of course I'm alive, he thought.

"Who did this sir? Who did this?"

"Tomás escaped." The words sounded strange. His tongue found its way around them with difficulty.

"He's dangerous. We have to stop him."

Who was speaking now?

"He's lost a lot of blood."

"Don't try to speak, sir. The situation's under control."

That was good. As long as everything was under control, Tomás wouldn't get far. The station was crawling with soldiers. The streets were full of them. Patrols were out around the clock, watching every corner, every public place, the face of every citizen who took his business into the world, the innocent and guilty alike. A wanted criminal didn't stand a chance. The whole country was under surveillance. *We're all being watched.* He could rest easy. The job would get done.

And as they lifted him and laid him flat, he thought of Nadia in her cell, staring up at him with those huge eyes, revealing nothing. It was galling to think of her tragedy playing itself out elsewhere, apart from him, after all the time he had spent studying her case. It was grossly unfair that he would never know where her journey ended.

They carried him off the train. He was being transferred to a wheeled gurney. Nobody spoke. He glimpsed faces that were full of concern. Looking up, he shuddered as the cold stark whiteness of the sky assaulted his eyes through the glass panels of the ceiling. He tried to move but there was something glued to the side of his head. Then he was outside. Drops of rain struck his face, and he was momentarily refreshed. The blare of sirens. The commotion was deafening. But it didn't have to be like this. Somewhere in the world were the peace and silence he craved. He wondered where that might be.

He saw him, Hector Tomás. He was running. He was getting away! Down that street. Into that passageway between those buildings. What were they thinking, letting him go? And he tried to warn them, but his mouth wouldn't speak, his arm wouldn't rise from his side, his finger wouldn't point, and with great reluctance he gave up the struggle. But this wasn't over. He would find Hector Tomás. He would get the answers he wanted. Nadia would tell him everything. Those murderers would be called to account for their crimes.

FORTY-SEVEN

The order has come down. In preparation for the transfer of power to a civilian government, thousands of prisoners all over the country are being moved. Many are taken in the dead of night. Others, like Nadia Wladanski, wait until morning to be removed from their cells, for there are only so many vehicles, only so many men who can be trusted to maintain a strict silence for the rest of their lives about what their military leaders have ordered them to do.

Because this operation is clandestine and sensitive. The vehicles are unmarked. The final destination is unknown, even to the men driving the trucks.

Nadia is roused by the abrupt clatter of the latch being drawn back. It is a cruel but familiar sound, one that normally causes her heart to accelerate and her body to stiffen with alarm. But the last interrogation took place a while ago. Though she has lost touch with divisions of time as she knew them for most of her life, it seems like many days since she was injected with fluids that make it feel like her skin is being peeling away layer by layer, or had electrodes attached to her eyelids, breasts, and genitals, or been dunked upside down in freezing water. She has no way of knowing if they have lost interest in her. She does not dare to hope for anything.

A man enters. Her only visitor lately has been the old man who brings the food—her mouth had flooded with saliva in anticipation. But she has never seen this man before. He is tall, dressed completely in black, and her first response is to flatten herself against the wall. Other than the old man with the food, the pain of interrogation is her only memory. It has to be one or the other. He grabs her arm, drags her from the filthy straw-filled pallet—the only object in the tiny cell other than a plastic bucket—and pushes her ahead of him into the corridor. Indifference is written on his face. He is neither gentle nor rough.

She is one of many. A voice barks at them to halt, and they are shackled together in twos by their hands and feet then herded along the corridor beneath a row of flickering lights and through a door leading into another dimly lit passageway. Here the stench of decay is overpowering. She pulls in a mouthful of dank air and tries to hold it, but she has no strength and coughs it out after only a few seconds. Everyone is coughing and gasping. But further along is another door. It is wide open and the bright light of day is waiting for her.

Cooler air hits her skin. She looks up at a white overcast sky and feels a drop of rain on her face. It makes her smile and in some place buried deep within her a memory stirs. She sees a girl with long shining black hair clutching a bag of schoolbooks. Beside her is a boy, also with dark hair. He is holding her hand. Her skin is very pale, his is darker. They are smiling. The blue sky is clear but for a single cloud, and this cloud is dropping rain on them as they walk. It is a warm, soft summer rain. They are getting wet, but it doesn't matter. There is pleasure in the moisture on their skin and comfort in the knowledge that the sun, when it emerges from behind the cloud, will dry them completely before they get home.

The memory dissolves. Her feet sting. The ground is strewn with stones. She keeps her eyes down and steps around them as best she can. Seconds later when she looks up, she sees a pair of dark green transport trucks sitting at the edge of the car park beside the wire fence. She is close enough to them now that her thoughts are overtaken by the rumble of their engines. Her eyes wander over the vastness of this alien world that is suddenly in front of her—sky, earth, air, trees, buildings, hills, distance. With mounting panic she glances over her shoulder towards the stone building they have just exited, sees the unsmiling faces of the men in black, the ragged procession she is part of. She stumbles and clutches at the hand beside her. With a curse, the woman shakes her off. The men in black prod them with their weapons. The pace quickens. Cries and whimpers rise up. "Silence!" a voice shouts, and instantly the sounds stop. Then they have crossed the short distance and are being loaded, two by two, into one of the trucks.

She feels safe again within the dim interior. But there are already people in here. The benches along each side of the truck's compartment are filled. Where can she go? Prodded by the men in black, prisoners pile in behind her. She spies an empty corner and yanks on the wire cord binding her to the woman who cursed at her. Murmurs and groans rise in volume as more prisoners are pushed into the already crowded compartment. They jostle and shove, trying to make space where there is none. Nadia pushes her way through, treading on feet and toes. The proximity of so much human flesh terrifies and disgusts her. Liquid leaps up her throat, thin and bitter to the taste. She drags her tether mate after her, pulls down on the cord. They sit on the floor, backs to the wall. Nadia gags, tries to swallow. Warmth from the body beside her seeps through the cloth of her shift, into her skin, but she cannot move away. Another body slumps to the floor in front of her and slides back on her feet, crowding her legs. And suddenly her corner of the truck reeks of human filth. She withdraws and tenses her muscles, resisting the intrusion. Somewhere a fight breaks out. She hears the smack of flesh on flesh, grunts and whimpers, a shrill cry.

"Stop it!"

She can't see what's going on but hears the stomp of boots, a crack, and a sharp intake of breath. The crowd shifts as a body hits the floor.

"You want me to shoot you?"

The loading is finished and the door of the truck slams with a crash. She hears a metallic slide and click as a bolt is pushed and secured into place.

Darkness and stillness descend abruptly and the rumble of the truck's engine leaps into the foreground. A new kind of fear tugs at her heart and she gathers her body in closer to herself, shrinking away from the others around her. But this is a mistake because at once the others expand to fill the space she has vacated, and the unwanted contact persists. In a few minutes the truck is in motion. As a single unit the tightly packed mass of prisoners shifts in response. She wearies of resisting the movement and holding her body stiff. She relaxes her muscles, but remains rigidly confined in the smaller space left to her. Humanity presses against her. There is no escape. She feels the restriction in her throat and lungs. Her limbs ache. Her heart is weary. There are tears in her eyes, but they are from exhaustion. She feels no urge to weep.

Bodies sway in response to the motion as the truck lurches over ruts, stops, starts, and swings around a series of sharp turns. After a gradual ascent she feels the truck gain speed, and soon it is gliding smoothly over an even surface.

No words are spoken. The silence is a momentary respite. Briefly she is calm—her misery eases. With a little effort she can pretend she is in her cell with the light off. But it is not long before the murmurs and whispers resume. One person is crying, then two, then three. The separate strands rise piercingly and weave around one another, blending to create a complex and discordant lament, a symphony of grief. Others join in. Nadia lifts her hands, stretching the cord to its limit, and bends her head down. She clamps her hands over her ears and presses herself into the corner.

Over time the air warms and thickens with all manner of bodily exhalation. Through her hands she hears the moans, retches, coughs, and wails of her companions. The movement around her is ceaseless. Cramped limbs shift in a futile search for comfort. The pushing becomes violent. It's as if the air itself has assumed animal form and is squirming, shoving, prodding, seeking breathing space of its own. Exhaustion moves into the base of her neck, a pervasive throbbing hunger for oblivion. She will settle for sleep, but this is impossible, and finally her strength fails and she must lower her arms, the final barricade between her and them. In this closed space, in this darkness, there are no boundaries. There is nothing left of her. She is consumed by them. They are her and she is them. They become one.

She curls up and presses her forehead to her knees. Labours for every breath.

The truck is no longer moving. She is awake. Has she slept?

The smell is everywhere. She feels suddenly that she is suffocating. Her frantic movements seem to rouse her tether mate, whose own movements cancel out each of hers. She tries to stand but there's so much weighing her down.

"Sit still!" The voice is a whisper. A plea.

She settles back into place. And then she notices the quiet, the stillness. What has happened?

"You are young, aren't you?" The woman leans her head towards Nadia. She feels the stale warmth of breath on her arm. She doesn't answer.

"I know. You don't have to say anything. But listen. Please, can you just listen?"

A deep intake of air.

"I went looking for my children. Julia and Ernesto. They are like you, young and impetuous. I had a chance to send them away. I still can't believe I didn't do it. God forgive me, I was selfish. I wanted them with me. I tried to keep a close eye on them. But they got involved in this business. And one day they didn't come home. I had no idea. To me it made no sense. But I was their mother so I went to the police. I went to their friends. Nobody would tell me anything. I made a poster with their photographs asking people to call me. But it was the police who came. They said I was causing trouble. They told me to stop. I refused. I'm a mother looking for her children. How can that be causing trouble? So I went on asking questions and bothering people. None of them would talk to me. I heard whispers, rumours that they were dead. I didn't want to believe it. None of it was real. But a mother has to know the truth about her children. Even knowing the worst is better than knowing nothing. I kept asking questions. Then in the mailbox I found an envelope. Inside it was a finger with a ring on it. My Julia's ring, the one my mother gave to me when I got married. I almost died that day. I wish I had died. I didn't know what to do. I called the newspaper and told them, and they said they would send someone to copy down my story. But instead of someone from the newspaper the police came and arrested me."

The woman pauses and beneath the silence Nadia detects the muffled drone of voices outside the truck. A slamming door creates a deep, resonating echo.

"I don't care what happens to me. It doesn't matter. There's no one left. But I want to know about Julia and Ernesto. I have that right. I've been in jail for two years. They did everything to me. I can't remember half of it. But the worst was when they said that if I had just kept quiet about my children when they told me to, they would have let them come home. But I had to go around making trouble, so they got rid of them. They said it was my fault. They blamed me. They blamed their mother."

Nadia strains to listen through the wall, to the voices outside the truck.

"I died that day. I truly did." Her voice fractures and fails.

Suddenly the woman's hand gropes for hers, finds it, grasps it.

"I would ask them to forgive me," she gasps, "because I killed them. But I can't ask them. I'm asking you. Can you forgive me? For killing my children?"

The woman's grip is firm as she lays her other hand on Nadia's and strokes and fondles it. Her instinct is to pull away, but the contact does not disgust her. She craves the solitude of her cell, but the woman's need has unlocked a door, and she cannot stop herself passing through. On the other side are images of the life she once lived: the girl Nadia laughing with her sisters, Carmel and Magda, at something one of them said. They are in a bedroom, taking turns brushing each other's hair. Their parents and the kisses and hugs they shared. She is small, sitting on her father's lap. They are eating dinner. Everything she loves is on the table: thick and savoury *barszcz czerwony,* the *smalec,* so fattening (how did Carmel keep her figure?), *żeberka w miodzie* (the honey sauce her favourite), *pierogi* with white sauce, crispy *placki ziemniaczane* on the side, and for dessert *szarlotka* or, if they had been good all week, *faworki* with extra sugar and ice cream. The aromas flood her senses and saliva gathers in her mouth. And there is Hector with them at the table, the first time so polite though she knew he didn't like the food. But he came back and learned. They are holding hands in the rain—it's the same vision she had outside the building—and she is kissing him, their tongues playing, the urgent thrust of bodies touching, rubbing, grinding. The shock of Enrique's eyes outlined in black—it made her knees weak to recall it. His kindnesses towards her.

She squeezes the woman's hand. *"Wybaczam wam,"* she says. *"Nie oskarżać siebie."*

The woman is weeping. They are in each other's arms.

"Wy będziecie widzieć oni znowu."

But the words are wrong. What's happened to her words?

"Wy musi im powiesz."

"You're foreign," the woman says. "You don't understand what I'm saying. I am sorry to burden you with this."

"Nie! Jestem tym samym jak wy!"

"Don't worry, my child. It's all right. It's all right."

The woman's arms draw her close. She grows quiet and allows her body to relax beneath the woman's caresses. She leans into the warmth. The pressure of other bodies resting against them is almost soothing. She cannot understand what has happened to the words in her head, but in some veiled recess of her mind she knows it does not matter. She knows that the woman has accepted her meaning into her heart and that she can resign the struggle with no loss of dignity.

They remain in a close embrace for whatever time is left. Her breathing slows and she almost falls asleep. And then, without warning, the bolt is drawn back with an abrupt clatter of metal on metal. The door is opened and she is momentarily blinded by the bright white light flooding the compartment.

Grumbles and protestations as people rouse themselves and raise their arms to shield their eyes.

"Silence!"

The voices fall away and the first prisoners climb down or are pulled from the compartment. The pressure of bodies lessens and they stand. The woman places her lips to Nadia's ear.

"Do not be afraid, my child. We are safe now. You will see."

Nadia nods.

Hand in hand, they proceed stiffly towards the light, avoiding a few lifeless bodies that succumbed to the conditions of their confinement. There are further murmurs and groans, sounds of bodies venting themselves, expressing their natural needs. Waiting for them as they climb down from the truck are a dozen or so men dressed in black holding automatic weapons. The light is coming from rows of spotlights attached to tall metal stands.

No one resists or questions what is happening. Nadia and the woman fall into step behind the other prisoners as they move slowly between the rows of lights.

They are in a huge building, like an auditorium. The ceiling hovers an impossible distance above them. When she looks over her shoulder, the truck appears puny, a toy abandoned within a space of infinite dimension.

Ahead of them is a table where three people in white lab coats are seated, a young woman and two older men. Prisoners are led to the table, quickly processed, and led away. She grows aware of a distant sound, a steady drone. She looks past the table and towards the far end of the building where an opening extends from floor level all the way to the ceiling, a tall narrow crack in the side of the structure. Through the crack she sees the black night sky.

Just before they reach the table she looks at the woman next to her whose hand is soft and warm in hers. She is taller than Nadia. Her hair, which straggles unkempt to her shoulders, is mostly grey. Her face is not old. She looks into Nadia's eyes and smiles.

Then they are next and she realizes these people are doctors. Everyone is getting an injection.

A soldier grasps the woman's arm. He turns it to expose the pale underside and holds it out straight. One of the men at the table is filling a syringe with clear liquid from a small vial. He hands the syringe to the other man. Meanwhile, the woman at the table is rubbing the skin of Nadia's companion's arm, at the inside of the elbow. The soldier holds the woman's arm steady as the man with the syringe pokes the needle into the skin and presses the plunger. The liquid disappears into the woman's arm. The soldier takes Nadia's arm. The woman at the table kneads the stringy flesh of her inner elbow while the syringe is refilled.

The woman murmurs, "My God, she's so thin." But no one takes notice.

The two men complete their procedure. The syringe is ready.

The woman glances over nervously. "Sorry. I can't find a vein."

Another memory leaps into Nadia's vision, of receiving inoculations at school. She can see herself, very small, standing before a similar table in a hallway filled with children of all ages whining and crying. But it is only as the needle pricks her skin that she thinks it odd that here, tonight, everyone is being injected with the same needle.

Pain shoots up her arm. She gasps and pulls against the soldier's grip. Clear liquid trickles to her wrist and dribbles to the floor.

The woman at the table has tears in her eyes. "I'm sorry," she says.

The man with the syringe grabs her arm, thumbs the skin briefly, and sticks the needle in. The remaining liquid vanishes without incident.

They are led away and someone else takes their place.

As they proceed hand in hand, following the others towards the gap in the side of the building, Nadia's fingers and toes start to tingle and she feels a soft fuzzy warmth flow into her arms and legs. A moment later she senses the woman struggling to maintain her grasp. The pressure of the hand in hers slackens and becomes limp. Nadia feels her own grip loosen, and then it doesn't matter. She is swept along by a soft, radiant wave of indifference. The rhythm of her steps slows, and all she can do is place one foot ahead of the other. They proceed like sleepwalkers, arms dangling at their sides. Soldiers appear from somewhere to help them along, and when they are outside someone unfastens their bindings. Nadia rubs her wrists, lifts a glance to the night sky. The air is cool. The stars wink at her. But her curiosity is overwhelmed by the dullness pressing on her brain, a blanket smothering her thoughts. An airplane is waiting, the whirl of its propellers creating a drone that blots out every other sound. The rear underside of the aircraft has been lowered, and they are escorted up the ramp into the airplane's gaping belly. Her feet slip between the rough corrugations and she stumbles, but the hand on her arm gently guides her along. Only a few more steps and she is being steadied and lowered to the floor. She curls her legs beneath her and tilts her head until it is resting against the wall. She is so tired, but she has no fear. All care and worry has left her. She opens her eyes. Weak ceiling lights reveal that the inside of the aircraft is an empty cylinder. There are no seats. The other prisoners rest as she does, slumped against the wall, against each other, or prone on the floor. The woman with the grey hair is beside her. Her eyelids are parted, but her eyes gaze blankly. There is a dead, wooden look about them.

Nadia opens her eyes again. There is a grinding of gears. The ramp is rising, closing like a set of jaws, swallowing the night. The plane's belly is full. Flesh and bone press against her, but it is not as cramped as the truck. There is no smell. The drone rises in pitch and volume. The plane shudders and begins to move. She adjusts her shoulder against the wall. Her body is weightless: she is aware of it, but it has gone somewhere and left her behind.

The drone of the plane fills every crevice of her sedated consciousness. She feels no anxiety as the force of its forward momentum presses her backward. They tilt upward and are airborne, climbing higher with each passing second. Her mind grapples vaguely with the notion that the journey will have a destination at the end of it, but she can barely formulate the thought before it scatters. When she closes her eyes a chaotic series of memories and images flits through her mind, but she cannot capture any single detail long enough to extract meaning from it. If only she could sleep. Then her eyes are open again. The woman seems to have drifted into some sort of waking slumber. Her head nods but her eyes are wide open and her lips are moving. For no particular reason Nadia reaches across the space that separates them and grasps her limp hand.

She takes in the murky interior of the plane, her eyes gaining and losing focus. The ragged bodies of other prisoners are strewn about like garbage. A man dressed in a bulky dark coat and gloves steps among them. Occasionally she lifts her head as if emerging out of a doze, unsure how much time has passed. The cold air has wakened her. The air is so cold it hurts to breathe. She can't stop her body shaking.

When next she looks up, there are fewer bodies about her on the floor, fewer leaning against the wall. Where are they being taken? The question brushes against the surface of her comprehension but leaves no impression.

Her bones ache from the cold.

The woman's hand slipping out of hers disturbs her fragile hold on sleep.

She is cold, so cold her body's protests are silenced.

The man in the heavy clothes has lifted the woman to her feet. Gently, he escorts her away, towards the front of the plane. The woman staggers, halts, leans on the man, then at his urging resumes her faltering progress. Nadia twists around, trying to keep them within sight, but when they reach a partition the man pulls some elastic material aside so the woman can pass through. He follows. It snaps back into place behind them.

She turns and closes her eyes.

She wakes to see the man standing over her. He reaches down, takes Nadia gently under the arm and lifts her to her feet. He says nothing and does not meet her eye, but she looks at him and sees that he is neither young nor old. He is not happy, but he is not sad either.

"*Jestem tym samym jak wy,*" she whispers, but cannot make herself heard above the drone of the plane.

He urges her forward and she does not resist. There is nothing in her that can make her resist. She is empty.

"*Jestem tym samym jak wy,*" she says again, and then the words she had tried to find when she talked to the woman come to her. "I am the same as you."

Now he looks at her, but says nothing.

"I am the same as you," she says.

At the partition, he reaches past her and draws the tight fabric aside so she can step through. The section of the plane they left behind was cold, but this tiny sterile enclosure is beyond cold. Her exposed skin is flayed raw and grows numb. A coarse wind squeezes tears from her eyes and whips the shift up, almost ripping it from her body. The roar of wind and engines is deafening. She clasps her arms around herself, but they are stick-thin and provide no warmth, no protection. Through the doorway she watches a few distant clouds drift serenely past. The night sky stares back with a predator's eye: cold, cruel, relentless.

The man is behind her. With powerful hands he grips her by the arms and holds her steady before the gaping doorway.

For a fleeting moment she is aware of a watery expanse that stretches from one horizon to the other. Then she is weightless. The world falls silent. She is safe now. Nothing can touch her.

FORTY-EIGHT

It was another grey day, cold and intermittently rainy—a creeping sort of cold, the kind of cold that seeps into the bones and causes an ache from the inside out. The constant and enveloping pain made it hard to concentrate, and Enrique often set his book aside, laying it face down on the arm of the chair. Staring out the window, he would fall into a doze and dream that his family had gathered around him. He was ill—he was dying—but Lucinda was fetching him a cup of tea. Julio was singing and playing his guitar (out of tune—there was really no hope). Dulciana had been baking bread, Cesara in her thick glasses, always reading, dark-eyed Rosaria had a new boyfriend, and poor Helena who always seemed to be coming down with something. Hector and Carlos were there too . . . they sat listening indulgently, smiles all around. Then, when Julio was done and the applause had faded away, they would sit down together for dinner. The meal would proceed, accompanied by stories and much laughter, and despite his weakened state he would preside over the feast that Lucinda had prepared with great dignity and benevolent authority, from time to time casting a gaze of appreciation and deep longing into his wife's eyes, which she would return, blushingly but boldly. Then, afterward, coffee and dessert, and finally, to bed with Lucinda, whose firm breasts and lithe body . . .

But inevitably he would awaken, startled into consciousness by some street noise, a shout or car horn or the rancorous whining of one of those infernal two-wheeled scooters. The book would be on the floor and the realization that he was sitting alone in a darkening room and that his family was gone would settle over him again, quietly, like a net from which he had spent the last of his strength trying to disentangle himself.

How the boy was spending his time in this fusty old flat was a question that confounded him, though with each passing day he was less inclined to concern himself with it. All that mattered was that the boy's home- and lovemaking skills were adequate and Enrique was seeing glimmers of interest in things intellectual. So there was potential for the arrange- ment to become satisfactory if not ideal, but only if he could find a way to limber up his limbs and recover some of his mobility. The boy—Diego Vasquez was his name—seemed content, and the current situation—with Enrique little more than an invalid—was preferable by far to almost any other in which he might find himself. A bondage house (Enrique was not familiar with the place) had come under new management and was in the process of shedding some of its assets. Eleven-year-old Diego would have been auctioned off to the highest bidder, but a man named Etienne Torres stepped in with a guaranteed sum on behalf of a friend, who wished to remain anonymous.

Somehow the new Dean of Arts and Sciences (the family friend hav- ing long since been put out to pasture) had gotten wind of his clandestine activities. In the course of investigating the allegations, someone with a master key had gone into his office and jimmied the lock of his private filing cabinet, where he kept his collection of erotic fiction, photos, and illicit publications, not to mention, most crucially, an address book. The Dean was now in possession of the incriminating material, and in order to make the embarrassment go away and avoid outright dismissal, he had found it necessary to accept a less than totally satisfactory retirement package from the university. In the meantime, his assistant Juan Carlos was sitting in the archivist's chair, the very position the jaundiced old bootlicker had coveted for years.

He did not know how he would have survived these last few months without Diego. The boy did all of the shopping and cleaning, helped him back and forth to the bathroom, watched over him as he crept about the flat, cooked most of their meals. In return, the freedoms Diego enjoyed after years of brutal servitude had brought a new glow to his skin and fleshed out his sunken cheeks.

Enrique's eyes snapped open just as the book slipped off the arm of the chair. He couldn't move fast enough and it hit the floor with a plop. After thirty years he was re-reading Smekal, the highly praised *Treatise on the Blood-Gold Anomaly*, but it was tough going. Tougher than he remembered.

The key in the lock had woken him. Diego was back.

Enrique tried to raise himself, but his stiff old bones were not cooperating. He let himself sink backward into the upholstery before giving it another try. Finally, his knees locked into place beneath him and, tottering, he was on his feet. He attempted to bend down to retrieve the book, but his back shrieked in protest and he left it where it had fallen. Why oh why was everything such a struggle?

"Diego! What is the news from the world today?"

The boy appeared around the corner gripping two plastic shopping bags. He was slim with tousled brown hair and looked younger than his eleven years, which to Enrique was a delightful bonus, and well-deserved too since through his generosity the boy now had a decent place to live. Diego had evidently hung his dripping poncho on the coat tree in the entryway, so Enrique's training was having an effect. He was wearing one of Julio's outfits—a black T-shirt with the white letters AC-DC emblazoned across his narrow chest, and a pair of jeans, which were just a tad short.

"I saw Señora Cabeza again," he said, smiling, almost bursting with excitement.

Enrique's smile fell away at the mention of this name. "Oh, and what does the old goat have to say for herself?"

"She says she hopes you're feeling better."

"And if that's true I'll eat my socks. She has always had it in for me. I don't know why. She says these things, you know, to get you to talk. She's a busybody. She just wants to know our business. But you don't have to tell her anything, do you?"

Diego was carrying the bags into the kitchen.

"No," he said. "But she's nice." Traces of doubt had deadened his tone. "I like her."

Enrique entered the kitchen a few steps behind the boy. Diego's last remark came out almost as a question, and Enrique let it slip by without comment. It was a troublesome balance he was trying to attain, taking a boy whose early years had left him with one certainty—that suspicion and fear are essential to survival—and teaching him social skills that would serve him later in life, but at the same time discouraging him from blurting out intimate knowledge to anyone with a friendly face and a kindly manner. He wanted Diego to be guarded but open, trusting but discreet—in sum, he wanted him to be normal. But he couldn't find a way to explain this in so many words without coming across as a tiresome pedant or a lunatic nitpicker. So for the time being he had to trust the boy's instincts and be prepared to take corrective measures in the event of the occasional gaffe.

They began unpacking the groceries.

"Well, maybe she's changed. But please don't go into her apartment again."

"I won't."

He ruffled the boy's hair and let his hand linger on the smooth skin of his neck. Last week the old witch had lured Diego into her rooms and sent him home with a plate of stale cookies. Enrique had pitched them into the trash and sent him downstairs immediately to return the empty plate.

"She saw the man across the street again."

Enrique stiffened.

"I saw him too."

Trying to keep the tremor out of his voice, Enrique replied, "Did you now?"

"Yes, he was just standing there. Like the last time. He was smoking."

"You didn't go near him I hope."

"He was across the street."

Enrique nodded. "So you say he's not with the police? How can you be sure?"

Diego shrugged. "He's sloppy looking. Like a raggedy man. He talks to himself and he wears sneakers. I'll bet he smells."

Enrique allowed himself to briefly echo Diego's chuckle, but in truth he could not share his young companion's light-hearted view of the matter. The assault had been months ago, but the nightmares and mistrust persisted. He wanted to believe that all was well, now that the military regime had stepped aside to allow a civilian government to take power. He wanted to believe that the persecution and surveillance was a thing of the past. But wanting to believe did not make it true. The "raggedy man" was, after all, a perfect disguise. The streets were crawling with them, malingerers whose homes in the hill towns had been damaged or destroyed in the conflict. They came into the city looking for something to eat, but he could not help wishing they would go back to where they came from. Petty crime was on the rise. The streets weren't safe. He did not like exposing the boy to such hazards, but he was unable to go out himself. And he needed Diego's younger, sharper eyes and ears at work for him. He needed him out there gathering intelligence, talking to shopkeepers and the likes of Señora Cabeza (God help us), and reporting back.

"Excellent!"

Enrique held aloft a tin of Italian tomatoes, the same brand his mother's cook had used in her beef stews. Even the label was the same. The return of a quality product gave him a warm feeling inside. With Italian tomatoes back on store shelves, things were indeed looking up.

"We'll make the pasta and tomatoes tonight, then, shall we? With fresh herbs?"

Diego gave him a shy smile.

They set about assembling the ingredients for their evening meal. Enrique would make a show of rapturous enthusiasm over supper. For the boy's benefit he would speak in a robust voice, tell funny stories and make them both laugh. He was still in mourning, but for the boy's sake he would dissemble and deceive. It would do neither of them any harm. How could he share his true feelings or say what he really thought? Diego knew nothing of his recent past and needed no more gloom and misery in his life. If Enrique were to resort to tears, he would do it later, after Diego had gone to bed. He would pour a brandy and sit in his chair in the dark and brood to his heart's content.

He had already wept copiously for his family and would grieve their loss for the rest of his days. Life had brought the rod down upon him and the lesson he had been taught was a harsh one. He knew now that a loss of such magnitude left a gaping wound that would not heal, and there were times when—alone in the dark, with only his thoughts for company—he envisioned the last breath leaving his body and embraced the moment like a lover.

But he was doing his best to move on.

He had been in hospital when it happened, and it was only after his release that he spoke to Javier and Josefina in Puerto Varas and learned that a band of thugs had entered their home in the night and taken Lucinda along with his remaining children. The pattern was chillingly familiar, reminding him of the night Carlos had been abducted and of the story Nadia had told about her parents being taken away: men dressed in black armed with automatic weapons, the unmarked van. But apart from the shock there was a part of him that was not surprised, that had been waiting, expecting this tragedy to occur. It was like a seed that this deeper part of him had known all along would germinate and grow and yield a terrible harvest, while he—incapacitated—could do nothing to avert it. After learning the truth he had not known what action to take, fearing to call further attention to himself and risk another beating, or make things worse by raising a fuss. But Javier had already begun the inquiry process and, aware of Enrique's health issues and understanding his fears, told him to wait before initiating an inquiry of his own. Roberto, Dulciana's husband, had also set an inquiry in motion. But then the military regime had left office, and in the ensuing confusion so much information had been lost. The new government was doing its best and had set up an entire ministry to look into the previous regime's abuses, which included locating civilians who had disappeared. The day before Diego's arrival Enrique had gone to the ministry offices and submitted the necessary forms, one for each missing family member, including Hector and Carlos, and one for Nadia as well, though the information he had was woefully incomplete (he was shocked by how little he knew about her). But as he passed the forms across the counter to an unsmiling young woman, and watched dozens of others doing the same, and then imagined hundreds if not thousands of identical forms being submitted at countless centres around the country, he felt his slender hopes bend perilously close to the breaking point beneath the weighty realization that the search had already failed, the struggle was already lost.

Enrique and Diego ate at the little kitchen table. The pasta was perhaps a bit *al dente* for Enrique's taste (he liked it softer). But the sauce was perfect: tangy with the lingering sweetness of the basil offsetting the oregano's bitter edge and the robust meatiness of the tomatoes, and a suggestion of heat from a small chilli pepper. Diego had brought crusty bread from the new bakery that had opened on Avenida Independencia near the Plaza des Patriotas (absurdly called Panadería de la Revolución), which they warmed in the oven right in the paper bag so that the crust stayed firm but the inside was springy and moist. At the table, they tore into the bread with their bare hands. The crumbs flew everywhere.

Absorbed by the food, they ate mostly in silence. Enrique sipped his wine (a five-year-old Mâcon-Villages) while Diego slurped a glass of milk. At times like this, when silence prevailed, one last conundrum occupied Enrique's mind: the weekly letters from Claudia that had resumed now that mail was moving again. To his great bewilderment she continued to extol Hector's virtues, recounting his exploits in the fields, his expert handling of the animals, his value to her in the kitchen, his deep attachment to the farm and love of the clean mountain air. Francisco was still strong and working from sun-up to sundown. Her legs troubled her sometimes, but with Hector there to help, and on and on. It had been four long years since he had delivered his son to the train bound for Envigado (though he had stalked off the platform in a rage, he had watched from the station waiting room to make sure Hector got safely on board). What was he to make of this latest barrage of communication? His own letters had been interrupted for the months of his hospitalization. But he had started writing the moment his hands were strong enough to hold a pen, making the reasonable assumption when he did that Hector had long since left the farm (he did not enclose a cheque). Claudia's letters began arriving shortly after he dropped the first of his into the letterbox, obviously too soon for her to have received it. Since then the floodgates had opened and he had received more than a dozen, each the same as the last—an uninterrupted stream of praise for Hector. Though frugality was his watchword as he assessed his retirement finances, he had felt obliged to pick up the payments where he had left off. And yet, disturbingly, despite her long-windedness, she had not acknowledged his news that Lucinda and the children had been abducted and that he feared the worst, and had not responded to his suggestion (phrased more emphatically with each missive) that since times were tight, some small evidence that Hector was still living under her roof would help him justify the expense. Was she even reading what he wrote? Why had Hector never written to his family? How could Francisco still work so hard when he was over a hundred? Why in God's name didn't they get a telephone? In recent letters he had bluntly put all these questions to her, but to no avail. It was puzzling and distressing. The only way to get to the bottom of it, he had decided, was to see for himself.

Enrique puffed contemplatively on his cigarette and sipped his wine. He sloshed it around his mouth, relishing the fruits and spices. This was another problem. He was rapidly depleting his stash of wine and brandy. Diego could buy most things they needed, even cigarettes. But Enrique would have to buy the booze.

"You do not mind living here, do you my boy?"

"I like it here," Diego said around a mouthful of food, smiling sheepishly at this *faux-pas* and swallowing. Enrique sometimes suffered pangs of doubt about the boy's sincerity, but the smile appeared genuine enough.

"I'm sorry for being such a decrepit old fool. But I promise, when I get my strength back, we'll go walking in the park. We'll go to the movies."

"I don't mind being inside."

Enrique nodded. "Yes, but right now the weather is cold and wet. When spring comes we'll both want to get out. I know I will. Now that I'm retired I have all kinds of time. We could take a trip. My aunt and uncle live in the south, near Envigado. Do you know where that is? We could visit them on their farm. It's near the mountains. Have you ever been on a farm?"

Diego shook his head.

"They have cows and pigs and chickens. They grow trees for fruit and my aunt bakes championship cakes and pies."

Diego stared at him, his bottom lip drooping, as if the concept Enrique was describing could not be more alien.

Enrique shrugged. "It's just a thought. They are both very old and it would be nice to see them before . . . before they are gone."

With a hunk of bread Diego cleaned the last smears of sauce from his plate.

"I used to visit them when I was your age. We took the train. I can still feel it, the rhythm of the train, swaying from side to side." Ah, the lure of nostalgia—it was so easy to fall into that trap. He had vowed he would never bore the child with tales of his uneventful past. Now, here he was. "It was so dusty and hot. I had lots of friends and we used to take off our clothes and swim in a stream. My parents took me there because they thought I was reading too many books." He shook his head and chortled lightly. "Perhaps they were right."

He picked up the bottle and emptied it into his glass.

"I like to read," Diego chirped.

"I know you do, my boy. I know you do." He had watched Diego leafing delightedly through comic books left behind by Hector and Julio. He had probably never seen anything like them. *Superman. The Flash.* Juvenile entertainments, no doubt stimulating in their unique way, but of no cerebral value whatsoever. "But don't you worry. We'll get some intellectual meat on those bones before too much longer. I can see you have a thirst for knowledge. You're like me when I was your age. Once you get started you'll never be able to stop."

Enrique sat back and allowed himself a moment to savour the wine. The tablecloth was covered with crumbs. They'd eaten the entire loaf.

There was a rumble in his stomach and Enrique placed his hand over his mouth in time to cover the belch.

He was proud of the boy and of what they had accomplished together in a short time. During their first days together Diego had been morbidly withdrawn, comfortable only in the bedroom seeing to Enrique's sensual needs. Making eye contact was difficult and conversation out of the question. But a few months later he was a trusted companion, a fully functional partner in the domestic routine—almost like a spouse—handling money and contributing to everyday household decisions, capable of a degree of independence that Enrique would have not have dreamed possible on the day he admitted the silent, evasive, diffident child into his home, holding in his hand a small tattered valise that contained all his belongings. But he still feared for the boy. Enrique was not in the best of health. What would happen when he died? It seemed callous to look towards the future when the scars left by recent losses were still raw and seeping, but he would have to do something about his will. The original document dated from shortly after he and Lucinda married and had last been revised when Julio was born. He couldn't remember who had drawn it up. In any event, everything had changed. Everyone named in it was gone. Claudia was his last remaining blood relative, but (to be frank) she and Francisco were so old they might as well be dead. He could leave everything to Diego. But who would make the arrangements? Who would guide the boy through the process? Who would see that he wasn't cheated? Enrique's greatest regret was that he had no dear and cherished friend, no trusted confidant, no intimate who might assume such a task and upon whom he could unburden himself without guile or reservation. Diego would become that faithful companion, but not for many years yet, and what if Enrique didn't live that long?

He rubbed his eyes. At night his ruminations turned mawkish. It was nothing to be ashamed of: just another of the hazards of getting old, of looking to the past for comfort more so than the future. But it was embarrassing. He loathed this weepy, sentimental side of himself, but alcohol always brought it out. Time to retire to the living room. There was no need for Diego to witness this.

"I'll let you get to the cleaning up then, shall I?"

Enrique pushed his chair back from the table and rose to his feet. Diego rushed to his side, steadying his shaky ascent with a hand on his elbow. Until recently Enrique had navigated his rooms with the aid of his father's old knobby wooden cane. It had come in handy at difficult moments. However, hoping to speed his recovery, he had disdained using it of late, relying on Diego to be there when he needed him. How else was he going to regain his strength? But no matter. He was soon standing unaided. He smiled and briefly stroked Diego's hair before leaving him to his task.

He settled himself in the chair and tried again to retrieve the Smekal volume from the floor where it had tumbled. He had started reading through the old works—for simple enjoyment of course, now that he had the time—but also with an eye towards tutoring the boy and gently initiating him into a world where speculating upon weighty abstractions such as radical spiritualism, esoteric ritualism, the body-spirit inter-regnum—that world where blissfully he had spent his own youth—was second nature. Gradually, assuredly, like a sculptor, he would shape the boy's intellect until his grasp of elusive theories and slippery concepts was every bit firm as his own. Then Diego would read through Enrique's notes and papers. This would light the fire. He was sure of it. He'd seen it in a dream: Diego as a young man, his lean handsome face illuminated by the light of a single candle, hunched over a desk, surrounded by stacks of books, his eyes ablaze during a moment of epiphany when the blinders drop away and everything becomes clear. That instant when, once and for all, he shuns worldly concerns and devotes his life to shepherding Enrique's work to the next level.

But that was for later. For now he sought only to distract himself, as, wheezing from the effort, he finally pinched the edge of the book's stiff cover between thumb and forefinger and successfully conveyed it into his lap. Maybe by spending a few moments with his beloved Smekal he could keep the tears from pushing through to the surface until after Diego was asleep.

Then he heard tapping. Someone was at the door.

Instantly sober, he pulled himself up. His heart thumped and for a second the rush of blood was all he could hear. They wouldn't hurt the boy. Surely they wouldn't hurt the boy.

But he was jumping to a conclusion, perhaps a false one. Maybe it was just someone from the building.

Diego had come out of the kitchen and was looking to Enrique for instruction. Neither of them spoke.

Again, a gentle, tentative tap on the door.

He had, of course, considered purchasing a weapon (a gun, a cricket bat), but had put it off. Now, glancing quickly from side to side, he settled on his father's cane, which stood unused in the brass umbrella stand beside the china cabinet.

Retrieving the cane, he signalled to Diego to keep back. He shuffled forward. In this instance he could not send a boy to do a man's job.

"Who's there?" he called in his best crotchety baritone as he rounded the corner, approaching the door along the narrow entryway. "It's late. What do you want?"

His question was met by silence. But no. There were sounds. Movements. Whispering, muttering. How many of them were there?

The building seemed to be asleep. As it did every night at about this time, the aeration system issued a sigh and expelled a stream of air with a whoosh.

His quaking hand reached forward as if of its own volition. He was curious. It was just some kids, mischief makers. He would put the run to them. Oh, yes.

He slid back the bolt and, gripping the knob, pulled the door until the security chain snapped taut. Someone was standing there, a shadowy hooded figure in an overcoat.

"Who are you? What do you want?"

The figure raised its head. Their eyes met through the narrow opening. And Enrique suffered a slowly dawning, punishing jolt of recognition.

"Hector?"

He unlatched the chain.

"Is this true? Can this be happening?"

Enrique stepped across the threshold and embraced his son, then stood back as they locked gazes. With his hands he gripped Hector's shoulders.

"You're all wet. Where have you been?"

Hector did not move or speak.

"What is it? What's wrong?"

Then Enrique noticed the murkiness of his son's eyes, the pupils shrunk to pinprick. It was as if he were sleepwalking, or under a spell. Hector's lips moved but the sounds were unintelligible.

"I can't hear what you're saying. What's wrong? Tell me."

Enrique leaned closer.

"You're sick, aren't you? Is that it? Hector, you don't need to do anything. You're home now."

But then, looking again into Hector's eyes, Enrique understood. He grabbed Hector's arm.

"Are you on something?" He had seen it before. Some of the boys he had spent time with. Sad, hopeless cases.

Hector pulled away.

"It's nothing to be ashamed of, my boy."

Enrique gripped his son by the elbow.

"It doesn't matter. Just come in. We'll get you well, my boy. We'll get you well."

Enrique did not see the knife. Hector made a single thrust. Enrique's mouth dropped open. His body folded on itself as a searing pain sliced upward through his midsection, a pain that swelled and blossomed into agony as Hector withdrew the blade. Enrique gasped and fought to breathe. With an upward glance he tried to speak, but all that emerged from his mouth was a strangled, gutted sound. And the way Hector was looking at him, did he have to ask? He knew why. Oh, he knew why. But did he really? He was overcome by doubt. Because when he looked into his son's eyes for the last time, he met the indifferent, preoccupied gaze of a killer.

He staggered backward and banged against the door, which was still ajar. It swung back and struck the wall. He gripped the doorknob to steady himself, but his legs gave out beneath him and he slid to the floor. His hand found the cane that had slipped from his grasp at the moment of recognition. He was aware of blood flowing freely and of Hector stepping over him and disappearing around the corner into the flat. He tried to call Diego's name but could not make any sounds. From within came a clatter of things being turned over and falling to the floor.

Then Diego was looking down at him, his expression veiled in shadow. Enrique tried to smile, to save the boy from fear.

"It's the raggedy man," Diego said and giggled foolishly. He broke off and lapsed into a confused silence.

Enrique swung his arm towards the hallway and grunted.

Go, he wanted to say. Run. Call for an ambulance. Scream out loud. Get help. Even Señora Cabeza would help if he asked her. Or just knock on doors until someone answered. Do something. Anything.

Diego backed away and disappeared into the flat.

Don't harm the boy, he thought as the agony melted and a strange calm took hold. Don't harm him. But when he pictured the boy for whose safety he pleaded, the face he saw was a strange amalgam of familiar features, Hector's and Diego's mingled into something that was both and neither at the same time.

His breathing grew shallow and uneven. He felt himself slipping, losing his grip on consciousness. If only he'd had time to prepare, he could have put things right. Time . . . there was never enough time. He was not afraid, but he was tired, weary of everything, of life itself. The world was spiralling downward and taking him with it. Maybe this was the moment he'd been waiting for, that in a dream he had embraced and held to his breast like a loved one. Maybe he should pray to God. Where on earth had that thought come from? If only he had the strength he would laugh at the absurdity. There was no God. He'd proven it years ago in one of his papers.

Hector appeared from around the corner. In each hand he held a plastic bag stuffed full. Enrique could not make out the contents. Without a glance in his direction Hector stepped around him into the hallway. Enrique listened to his steps recede and fade away into silence.

Then he saw Diego, his beautiful boy. Enrique tried to lift his arm, to signal that he should come to him, but it was heavy and his hand was sticky. He could not pry his fingers away from the cane. The sludgy, slimy warmth of blood. It was repulsive.

Enrique's glazed eyes absorbed the scene as Diego set his little valise on the floor. The boy went back into the apartment, and when he returned a moment later he was holding a coffee tin, the tin in which Enrique kept his hoard of cash, the tin that was always locked away, in a secret compartment in his desk. Enrique had never shown Diego where it was kept.

Diego opened the valise and put the tin inside. He closed up the valise and lifted his poncho from the coat tree. He put it on. Then he searched the pockets of Enrique's coat until he found his wallet. He slipped the wallet into the pocket of the poncho.

Enrique could not move. Each slow breath rattled in his throat. He knew the moment was approaching, the moment when his body would give out and his heart would stop. For all the thinking he had done in his life, now that it was upon him he did not know what to think about this moment. It perplexed him. Should he be worried? Happy? Sad? He was none of these. Maybe it was simply time for him to go.

Enrique's eyes followed Diego as the boy stepped nimbly around the glistening pool of blood and disappeared down the hall. There was nothing left for him to do. He relaxed and listened to the anguished rasp of his own breathing. Then his burden lifted and everything was quiet.

ACKNOWLEDGEMENTS

Thank you for advice and encouragement: Richard Cumyn, Brian Bartlett, Isabel Huggan, Alistair MacLeod, Antanas Sileika, Doris Cowan, Steven Heighton, Steve Skurka, Mary Beth Hughes, Michelle Butler-Hallett, Shari Lepeña, Stephen Patrick Clare, Deborah-Anne Tunney, Valerie Compton, Andy Wainwright, Ryan Turner, Dorothy Allison.

I wish to acknowledge the generous support of the Canada Council for the Arts.

Thank you to Mrs Drue Heinz and the Trustees of Hawthornden Castle and to the Corporation of Yaddo for residencies during which portions of this novel were written.

Special thanks to my Hawthornden Castle colleagues for sharing and listening: Alfred Corn, John Greening, Beena Kamlani, Sophie Mayer, Fiona Shaw, Chiew-Siah Tei.

Chris Bucci of Anne McDermid & Associates found a home for *Hector Tomás* at Freehand Books. Sarah Ivany and Robyn Read have given this book its final form.

Jim Holloway of the Spanish Department at Dalhousie University was an early supporter of this project when I had no expectation that it would ever be completed let alone see the light of day. His knowledge of Latin American history and culture informs the text in ways that defy easy description. Tragically he did not live to see the novel completed. This is my fault for taking so long. His intelligent and generous spirit is sorely missed.

This novel goes to some very dark places and my wife Collette endured the writing process with patience and grace.

IAN COLFORD is a fiction writer living in Halifax, Nova Scotia. He previously served on the executive board of the Writers' Federation of Nova Scotia, and in 1998 he selected and edited a collection of stories by Maritime writers called *Water Studies*. Written over eight years, *The Crimes of Hector Tomás* was completed with the help of two Canada Council grants and residencies at the Hawthornden Castle International Retreat for Writers and Yaddo, the artists' colony in Saratoga Springs, New York. *Evidence,* his first collection of short fiction, was published in 2008 by Porcupine's Quill.